Praise for Grace H

"A delightful romp! *His Delightful Lady Delia* is full of yearning and humor and just the right touch of old-fashioned Victorian melodrama. Delia's upstanding character and her quest for acceptance make her an endearing heroine, and Kit offers dash and integrity and a trace of vulnerability. Enjoy!"

Sarah Sundin, bestselling author
of *Until Leaves Fall in Paris*

"*Her Darling Mr. Day* is a delightful and charming romantic romp. Grace Hitchcock has created wonderful characters who face mystery and adventure while falling in love. I know my readers will find this novel as endearing as I did and highly recommend it."

Tracie Peterson, bestselling author
of the Ladies of the Lake series

"Grace Hitchcock does an excellent job of weaving history of the era and Louisiana region into the romance with well-drawn characters, who came alive in their first scene and stole their way into this reader's heart. A gutsy heroine with determination to spare, trapped in society's rules of the day, had me cheering for her from the beginning. *Her Darling Mr. Day* kept me reading when other things needed doing."

Lauraine Snelling, bestselling author
of the Red River of the North series

"Delightfully original! Set during the glittering Gilded Age, *My Dear Miss Dupré* is a captivating story that will charm readers from the first page until the last. Grace Hitchcock is a writer to watch!"

Jen Turano, *USA Today* bestselling author

"Sparkling with vivacious energy, this romance launches Hitchcock's AMERICAN ROYALTY series. . . . Fans of TV's *The Bachelorette* will adore this historical spin on competitive courtship that features all the glitz, glamour, and drama that the Gilded Age brought to New York City's elite."

Booklist on *My Dear Miss Dupré*

"To the modern reader, the plot of this book is reminiscent of the popular reality show *The Bachelorette*. In what is a unique take, author Grace Hitchcock has combined the modern with the old-fashioned by setting her book at the height of America's Gilded Age. . . . Overall, the book is amusing and entertaining. The characters are interesting and possess great depth."

Historical Novels Review on *My Dear Miss Dupré*

His Delightful
LADY DELIA

Books by Grace Hitchcock

AMERICAN ROYALTY

My Dear Miss Dupré

Her Darling Mr. Day

His Delightful Lady Delia

AMERICAN ROYALTY
BOOK THREE

His Delightful
LADY DELIA

GRACE HITCHCOCK

BETHANYHOUSE
a division of Baker Publishing Group
Minneapolis, Minnesota

© 2022 by Grace Hitchcock

Published by Bethany House Publishers
11400 Hampshire Avenue South
Minneapolis, Minnesota 55438
www.bethanyhouse.com

Bethany House Publishers is a division of
Baker Publishing Group, Grand Rapids, Michigan

All rights reserved. No part of this publication may be reproduced, stored in a retrieval system, or transmitted in any form or by any means—for example, electronic, photocopy, recording—without the prior written permission of the publisher. The only exception is brief quotations in printed reviews.

Library of Congress Cataloging-in-Publication Data
Names: Hitchcock, Grace, author.
Title: His delightful Lady Delia / Grace Hitchcock.
Description: Minneapolis, Minnesota : Bethany House, a division of Baker Publishing Group, [2022] | Series: American royalty ; 3
Identifiers: LCCN 2022020230 | ISBN 9780764237997 (paperback) | ISBN 9780764240850 (casebound) | ISBN 9781493439072 (ebook)
Subjects: LCGFT: Novels.
Classification: LCC PS3608.I834 H57 2022 | DDC 813/.6—dc23
LC record available at https://lccn.loc.gov/2022020230

Scripture quotations are from the King James Version of the Bible.

This is a work of fiction. Names, characters, incidents, and dialogues are products of the author's imagination and are not to be construed as real. Any resemblance to actual events or persons, living or dead, is entirely coincidental.

Cover design by Create Design Publish LLC, Minneapolis, Minnesota / Jon Godfredson

Author is represented by The Steve Laube Agency.

22 23 24 25 26 27 28 7 6 5 4 3 2 1

For my Angel Baby

Because of the hope we have in Jesus Christ,
we will hold each other again.
Know you are treasured and loved beyond measure.

With all my heart,
Mama

Whosoever shall confess that Jesus is the Son of God, God dwelleth in him, and he in God. And we have known and believed the love that God hath to us. God is love; and he that dwelleth in love dwelleth in God, and God in him. Herein is our love made perfect, that we may have boldness in the day of judgment: because as he is, so are we in this world. There is no fear in love; but perfect love casteth out fear: because fear hath torment. He that feareth is not made perfect in love. We love him, because he first loved us.

1 John 4:15–19

Let me not to the marriage of true minds
Admit impediments. Love is not love
Which alters when it alteration finds,
Or bends with the remover to remove.
O no! it is an ever-fixed mark
That looks on tempests and is never shaken;
It is the star to every wand'ring bark,
Whose worth's unknown, although his height be taken.
Love's not Time's fool, though rosy lips and cheeks
Within his bending sickle's compass come;
Love alters not with his brief hours and weeks,
But bears it out even to the edge of doom.
If this be error and upon me prov'd,
I never writ, nor no man ever lov'd.

William Shakespeare, "Sonnet 116"

One

NEW YORK CITY
OCTOBER 1883

Madre had lost her voice at last. And while the news had initially struck joy in Delia Vittoria's heart, she now repented most heartily as she paced in the wings between the walls of faded burgundy velvet of the Academy of Music's curtain. The hum of the audience and the strumming of the instruments warming up filled her senses. After five years as her prima donna mother's soprano understudy, Delia had thought she would be ready for the limelight when the time came, especially since she had been all but banished to the ensemble for years. She clasped her trembling fingers. She couldn't allow herself to give in to her nerves or they would affect her voice and her career would be over in a single night. Maestro Rossi would be furious if she failed after all the hours he had invested in her.

Maybe no one will be here for opening night, what with the Metropolitan Opera House's grand opening being to-night, as well. She peeked through the crack between the curtains, and her stomach dropped as she spotted Mr. and Mrs. Astor taking their seats in their rose-lined gilded opera box. The pair was never there for the opening act. But Delia supposed that when the rival opera house was opening the same night, Mrs. Caroline Astor wished her support for the Knickerbockers' exclusive opera house to be evident, and judging from the sixteen other boxes filled with guests, Mrs. Astor had used her influence as the leading matron in society. If Delia faltered, all in society would know by midnight, as every member of the elite set had their pick of opera balls to attend throughout the city and would no doubt discuss Delia's unexpected appearance.

Her pulse hammering in her ears, she whirled away from the curtain and nearly ran into an ensemble member dashing to his place on the opposite side of the stage. She focused on what Maestro Rossi had told her to do should she be overtaken by nerves. *Breathe in. Breathe out.* She closed her eyes and imagined herself not in the wings but alone with her teacher. This was just another lesson, one of thousands—in front of thousands. Her stomach churned. This exercise was not working. *Lord, help me.*

The instruments silenced, and as she closed her eyes again, she could envision the rustling coming from last-minute guests finding their seats, their murmurs echoing off the horseshoe of exclusive boxes lining the walls of the Academy that held New York's elite. The curtains drew back as the prelude began for Bellini's *La Sonnambula*, *The Sleepwalker*, and Lisa's cavatina followed, the company streaming onstage while Delia doubled over, feeling she might actually toss her accounts now that her entrance was rapidly approaching.

Four company men took their positions, gripping the

horse shafts of the milk cart in which she was supposed to stand and ride onto the stage while performing her aria. Madre had done it countless times as Amina, the young bride-to-be in Bellini's opera. Delia could not fail. She swallowed back a groan and smacked her cheeks in rapid succession. The bride was not supposed to appear green, rather fresh-faced and rosy-cheeked. She grasped the nearest actor's hand beside the milk cart, who assisted her inside. The men adjusted their hold on the shafts, and she drew in a sharp breath through gritted teeth at the sudden movement. The actor sent her a reassuring wink as she spread her feet apart to keep her balance, clasping her hands to her chest, praying she looked for all the world to be a girl in love, even though she had no experience of such things in her nearly four and twenty years.

One of the girls in charge of costuming flitted past, only to whirl about and point to Delia's hair, grimacing. Delia swept her hands over the overlarge hairstyle, her ebony locks arranged and puffed to perfection. Her fingers found the loose flower, and she tucked the blossom back into place, resumed her position and plastered on a smile to cover her nerves.

The milk cart was tugged forward, and she almost lost her footing but then gripped the floorboards in her slippered feet. *I will not fall.* The cart jolted her again as it crossed through the wings and onto the stage. She spread her arms wide to keep from stumbling and decided to hold the position to fool the audience into thinking she had already faltered. She fought against squinting past the lights to see who was in the audience, yet she had performed enough as a member of the choir to know who would be there and where. Instead, she focused on the massive crystal chandelier overhead and allowed the music to flow through her, and in that moment all faded into nothingness as she became the music.

Her voice rang true in the high notes, stayed strong throughout, and when the aria faded, the applause of the crowd woke her, lifting her from her hazy dream. The applause did not dim, and Delia allowed herself a glance to Mrs. Astor, who lifted her hands to shoulder level and clapped, nodding her head once, which had the rest of the women in society rising to their feet, applauding her, and some of the single gentlemen in the nearest boxes throwing roses at her feet.

Delia could not rest in the moment, though, as Amina's love, Elvino, began their duet. The rest of Act I was an elated blur that ended in thunderous applause after her second love duet. She rushed from the stage for her costume change for the famed sleepwalking scene. Flowers rained in her path, her slippers crushing delicate blooms, even as she took pains to avoid stepping on them. In the wings, her friends in the company squeezed her hand as she went to change in her mother's dressing room, which was already overflowing with roses and bouquets of fall blooms. Her cheeks heated, knowing that the flowers were from gentlemen admirers.

She stripped off her gown and stepped into the nightgown that had, unfortunately, not been fitted to her, and the train was several inches too long. But the waist fit just right, even though the bodice was almost too confining to draw a full breath.

"You are doing well." Hester, her mother's maid, tugged the strings at the back of Delia's nightgown, securing it. "Now, for the sleepwalking scene, just execute it as you did in your rehearsal."

"You mean the one where I wasn't even allowed to mark the movements onstage until after Madre left the Academy?"

"Yes, but in the chorus you've seen her perform hundreds of nights. Simply do what she does, only better." Hester handed her a glass of water.

"It's difficult to improve upon a star." Delia downed the water and hurried to apply more rouge where she had thoughtlessly ran a hand over her cheek on her way backstage.

"Even though your mother is called the next Jenny Lind, it doesn't make her untouchable, especially with her—uh, choices of late."

Delia quickly dressed her hair with half atop her head and the rest flowing to her waist like a waterfall. The idea of her sleepwalking scene where she walked the narrow plank extending from the stage over the orchestra pit sent her stomach into tumbles. Still, she had to perform it without a mistake or she would never sing again—at least not at the Academy.

Delia jumped at the sharp knock on the door. Thinking it was the stage call, she threw open the door to find a waiter in the opera house's scarlet livery bowing to her, a note pinched between his extended gloved fingers.

"Miss Vittoria, I have a message for you." He gave her the note. "And please allow me to convey my compliments on your wonderful performance."

"Thank you." She closed the door as the waiter returned to his position. She flipped the letter over, searching for a name, the weight of the luxurious paper supporting the wealth behind it.

"The mystery will end as soon as you open it," Hester chided, flapping her hands and motioning for her to hurry and open it. "You don't have much time."

Delia opened it and read aloud. "'My dear Lady Vittoria, please attend my ball tomorrow night at the mansion as my honored guest. Best wishes, Caroline Webster Schermerhorn Astor.'"

"What an honor, miss." Hester pressed her hands to her ample bosom. "Your mother best not find out about this. Imagine what she might do if—"

"No, it would not do for her to find out," Delia agreed as she tucked the letter inside her reticule.

"No time to worry about that, ladies. Amina's sleepwalking is about to begin!" a stagehand called from the door.

Delia drew in a deep breath, whispered a prayer that she would not fall off the plank and into the orchestra pit, and rushed toward the stage.

Kit Quincy never missed an opening night at the Academy of Music, which was by far the most auspicious night as it marked the beginning of the winter season of society. But when he received his sister's frantic letter just moments before the understudy's entrance, Kit had no choice but to whisper his excuses to his friends and hotel manager, Mr. and Mrs. Ramsey Gunn, who had joined him for the evening, slip from his seat during the prelude, and ride for the Lowes' residence. Uncle Elmer or Ramsey would have to fill him in on the performance later.

Kit waited for the carriage to slow and then leapt out onto the sidewalk, pulling the collar of his opera cape closer in the crisp foggy evening and glancing up to the Lowes' brownstone with only the gaslights on the second floor flickering through the lace curtains.

"Return home," he called to his driver. "No need for you to catch your death waiting for me."

The elderly driver tipped his hat, hunching his shoulders against the icy wind cutting between the rows of houses. "Thank you, Mr. Quincy. Shall I return in an hour to fetch you?"

"No need. I'll have one of the Lowes' grooms bring me home if it begins to rain." He looked to the sky. "Or sleet. Otherwise I will hike back."

"Very good, sir." The driver turned the carriage and departed.

Kit trotted up the gray stone steps and twisted the bell. He took shelter in the doorway and waited, the fog turning into a thick mist and coating his silk lapels. Kit checked his pocket watch in the electric streetlights on Fifth Avenue. *Nine of the clock? And the downstairs lights are already dimmed?* He squinted through the sidelight window but didn't see anyone coming. He twisted the bell a second time, and just as he was considering ducking through the servants' entrance, he made out the willowy figure of a woman in an opera gown descending the stairs, kerosene lamp in hand that illuminated the tear-stained face of his parents' ward, whom he considered his sister. She set the lamp on a nearby table and fumbled with the trio of locks.

"Jocelyn?" Kit ducked into the marble foyer, the wind blowing a pile of invitations from the round table in the center before he could close the door. He scooped up the invitations and deposited them atop the silver letter tray. "Whatever is the matter? And why are you answering the door? Surely, your servants—"

"I sent them away for the night." She fell into his arms, sobbing. "I didn't want them to know!"

"What happened?" Kit placed her at arm's length, assessing her for any signs of harm, even though he knew that Lucian Lowe would never hurt his wife. "Jocelyn, I cannot help you if you do not cease your tears. Tell me so I can attend to the matter." He fished out a handkerchief from his pocket and pressed the folded square into her shuddering palm.

"You must fetch him for me." She wiped under her eyes. "Promise me you will?"

Kit's insides burned. Whoever hurt his kindhearted sister would pay—and pay dearly. "Who? Where is Lucian?"

"Who else could hurt me like this?" Her voice cracked. "I am not a weak woman, but this . . . this is more than even *I* can take. Must you make me say it?" Jocelyn pulled away from him, throwing open the parlor doors and striding into the dark room.

Kit clenched his fists in an attempt to squelch his rising anger, which would only cause his sister more distress, and retrieved the lamp from the foyer table and followed. Jocelyn turned from her desk in the corner of the room with a packet of letters tied with a crimson velvet ribbon and sank onto the settee, running a finger over the ribbon. Her bottom lip trembled.

Kit leaned against the doorframe and waited until a single tear traced down her pale cheek. "Where can I find your husband?"

She jolted, her head snapping up. She shook the clouds from her head and answered, "H-he sent word that he would dine at the club, but it is opening night." She released a dry laugh. "Lucian would never miss the chance to be with the city's darling over me, and I know the moment the clock strikes eleven o'clock that he will be rushing to Gramercy Park for his clandestine meeting with that Italian opera diva, even though he vowed never to see her again." She wiped her nose with the back of her handkerchief.

Everything in Kit urged him to find Lucian and beat him senseless. Instead, he crossed the room and sat beside her, taking her hand in both of his, intent on staying until her sobbing abated. Yet one look at her swelling belly and red-rimmed eyes and he lost the last morsel of fortitude he possessed. "Am I allowed to throttle him, Jocelyn? He cannot treat you and his child with such callousness."

"You are a true brother to rise to my defense and very sweet." She squeezed his arm, her other hand absentmindedly resting on her stomach.

"There is nothing 'sweet' regarding my objective. The man has pained you, and he will be held accountable for his infidelity."

A flash of concern crossed her features. "He may be telling the truth. Best check the club first, and if you do find him there, talk with him. Plead with him to remain faithful to me . . . to remember his promise to forsake *her*. I cannot bear the thought of him with another woman." She rubbed her temples, closing her eyes as her body trembled. "But it is hard to compete with that Vittoria woman he has secretly been seeing since long before we married. For five years I've been unwittingly *sharing* my husband with another." She grasped his hands, brokenness lining her every movement.

He swallowed his retort, unable to voice his true thoughts on the matter—to call his cousin the things he wished, which would burn the lady's ears. "How long have you known about Signora Vittoria?"

She picked at the cluster of yellow silk flowers at her waist. "I discovered his duplicity this summer, but he swore to me it was over."

Kit grunted. Apparently, he did not know his cousin beyond the boardroom. A few so-called gentlemen in his acquaintance possessed such secrets, but until now, it had never been in his power to right the wrongs done to their innocent brides. "Give me the address, Jocelyn."

She pulled the ribbon securing the letters and held out the top one to him, the address scrawled on the front to a Giovanna Vittoria. "I found this on his letter tray, to go out with the post several days ago. I confronted him, and he promised he had not seen her, that it was merely a moment of weakness that had brought it about after his seeing the poster advertising the latest opera. He said he was only wishing her well. But I found these in his library, tucked into a copy of a history of operas."

He pulled the envelope from her fingertips. Rising, he unfolded the letter, brows lifting at the script in Italian.

"He knows I cannot read it. I studied French, not Italian."

From the smattering of words he could understand, he crumpled the note. "It is most likely for the best. *La Sonnambula* shall end at eleven of the clock, so perhaps I can catch him between the theater and the diva's home. But in case he is telling the truth, I will check the club first." He pulled the bell cord. "We will send for some tea to help calm you while I fetch him."

"The servants are gone," she reminded him, the vacant look in her eyes betraying her utter exhaustion.

"Then I shall make it myself." He shrugged off his cape, draping it over the back of a chair. "You need tea."

"You know how to make tea?" Her lips curved in a smile. "How domestic of you."

"A degree of domesticity is a necessity on a ship. I've spent many a month sailing, during which times I learned to take care of myself." He turned up the parlor gaslight and used the lamp to guide himself to the kitchens. He had gotten lost in thought of how to deal with Lowe, and the tea turned out a little too strong, but he managed to find a tray and set her a nice tea service with a slice of bread. After bringing it to her and calming her enough for him to leave her alone, he tugged on his cape.

Knowing hailing a cab would be next to impossible at this time of night, he trotted to the stables and didn't bother waking the groom but saddled two of Lowe's horses for the journey to the club and the three-mile ride to Gramercy Park. He didn't want to take the chance of Lowe getting away in a carriage. How an opera singer could have obtained a residence in such an elite neighborhood, directly across the street from the park, he had no idea, but that was neither here nor there. What kind of woman was so brazen as to invite a married man into her home for all to see? Well, he knew what people called her sort. He shook his head and tugged the girth of each saddle tight once more.

With only an hour to spare before the performance ended, Kit set off into the night for the club to search for Lucian in the vain hope that his cousin was indeed *not* with that woman. His efforts proved fruitless and more than a bit annoying as he was caught by not one but two professional acquaintances, who were avoiding the social scene of the opera, both seeking advice on European hotel property investments. As there was no polite way to extricate himself, he was forced to cut the conversation short, no doubt offending them.

When he finally approached the prima donna's residence, the streets were clogged with the carriages of the well-to-dos returning from their night at the opera, all heading to one party or another to continue the festivities. Deciding it was best not to confront Lowe when there were so many witnesses, he directed the horses beneath a willow tree, attempting to blend in with the darkness and wishing he had worn a cloak to keep the mist from soaking him through. His opera ensemble would be ruined, but that mattered precious little when Jocelyn's happiness was on the line.

The brush of the willow branches on his sleeve brought his gaze to the remaining leaves bending low, offering him protection from the wind. He had always considered willows to be a sad sort of tree, until he had courted a woman christened with the same name. He smiled as he broke off a leaf and rolled it between his palms, the horse shifting beneath him. His time courting his dear Miss Dupré had been both thrilling and odd, as he was in a competition for her hand along with twenty-nine other suitors. And while she had stolen a piece of his heart, he did not regret leaving the competition. At nearly forty, Kit finally came to the conclusion that he was entirely too old for her . . . though some in his circle would say that fourteen years was nothing to keep a marriage from occurring.

The gaslights roared to life in what he assumed was the parlor of the residence in question while those in the surrounding houses dimmed as the residents retired for the evening, and others were still bright where parties continued. *Can't linger any longer, old boy. Time for action.* Kit guided the horses in front of the brownstone and fastened the reins to the hitching post. He took the stairs two at a time and pounded on the door. His anger rose with his accusations at the sound of footsteps approaching, but when it opened, he blinked at the sight of a lady in a sapphire gown. Her beauty stunted his speech.

Her ebony tresses were arranged into a loose coiffure that left tendrils to frame her face, emphasizing her wide, brilliant green eyes and full rosy lips. Her cheeks appeared to be a lovely olive tone, but they were heavily rouged, most likely from her performance tonight. It was bad enough to wear such cosmetics on the stage, but to not even wash her face before she left the opera house? It spoke ill of her nature. Her nature being why he was here and *why* she had most likely left on the cosmetics. The beauty of the woman turned sour as he was reminded that she was a loose opera singer and therefore was not to be trusted in polite society. "You." He ground out the word.

"Excuse me?" Her brow furrowed, taken aback at his tone.

"Hello, Cousin," said a slurred voice from behind the door.

The door opened fully, and his appraisal of the woman abruptly ended at the sight of Lucian at her side, a grin plastered on his face. He blinked rapidly against his own stupor as he nearly stumbled headlong out the front door. Her arm instantly anchored him about his waist. *Such blatant familiarity. How can Lowe act in such a manner, especially with a wife at home?* Certainly, Jocelyn was a bit tightly strung, but when Lowe had declared his undying love, Kit had approved the match, albeit warily, threatening that if Lowe ever hurt his adopted sister, there would be trouble. *Well, now there's trouble.* Kit clenched his fists. "Do you have any idea of how much pain you are causing?" He narrowed his eyes at the woman. "Surely there is another you could ensnare—someone who is preferably *unmarried.*"

"Pardon me?" She gasped, shrinking back, but it only pulled her closer to Lowe as he wrapped his arm over her shoulders.

"You *are* Signora Vittoria?" Kit shouted before recalling the neighbors. If they didn't already know of Lowe's infidelity, they would soon enough if he didn't control his temper.

"I'm *Miss* Vittoria," she hissed, brows arching.

Even her title is a lie, then. "Well then, *Miss* Vittoria, you should be ashamed for entertaining a *married* gentleman. Have you no sense of honor or common decency, or do you think because of your occupation you can get away with such harlotry?"

Her cheeks' color deepened, and he began to think perhaps it was not rouge after all but her natural heightened color. The color of guilt.

"How dare you come to my home and—"

"Do not speak of *daring* when you have my cousin's arm draped over your shoulders." Kit gripped the brim of his hat so tightly it cracked. He tossed it in the pathetic shrubbery. *Let her servants fetch it out.*

"Enough of this. Take him." She pushed Lowe out the door, the man nearly plunging headlong down the steps before Kit grasped his flailing arm.

"Don't be like that, *piccola* Delia." Lowe's words slurred as he ran a hand over his grin.

"Do not call me *little* Delia." She turned her glare on Kit. "And, sir, I may share my mother's surname and her voice, but I do *not* approve of her choices and would *never* entertain a man such as him," Miss Vittoria spat, tossing Lucian's hat and coat out onto the stone steps, a sleeve landing in an icy puddle.

Kit stiffened. No one had mentioned a mother.

"It is a term of endearment." Lucian waxed on despite her obvious desire for them to depart, what with the coat and gentleman tossing. "I love your mother and would make a great father to you, even if you are rather too old to be my daughter—which is why calling you *piccola* makes me feel more fatherly toward you, as I have every intention—"

"And what of your wife?" Miss Vittoria drew herself up. Her full height would not even reach Kit's shoulders. "If *you* had any honor at all, you would cease this pursuit of her like I have asked you every single time I have found you here."

"Your mother," Kit managed, feeling the blood rush in his ears.

"Yes. Did it not occur to you that there are *two* ladies Vittoria in residence here?"

He gaped at her, the stupidity of his assumption striking him. "Surely, not both of them can be opera stars." He looked to Lowe, who shrugged, still grinning from his time in the cups.

Her eyes sparked as she tilted her chin, looking down her nose at him. "I wouldn't call myself a diva quite yet. I am her understudy, Mr. Quincy."

His brows rose at his name on her lips before remembering that like most New Yorkers, she must have read about him and the outlandish competition in the papers, seen his picture even though he had always been in the background of the sketches of the famed Willow Dupré and her suitors.

"I would. If your voice is anything like your mother's." Mr. Lowe grinned. "Your mother sings like an angel. My angel."

"That's enough out of you." Kit drew Lucian's arm over his neck and hauled him down the steps, looking back up at the beauty, his gut wrenching at the offense he had placed at her feet. "I am sincerely sorry for everything, Miss Vittoria."

"Not as sorry as I," she said, closing the door and shutting them out.

Two

Unlike her mother's usual habit, Delia did not sleep the next morning away after her performance. She sprinted downstairs and out the front door, wrapping her embroidered shawl about the navy puffed sleeves of her day gown.

"*Buongiorno*, Amico." She greeted the newspaper boy on the corner of Gramercy Park North and handed her young friend a coin.

"*Buongiorno*, Signorina Vittoria!" He pocketed the coin and handed her the paper. "It's good news." He winked at her before turning to the neighborhood servants, approaching to fetch papers for their employers.

Delia trotted back, hopping over a few puddles left over from last night's rain to her front steps. She sank down on the top step, the velvet appliqué flowers on her long overskirt billowing out and knocking into the glass bottles the milkman had left for their breakfast. She shifted away from the bottles and tore through the pages, skimming the headlines pronouncing some Wellington gentleman guilty of horrid crimes and searching instead for a headline about the opera.

Ignoring the cold seeping through her skirts, she paused only when she spotted the articles on the warring opera houses. She closed her eyes before fully reading the headline. Besides knocking over a flowerpot onstage, she had performed flawlessly. *Papá, let the critics think I did well. Let me not have failed before I've even begun.* She drew in a shaky breath and began reading.

Even though the article focused mostly on the new Metropolitan Opera House and how the new-money elite Vanderbilt family and the rest of the *nouveaux riches* at last had their coveted box seats in an opera house far grander than the old Academy of Music, the final lines mentioned *her* name! Delia gasped as she ran her fingertips over the tiny print praising her and calling for more. The writer mentioned that after the fourth attempt to close the curtain for the night, the director, Mr. Mapleson, had to intervene to cease the encores and escort her from the stage as the lights dimmed. She pressed the paper to her heart. She would buy another copy and send it to Father. Maybe if he read that she'd been a success, he would come home at last.

At the tapping on the windowpane, she turned to find Hester shaking her head at her, her oversized nose leaving condensation where her breath touched. Hester pointed to the bottles of milk and then to the breakfast room, then ambled off.

Not wishing to be the source of the park's gossip again, Delia grasped the two bottles and slipped inside, setting one bottle on the table and trotting down the creaking wooden steps to the kitchen where she placed the second on the counter, smiling her greeting to Madre's only friend from her days in the Italian company's chorus, Elena, who was their rather untalented cook. But that was what happened when one lacked funds to pay a decent chef. "*Buongiorno.*"

Elena nodded and waved Delia over with a wooden spoon, thick with clumps of mushy oats at the top as she pushed the china serving tureen toward Delia. "Take this to the table. Oh, and I made you a cup of coffee already, *piccola* Delia."

"Thank you, Elena." Delia pressed her hand to her stomach and dutifully lifted the tureen and trudged up to the breakfast room, knowing what awaited her in the china pot. She vaguely remembered the Italian delights their former chef once created—frittatas, ricotta cakes, fresh brioche. Delia scooped the sticky mess into her bowl. At least the coffee was still superior to most shops in the area. She eyed her steaming cup but didn't reach for it, lest the barely tolerable oats become inedible after the first sip. She pushed her flavorless oatmeal about her bowl and ate in the tiny room that faced the park, daydreaming of the paper's praise, hope blooming in her heart that she might at last begin her career now that she had debuted.

Something in the bushes below the window caught her eye. Leaning over the sill, she spotted a crushed top hat. The events of last night sprang to mind. She *had* thought Kit Quincy a handsome man before he began yelling at her, judging from his pictures in the paper, where his attention was always adoringly on his dear Miss Willow Dupré. When Delia had read that he'd been cut from Miss Dupré's competition, she was heartbroken for him, as he had been her choice for the lady. Though Delia might have given in to the dream that the striking gentleman would one day call upon her, never in a hundred years had she expected New York's most dashing bachelor to end up on her doorstep, thinking she was Madre *and* a husband thief. Shame burned her cheeks, and the oats lost whatever allure they'd possessed.

She dropped the worn silver spoon into the chipped china bowl and reached for the one thing Elena excelled at making and what had earned her the position in the first place—delightful Italian coffee. She dragged her chair to the front window to savor her coffee over the paper but froze at the sight of her mother in the doorway in her lace-trimmed dressing robe, her thick ebony braid draped over her shoulder, hanging to her waist.

"Daydreaming again, Daughter? What is it this time? The stage, I imagine?" Madre crooned, her exquisite accent dipping and inflecting each word. Her bright eyes sparkled. "And from what Mr. Lowe informed me, you were quite the star." She grasped Delia's hands in her own. "Well done, my dear. Why, if I didn't look so young, we could have the mother and daughter roles in the operas, but perhaps now you can at least have the secondary role!" She seized her into an embrace. "I knew that once you got over your stage fright, you would do wonders."

"You were never ill before," Delia said. "I haven't been allowed to audition to sing in a lead role since I took over as your understudy."

"I shall do my best to make a slow recovery so you can sing at least twice more." Madre laughed, her voice cracking. "And what was that commotion last night?"

Delia's shoulders tensed. Why did she have to bring it up? "It was nothing."

"It sounded as if the police were taking down our very door." Madre lifted Delia's cup from her and took a sip, closing her eyes at the brew.

"I arrived home to find Mr. Lowe asleep on our divan." Delia reclaimed her cup, stood at the window and took a long sip, watching for anyone attempting to peek into their home after last night. Gramercy Park was no place to keep secrets, and she had no doubt that Mr. Quincy's shouting gave the residents even more fodder for their gossip of the ladies Vittoria. "You promised you would at least *try* to keep up appearances, Madre."

She waved her off. "I was *ill*, and Mr. Lowe arrived unexpectedly and *quite* inebriated. What was I supposed to do? Turn him away and let his protests raise the shades of the park?" she rasped, her voice not yet healed. "Yet I suppose that gentleman did just that in the end."

"Yes, I suppose he did." Delia crossed her arms, doubting Mr. Lowe's appearance was unexpected. It was *always* unexpected.

Madre peered into the china pot, her lip curling at the oats within as if it, too, was a surprise. "Well, let us skip the unpleasantness of your scolding me and head straight into how the Academy missed me and the audience demanded a reimbursement, as your voice is not as refined as mine." She winked and tapped the rim of her cup.

Delia did not take her mother's lure but instead reached for the *cuccuma*, the copper coffeepot, and put it in front of her mother, then moved about the room, picking up dirty teacups and setting them on the tea cart, straightening magazines on the table and stacking novels into a neat pile to return to Father's library. As with her taste in men, Madre took nibbles of books as if they were bonbons, tossing them about whatever room she resided in, until she found one she liked and then took her time savoring it.

"I really do wish to hear of your success." Madre poured herself a cup. "*Dimmi.*"

"The company was certainly nervous for me to take to the stage as the lead." Delia set her empty cup on the cart. "But they were supportive."

Madre stirred a second spoonful of sugar into her cup, clinking her spoon in applause. "*Brava!* They won't have to close the doors until I am well enough to sing after all. And Mrs. Astor?" She gritted her teeth. "I do hope it did not crush you too much when she departed after her resilient stance against the new opera house. She is very hard to please."

Delia returned to the window, watching a group of children skip down toward the park. "Mrs. Astor didn't leave."

Madre paused in twirling the end of her braid. "What do you mean?" She straightened, dark eyes flashing and reading what Delia did not reveal. "Mrs. Astor *acknowledged* you, didn't she?"

"Your voice, Madre," Delia chided, the precious envelope from the Astors weighing heavily in her pocket, "you'll never recover at this rate."

"It is only a bad cold. Calm yourself." Madre's gaze went to the slight wrinkle in Delia's formfitting gown. "She gave you something. What is it?"

Delia slowly withdrew it and sighed as Madre snatched it from her, tearing it open, damaging the fine paper, her frown deepening as she read. "How could Mrs. Astor find such interest in you as to invite you to an opera ball? I have never been invited to her house before . . . or any of the society matrons' houses after your father left, and *never* to an opera ball in my honor."

Delia smothered her rebuttal, for she could never state the

palpable truth. If her mother did not have Mr. Lowe as her caller and the scores of gentlemen before him, who were no doubt connected to Mrs. Astor's elite set of matrons, Madre would have been accepted as a refreshing novelty in society for at least a season. "It is not Mrs. Astor's annual opera ball—just one of the society balls she is hosting."

"Just one of the society balls? Do you hear yourself?" Madre's eyes welled, and she allowed the paper to fall from her fingertips and onto the worn Persian rug that was stained in places where Madre had lost control of her temper and smashed her cups in a passion. "Do you not think that I know my Mr. Lowe will be there? And even though we have been together for years, he cannot acknowledge me?"

I cannot imagine why. She pressed her lips shut, unable to question her mother's affection for the gentleman.

"As always, I am to be forgotten." She sighed, cupping Delia's cheek in her smooth hand. "I am proud of your success, *stellina*. Truly I am, but do not forget, Daughter, a star rarely stays in the heavens forever, but more often than not, fades into the unknown. A place that was once not so intolerable becomes unbearable once you have tasted glory." Madre grasped her teacup and slipped from the room, her footfalls on the stairs growing faint as she climbed toward her bedroom on the third floor.

Delia shook off the gloom left in Madre's wake. If she was to attend Mrs. Astor's party tonight after her performance, she was going to need a dinner gown from a store on Ladies' Mile. Delia removed her simple chapeau from the hall tree, threaded the pin through the grosgrain ribbon, and stepped out of her family's brownstone in Gramercy Park that her father had purchased for them before his first trip to London that was only supposed to last for the summer—a visit that had now extended nearly two decades. She had not seen Serenus Hearst since.

He had been promising a return from England since he left, but it seemed that every time a ticket had been purchased, something had called him away. Once her paternal grandmother passed away and the divorce papers arrived, the promises of returning faded to almost nothing. She had asked her mother a few times why he never returned home, until Madre had burst into sobs. That evening Madre received her first gentleman caller without another woman present.

Delia retrieved the skeleton key from her reticule and fit it into the front door lock. They could not employ any staff other than Hester and Elena, for Madre enjoyed her jewels and baubles too much to economize, and Father would only send an allotted amount that would run out each month if Delia did not hide half of it. But Madre had told her to never mind, as their neighbors would think they were true Knickerbockers with their frugality, what with their not even owning a carriage, and the nearby livery would supply them with whatever they needed.

Delia didn't bother reminding her mother that no one would think that of them, not with their olive complexions and dark hair setting them apart from the rest of the residents. Their Italian heritage would never allow anyone to forget the scandal of an English gentleman who married an opera singer, set them up in society and then abandoned them, society at once following suit, for if an English gentleman divorced his wife, there must be good cause.

It was only through Delia's pay from the opera house that

they had enough to make ends meet. And it was because of how they acquired their money, along with the lack of a father and husband, that no one in the park would even speak with them, let alone invite them to dinner. The only slightly affable family in the neighborhood, the Wingfields, had married off three of their five daughters this summer, which meant Delia would be without a friendly face for the rest of her time in Gramercy Park. She passed the Wingfield home, staring at the tall windows through which she used to catch glimpses of the happy family within. Would Flora Wingfield miss her, or did she even realize how much Delia coveted those chance friendly greetings and stolen tête-à-têtes as she strolled to the Academy of Music every morning for her lesson and rehearsals?

She rounded the corner and smacked into the chest of a gentleman. Her cheeks bloomed as his hands gripped her shoulders, righting her. Mumbling her thanks, she pulled back, but his hands kept a firm grip on her. The last thing she wished the matrons to see was herself in the arms of a man, even if it was to keep her from tripping into the street before a team of horses.

"Where are you off to in such a hurry?" the man asked, his hands grazing down her navy puffed sleeves to her elbows.

She jerked her head up, a searing word on her lips that died at the sight of him. She recognized him as the gentleman who had been lingering outside the Academy for weeks now, always with a bouquet in hand, waiting for her mother to pass by. She shook his hands off of her. "Thank you for your assistance. Good day." She slipped around the vulture, her heels clicking a staccato beat.

"I cannot possibly leave your side without assurances that

you are well, Miss Vittoria," he said, trotting next to her to keep up with her pace.

She paled, thinking that the only way he could possibly know her name was if he knew her mother, and if he knew her, then he might be under the impression that she was a lady of similar tastes.

"Your performance in *La Sonnambula* last night was impeccable."

Ah! So that's how he knows me. Her shoulders eased, but the relief was short-lived as he grinned, seeing how his words had slowed her frantic stride.

"You were even better than your mother." He chuckled. "Mr. Lowe has mentioned to me on several occasions about his *time* with your mother."

His words slapped her. "I do not know what you are talking about, sir. Now, if you'll excuse me, I must be on my way."

"Come now, surely you have seen me before." He chasséd sideways to continue following her. "It does not do well for you to be so unkind to a patron of the Academy."

She gripped the brim of her hat and darted across the street, dodging milk carts, carriages, riders, and a freight wagon.

"Miss Vittoria?" A masculine voice called to her above the clatter of the street and shouts of vendors selling their wares.

She grimaced, praying that it was not another of her mother's admirers. *If I don't look, I can't acknowledge him.* She bustled toward the Ladies' Mile shops, eager to leave all gentlemen undeserving of the title behind.

"Miss Vittoria!" he called again, louder this time.

Blast. She picked up her pace, which was rather difficult given she was lost in a sea of swaying bustles and yards of fabric getting in her way. She knocked into one lady and earned such a glare that Delia forgot herself and twirled away, facing the gentleman in question, who had her scowl melting despite her best efforts. "Mr. Quincy?"

He lifted his hat to her, his gaze on Delia. "How fortunate. I was picking up a notion for my sister and—"

"Then it is a good thing you came to the Ladies' Mile. There are plenty of notions for the choosing. Excuse me." Delia slipped inside one of the buildings, not caring to hear what he had to say—no matter how handsome she found him.

Kit couldn't believe the young woman had just given him the cut direct. Well, maybe not the full force of the cut direct, but she had left him standing with his traveler hat in hand, the women on the sidewalk rustling around him, sending him pitying glances. He hadn't even been given the chance to finish his apology.

He peered through Blanchard's dress shop to watch Delia approach the clerk, pointing to a dress in the window. He shifted behind the shop's front wall so she could not spot him spying on her. He gritted his teeth, shaking his head. *What am I doing? Acting like a man fresh from the university?* As he shoved away from the storefront, he couldn't help but glance behind him to see the clerk stepping into the display to lift the elegant emerald gown from its place. Miss Vittoria's eyes were bright with anticipation, her cheeks rosy.

Kit tore himself from the window and her enchanting countenance. He had to find a way to make amends for his tactless and diabolical assumption that *she* was the opera star who was pulling his cousin from his wife's arms. His attention shifted to the flower shop next door. What better way was there to apologize than to send flowers to the woman's dressing room after a performance?

He pushed open the door, the bell overhead announcing his arrival as the scent of hundreds of blooms greeted him. The hardwood floors squeaked underfoot as he meandered about the shop. Then the curtain behind the counter parted, and a rotund woman in an apron emerged with a smile on her face.

"Mr. Quincy!" she exclaimed. "What can I do for you?"

He blinked. He had yet to get used to the fact that people knew him from Willow's highly publicized competition for a husband. "Yes, ma'am. I am hoping to send a bouquet that conveys sorrow over my actions. What do you suggest in the way of bearing that message through the bloom?"

"Well, I have some lovely *Geranium phaeum*." The woman moved to a side display and lifted out a small bunch, tracing her finger just over the petals. "The dark purple petals are nearly black on the end to suggest sadness and sorrow."

He scrunched his lips to the side. "Hmm, well, perhaps something that conveys that I believe her to be pure of heart, as well."

The woman narrowed her gaze behind her spectacles. "You accused a young lady of having an impure heart?" Her voice rose at the last part, bringing a young clerk from the back room.

"It was an accident, I assure you." He inwardly cringed at their judgment that he completely deserved.

The woman set a notepad on the counter, her pencil tapping the pad. "I'm afraid that just flowers will not do the trick for reconciliation. Perhaps you would like to have the chocolatier next door include a box of his fine chocolates?" She gestured to the young man behind her. "My nephew's chocolate is unrivaled."

"I suppose it couldn't hurt to try." He nodded his thanks to her and the young man, who returned to the back again, and Kit could see through the fluttering of the curtain dividing the front from the back office that the shops were joined by a door.

"No, it certainly could not hurt. I have a few options for you in stock from my greenhouses. You may want to try a purple iris to convey faith in her pure heart. It also speaks of the importance of friendship."

"That's the one!" While Kit doubted he and the lady Vittoria would ever enjoy a friendship given their vastly different circles, he found himself wishing he *could* be friends with the young woman, who was unlike every socialite he had ever encountered.

"And might I suggest pairing it with a bloom to express your regret? A purple *Verbena officinalis* means that you are sincerely sorry." She lifted a bunch of long stems with equally long, pointed blooms that looked rather scraggly to him, but surely the woman did not send out scraggly bouquets.

"Please arrange the bouquet and have it sent to this location at seven o'clock," he said as he scribbled down the Academy's address, directing them to be delivered to Delia's dressing room.

"What about a note?" She pushed a small card toward him.

He jotted down his apology, and when he considered again the blooms gathered in the woman's hand, he had quite decided that the verbena were entirely too scraggly. He snapped his fingers as if just thinking of something. "Oh! Could you add some purple or lavender roses to balance the bouquet? The combination of verbena and iris seems a bit odd to me." He slid a few bills over to her.

"Of course. I will have them delivered on the hour." She tucked her pencil behind her ear, her lips pursed. "And my arrangements are never odd. Good luck with the young lady, Mr. Quincy. You are going to need it."

Kit glanced back at her. Had he inadvertently insulted a second woman in the span of twenty-four hours? But as she was already heading to the back to arrange his order, he did not ask but hurried outside onto the sidewalk. Unable to keep himself from walking next door, he caught a glimpse of Miss Vittoria before deciding to head to his hotel to check with the staff and go over the books for the week. He should have gone first thing this morning, but his errand for his sister had kept him.

Jocelyn! Seeing Miss Vittoria had completely driven from his thoughts the need to pick up a confection for his sister to cheer her rumpled spirits. *Well, perhaps a box of handkerchiefs instead of a jewel would work.* He grinned and entered Blanchard's, the bell overhead jingling. He moved to the shelves lining the walls that were filled with all sorts of lace frippery.

"Can I help you, sir?" A shopgirl in a cream-and-navy-striped uniform approached him, hands folded in front of her.

"I require a box of your finest handkerchiefs."

"We have several options, sir." She smiled, dimples appearing, which of course brought Miss Vittoria to the forefront of his mind.

He risked a glance over his shoulder, enjoying Miss Vittoria's enthusiasm over a row of reticules the clerk was displaying for her. "I trust your judgment. Pick what you think is prettiest."

The shopgirl reached for a pale pink box on the middle shelf and pulled back the tissue, revealing elegant lacy squares he was certain any lady would love to buy.

"These are perfect. I'll take them with me."

She murmured the sum, and he handed her the bills and accepted the box, his attention returning to Miss Vittoria, who was excitedly pointing to a selection of gloves in the glass display. As if feeling his eyes on her, she turned and met his gaze for half a second before lifting her pretty nose and officially giving him, Kit Quincy, the cut direct.

Three

After another successful performance, Delia could hardly maneuver through the meadow of flowers filling her dressing room. But one bouquet atop her vanity caught her eye as she set it aside to arrange her hair for Mrs. Astor's ball. Purple iris, roses, and a stringy bloom that smelled delightful, though she had little idea of its name. She pulled the pretty card trimmed in painted pink ribbons nestled in the blooms.

Forgive me, my lady?
Kit Quincy

She sighed. The man was persistent. She tossed the card on the dresser and readied for the party before stepping into her new emerald gown. Having no jewels for her hair besides her costume jewelry, she snapped off a few of the purple roses from Kit's bouquet, tucking a trio of them into her low coiffure. Satisfied with her appearance, she wove through the throngs of reporters and into the night to hail a carriage.

She smoothed the front of her lovely, albeit simple gown

that she had purchased ready-made at Blanchard's dress shop using nearly all her savings. The ottoman silk and velvet evening gown's modest cut were nothing like the showy costumes Madre donned on her evenings out, but that had been Delia's intent. She didn't wish to be seen as a woman of the stage as society surely viewed her mother, and so she had chosen this piece that the company's seamstress had kindly altered by adding gold lace at her shoulders, down the scooped neckline, and at the hem, transforming it into what ladies called a "confection."

The lights blazed from every level of the Astors' overly wide brownstone on the corner of Thirty-Fourth Street and Fifth Avenue. It was rather austere save for the Corinthian pilasters on either side of the front door and the architraves atop each first-floor window. Yet the gray freestone of the half-raised basement added some texture against the imposing bricks of the mansion.

Having no idea where she was welcome to enter the Astors' home, she directed the driver to deliver her to the rear servants' entrance. Peering up at the massive brownstone through the carriage window, she fought to stay the tremble in her hands. Still, as terrified as she had been to assume the role of Amina, somehow this felt ten times worse. Regardless, she could not disappoint her friends at the opera house, for the company was depending on her to save their positions at the Academy, as rumors were already swirling about the magnificence of the new Metropolitan Opera House.

Summoning all her courage, Delia departed the safety of the carriage and pressed a coin into the driver's open palm. She drew in a deep breath. "Papá," she whispered to the heavens, "help me not to make a fool of myself, Lord."

She jumped at the peals of laughter floating down from the open windows above her. "Breathe, Delia," she chided herself and, before she could change her mind, charged for the side door, twisted the bell, and folded her hands in front of her skirts. She nearly laughed at the shouts above the clanging of trays and pots that followed her ring, but all humor vanished when the door was tugged open by a man in white breeches and a livery coat the same shade as her gown.

Marvelous. My first outing into society and I match the staff. She had heard of socialites being ostracized for less. She held her head up high. "Good evening."

He held the door open wide with his forefinger, his crimson vest pulling at the brass buttons with a crest upon them that could only be of the Astor family. "Miss Vittoria? Whatever are you doing at our entrance?"

She blinked. "You know who I am?"

He grinned and swept his arm into the hall. "Everyone in the city has heard of you. And besides, Mrs. Astor has the staff expecting you after your appearance onstage. Please, come inside before it begins raining. The name's Neil." He held his gloved hand out to assist her over the threshold, which was entirely needed as her gown was far more cumbersome than anticipated.

The scent of fine food filled her senses, sending her mouth to watering. She had heard the elite set had their dinner late, but she hadn't allowed herself to hope that she could partake in the delicacies. The bustling hall had her darting to the wall to avoid a tray to the head as staff rushed upstairs.

"Sorry, miss!" the footman called over his shoulder.

"Anyone else would have known where to stand, but we never have your sort down here," Neil commented.

"Oh," she replied. Did he mean she was thought of as set apart, elite . . . or a tainted opera singer? *Does it matter?*

The hall was open to the kitchen, where servants rushed about preparing trays to be sent up with a red-faced cook waving her thick arms, wielding a pot lid in one hand and in the other a wooden spoon with a red sauce dripping from it as she instructed the kitchen maids. A door behind her swung open, and the footman gently tugged her back against the opposite wall as a maid scurried out in tears and a severely dressed woman exited the office, her chatelaine of keys jangling at her side, proclaiming her position as housekeeper. Her frown lines deepened at the sight of Delia.

"Miss Vittoria, you were supposed to go to the front door." She narrowed her gaze at the footman. "Which you knew, Neil."

"Her beauty drew it straight out of my mind, ma'am." He clasped his hands behind his coattails.

Delia squirmed under his compliments. Madre and Hester bestowed them, but no one else at the Academy dared to compliment any other soprano or mezzo-soprano but Madre, lest the diva find out. Truly, Madre's voice was unparalleled, even by her own daughter's—at least until this week, according to the papers—a fact that left Delia reeling and her mother's compliments sounding strained.

"It was my mistake." Delia moved to retreat out the rear door, the thunder's rumble sounding down the hall.

"Her carriage is gone. She cannot be seen entering the party on foot," the footman said to the housekeeper. "Not soaked through."

The housekeeper sighed. "See her through and pray you do not lose your position. Mrs. Astor has dismissed servants for less." She turned to Delia, her frown lessening. "The butler was supposed to instruct you upon your entrance, but I suppose the task falls to me now."

Delia opened her mouth to apologize, but the housekeeper continued without a second beat. "When you hear the music, you are to sing."

"Do you know when that will be? I shall need to warm my voice. What song—?"

"I'm certain a night of singing has your voice warmed enough." She cut her off and motioned them forward. "Best not keep the lady of the house and the party waiting any longer. You are twenty minutes later than they expected, and I can assure you, the ladies are growing restless waiting for the dancing to commence—which they cannot begin before the guest of honor arrives, allowing them to open the ball."

"They do not expect me to open with the quadrille, do they?" Her heart crashed against her ribs. She vaguely recalled the dance from learning it for an opera years ago, but she certainly was not fluent enough to complete it without error.

The housekeeper rolled her eyes. "Undoubtedly not. They merely wish to honor you by waiting. Now, if you'll excuse me, I must check with the cook about the timing of the soufflé."

Neil chatted the entirety of the way up the winding servants' stairs to the second floor where he opened the door into the main hall, leading her into the ballroom. Her response to his questions died on her lips at the raw splendor of the room with its silk-lined walls and priceless works of art, all lit by a massive crystal chandelier. Guests paused in their conversations as Delia's heels sounded on the polished parquet floor. It was the quartet playing in the corner that brought her out of her stupor long enough to spy the clusters of ladies looking eagerly to the dance floor.

The females in attendance eyed her with interest, the matrons clinging a bit tighter to their husbands and eligible sons, something she had grown accustomed to long ago. Her gaze landed on Mrs. Astor, seated upon a satin settee of royal blue. The humming of the instruments halted at Mrs. Astor's rising.

Mrs. Astor crossed the room in a slow, deliberate manner that had all studying her. "Miss Vittoria, thank you for joining us tonight." She nodded to Delia.

"Mrs. Astor, it is an honor to have been invited to sing for you all." Delia curtsied prettily as she had been taught in her etiquette classes with Hester.

"Yes, well, we must see to it that our beloved Academy stays the beacon of success it has been for years." She waved a tall, brown-haired woman in a bright yellow brocaded gown forward with her silk fan. "Allow me to introduce you to Miss Mildred Ford. Millie, will you see to it that Miss Vittoria makes the rounds? I want *everyone* to meet her." Her gaze flitted over Delia's gown, a pained twinge appearing at the corner of her lips.

Miss Ford curtsied, sending Delia a wink as Mrs. Astor sauntered off, effectively dismissing Delia. "Take a breath, Miss Vittoria, you have already won."

"Have I?" Delia released a nervous laugh. "I feel rather out of place."

"You are here, and Mrs. Astor went out of her way to not only invite you to her exclusive ball but to leave her throne to greet you," she whispered, no animosity hiding behind her sparkling eyes. "Besides, I *know* Mrs. Astor's plans for saving the Academy, and believe me, they are quite marvelous. And *you* are the key."

"Marvelous? But she doesn't even know me. How can she have plans for me?" Her stomach churned. She should've eaten something before coming.

"Yes, well, she doesn't have to know you. After hearing your voice, she has quite decided that you are the instrument she needs, which is slightly prosaic but will greatly benefit you in any event." Miss Ford threaded her arm through Delia's, pulling her close to her side. "Now, who shall we introduce you to?" She studied the room, tapping her fan to her lips. "Any preference? Or do you harbor a secret love for anyone in particular whom you would care to meet?"

Her cheeks flamed. "I possess no secret love, I assure you."

Miss Ford chuckled. "Good, because it is far more useful to the plan if your heart is not already otherwise engaged."

A plan for my heart? What exactly does Mrs. Astor have in mind? Swallowing back her apprehension, she pasted on a smile. "Please choose someone pleasant but who would not view me as an exhibit."

"Well, that does narrow it down a bit." Miss Ford gestured toward a gentleman standing by the crystal punch bowl. "Mr. Pruett is affable, or perhaps we should start you off with another lady so we will not seem as if we are trying to match you from the start?"

"Match me?" Her voice squeaked. "Heavens no. I just began my career and have no intention of marrying anytime soon." *If at all.*

Miss Ford lifted her brows. "His sister then—they are a generally wonderful family." She guided Delia over to a young lady, who hardly seemed old enough to be out in society. "Miss Pruett, please meet Miss Delia Vittoria, the Academy's rising star."

The lady's eyes widened as she set aside her appetizer. "Miss Vittoria, I was present during your performance on opening night in my friend's box, and oh my, there has never been a more graceful, elegant Amina than you!" she gushed, putting Delia at ease as she clasped her hands to her heart. "Elvino has never been so convincing in his love for his counterpart before." Miss Pruett motioned to a gentleman nearby. "Why, Mr. Kemp was right there with me as I was keeping company with his sister for the whole of the performance. Mr. Kemp, what did you think of our dear Miss Vittoria?"

He shrugged. "I thought your interpretation was pleasant enough, but judging from the papers, I should have seen the grandeur of the new opera house. It will never open again for the first time. If Mother hadn't been so insistent, I could have gone."

Delia covered her wounds with a smile. She should be used to it by now, but people's dismissal of her feelings simply because of her lack of status never did seem to get any easier. "Well, there is always another performance, so you may have further opportunity to witness the wonders of the new house," Delia offered.

"Yes, but not a *first* opening night, you see." He lifted his glass to them and ambled away, greeting a cluster of ladies who eagerly accepted his attention.

Miss Pruett's cheeks bloomed. "He is perfectly horrid sometimes and he shall not get away with it. I will be informing his sister of his uncouth behavior. Excuse me." She brushed past them, flipping her skirts behind her.

"So sorry about Mr. Kemp." Miss Ford parked Delia by the ornate pair of dining room doors. "Dinner will be served just after your song. I am going to fetch your partner in the crowd so I can introduce you."

"Please don't leave me," Delia whispered, her desperation for a friendly face keeping her propriety away. "Can't you be my partner for dinner?"

Miss Ford patted her hand. "It isn't done for us to sit side by side. Not all of our gentlemen are like Mr. Kemp." She lowered her voice. "While we are speaking of unpleasantness, avoid the Lovett family, even though they should be tripping over themselves to get to you."

"Oh, I know of them. They are always one of the first to depart if they find the opera lacking." Delia looked about for the family members, picking out the eldest son in the crowd. "But why are they on the outskirts of society? They are an old family." If society could cut one of their own for a misstep, what would they do to Delia's career if they discovered Madre's companion of the past seven years was one of their husbands? And she had already spotted a handful of gentlemen who had attempted to woo her away from Mr. Lowe.

Miss Ford waved her hand dismissively. "It is a long story. But know that they should be doing everything in their power to keep on the Astors' good side, as Mrs. Vanderbilt threw the Lovetts out of her circle for their son's duplicitous actions against the Dupré family. They are on precarious ground being included as part of the Four Hundred. Mrs. Astor says she cannot fit any more into her ballroom, and simply put, they are not the most pleasant of people to be around, no matter how much they pretend to be gregarious. But anyway, don't worry. I'll be back in a shake of a lady's silk fan."

Standing alone was far more pitiable than studying art alone, so Delia strolled along the silk-lined walls, viewing each piece. She had successfully reached the end of the hall without being stopped and paused beside the massive fireplace that was flanked by two antique globes. She was tempted to give the nearest globe a spin when she heard footsteps behind her.

"Miss Vittoria, I wouldn't touch them. Mr. Astor is particular about his antiquities," a deep, familiar voice sounded behind her.

She closed her eyes and drew a breath before turning a bright smile to him to hide her true ire. His dark hair brushed against his broad shoulders, and she had to admit that he was born to wear his evening tails, making him far too handsome for his own good. *Why haven't these women snatched you up?*

"I didn't expect to see you so soon," Mr. Quincy ventured slowly as if he were afraid she would turn from him again. He glanced over his shoulder and risked a second step closer. "You aren't going to run from me again, are you?"

Well, she had tried giving him the cut direct. Perhaps if she forgave him, he would leave her alone. It would not speak well of her to ignore Mr. Quincy's apologies, especially not if anyone overheard them, for then the rumors circulating about her mother's indiscretions would be confirmed. "Thank you for the flowers."

"I am forgiven, then?" His dark brows crinkled, and to her astonishment, she could read true remorse for his actions.

She lowered her voice. "You believe me when I say I am innocent?"

"I do." He ran his hand over the back of his neck. "I have

not ceased thinking of my horrid claim since last night. And if you had a brother or father near, I'd be challenged to a duel—even if it is outlawed."

"Then it is a good thing I have neither father nor brother, so you may not risk your pretty face from being marred." She extended her hand to him. "You are forgiven."

He grinned and caught her hand, but instead of shaking it, he turned over her gloved hand and pressed a kiss atop it. "So, you think I'm pretty?"

"Did I say that?" Her cheeks warmed as she inched away from him and folded her hands in front of the gathers of her overskirt. She looked about the room and, finding no one else looking nearly as friendly as the dashing Mr. Kit Quincy, turned back to her companion, who had returned to looking far too remorseful, which would likely bring someone into the conversation who would ask him why he was so despondent. *That will not do at all.* "While I did receive your flowers, I did not see you in your box. If you were truly remorseful, you would have tossed blooms at my feet," she teased to chase away the serious crease in his forehead.

His grin returned as he leaned against the mantel. "I am quite remiss, though I must say I'm stunned that you know the Quincy box."

She laughed. "While you attend opening nights and every Monday, I have lived at the Academy nearly the entirety of my life and am there for most of the day, save for when I must return home for rest. I know when the families do not attend."

"While I only attend society's required number of performances, I still possess a great love of the Academy. My mother always kept me company during the performances." He cleared his throat and shoved his hands into his pockets. "When I attend, I feel close to her."

"I'm glad you are continuing the tradition after her loss. The company was greatly saddened when she passed. Olympia Quincy was not only a generous patroness but also a kind woman to all who crossed her path."

"Thank you. She was a dear friend who has been sorely missed these past two years." He chuckled, grimacing. "A dear friend who would have been mortified that I did not see your Amina on opening night. And though I was unable to attend that first night . . . due to circumstances you are well aware of that extended into this evening, and I had tonight's ball already planned, I will attend the Academy tomorrow to hear you sing in your role in *La Sonnambula* before the next opera begins."

She held up her hand. "I doubt you will have to go through that trouble, as Mrs. Astor wishes me to sing tonight."

"I wouldn't dream of missing you as Amina." He accepted a glass from a passing footman, extending a second to her that she accepted with a nod of thanks. "And besides, I wish to show my support of the opera house. I agree with Mrs. Astor that it would be a shame for the Academy to fall to the wayside simply because of a new opera house opening."

She silently thanked him for his support with a smile and took a dainty sip of the liquid, testing it against her throat. The acidity of the punch bit her. She looked for the footman to return her drink, but he had already moved into the crowd. "I heard the Metropolitan Opera House is lovely."

He shrugged. "But I've also heard the acoustics leave something to be desired, which in my opinion is *everything* when it comes to an opera. What does it matter if the gilded boxes are gleaming when quality is sacrificed?"

"Well, at least the patrons can all see the stage, which cannot be said for the Academy," she murmured and swirled the contents in her cup. "So, as you are here tonight for Mrs. Astor's party, am I correct in assuming that you side with the Knickerbockers? To keep the opera boxes for the old rich only and keep the parvenus separate?"

Kit lifted a single finger and hovered it over the globe. "Do I dare?"

"You may be joining the ranks of Mr. Lovett and his family if you do," Delia teased, even though for some odd reason she longed to give it a spin herself.

He did, and the globe let out a loud squeak with each turn of the world, drawing the attention of an elderly lady, who sent him a scowl.

Kit grasped Delia's elbow and promptly steered her toward a painting, pointing to it in feigned interest.

"Is she still looking?" he asked out of the side of his mouth.

Delia dared a peek. "We are safe."

He drew her arm through his, pulling her closer. "Good, because what I am about to tell you would surely see me banned. I side with keeping the Academy afloat *not* because of Mrs. Astor's reasoning but because the memories of my mother are most alive when I am there, sitting in her very seat, listening to the operas she loved with the ancient sets that she saw herself. With the Metropolitan opening, the Academy could easily close its doors should the Metropolitan succeed with the nouveaux riches, though I fear the old money's pride will be the Academy's downfall. Personally, I do not care for keeping people out simply because their money is new. It is not right." He leaned toward her. "But let's keep that our little secret, lest the Academy rescind my box."

"I doubt they would attempt such a thing. Your family has owned that box since the Academy first opened. It would not bode well for them to threaten their loyal patrons like that."

"If I am in danger from the patrons for my ideology, will you rescue me as a pledge of friendship?" Mr. Quincy grinned. "Perhaps you could threaten to become the diva for the enemy unless they keep me?"

Delia lifted her glass. "To friendship."

He clinked his glass against hers, and there was a flash of something behind his eyes she did not quite understand but felt in her heart that she had just agreed to a friendship that could change everything.

Mr. Quincy drained his cup and relinquished both of their glasses to Neil, who sent Delia a wink. Mr. Quincy shoved his hands into his pockets. "So, when did you arrive to the party? I didn't see you come through the front, and I know Mrs. Astor always enjoys a certain level of pomp for the honored guests by having them walk through her three reception rooms before being greeted. Did you not have an escort?"

"I hired a carriage and had them drop me around back," Delia admitted.

His brows rose. "You do not own one?" he asked as if it were the oddest thing about her statement.

"There is no need. I am able to walk to and from the Academy."

"To Gramercy Park," he supplied.

"Yes, my father chose it because of the proximity to the Academy." Delia looked up at the art lining the two-story ballroom, eager to end this personal line of questioning. The coved ceiling's motif begged for her attention, but she supposed it would not do to crane one's neck to avoid a conversation, so she settled on strolling.

Mr. Kit followed her. "My condolences for your loss. It must have been hard to experience that at such a young age."

She tilted her head. "What loss?" When she saw the direction she was taking them, she halted before they reached a marble statue that made her cheeks flame. She whirled away lest Mr. Quincy think her goal had been to study the scandalous piece that was in sore need of clothing.

"Your father?"

Delia shook her head and snatched a puff pastry ball from a passing footman. She turned it between her fingers, wondering if its savory contents were worth the risk of foul breath to evade questions, but perhaps bad breath could do the trick just as well. "I understand how you might believe that is the case, but he is alive and well and living in England." She bit into it and nearly sighed at the delightful lobster within.

He cleared his throat. "It seems that I have put my foot in my mouth twice in a row now."

"Let's not try for a third, then." She smiled to let him know she was teasing, despite her desperation to get away from him and his questions. If he continued, he might discover more about her family, and when he spread the findings that she had taken such care to hide from society, all would learn of their shame. Friendship or not, she could not allow society to know what went on behind closed doors in Gramercy Park.

"I see you've found each other." Miss Ford grinned, and at

their quizzical glances, she added, "Mr. Quincy is your escort for dinner, Miss Vittoria, but first I was instructed to tell you that you are to sing from Act II, *Ah! non credea mirarti*, after the opening quadrille. Mrs. Astor said that you can warm your voice in the servants' hall while the dancing goes on." She motioned to Neil behind her, who seemed more than a little eager to escort Delia once more.

She dutifully followed Neil back into the dimly lit servants' hall, cheeks flaming. It was not as if she hadn't warmed her voice up a thousand times in front of people, but the sputtering, guttural noises that were required to warm her voice sounded like they belonged in the wild and not in the servants' basement. It hardly seemed fair to burden the staff with hearing her, and what made matters worse was that Neil didn't seem to intend to leave her as he leaned against the doorframe and watched her pace back and forth while keeping her focus on the maestro's techniques.

Her mother's voice had been the toast of the city when she was younger, without much training, but it was due to her lack of training that she had almost spoiled her voice. If it hadn't been for the maestro forcing her to silence her voice for months before practicing with her, she most likely would have never recovered her voice to sing before the prince, and then she would have never met her father. And so Delia shoved aside her embarrassment and warmed her vocal cords, going through the various contortions to prepare for the complicated song from Act II that she had known by heart since childhood.

Four

Kit had thought Miss Vittoria to be a beauty before her voice filled the ballroom, but there before the Four Hundred she was transformed into a poised lady, radiant with purpose, her voice resplendent. He watched her full lips as they formed each word, drawing them out. Then, as her voice faded into a caress, his heart dipped, having never witnessed such an enchanting aria.

Thunderous applause marked the elite's adoration, and Kit strode to her side to escort her from the stage. However, it seemed that every available gentleman in the room had the same idea as they rushed toward her, eyes bright with admiration, while socialites and their mothers scowled behind them. But as Mrs. Astor had invited Miss Vittoria, they had little choice but to stand back and keep their opinions for the privacy of their own parlors.

The lady of the hour ducked her head at their compliments, and when Kit reached through the press of gentlemen to take her hand, Miss Vittoria's gaze flitted up to meet his. "Excuse me, sirs, but my dinner partner has arrived to claim me."

The gentlemen protested as she rested her hand atop his

palm. Her hand fit delightfully well into his. "You were positively enchanting, Miss Vittoria."

"Thank you," she whispered as he guided her to the corner with its petite forest of potted palms that added a touch of the old way of the Knickerbocker families with its simplicity. "I am used to being behind the curtains or as an extra on the stage in the ensemble, never in the center. I am not well equipped to handle admirers yet."

"I'll take care of you," Kit promised, then added with a wink, "After all, I *am* your escort for dinner."

"Yes, and speaking of escorting . . ." Mrs. Astor caught up to them, sending Miss Vittoria springing closer to him, which had him grinning.

He quite liked having Miss Vittoria on his arm.

"I have been discussing a plan with an intimate circle and I have decided that, in order to save the Academy, what we need is something sensational, driving anyone who owns boxes into the opera not only on the customary Monday and Friday evenings but for nearly every performance," Mrs. Astor whispered. "Therefore bringing in more of the Knickerbockers like Mr. Wingfield and his flock of girls. His renewed attention would bring a great deal of patronage."

"Miss Vittoria's voice will bring them soon enough as word circulates," Kit said.

Miss Vittoria smiled but remained silent, eyes fixed on her greatest patroness.

Mrs. Astor waved him off. "Yes, yes, she will be our instrument, but we need something *more*." She motioned Millie Ford to join them. "Now that I have the two of them together, you explain everything, my dear. I can't have word circulate that I was the one behind this little scheme to save the Academy. Millie will explain everything." She lifted her fan in greeting to a lady across the way and sauntered off.

"Whatever does she mean? And what does it possibly have to do with Mr. Quincy acting as my dinner escort tonight?" Miss Vittoria grasped Millie's arm in the manner of a friend. *Females certainly seem to form attachments sooner than gentlemen.* He felt a twinge of jealousy that while he had attempted to become friends with the singer for days, Millie had only just met Miss Vittoria. *I suppose it* does *help when one does not accuse one of being a woman of ill repute.* Yet Miss Vittoria had indeed chosen wisely if she had Millie as a friend.

The music for the second quadrille began, and the floor bustled into action as the dancers took their places while onlookers encircled the four couples.

Millie's eyes sparkled as she pulled them behind the potted palms. "Before I disclose our plan to you, I need you both to vow not to breathe a word of it, even if you refuse the plan, which would be most inconvenient if you did—especially for you, Kit."

"Millie, must everything be *so* dramatic with you at all times?" Kit chuckled and looked to Miss Vittoria, explaining, "We have been fast friends for three decades, and whenever I got into a troublesome situation, it was usually because Miss Ford here decided to have an adventure." He lowered his voice to Millie. "Don't you think we should be well beyond our scheming days?"

"Never." Millie rolled her eyes. "Where is your sense of adventure? You are only as old as you think you are, Kit." She grasped both their elbows to close their intimate circle. "We need the phantom to return."

"The phantom?" Miss Vittoria gasped. "But didn't he *burn down* the original opera house?"

Millie shrugged. "That was what the police claimed, but as there were no witnesses, they may have decided to lay the blame at his feet because it was most convenient."

"They claimed it to be the phantom because it was most likely the truth, Mildred," Kit retorted, using the name he knew she hated.

She wrinkled her nose at him. "Conjecture that would never stand in the court of law."

"He hasn't been heard of in years, not since my mother . . ." Miss Vittoria's words faded as if an old story had flared in her memory. "That was but a rumor, a fantastical story to drive people to see my mother take over as diva of the new Academy."

Millie shook her head. "It wasn't a rumor. Now, I was just a debutante when it happened, yet I witnessed his obsession. Your mother wished to reclaim her position as prima donna after her time away when she married. But the directors disagreed, which brought about the first sighting of the phantom, who threatened to set fire to the opera house if she was not appointed the position. And we all know *someone* eventually did burn down the building and the phantom only disappeared when his wishes were fulfilled that your mother be appointed diva. Once the Academy was rebuilt and she began her reign, it was then the phantom faded away and everyone seemed to forget him. Still, I'll never forget the terror of the phantom appearing in the rafters above the prima donna's head, wondering if it was love that had driven him to such madness or something else entirely."

Kit scowled. "I remember it as well, and it was not love but obsession."

Millie scratched her head with her little finger. "Well then, I don't know *why* I am repeating myself, because you obviously know all this as her daughter, and Kit was there. Anyway, after witnessing your performances, it was decided by the patronesses that it is time for a new reign."

And by patronesses, Kit had no doubt she meant Jocelyn. He glanced about the room for his sister, feeling guilty that he had not thought to check for her yet. But in the mass of hundreds of guests, she was not to be found—no doubt due to Mr. Lowe's actions keeping her spirits low.

Millie grinned. "So I came up with the idea and presented it to a certain patroness that the return of the phantom would be a wonderful way to bring attention to our dear Academy once more, and she agreed."

"And how do you suppose we go about alerting the phantom? We cannot rightly send him a telegram." Kit chuckled. "Unless you have discovered his address?"

Millie laughed into her fan. "Oh, my dear Kit, you have not lost your sense of humor, despite your towering years. To answer your question, no, but that, my dear fellow, is where you come into the plan."

"Me?" Kit lifted a brow, not caring for where this was leading.

"Well, I don't have you present for this conversation for nothing." She giggled like a schoolgirl and clapped her hands in delight. "Now, this is the delicious part."

Oh no. "Millie . . . what have you done?"

"You, Kit Quincy, are to be the *new* phantom who haunts as if you were the original."

Kit's jaw dropped. "You cannot be serious."

"But instead of inspiring fear and issuing threats, you are to be an utter romantic, leaving the female populace swooning for more of your gallantry."

Miss Vittoria pressed her hand to her mouth, her shoulders shaking from suppressed laughter.

Millie did not notice as she pressed onward. "You may not be aware of this, but the phantom requested to have your box that season he first appeared. He paid a handsome donation for it too, but the Quincy name meant everything to the Academy."

"Truly?" Kit straightened. "Surely someone has records of his donation. He should have been arrested after the fire he set in the basement spread to the neighboring buildings."

"The phantom must have requested that box under a *nom de plume*, and even if he had used his true identity, those records were destroyed long ago in the fire. No one would recall either, as the name was one of hundreds pouring in at the time, donating and requesting to purchase boxes, but only the elite of society were chosen."

Kit crossed his arms and leaned against the room's second fireplace's carved garland, running his fingers over the acanthus leaves. "I do not like the idea of deceiving people I know—my friends. This is nonsensical. I will not be party to—"

Millie gritted her teeth and turned him away from Miss Vittoria, whispering, "We thought you might say that—which is why I am sorry I raised the topic of your being the phantom in the first place, because a certain investor of yours agreed to call in his portion if you do not comply."

"What? I took William Waldorf Astor's loan because he

wished to learn about the hotel business," he hissed. "I would have never sunk so much into the building of the second hotel in Charleston if he hadn't approached *me*." Kit's muscles in his neck tightened. Nearly everything he had was currently in the building of his second hotel.

"You know how Mrs. Astor doesn't get along with her nephew, yet she has something on him that made him agree to it," she whispered. "But I am not supposed to know that, so do not breathe a word of it. The veil of their dislike must not be drawn."

"If William calls it in, I could lose my hotels." He tugged his fingers through his hair. He should have read that document more closely, but he had trusted Astor. He had nothing besides his residences and yacht to liquidate in order to pay back William. Still, the timing of the issue could prove disastrous. He could be ruined as they would have to be sold at a loss to pay the man back. And they were more than just deeds—they were the memories of his mother and father. He grunted. Uncle Elmer had been right. He had been a fool to invest so heavily in his business and overextend himself by accepting the loan. "So, if I agree, the loan will continue to be paid off at the agreed-upon rate?"

"What are you two saying?" Miss Vittoria interjected. "Why are you looking so distraught, Mr. Quincy?"

He didn't need to burden her with his stupidity of not protecting himself better because of his friendship with the family. "It's nothing."

Miss Vittoria's brow furrowed. "It's obviously *not* nothing. Oh, this is all my fault. I should have listened to Madre and never have come tonight."

Millie sighed. "If it hadn't been you, it would have been

someone else, I'm afraid." Millie grasped his arm. "This will serve a greater purpose, Kit. You will not only save your mother's legacy but will also send Miss Vittoria's career into a thing of legend."

"I do not think I can rightly profit from such chicanery," Miss Vittoria said. "It may sound rather idealistic, but I would prefer to rise on my own merit."

Millie's gaze darted to Miss Vittoria. "Frankly, my dear, in light of your mother's recent indiscretion, Signora Vittoria's reign is coming to a close."

The blood drained from Miss Vittoria's face. "Y-you've heard?" She flashed a look to Kit. "Did you—?"

"No! A gentleman never gossips about such things." *If Millie knows . . . how many others do, as well?* He well knew the damage a tarnished reputation in a family could cause, no matter how hard one attempted to keep it from soiling one's own . . . guilty by association, and *he* had proclaimed Miss Vittoria guilty before even speaking with her.

"Well, your mother could not expect to remain untouchable forever, not with choosing Mr. Lowe as her conquest."

Miss Vittoria looked down to the fan she was clenching in her fist, her shoulders slumping. "Madre relies too much on her voice to save her."

"It has in the past, but she crossed the wrong patroness." Millie shook her head.

"If I accept your offer, won't I be unseating my very own mother?"

"Her fate has already been determined. It may not go into effect until next week, but she will be removed as prima donna. By taking the role, you are rather solidifying your family's legacy. Your mother should be proud of you for saving the family's name." Millie laid a hand on her arm as if to reassure Miss Vittoria.

"You do not know my mother," she murmured under her breath, barely loud enough for him to hear. She added, "But you are correct in that she has been unwise and well knew how patronage could change the course of one's career—for better or for worse." She pressed her lips into a thin line. "And you are certain they would be replacing my mother even if I did not agree to this plan?"

"I know you are worried about your mother, but understand that this will happen with or without you as diva."

Delia raised her gloved hand to her cheek. "I see."

Millie turned to him. "And, Kit, if you are still hesitating, remember you owe Mrs. Astor for the recommendation to Mr. and Mrs. Dupré to invite you to join their competition." Millie lifted a single brow. "Would you refuse to repay a debt?"

"A recommendation which very nearly ended in heartbreak." Kit chuckled to lighten his words, feeling Miss Vittoria's curious gaze on him.

"'Tis all in the name of theater. It's a *play*." Millie patted him on the arm with her fan. "And I well remember how you loved to join in the tableau games. It is a small price to pay to keep your hotel safe." She turned to Miss Vittoria. "Think not of this as 'chicanery,' as you call it, Miss Vittoria, but as part of the play. Anyone who is anyone will be filling their boxes for a chance to see the phantom in action, for the night of his appearance will be ever-changing, and the papers will cover the story, no matter that it is a third or sixth time you have performed *La Sonnambula*. Admit it, Miss Vittoria and Kit. It's a brilliant plan."

Kit shifted in his dinner jacket, even as the idea began to grow upon him that as part of the *play*, it wasn't truly wrong and it would give him the chance to counter with the Astors, creating a clause in the loan's contract that kept them from ever calling in the loan—though now he would do all in his power to repay the debt by next summer. "I can see its merit, but again, the deceit."

"My dear boy, our mothers were the dearest friends of friends." Millie rested a hand on his arm.

"They spoke but thrice a year," Kit corrected with a snort.

"Time spent together does not judge the weight of one's affection toward a friend. And I *know* our mothers would have loved such a lark. And again, it will ensure Miss Vittoria's position, who is too young to lose everything due to the politics of opera when she should only be concerned with the art."

He looked to Miss Vittoria, his jaw tightening. Her voice rivaled that of the famous Jenny Lind. She needed only a season before she burned too brightly for the Academy and would be asked to tour, he was certain of it. But she needed that season first or else she might never see the stages across the world. And if he did not agree to this plan, his dream, as well as hers, could very well be crushed. "Yes, it would be a shame," he finally said.

Miss Vittoria dipped her head at his praise, but he caught the pleased smile she was attempting to hide. "Won't Mr. Quincy be liable to suspicion if he is there when the phantom isn't and vice versa?"

"To bolster his role in all of this and keep people from suspecting him, he will become your patron." She turned to Kit. "Which is believable given your charity donations.

Not only will you support her work monetarily but you will also become her escort into society to show Mrs. Astor's approval. Miss Vittoria will be accepted by all in New York, which Mrs. Astor's rival, Mrs. Vanderbilt, well remembers is next to impossible." She leaned toward them and in a conspiratorial whisper said, "Mrs. Astor still has not forgiven Mrs. Vanderbilt for forcing her hand in making her visit Mrs. Vanderbilt's home—and therefore acknowledging her as a society matron—for her daughter, Carrie, to attend that costume ball of Mrs. Vanderbilt's and take part in the star quadrille." She shuddered. "I well know that when a daughter is being slighted, a mother will do nearly anything, even swallow her pride, to right the situation."

Kit sighed. "You are neither married nor a mother or aunt."

"I can *imagine*, Kit, all right? Now, are you going to help Miss Vittoria or leave her to face her fate alone and risk your business?"

"Your business is at stake? Oh, Kit, I am so sorry." Miss Vittoria covered her mouth with her hand, remorse flooding her countenance.

Kit could feel the last bit of resolve crumble with her calling him by name. Despite his beginning with Miss Vittoria, he would prove himself to be kind, compassionate, and above all, *repentant* of the way he had severely judged her. And after hearing her sing tonight, she had awoken something in him. No, he certainly did not wish to leave her alone, nor lose his successful business. "It is not your fault."

Millie placed Miss Vittoria's hand atop his, the diva's touch sending a flare up his arm.

"The fate of the Academy of Music rests in your hands, Kit," Millie added somberly.

"And Mrs. Astor stands fully behind this outlandish idea?" He looked over to the regal lady.

Millie winked at him. "I can neither confirm nor deny it, but I know that we must decide everything from here on out between us three, for she cannot be seen as party to this. However, we will have her approval and therefore we will find our tasks much easier to accomplish."

The quadrille concluded, and the dinner gong sounded, sending all to their partners.

Millie patted his arm. "Now, I must see to my escort, lest he think I gave him the slip like last week. You two probably shouldn't discuss this conversation at dinner, given the delicate nature of our topic." With a whisk of her brocade skirts, Millie abandoned them.

Miss Vittoria's hand still rested on his arm, her touch searing through his jacket. "Shall we go in to dinner?"

At her nod, Kit expertly wove them through the crowd, earning scowls from the single ladies in the ballroom, which made him send Miss Vittoria a smile to help steady her nerves. Her gritted-teeth expression of enduring a great trial made his chest swell with suppressed laughter. "So, you can sing in front of all, but being escorted into dinner by me is a trial?"

"Never. It is an honor. It is only . . ." She rose on her tiptoes to whisper in his ear, "I have never been to a ball before and I'm not quite certain what to expect."

He halted in the line, the couple behind him grumbling at the unnecessary stop. "What? Never?"

"Madre does not exactly have a lot of friends." She looked to the quartet and sent them a smile and a little wave at her waist, unknowingly displaying her kind heart. "When she married my father, she abandoned whatever little family and friends she possessed in the Italian district. I have no idea if I have any relatives there, as she refuses to speak of them. And after my father left, she didn't seem to have any friends from that period in her life either. Being a prima donna, well, one does not become a diva without isolating herself from all peers, not if one is like my mother and thinks the rest of the company is beneath her."

"But you don't think that way, do you?" he asked as they entered the oak-paneled dining room. He held the back of her chair under one of the Flemish tapestries, noticing Mrs. Astor had selected the gold plates for tonight in another move to display her support of Miss Vittoria, even if she had proclaimed to Miss Vittoria's face that she was little more than a means to an end.

"Oh no. The company is my family. They know more about me than my own father." She assumed her seat, looking at Mr. and Mrs. Astor at the head of the table, almost nervously as she studied the place setting before her—namely the silverware.

At the arrival of the first course, she worried her bottom lip at which spoon to choose. Kit slowly moved his finger along the line of spoons, landed on the correct utensil, and picked it up, earning a dimpled smile from the beauty.

The conversation hummed about them, and as most inclined their attention to Mrs. Astor's side of the table, Kit was able to wordlessly cue Miss Vittoria on the table etiquette—until the conversation turned and he was forced to leave her to Mr. Pruett. The man was still seeking a bride after the spring's competition for Willow's hand, but knowing the gentleman was extraordinarily kindhearted, Kit had little reason to fear for Miss Vittoria's comfort. Instead, he turned to Millie.

"So, have you two decided?" Millie asked, spearing her partridge and truffles, slicing through the meat. "I need to let Mrs. Astor know by the end of the night."

He lifted his brows. "We haven't discussed it . . . as you suggested."

"I meant to discreetly discuss it. Really, Kit, do you not know me at all after all these years of spending dinner party after ball after luncheon together? Ask her now," she scolded and took a dainty bite, humming at the morsel.

"That is hardly discreet, as the conversation has turned," Kit murmured, finishing his plate while Millie took another bite.

She lifted her hand to hide her mouthful and answered, "Whisper it in her ear. It will draw attention, yes, but it will show that Miss Vittoria has caught your eye. If you are to act as her patron, you'd better get to the acting part of it."

Kit sighed, then arranged his expression into that of a young pup and turned to Miss Vittoria, whispering in her ear, "Miss Vittoria?"

She fairly jumped out of her seat, her fork tilting and coming perilously close to soiling her gown.

"Miss Ford requires an answer. Are we agreeable to her plan?"

She dabbed her napkin at the corner of her mouth, blocking her lips from Mr. Pruett. "Well, as Mr. Pruett just informed me of some rather convincing tales of the grandeur of the Metropolitan and its prowess over the Academy, I believe I must answer in the affirmative in order to save my company."

"Truly?" Was he really going to do this? Was he, the confirmed bachelor, going to squire this beauty about town and so save them both? At the excitement sparking behind her dark eyes that was echoed in his heart, he knew it would be no hardship.

Miss Vittoria smiled. "It seems we are to be great friends indeed, Mr. Quincy."

Five

The mist was becoming heavier as Delia fumbled for the keys in her new reticule. Kit stood behind her on the front step, keeping guard over her after Mrs. Astor's enlightening dinner. Never had she enjoyed such an evening, nor been out until three in the morning! Even though it had started rather demoralizing with Mr. Kemp's appraisal of her voice, it ended splendidly, for the dashing Mr. Kit was to be her escort for the season.

Her cheeks warmed at the thought of his paying call in broad daylight and applauding her in his burgundy velvet and gold box, showering her with blooms for all to see. *If only he had asked me to dance, my night would have been complete.* She rolled her eyes at her ridiculous daydream and retrieved the key. *Stop it. You know he is only doing this for that loan he mentioned and the Academy, for the memory of his mother and for the Knickerbocker society matrons.*

She had wished to press him more about the loan that had pushed him to join her in saving the Academy, but as he'd already agreed, she saw little point in pressing the matter tonight. Whatever was at risk for him, she would not fail him—not after he had been so kind to her.

Hoarse laughter flowed from the parlor window. Madre was entertaining Mr. Lowe again after Delia had informed Madre of Mrs. Lowe's delicate condition. The skeleton key in her hand trembled on its way to the lock. Delia braced herself, praying that Kit did not hear it for fear it would spoil their evening. She hadn't realized she had frozen in place until Kit's hand wrapped around the key, gently taking it from her stiff fingers and unlocking the door.

"What must you think of me, Mr. Quincy?" She pressed her hand against the door, the other pausing on the latch as she fought for equanimity.

"I think Lowe stopped by after a party and that your mother's actions are just that, Miss Vittoria—your mother's. This situation is not your fault." His strong hand rested on her shoulder, gently turning her to him.

She looked up to find only kindness lining his expression. She lifted a hand to her mouth, tears filling her eyes. This was why she did not have friends apart from the Academy, for if any one person witnessed her shame and mortification over her mother's behavior, news would spread faster than she could control. It was easier to be alone to manage her shame, when all she had to do was escape upstairs and drown out the laughter around the old upright piano on her level of rooms. "It doesn't make it any easier to bear, knowing—"

"If there is one good thing that will come from our little charade, people will see you for *your* own merit and judge you for your actions and not those of your relations." He held the door open for her. The foyer was lit by a single gaslight, and tonight's flowers from her dressing room now filled the room, spilling over the round table, occupying every corner, even sitting on the marble floor. For a brief moment, Delia could imagine that she and Kit had happened upon a field of wildflowers far from this house of shame. *Stop it, Delia. And his name is not* Kit *to you. It is Mr. Quincy.* She swiped at her eyes with her thumb, rubbing the traces of tears away, and straightened her shoulders. No more dreaming. The only dream she could afford was her career.

Kit laughed, gesturing to the sea of flowers. "I see mine was not the only offering tonight, nor the most extravagant."

Delia turned about, displaying the roses in her hair for him. "Simplicity is what I prefer."

"I noticed, and it gave me hope that you not only liked them, but you forgave me." He moved his cane from hand to hand. "But I do not think you need to worry so much about what people think of you based on your mother anymore. By having Mrs. Astor's approval of your career, and I daresay without meaning to sound arrogant, with myself acting as your escort, you will be received with honor by the end of the season. People will clamor for your appearance."

"And for that I will be forever grateful. You understand, however, that I cannot admit to being in your debt. For being in debt to a man does not become a lady."

Kit's neck reddened. "I would never presume such a thing, Miss Vittoria."

If her mother knew of their plans, she would question why Mr. Quincy would go along with this scheme. Delia sent him a sideways glance, noting the lines about his eyes, and wondered who had put those lines there. And the silver streaks at his temples? He was all the more handsome for them. In her brief time with him, she was finding Mr. Quincy was too kind, too pure of heart to be like the others. *And like the others, time will tell,* her incredulous heart whispered. "I know, but I must say it nonetheless." She gestured to the parlor door. "For you can see by my upbringing, gentlemen rarely bestowed gifts to my mother without expecting something in return."

"I can tell from spending a single evening with you that you do not take after your mother's taste in men." He paused. "You must know that if it is indeed Lowe in the parlor, I will be forced to drag him out. I will attempt to do so without ado."

Delia had little doubt that it was anyone else but Mr. Lowe, as Madre had kept him about for nearly seven years now, though she wouldn't divulge that to Kit. With a sigh, she turned the parlor's handle, cringing at the man's voice on the other side of the door that she knew far too well. She found Madre in her extravagant receiving wrap, her arms draped over Lucian's shoulders as he played Madre's favorite aria from *La Sonnambula*.

"Lucian Lowe," Kit thundered, his brows lowered to a point as he fairly charged into the room with clenched fists. The gentleman from moments before vanished. "You gave me your word as a gentleman, sir."

Lucian, sober this time, continued to play while Madre reclined on her settee, drawing her wrap closer. "You see, I love Giovanna Vittoria, and one cannot simply dismiss love, Cousin."

Kit scowled at him, gripping his cane in both fists, his knuckles whitening. Kit's displeasure caused Lucian's fingers to stumble over the chord. "The same was declared over my sister five years ago. How could you do this to Jocelyn?"

Delia's stomach roiled as the rich food twisted her insides in pain, along with the realization that Mr. Quincy was not only this man's cousin but also his brother-in-law.

"A man can love two women at the same time," Lucian replied, rising from the piano and resting his hand on Madre's shoulder.

"Not well, nor in the manner they deserve—with respect."

Delia grasped the back of the shabby turquoise-colored divan for support. How could she not have known? The dream she had allowed to bloom in her heart curled in on itself. *Mr. Quincy must despise my mother.* A man couldn't get past such a sin against a beloved sister—no matter how kind, and no matter his pretty speech. He most likely would never see Delia apart from her mother and his sister's pain. The two would be forever intertwined.

"I see, Quincy, that we fancy the same type of woman." Lowe looked into Madre's eyes with admiration. "Talented, extraordinary, Italian beauties."

"Luciano, *caro mio*. You are too kind, my dear." Madre rose to brush his jaw with the back of her hand.

Kit pointed the head of his cane at Mr. Lowe. "Go home, Lowe, before I forget myself in front of a lady."

Madre laughed. "How gallant of you, Mr. Quincy."

He narrowed his gaze at her and turned to Delia, his meaning clear as her tinkling laughter died. In his eyes, Delia was the only lady present. Despite her pleasure that he still thought her such, she couldn't help but feel for her mother, even if Madre had brought it upon herself.

Madre's dark curls about her face began to tremble. "Are you going to stand there and allow him to insult me, Luciano?"

Lucian stepped back and cracked his knuckles, studying his opponent as if weighing if Mr. Quincy would throw a punch. "I was about to depart anyway. Mrs. Astor's party is ending, so my shield of guise shall be taken if I linger."

Kit lowered his cane. "And do not return or it will not end well for your career, Signora Vittoria."

Madre laughed as she ran her fingers over Mr. Lowe's shoulders. "Is that a threat, Mr. Quincy? How ungentlemanly of you."

"He is not the one making the threat, Madre," Delia interjected, moving to her mother's side, clasping her hand. "Please. You must listen to him. I think that it is best that you and Mr. Lowe do not see each other again."

Madre straightened to her full height, and as she was rather tall, she towered over Delia. "As I have said before, you will not dictate how I live in my own home."

"If Father were here, Mr. Lowe would not dream of—"

"But he is *not* here, and he never will be." Her voice cracked, and she pressed her fingers to her temple and drew in a steadying breath. "And you know nothing of the reason he abandoned us. If you did, I doubt you would ever speak of him again with such deference." Madre crossed the room and took her by the arm. "Go to bed, Delia. You have lessons in the morning, *cara mia*, though I doubt you will be performing. My voice has returned."

Kit took a step forward. "I will not warn you a third time to stay away, Lucian. You know what I am capable of."

Madre clapped twice at her. "Now, Delia, *vai via*!"

If only she could *go away* from this situation, but Delia would not leave her side—not when Kit was looking so murderously at his cousin.

Lucian pressed a kiss to Madre's forehead. "Farewell, my darling."

Kit glared at Lucian, grabbed their top hats and cloaks, and the two of them retreated from the heavy rain to the carriage. Before stepping in, Kit looked over his shoulder to Delia and sent her an apologetic smile. Lifting his hat to her and her mother, he slipped inside and shut the door, and the carriage disappeared into the deluge.

Delia cringed, and without a single word to her mother, despite Madre calling to her, she escaped up the stairs to the third story that held her rooms and Hester's, along with a small room that was deemed the guest room, though they never entertained any guests. Elena stayed with her husband but returned every morning to make coffee and prepare the meals.

Hester leaned against the doorframe across the hall from Delia's rooms. Her wiry gray hair framing her face was rolled in cloths that bunched up at both sides, the gray disappearing into the blond braid that swayed beyond her waist. She set her glasses on the tip of her nose. "You were out late. Must have been a good party. I am sorry it ended the way it did."

Delia covered her face with her hands, leaning into Hester's outstretched arms. "Oh, Hester. It was such a lovely evening, one that Madre saw fit to crush."

Hester drew an arm around Delia's waist and, with her other hand, patted Delia's shoulder. "I tried to have her refuse Mr. Lowe, but you know that if I push, I will lose my position, despite my years with the family."

"You are more my family than anyone ever could be, Hester."

"You know that your mother loves you." Hester patted her shoulder again.

"Then why does she do this? She has us—aren't we enough?" Delia swiped at her cheeks, angry with herself for crying. But seeing her mother with Lucian in front of Kit was all too much.

"I'm by no means excusing her behavior, but your mother has never gotten over the hurt of your father leaving. I think she is trying to fill the void he left in her heart." Hester sighed and guided her into Delia's rather large chamber with its pretty pale mint walls of faded silk, lined in creamy molding she was told her father had selected for her. The darling furniture it had once contained and that she had long since outgrown had been sold, and in its place were worn secondhand pieces that did not match. Though her bed frame was plain, it was made of sturdy walnut. She had painted her armoire white to cover the stains and chips, but as she didn't know very well what she was doing, the door always stuck and its drawers were near to impossible to open at first. Now, after years of use, just a tug did the job.

Her prized possession sat at the bay window facing the park, a lovely upright piano. It had taken a pulley system and a new set of windows to have the instrument moved into her room. The piano was a gift from her father, who had it sent to her on her thirteenth birthday—after she wrote him, telling him of her decision to pursue becoming an opera star. Beside her bed, a chipped vase bore more flowers from her performance, in bright yellows and oranges with evergreen branches mixed into the arrangement.

"Thank you. They help brighten the room," Delia commented as she pulled off her gloves. She drew the shades against the lightning and rain, hoping Kit had made it safely home.

Hester nodded and helped her undress and ready herself for bed, lastly running the wooden comb through Delia's locks. Her guttural humming began, and Delia closed her eyes, allowing herself to sway with the hymn "Jesus, Lover of My Soul." Maestro Rossi and Madre always silenced Hester's unusual voice, declaring it horrid and without tune, but to Delia it was the voice of the grandmother she longed to possess, and to her there was not a superior soprano to be had.

"'Other refuge have I none, hangs my helpless soul on Thee: leave, O leave me not alone. Still support and comfort me: all my trust on Thee is stayed. All my help from Thee I bring. Cover my defenseless head with the shadow of Thy wing,'" she finished, warbling the verses. She pressed a kiss atop her charge's hair, just as she had done since taking on the role of nanny, shortly after Father had left and the first nanny packed her bags along with him.

She returned the combs to the vanity and drew back the coverlet. "Just remember, Delia, your worth does not hang on the dithering praises of society. Keep your trust in Jesus and He will never leave you. He will cover you with the shadow of His fatherly wing and protect you. As a believer, you are a child of God and will forever know to whom you belong—not to a mother with scandal dripping from her name, not to society, not to that wayward father of yours, but to God alone." She tapped the Bible on the nightstand. "I marked a passage for you that I think goes well with this week's new hymn we learned in our choir meeting that you missed, which you need to practice before Sunday. Tell me what you think about it tomorrow."

Six

After leaving Lucian in his sister's care, Kit did not sleep well. Every time he closed his eyes, he was greeted with visions of the phantom of old—the one who incited fear. And when Kit finally unmasked the villain haunting him, the man was himself. Unnerved, he at last gave up on the idea of sleeping and, as the rain had finally ended, quickly dressed to ride to his hotel.

Kit directed his horse through Central Park in the direction of the Olympia Grande, basking in the sunrise as it banished the fog rolling over the grassy mounds, the mockingbirds twittering and calling to one another. The only other sounds to be heard were the footfalls of his horse's hooves on the gravel path and the occasional splashing through a mud puddle. By the time he reached the hotel, prayers and nature had made his soul tranquil once more and he was ready to solve the problems of the staff.

"You are here early!" Ramsey Gunn called to him from the front desk, where a cluster of clerks scattered at once at his nod of dismissal. "I thought the whole point of hiring me as your hotel manager was so that you could take long mornings and trips across the seas in that yacht of yours."

Kit laughed and handed his hat and riding crop to the bellhop. "That is the curse of the driven man. Even if one finds success, there is always more success to be had." He nodded toward the elevators. "I am here to see how the finishing touches for the rooftop garden are coming along for tonight's party."

Ramsey grinned. "Let's just say that you are going to put Rudolf Aronson's rooftop garden out of everyone's minds."

"Excellent." Kit fought to remain professional and not slap Ramsey on the back at hearing the news. His rooftop garden would be one of the first in New York City after Aronson's, who had unveiled his own roof garden atop his newly built casino over on Broadway. But Kit's undisclosed project was sure to bring the hotels of New York to attention with his latest attraction. "Will it be ready?"

"It will be close. The crew will finish up by noon, after which the staff will ready it for your sister's opera ball tonight." Ramsey lifted his notebook, running his index finger over the columns. "I have a few things to check over. Would you mind reviewing the financial ledger before I go to the bank . . . ?" His words dropped off as he stared behind Kit. "What in the world is *she* doing here?"

Startled at his friend's animosity toward a woman, Kit turned, his jaw dropping.

"Hello, Christopher." His former fiancée smiled at him, her crystal blue eyes sparkling as if she were delighted to see him.

She held her hands out to him, and he had little choice but to accept them in his. She pressed a kiss to his cheek, the touch nearly searing him.

"Alice Lexington? What are you doing back in the States? I mean, *Lady Ellyson*."

"No need to stand on such familiarity, Christopher." She flipped open her lavender fan, batting it slowly. "It would be refreshing to hear my girlhood sobriquet once more. You may call me Elsie, as you always have."

"May I?" He released a chuckle and ran his fingers through his hair, glancing at Ramsey, who had not ceased frowning at her.

Elsie nodded to Ramsey. "Mr. Gunn. I am glad to see that you two are still close."

"Someone had to be," he retorted. "After you broke him in favor of adventure and that British title."

Kit glared at Ramsey. "She did not *break* me, Ramsey. Don't you have something pressing that you need to see to?"

Ramsey shot a glance at Elsie before slowly nodding. "I do, but I'll be right over there the whole time." He pointed to the front desk. He leaned to Kit and muttered, "Cough twice if you need me."

A flicker of apprehension crossed over her now-tanned cheeks as Ramsey departed, sending surreptitious glances over his shoulder at the pair of them. "You will speak with me, won't you, Christopher? I came down here to see you."

"Of course, Lady Ellyson." He grasped her elbow and guided her to the corner of the lobby to the large circular conversation settee and waited for her to take a seat before joining her. "Pardon my manners. I was only shocked. May I ask *why* you are here to see me? You haven't left India since you stepped off that boat."

"Things changed." She gestured to her gown.

Kit ran his hand over his jaw, feeling ten different kinds

of the fool for not spying the obvious, and judging from the shade of lavender she was wearing, she was just coming out of mourning. He was too caught up in his own thoughts to see the pain before him. "Oh no. Elsie. No." His heart ached for her. "Was it your parents?"

She stared at her folded hands in her lap, her knuckles tightening and pulling against the kid gloves. "I lost my Dawson."

Kit's heart clenched. The loss of his mother had been difficult, and while he had not experienced the loss of a spouse, he had experienced a future—or two—dying. He placed his hand over hers, offering her his strength. "To lose a spouse . . . I cannot imagine the pain. I am so sorry to hear of your loss, Elsie."

"Thank you. It's been difficult, but I feel the change of scenery will help my son, Thomas, as I learn to adjust. And after Dawson's death, I regretted how I treated you. Being married gives one an altered perspective on life and love. With Dawson, our home was always filled with wonder and adventure." She looked up at him through those thick lashes he could never forget. "Much like how our love began." She shook her head. "But that sense of adventure took him from me and our little chap far too early . . . as it took me from you."

He lifted his brow, unable to mask his surprise. At the end of their relationship, she had not disguised her scorn for him and his unadventurous ways.

"Lord Ellyson passed nearly a year ago and the pain never ceases, which made me think of the pain you must have endured when I left you."

"I hardly think you can compare my heart, which has never

known a day of marriage, to yours, a widow after nearly fifteen years of marriage." At the flash of hurt in her expression, he amended, "But yes, it wasn't easy in those early days after you left."

"I regret the way I ended things. You know that I didn't mean what I said then."

You could have fooled me. He could recall the scene in its entirety. She'd been wearing a scarlet gown and had yellow flowers in her chapeau, and her eyes were flashing angrily at him for chasing her down to the docks after receiving her note. She wanted to slip away without a parting. But when he had attempted to dissuade her from leaving with her parents and once more refused to join her, she cut him down, declaring him wanting. No matter that they had been sweethearts for years. No matter that she had promised she would wait for him to finish at the university before expecting marriage and adventure. Apparently, they had vastly different ideas on what exactly *adventure* entailed. For Kit, it had been a plan to build a hotel business along the East Coast. For Elsie, it was India. "Didn't you?"

"I was a romantic. I wanted you to give up everything and join me. And when you didn't board the ship, I lashed out to the only gentleman who had ever loved me." Elsie squeezed his hand, her blue eyes lovely as ever. "You were my first love, you know?"

"If love means that you can abandon said love for someone with a heart for adventure, then certainly I knew you loved me," he said, disliking this feeling and the memories she was bringing forth.

"I know I did not handle myself well when I broke it off. Now that I have had years to contemplate what I was feeling, I realized that sometimes, if you love someone, you must let them go. I knew that if I did not travel to India, I would come to resent you. And that was something I could never do, not when you had always been so impossibly kind to me."

He did not like being brought back to that place where his heart was so full of hurt. He was not some love-scorned boy. He had grown into himself, and he liked who he had become. "Why are you telling me this now?"

"Because I've discovered that life is too short to live with bad blood between ones who were once such close friends," she whispered, smiling at him in the old way that once had him melting at her command. "And when I discovered you were single, I thought—"

"That I was pining for you?" He chuckled. "It shouldn't come as a surprise to you that I am not some heartsore lover. I simply have been enjoying my bachelorhood."

"Always a homebody." She smiled, softening her words.

"You make it sound as if I never leave New York, when you are fully aware I spend my summers in Newport, my winters in New York, and my springs in Charleston. And I do travel extensively in my yacht to each home."

"Forgive me." She rose, clutching her reticule, Kit rising with her. "I did not come here to argue but merely to tell you I am home to stay, and I so desperately wish to be friends again."

Kit coughed twice into his fist. "Then we shall be."

Ramsey trotted over to him. "Kit? We have quite the pressing matter. Would you excuse us, Lady Ellyson?"

And with a nod to the lady who had once crushed his heart underfoot, Kit escaped to the safety of the hotel office.

Despite the late night at the Astors' ball and dragging herself out from under her coverlet, Delia arrived at the Academy five minutes before her appointment with the maestro at eleven of the clock. She waved to the Academy's staff and company members, weaving through the stacks of theatrical property, trunks of costuming and the possessions of the company on her way to the maestro's music room. She slipped into the darkened room, careful to avoid the stacks of sheet music scattered about. The chamber was lit only by a single hurricane lamp that rested upon the grand piano, where Maestro Rossi sat, his stiff back to her, the whiskers of his muttonchops peeking around his cheeks.

When Delia was a child and they had first begun their lessons at her mother's insistence, Delia always attempted to strike up a conversation, but Maestro Rossi never engaged beyond the lesson, as if any more time in her presence was painful. And so she respected the maestro's requirement of silence beyond the music and greeted him with a nod, taking her place beside the piano and beginning her scales as she warmed her voice.

The practice was fairly all muscle memory, which did not keep her mind from drifting back to Mr. Kit Quincy and their quest to save the Academy. While she did not approve of the layers of deceit, she saw the merit of the act and appreciated the theatrics that would hopefully save her dear Italian company from being tossed into the street, unemployed, all thanks to the shimmering new opera house.

"Again, Miss Vittoria," Maestro Rossi barked. "You are *not* concentrating. Two successful performances do not warrant a third. *Practice.* That is what ensures another perfect performance, but even then, it will not be perfect if you are not present in body, soul, and *mind.* Now, sing with all of yourself and do not hold back or our lessons will end for the day."

"There you are, Delia." Madre sailed into the room, tugging her fingers free from her gloves, her scarlet skirts whisking in her haste.

"Confound it all." Maestro Rossi harrumphed and slammed down the fallboard, making Delia jump at the jarring discord. "Does no one respect the sacredness of the lesson?"

Delia folded her trembling hands before her skirts. She had made a deal to save the Academy, but at the cost of Madre having to step down as lead, who had encouraged her talent in the first place. It was certainly easier to be vexed with her at night when the mother she knew disappeared, but in the opera house, there were too many happy memories scattered about for her *not* to feel culpable. "Madre, I thought I left you resting."

Madre caressed her cheek in passing and gave the maestro a slow, soothing smile, running her gloves through her open palm. "That is enough practice for one day, Maestro. Delia won't need it for tonight, as *I* have been cleared by my doctor and will be reclaiming my throne and the lead role as Amina."

"Back in the sixties when you were my pupil, you would not have *dared* to voice a comment such as that." He scowled, his wiry eyebrows lowering to a point. "She is done when I say she is done."

"And a gentleman should never remind anyone of a lady's age." She gently kissed his withered cheek. "Now, be a dear and dismiss her so we can begin our practice. I'm afraid my voice needs it after all this resting."

"Delia will be finished once she completes this aria," Maestro Rossi replied, resuming his seat.

"Another aria? Would you allow me to demonstrate for you how it is done, *cara mia*, like the old days?" She removed her wrap and slid the pin from her chapeau, setting each atop the piano, which had the maestro's scowl deepening as he muttered about protecting the finish of the instrument.

Never one to deny Giovanna Vittoria anything, the maestro obligingly flung open the fallboard and led into the aria. Madre rolled back her shoulders and drew in a deep breath.

Delia was no match for Madre's cultured, experienced voice. Nonetheless, the papers had called Delia's voice quite refreshing, although her mother's acting was deemed to be far superior. Madre could cry and sing at the same time. If Delia attempted such a feat, well, it would not end so prettily.

As the last note faded, Madre turned an impassioned smile upon her, her chest heaving from the exercise. "You are talented, Daughter, but I know what the audience wants and expects. They are in love with the novelty of your voice, yet that will fade in time, and soon they will long for my polished voice, as well as my fine acting and dancing. These are areas in which you must practice. Therefore, I have arranged for you to attend a weekly ballet class with Madame Dumas."

"Thank you, Madre," she said. While Madre never listened regarding her choice in men, she never neglected Delia's talent—even if it meant that Delia would one day be given the lead roles.

"Dancing lessons?" Giuseppe Rossi grinned from the doorway, his hair brushed into a thick dark pompadour.

"Jealousy is not becoming on you, Signora Vittoria, especially not when it is directed at your daughter."

As always, Madre smiled at him, never minding his sharp tone. "Oh, Giuseppe, always such a tease, as if I could ever be jealous of my own daughter. Granted, she may take the lead in a few years when I finally begin to show my age." She ran the back of her hand up her cheek, laughing. "But I must prepare Delia for when I take on the more mature roles."

"Not according to the papers. Seems after seeing her performance, they are ready for you to take on those, what did you call them, *mature roles*?"

Her gaze fell on the headline Giuseppe held up and pointed to with glee. "But she isn't ready. Besides this week, her only experience has been in the ensemble and her church choir."

Giuseppe leaned against the doorframe, the paper gripped between his fingers to display the headline. "Says in here that her voice is ethereal."

"That's enough out of you, Giuseppe." Maestro Rossi frowned at his son and rose from his place at the piano, but Giuseppe was too busy bickering with Madre to hear. The maestro's eyes met Delia's, and in that second she could read his raw loathing of her that she suspected was there all along. "She will never replace Giovanna. She is nothing to her."

Delia refused to shrink back at his comment—that this man who had been her only father figure would reject her. She closed her eyes against his stare and recalled the beginning verses from Psalm 61 that Hester had marked for her. *"From the end of the earth will I cry unto thee, when my heart is overwhelmed: lead me to the rock that is higher than I. For thou hast been a shelter for me, and a strong tower from the enemy . . . I will trust in the covert of thy wings*

. . . For thou, O God, hast heard my vows: thou hast given me the heritage of those that fear thy name." She lifted her chin. Her father might not have wanted her, nor this man she had known since birth, but she didn't have to allow that knowledge to crush her.

Not wishing to stay for the brewing storm, Delia gathered her things. "I must go. *Grazie* for the lesson, Maestro Rossi." She flew from the room, anger and confusion charging her every step. Madre prized being the star, but what maestro wouldn't want his pupil to do well? *Papá, Lord, why do his words still hurt, even when I know the truth of who I belong to?* Her tears choked her prayer. *And what am I to do when Madre has done nothing but support me? How am I going to go through with Mrs. Astor's plan?*

"Delia!" Lorenzo called from overhead.

She swiped at her cheeks and nearly gasped at the sight of him above the proscenium arch on the wooden plank walkway, his foot and arm wrapped about a thick rope as he adjusted a theatrical set piece for the opening scene that must have come loose the night before. She had never gotten used to workers dangling fifty feet from the deck on the walkway that allowed the crewmen to work above the stage without fear, complete with ropes for them to hold on to if the position called for it. And for the most dangerous of positions, they turned to the harnesses the actors used for flying scenes on the platform at the highest point in the house.

She strode onto the stage, her heels clicking off the hardwood and echoing in the empty theater. Even without guests, the stage thrilled her. She looked up at him. "Did you want something, Lorenzo?"

He grinned down at her, his teeth stark against his olive

complexion. He gripped the rope and leapt off the boardwalk, the pulley system sending him down with ease as the sandbags lifted from the wings. His boots landed with a thud on the stage, towering over her. "You were *magnifica* last night. Even my ma said so, and you know that was hard-won, as she has been in the ensemble supporting your mother for as long as I can remember."

Delia dipped her head at her childhood friend's praise. "Thank you, but you didn't have to come down just for that."

He shrugged. "I was done, and besides, I like swinging down for an audience that was certain to find it impressive." He winked at her. "And did you?"

"If I did, I don't think I should tell you, for you may take it as encouragement," Delia replied, running her fingers over the brim of her hat to keep from looking him in the eyes.

"That you might step out with me?" Lorenzo rolled his broad shoulders. "Come on, Delia, you know I am tougher than a few rejections, and I like the challenge of getting you to choose me over your career."

"We have been friends a long time, Lorenzo, and you know I will not change my mind. I have long since chosen my career and cannot give up on it now, especially with it only just beginning." She rested her hand on his arm, her fingertips meeting with his corded muscle from years of working the ropes. "You should try asking Bianca. She set her cap for you months ago."

His brows shot up. "Has she now? Well, if Bianca magically turns into Delia, be sure to let me know."

"Lorenzo," she scolded. "Bianca is a lovely girl."

"Absolutely. Just not for me." He grasped her hand, and before she could tug it away, he placed a kiss atop it. "There is only you."

"Lorenzo!" Another stagehand called, distracting him enough for Delia to escape from the Academy.

Hat in hand, she leaned against the building and closed her eyes against her tears and concentrated on the clattering wheels of Irving Place. The milling throng outside aided in drowning out all thoughts but one, leaving her head clear at last. *Do not be surprised, Delia. The maestro has always found a way to climb to the top rung of the stage, even if it means crushing his own pupil in the process.*

The sting from that first slight three years ago still hurt when Delia was being considered to play the lead soprano for a young woman's part, as it was mentioned in hushed tones that Signora Vittoria might be too mature for the part. The maestro convinced Madre to have Delia sent away to the seaside for the summer for the so-called health of her voice, effectively banishing her to the back of the ensemble when she returned. He had played on Madre's fears that what had happened to her overworked voice in her youth could happen to her daughter. *What will he attempt in repercussion when the patronesses have Madre dethroned?*

"Miss Vittoria?" Mr. Quincy's voice drew her eyes open as a thrill washed through her.

Her heart fluttered at the sight of his dark hair pulled back into what she could only describe as a swashbuckling queue. She had always adored the pirate garb when used on set.

"Are you well?" he asked, his brilliant eyes calling to her despite the warning flaring within her.

"Just taking a breath of fresh air, Mr. Quincy." *Which is much needed when you keep stealing mine away.* She threaded her hatpin through her hair. *Distract yourself!*

"Shall we walk?" He extended his arm to her. "If we are

to be partners in crime, we should at least call each other by our given names, do you not agree?"

"Very well, but only in private." She wrapped her hands about his arm. She had performed promenades onstage, sung love duets, and dressed as a bride, but such things did not compare to the feel of Kit's arm that exuded power and protection. "You may call me Delia, but as the Italian pronunciation for Delia is rather a mouthful for most, you may call me Lia." She released the pet name that only her closest of friends called her, studying his face to gauge his reaction.

"What a lovely sobriquet." He grasped her hand. "It is wonderful to meet you, Lia. You must call me Kit."

"Kit," she replied, trying on his name, even though that is what she had begun to address him in her heart. "Is that short for Christopher?"

He nodded. "My father was called Christopher, so to avoid confusion I was addressed as Kit as a boy, and well, after he died, no other name seemed to fit."

"Kit. I like it." Other men might not be able to carry a sobriquet so well. But Kit, well, she had never met a man so broad in the shoulders and could tell by the brief moments her hand had rested on his arm that they were hardened from years of sailing in the sun. Though a gentleman, he was unlike any other she had encountered. *He is the quintessence of manliness.* At *that* highly inappropriate thought, she felt heat greet the tips of her ears, climbing down to her collar.

"Where were you off to, Lia?" His voice anchored her and brought her safely into harbor from the fearfully unfamiliar place she had allowed her mind to wander.

She felt the cloth bottom of her reticule. The lone coin in her purse made it hardly worth carrying, but for appearances' sake, she did. She had no funds for shopping, but perhaps she could spend her coin on a sweet. Her stomach rumbled at the thought, reminding her of the pathetic breakfast she had eaten this morning. But such a wound from Maestro Rossi required something more substantial. "I have a craving for ice cream."

"Ice cream? In this weather? My knees tell me it is going to snow tonight."

She laughed. "Cold weather is the *best* time for ice cream."

"Well, then I must test this for myself. Have you tried Horton's Ice Cream?"

"I have not, but some of the company enjoys going there after rehearsals. I believe the closest one is on Broadway—if you don't mind the wind and a mile-and-a-half walk."

"Actually, I prefer the Horton's on Fourth Avenue, and we can enjoy a walk in the park afterward."

While the idea sounded delightful, she had worn her heeled shoes today. "We can't possibly walk all the way to Fourth—"

He whistled through his teeth, lifting his arm and hailing a cabriolet. "We ride!"

Lorenzo trotted out of the building, his broad chest pulling against his shirt, his hammer still in hand. His look of anticipation dropped at the sight of her arm around Kit's. Lorenzo's hurt expression hardened into anger. "So you refuse to step out with me because you are supposedly focusing on your career, but now I see I am not good enough for you."

Kit looked to her and then the company's crewman but stayed silent.

"Lorenzo, this isn't—"

"Isn't it?" His dark eyes clouded.

"I did not speak untruthfully." When she had first spoken the words long before opening night, she hadn't known she would be thrown into the path of Mr. Kit Quincy, but even if she had, she hadn't any interest in Lorenzo beyond their tumultuous friendship, and yet her telling him so would hardly make the situation better.

"I don't know which is worse, that you would lie to my face or that you'd choose a gent like him over me." He gestured toward Kit with his hammer and shook his head. "You are more like your mother than I thought."

Delia flinched. He knew what that meant to her. They all did.

Kit dropped her hand and stepped forward. "Sir, you are out of line."

"I am no *sir*," insisted Lorenzo, "and Lia should know better than to trust someone like you."

Kit grunted. "I would never hurt her."

"Says every gent who ever looked at an opera singer or a company girl."

Kit scowled, his fists clenching, but Delia pulled on his arm, keeping him from escalating the situation.

"He won't see reason," she whispered, and though she could sense Kit's anger, he complied and helped her into the carriage.

Once inside, she'd expected him to say something on the matter and so was pleasantly surprised when instead he settled back in his seat and offered her a smile, putting aside his feelings in order to make her more at ease.

"Well, now I have firsthand experience on how it feels to be falsely accused of immoral behavior." He raked his fingers through his hair and settled his hat on his lap. "I truly am sorry for the way we met."

"I have long since forgiven you, Kit, and do not take to heart what Lorenzo said. He simply cannot abide my choice to stay single."

His brows rose. "I see. I had thought with your growing up on the stage, you would have no end of admirers, especially now that you are the prima donna."

"I'm not prima donna anymore," she admitted as the carriage slowed on Fourth Avenue. "Madre is taking over tonight."

"The patronesses will not approve. I believe they have already written to the board," Kit said as he helped her down from the carriage in front of the ice cream parlor. "They would not have allowed Signora Vittoria to dictate that unless it was a part of their master plan."

"Mr. Quincy!" Millie Ford called from down the sidewalk, holding onto her matching orange chapeau as the elongated feather twirled in its battle with the wind. "What a piece of luck. I was just discussing with our dear Mrs. Linwood your infatuation with the singer Mrs. Astor is so taken with, and Mrs. Linwood was eager to make Miss Vittoria's acquaintance. Miss Vittoria, may I present Mrs. Linwood?"

Delia hid her surprise and dipped into a curtsy. "Mrs. Linwood."

The lady nodded her head in return. "When I heard Mrs. Astor *and* Mr. Quincy have become your patroness and patron, I had to meet you. I know it is abominably late notice, but I am having a dinner party and I just had the thought of what a delightful treat it would be to have you sing us out of dinner, given that you will most likely be leaving the theater by the time dinner is over. The guests will be in awe that I have managed to secure you after Mrs. Astor. Oh, do say you will come!" she fairly gushed, grasping Delia's hand in her own.

If she was ever to have a chance at securing the lead role on her own merit, Delia needed to garner attention. She would need a new dress for the event, but as she couldn't afford a new one just yet, perhaps she could have one of the stage dresses on loan and have it fitted to her. "I would be honored, Mrs. Linwood."

Mrs. Linwood patted her arm. "Lovely. I am so glad Miss Ford brought me into this little secret of ours. Until next week. Oh, and Miss Vittoria? *Do* use the front door." She giggled into her gloved hand.

"Yes, do." Millie giggled too and embraced her, tucked a note into Kit's jacket pocket, and chasséd away.

Kit lifted his brow at the back of the ladies and unfolded the note. "'Await further instructions. Miss Vittoria's career is safe with us.'"

"Thank goodness." She tugged open the ice cream parlor door, the bell overhead jingling and announcing their presence to the proprietor. She drew a deep breath of the sweet scents of vanilla, chocolate, and caramel. Yes, ice cream would certainly help dull the pain of her abysmal morning.

Kit grasped the door above her head, holding it for her. "You have me now and the patronesses. Your career will be well looked after."

Delia peered at the blackboard above the counter even though she knew what she would order.

Kit clasped his hands behind his back, reading it for himself. "What shall I order for you?"

"You've already paid for the carriage, Kit—I couldn't accept more."

His laughter warmed her heart, making her feel quite special that she was the one who was making him happy. "My delightful lady, this is how a gentleman squires a lady about town. What kind of gentleman would I be to escort you to an ice cream parlor and then make you pay?"

She dipped her head. "Very well. But you must guess my favorite flavor."

He grinned and ordered two chocolates while Delia took a seat at the bay window, enjoying watching the pedestrians bustling down the sidewalk, wondering of their different stories.

He slipped into the wooden chair across from her and slid over a glass dish with a spoon. "Did I guess correctly?"

She took a spoonful of the rich dark chocolate, closing her eyes at the impeccable flavor of Horton's ice cream.

"That good?" He laughed, taking a massive spoonful.

"Divine." She took a second and a third bite. "Hester is a great fan of chocolate, too. I must bring her back here soon."

He rose from the little round table and headed for the counter. "A brick of your chocolate ice cream, please."

"Kit! I couldn't possibly eat this whole dish, much less a brick." She protested as he paid the man in the mottled apron, although in truth she was certain she could lick the glass dish clean, it was so delightful.

Kit set the white rectangular carton on the table, which was tied with a brown string for ease of carrying. He pointed to the advertisement on the wall behind the counter. "It says there that their bricks are 'super frozen' and can last up to an hour. It's for your Hester to enjoy tonight while you perform."

"That is incredibly thoughtful of you, Kit." She reached

across the table and grasped his hand for half a second, the spark of his touch sending her arm shooting back. Her gaze flitted to his, hoping he hadn't noticed. He grinned, revealing those dimples. He most certainly *had* noticed.

He gave a shallow sigh. "And it seems that my own thoughtfulness will be my downfall, for now you will have to return home before the hour is up and it melts, taking your wonderful company away from me."

Such a kindness required payment, but the only thing she could offer was her time. She could use her coin to take the trolley home and still have time for the brick of ice cream to remain frozen. "Then let us take a half-hour walk and enjoy the last of the fall foliage before tonight's snowfall, and then I must return home to save the ice cream."

Without waiting for him to hold her chair for fear that his possible touch might cause her to become undone, she hastily scooted back with the ice cream box in her hands when her heel caught on the chair leg. Dropping the box to catch herself with her hands, she tumbled backward. Her heel cracked as her derrière hit the floor, her bustle collapsing and a fierce cold greeting her bloomers.

Seven

Delia!" Kit knelt at Delia's side, one hand on her waist and the other grasping her hand. "Are you hurt?"

"Just my pride," she answered, her cheeks already ablaze with that darling shade of pink. With his aid, she rose while gripping the back of the chair.

He ran his hand over his face to stifle his laughter. "And apparently our ice cream."

Delia whipped around and gasped at the smashed-in box of ice cream that certainly had not been a solid brick. "If the box burst open, then . . . ?" Her eyes grew wide as her hand traveled to her bustle, her fingertips coming back covered in chocolate ice cream. "No. Kit, please tell me it is not all this bad?"

He twisted around her and allowed his eyes to glimpse at her bustle before quickly returning to her face. It was quite bad. He grimaced. "I'm afraid the chocolate coverage is extensive."

She pressed her hands to her cheeks and took a wobbling step toward the chair.

He grasped her elbow. "What's wrong with your foot?"

She sighed. "My shoe heel broke. It hasn't detached itself but is hanging to the side, making it nearly impossible to walk." She buried her face in her hands. "I doubt a hired carriage would allow me inside with this on my . . . well, on my gown."

Seeing no other course of action, Kit swept the lady into his arms, her petite hands wrapping about his neck.

"Kit! What are you—?"

"The Olympia Grande hotel is only two blocks away on Fifth Avenue. We can send for a fresh gown and shoes once we are there." She was remarkably light in his arms.

"I couldn't possibly go inside such a fine establishment on a normal day, much less with my bustle covered in chocolate and with a missing heel." Delia lifted her shoe to illustrate her point, displaying its well-worn leather on her dainty foot. It was little wonder the thing had broken when the pair should have been tossed in the rubbish bin.

"Of course you can."

"You do not understand." She squirmed in his arms. "They will most assuredly wish me to depart, as I have never let a room there, and I have no desire to be thrown out of the building, garnering further humiliation."

He grinned down at her. She didn't know. Nearly all of New York knew he owned the Olympia Grande hotel and was almost finished building yet another in Charleston. "Trust me. They won't mind."

"How would you know? Do you know the staff at the Olympia?"

He swallowed his laughter. "Because the manager happens to be my best friend."

She ceased her struggle. "And you are certain I can wait there?"

"I would stake my fortune on it."

"Very well then, Mr. Quincy, lead the way."

The proprietor of the ice cream parlor gasped from the back-room doorway. He dropped his armful of boxed ice creams onto the counter and hurried around to their side. "Is the lady well?"

Kit reassured the man, nodded his thanks for the proprietor holding the door, and stepped onto the sidewalk amid a sea of people. The sight of a woman in Kit's arms drew stares, and most parted for them on the walk, a few men guffawing and women tittering into their gloved hands, all pointing to them until Delia tucked her face into his shoulder, groaning.

"Your ankle doesn't hurt, does it?" he asked, unable to keep the concern from his voice.

"I wish it did. Maybe then I'd at least feel better about being seen in such a position. Why did I have to wear my ivory walking suit? Why couldn't I have chosen my sensible muted brown?"

He swallowed his laughter that would surely only send her to squirm out of his arms again. "Never fear, for it is hidden on my jacket. To everyone seeing us, they only see a woman in a man's arms."

"Which isn't scandalous in the least," she groaned, and then her eyes widened. "Your jacket! It will be ruined. I'm afraid I was only thinking of escaping this situation for myself and didn't think—"

"I have plenty of jackets, and this one is honored to sacrifice itself for such a beauty as yourself."

"I imagine you to be quite the clotheshorse at heart. I have not seen you wear the same clothes more than twice, even though you exude an air of not caring—which befits your manliness."

"My manliness? I am happy you think me so dashing," he whispered, their proximity blurring carefully constructed lines.

"I do." Her fingers twitched on his neck. "You are the most—"

"Mr. Quincy!" A doorman in emerald livery trimmed in gold trotted toward them. "Sir, do you require assistance?"

"Just with the door," Kit replied.

"Of course, sir." He rushed back to his station and held the door for them. The instant they crossed the threshold onto the polished marble floor, Kit's staff smiled their greetings, bowed, and offered assistance that he denied needing, even though his arms were slightly burning.

"Kit, where will I hide out?" she whispered. "I cannot sit on the velvet furnishings. I'd ruin them for sure."

"I've an idea." He headed toward the elevators, calling over his shoulder to the bellboy shadowing them, "Send two or three staff to the alleys as well as the head housekeeper."

"Right away, sir." The boy darted off.

The operator nodded to them, concern in his eyes directed toward Delia.

"To the lower level, please," Kit instructed. "Bowling alley." They would be out of the way down there, as his staff were busy readying the hotel to receive the four hundred guests arriving for the party at half past eleven of the clock tonight.

"It's not open yet, sir," the operator replied, but then he hastily pulled the levers. "But of course you know that, Mr. Quincy."

The elevator jerked into motion, and Delia's grip tightened on his neck. "They really do know you here. You come here that often?"

"Nearly every day. I really should give up my residence on Madison Avenue and take up a flat here." He laughed. "Did you think I exaggerated?"

"Of course not, but I wasn't expecting the entire staff to know you. I thought for certain they would at least question my appearance, but they do not seem to mind at all." Her gaze flitted to the operator, who professionally ignored their conversation, staring at the numbers on the elevator as if mesmerized by them.

The elevator halted, and the operator opened the iron doors for them and promptly turned the gaslights on completely, brightening the room and showcasing four polished hardwood lanes. Then the elevator doors closed, and with a groan it disappeared upstairs once more.

She pulled her hands from his neck, twisting them in her lap. "We are asking for far too much. We aren't even paying customers."

Kit gingerly set her down atop a wooden chair at a table that was devoid of any frippery for his gentlemen guests to enjoy during their stay. "They don't mind."

"We will not mind because Kit Quincy owns the Olympia Grande hotels," a stocky gentleman said as he stepped off the elevator with two staff and Kit's head housekeeper.

"Ramsey Gunn, you were not supposed to say that," Kit scolded.

Delia gaped at him, staying firmly planted in the chair. "I thought you said the manager is your best friend."

"I would hope so, as we have been friends since boyhood and sparring partners for the past two decades."

Kit narrowed his gaze at Ramsey, yet Delia did not seem at all fazed. He shook his head and made the introductions, taking Ramsey's notepad and pencil from him. Kit jotted down a note to Hester on what to send. He folded it and gave the bellboy the address with instructions to wait for the items while the staff hustled about the place, lighting the remaining gaslights, a third appearing to deliver a silver tea service.

Delia smiled at the staff, discreetly removed her shoes, and focused on her stockinged toes peeking out from under her ivory skirts. She glanced back at Mrs. Jenkins, who settled into a chair and folded her hands on her lap.

"Well, while we wait for the items, shall we play a round of bowling?" Kit asked. "We will be chaperoned," he assured her. Ramsey had departed with all the footmen save one, who took his place at the end of the nearest lane beside the pins to reset them as needed. Kit leaned toward her. "And remember, I am supposed to be smitten with you, so by participating in an activity with you in front of Mrs. Jenkins, whose sole hobby is gossiping, the rumor will spread across New York by dinnertime."

"Very well." Delia rose, displaying the back of her gown.

Mrs. Jenkins gasped before she could cover her surprise and picked up a newspaper.

With a sigh, Delia said, "Hopefully, she will leave out the part about the state of my dress."

Kit chuckled and lifted a bowling ball from the wooden rack along the wall. "Come, Miss Vittoria, allow me to show you how to play." He demonstrated with his feet planted together before striding toward the lane and drawing his hand back and releasing the ball in a single swinging motion. Kit sent the ball rolling toward the pins, scattering half of them to the sides.

Delia clapped, then in her stockinged feet stepped up to the second lane as the remaining footman reset the pins on the first lane. Mimicking Kit, she attempted to roll the ball but instead sent it flying behind her toward poor Mrs. Jenkins, who cried out in terror and moved another few chairs away for safety's sake.

"So sorry, Mrs. Jenkins," Delia called before turning a grimacing look at Kit. "Her story is getting more outlandish as we speak."

"Never fear. You'll get the hang of it, I'm sure," Kit said, stepping behind her. "May I show you?"

At her nod, Kit wrapped his arms around her, helping her hold the ball in one hand and then guiding her elbow to rest on her hip while using her other hand to support the ball and guide it. Her hair brushed against his cheek, and the lavender scent nearly made him forget where they were.

"Now what?"

Her question brought him back with a cough. Her delicate perfume was entirely too intoxicating for a man to bear. "Drop your right shoulder forward. Now, swing your arm and release the ball in one motion." He stepped away and watched as she copied what he told her and executed a perfect swing. Seconds later, the pins scattered every which way. His jaw dropped. "I am an excellent teacher."

After her fifth strike in a row, Kit crossed his arms. "Never bowled, eh? I believe I have been taken."

She grinned as she marked her score on the board, her stockinged feet padding against the hardwood floor. He hoped she wasn't cold despite the fire the staff had set in the stone fireplace along the mahogany-paneled wall of the bowling alley.

"I didn't say that. I used to go to Bowling Green Park with my father every Saturday morning as a girl, where I watched *and* played. Or so I was told by Hester, who continued to bring me every Saturday until I began at the Academy."

He shook his head, tsking. "Then why did you have me instruct you but to laugh at me, even though I rescued you?"

She accepted another bowling ball from him, their fingertips grazing one another. "Or mayhap I pretended not to know what I was doing in order for you to teach me."

Is she acting for Mrs. Jenkins or does she mean it? He grinned. "Why, Miss Vittoria."

She straightened and stepped back as if she at once regretted her confession. "Thank you for rescuing me, Mr. Kit."

"Always, my lady." He grasped her hand and pressed a kiss atop it.

A woman gasped from behind them. "Christopher?"

Delia stiffened as Kit straightened and asked, "Elsie, what are you doing back here?"

"I left my parasol in the lobby and was told you were down here." Her gaze narrowed on the lovely woman beside him. "Should I be jealous?"

Delia looked to him, then to the woman, her cheeks reddening as she jerked her hand out of Kit's. "I'll wait for my things in the retiring room upstairs. Excuse me."

"It's not like that. Miss Vittoria—" But before he could finish explaining, she had already whisked herself away.

Elsie smiled and joined him. "I have a few moments before my next appointment. Why don't you show me how the sport is played?"

"I don't think that is a good idea." He stuffed his hands into his pockets and looked over his shoulder to see Delia disappear into the elevator, her ire evident in her scowl.

Elsie's full lips parted. "No? I thought you promised that we could be friends?"

With a sigh, Kit stepped behind her. Hopefully he would have a chance to explain everything to Delia tonight after his first public appearance as her devoted suitor.

Eight

"You mean to tell me you are doing this phantom bit for a woman you just met?" Ramsey Gunn paused in their intense bout of wrestling at the Gentlemen's Athletic Club to scrub a towel over his chest and beard, tossing it on the wooden bench lining the walls and striding back into the painted ring on the cushioned mat. Grunts and sounds of the sport filled the chamber, as well as the pungent smell of training bodies that had grown with the number of gentlemen arriving after a long day of working. If most of the gentlemen were to survive an evening of dinner parties, operas, and balls, they first needed to sweat.

"Is that so hard to believe?" Kit panted, lowered his stance, and shot for his best friend's legs, driving his forehead into Ramsey's sternum and locking his hands behind the man's knees before slamming him to the floor.

Ramsey fought against Kit's tightening lock, but Kit drove his legs to apply colossal pressure and flipped Ramsey. Digging his soft leather shoes into the mat, Kit forced both of Ramsey's shoulders down, pinning him to the mat and effectively winning the match. Kit released a whoop and shoved off Ramsey's chest as he stood, resuming his staggered stance with his right foot in front and his left behind him, arms raised at the ready before him. "Again!"

"Question." Drawing deep breaths, Ramsey gathered his knees to his chest and rolled himself to a standing position. "If the phantom appears when you are always vacant and you are supposed to be her beau, what's to keep people from figuring it out that it's you?"

Kit motioned for Ramsey to assume the stance for another match between them. "That's why I was going to have you seen dashing about in the costume on occasion, with myself in my seat. From far away, the audience will not be able to make out our height difference."

Ramsey laughed. "You must consider her to be one pretty prima donna."

"What does that have to do with it?"

"Nearly *everything* to draw a gentleman into such a caper. From the sound of it, you are enchanted by more than just her looks. Mayhap her voice? Is she a siren?"

Kit shot forward and seized hold of Ramsey's neck, securing a collar tie with his forearm against the side of the neck and his hand gripping the back at the same time.

"Admit it, you like this girl," Ramsey grunted, then rammed his forehead into Kit's, jolting Kit and causing him to lose precious ground and his advantage. Kit shook the stars from his eyes as he shifted from foot to foot, flicking his hands to wake himself as Ramsey assumed his stance again. Though Kit was taller than his friend, Ramsey was stocky with a strength that was nearly equal, and yet Kit had been wrestling far longer than Ramsey. He feigned a dart to the left and then grasped Ramsey by the elbow, positioning his hip to the back of Ramsey's and hurling him over his shoulder.

Ramsey slammed against the cushioned floor, the other gentlemen wrestling in the chamber groaning for him and cheering for Kit. Ramsey slowly raised himself to his knees, squeezing his neck, his expression pained. "You cannot avoid my question forever. She's either a siren or she has something over you. Now, which is it?"

"Both." Panting, Kit wiped his brow and explained Mrs. Astor's ultimatum that had Ramsey scowling. "And I was abominably rude to the lady the first time we met, so I wish to make amends."

Ramsey stretched his neck. "How rude?"

"As rude as one can be." Kit gritted his teeth. "I may have mistaken Miss Vittoria for her mother and accused her of being a woman of ill repute."

Ramsey's jaw dropped. "Well then, it appears you do indeed owe this young lady reparation for your odious behavior."

"Indeed. I do not wish to be thought ill of by her." He swung his arms in front of his chest, keeping his muscles warm.

"You fancy her, don't you?" Ramsey grinned. "I saw the way you carried her inside your hotel for all to see. The staff and guests are humming with the romance of it all, that the elusive Mr. Kit Quincy has found his lady love at last."

Kit raked his fingers through his dampened hair. "Fancy her? What are we, two boys in the schoolyard?"

"And yet you do not deny it." Ramsey hooted, drawing the attention of those on the surrounding mats. "The great Kit Quincy has fallen at last!"

"Shut it." Kit rolled his eyes, reaching for his towel and running it over his face to keep his reddening cheeks hidden.

Ramsey slapped him on the bare back so forcefully that Kit knew he had left an impression behind. "No need for embarrassment, old boy."

"We are the same age, Ramsey." Kit flicked the towel at him, its end snapping.

His friend easily dodged the towel. "Yes, but as I am happily married with two strapping young boys, I am eager to see you settled. With your permission, I will tell my wife everything so she knows I haven't lost my mind in donning a cape for you."

"Granted. I trust Mrs. Gunn, but *no one else* may know."

Ramsey nodded solemnly. "Of course. Now, allow me to give you all the tips I've ever used with my Rose to woo her into somehow falling in love with a clod like me."

"Isn't it so much better not to have the pressures of the success of the evening resting on your shoulders?" Madre smiled up at her from the vanity in an attempt to make Delia feel better about becoming the understudy once more. She knew as well as Delia that now she had tasted the lead role, Delia craved more. "Perhaps when you start your dance lessons with Madame Dumas, more roles will become available for you."

She gave Madre a halfhearted smile. But Madre didn't notice, as she was applying her lip rouge, dabbing with her pinky, her lovely olive complexion hardly visible under all the stage paint. She wiped away the residue on her finger with a handkerchief, tossing the crumpled cloth onto the vanity. She rose, shrugging out of her costume of the Swiss maiden and tugging on the nightgown, adjusting it to the best advantage for her décolletage.

When will the patronesses remember their promise? Delia swallowed back the shame of being shuffled to the side once more after her mother's recovery, and the guilt for wishing to take her own mother's role. Despite her knowing the fate of her mother's career at the Academy, she couldn't help but long for her time in the spotlight to begin in earnest, when she could prove that she was worthy of the title prima donna.

As the opera progressed to the sleepwalking scene, it was becoming more difficult to trust the rich, who had always looked down on her kind. *I should prepare myself to be the understudy again,* Delia chided herself, knowing the favor of the elite shifted constantly. And she couldn't help but recall spying Kit and that Elsie woman in the exact same instructing position as he had been in with her just moments before, as if holding Delia had meant nothing. She shook the memory from her head. She had never needed a man before and she certainly would not start now. Her relationship with Kit was just as much of a play as her arias onstage.

"Delia, *aiuto*!" Madre gestured for Delia to help her tie the nightgown's back. "*Per favore*. I cannot do it on my own."

"*Sì, Madre*." She ran her fingers along the length of the laces, pulling, tugging, and puffing the nightgown to perfection.

"*Bene*." Madre nodded her approval. "Now, if you'll excuse me, I have a performance to execute." She rolled back her shoulders and adjusted the puffed sleeves one last time, then flung open the door to be escorted to the stage in a cloud of assistants.

Delia dutifully followed her to the burgundy velvet wings

of the stage, watching as Madre held her arms out as if in a dream for her sleepwalking scene, the applause filling the house as she crossed the beams between the set's houses to the count's room at the village inn.

Despite her disappointment, Delia swayed with her mother's dulcet voice. A commotion behind her caught her ear, and she whipped about to spot the offending person who dared to jeopardize her mother's performance with their backstage din. Fists clenched, she strode toward the noise, the sharp scolding on her tongue fading the instant she saw not drunken crewmen, but a great lady in a shimmering gown of burgundy and gold with diamonds dripping from her throat.

She stared down at Delia, lips pursed as her diamond earrings trembled with her suppressed rage. "Do you know who I am?"

She felt the blood drain from her face at the sight of Mr. Lucian Lowe's wife, and visions of Madre being dragged from the stage in the middle of her aria spun in her head. *Papá, I know Madre was wrong, but, Lord, please don't let Madre be humiliated in front of all of New York. Please spare her.*

"Yes, Mrs. Lowe." She gave a shallow curtsy.

"Then you know I may stand here if I wish." She narrowed her eyes at the stage manager. "Please inform him."

"Mrs. Lowe," the stage manager whispered, hat in hand, "I beg your forgiveness at my insistence. If you could only wait until intermission—"

"I will wait until the end of this aria, but that is all. I will await *her* in the dressing room. Show me, sir." Mrs. Lowe turned back to Delia, and with a flick of her wrist, she bade Delia to follow them.

"Yes, Mrs. Lowe," he murmured, leading the way, his limping gait slowing them a bit.

Delia followed behind, weaving around stagehands, dancers, and other random bits of theatrical property, ignoring the stares and looks of concern.

Someone caught her elbow.

"What is going on, Lia?" Lorenzo whispered, his hand on a rope that was attached to the moon prop he was supposed to lift from the stage in a moment.

"I can't tell you now," she said, shaking off his grip. At his hurt expression, she added, "I will let you know all that transpires later." She hurried to her mother's dressing room.

The stagehand opened the door, the dressing room already littered with hundreds of roses from Madre's admirers. Delia breathed a silent prayer of thanks that they were now away from the audience. She ached to shut the door and keep the company from hearing, but the stage manager stood with his cap in hand, wringing it, for he knew as well as Delia how closely Madre guarded her dressing room.

Mrs. Lowe lifted a brow at the vanity, where a bright bouquet of marigolds had been placed, their meaning clear. She snatched the note off the bouquet, her cheeks flushing at the sender's initials. The note had been written in Italian. "You see? Even now, my husband betrays me for that siren." She grabbed the marigolds and flung them at the wall, the golden blooms scattering across the floor. "Passion, indeed. Why does he even bother with covert languages like flowers and writing only in Italian?" She crumpled the note and tossed it into the room's wastebasket. "This *will* end. I will no longer stand idly by while he makes a fool of me." She rested her hand on her abdomen. "I cannot. Not when we at last have a child coming."

Shame over her mother's actions filled Delia anew. "I've begged her many times."

Mrs. Lowe's expression softened. "I know, my brother has told me. And speaking of my brother, I understand Kit Quincy has deemed to be your patron as well as the flock of patronesses. But do you know who has been your mother's greatest patron for the past decade?" She moved about the room, picking up a string of costume jewelry and casting it back atop the dresser, dusting her hands free.

Delia could hazard a guess that it was Mr. Lowe. She folded her hands in front of her gown, fighting the tremors threating to overtake her. "I, uh . . ."

"My apologies." She lifted her hand. "It is too much for me to ask it of a young lady such as yourself, so allow me." She moved back to the vanity, picking up a folded frame, her nose wrinkling at the sight of Mr. Lowe on one side. Mr. Lowe had given the framed pictures to her years ago, but Madre had placed a picture of Father over the one of her.

Delia stiffened as Mrs. Lowe cracked the frame in half, leaving Father's picture alone on the vanity, gripping the other half in her arm.

"Mr. Lowe may have chosen to patronize her, but my birth father, being a modern American millionaire, took great care with my fortune in his will. *I* control the entirety of my fortune, and Mr. Lowe has been taking advantage of my brother's and my goodwill long enough, especially when certain facts have come to light." Her gaze rested on the ruined marigold petals on the floor. "The Academy fawns over the Astors, but *I* am the Academy's greatest patroness, and I will no longer be shamed."

"Mrs. Lowe, I sincerely apologize for my mother's actions," Delia whispered, desperate to keep the secret from destroying them all. Her attention shifted to the crewman standing just a pace away, his ruddy ears revealing that he was all too aware of what Mrs. Lowe was saying. "Could we perhaps discuss this after the performance in *private* at our Gramercy Park residence? To protect not only your family's reputation, but the Academy's as well?"

Mrs. Lowe studied her and shook her head. "I have much business to attend to here." She snapped her fingers at her lady's maid, who stepped from the shadows with a long box in her hands. "Come, and close the door behind you."

But as the maid moved to close the door, Madre shoved past the maid, sending her a scowl as she sailed into the room, a fresh bouquet of marigolds draped over her arm. "Help me change my hair, *cara mia*." She tossed the blooms into Delia's arms and came to a halt upon finding they were not alone. "Mrs. Lowe."

Mrs. Lowe's outrage was evident in her pressed lips and stiff posture, but she kept her hands folded neatly around her fan. "I have come to inform you that you have just given your final performance at the Academy."

Delia straightened, awaiting Madre's wrath, the guilt at once resurging that she had not warned her mother.

Giovanna Vittoria clenched her fists at her sides before relaxing them with a smile. "While I understand your frustration, I cannot keep Mr. Lowe from coming to me any more than you can keep him from leaving you."

Delia whirled on her mother. "*Vergognati!*"

Mrs. Lowe's face turned crimson. "How dare you?"

"I am *not* ashamed of myself, Daughter." Madre stayed Delia with a single finger lifted, keeping her gaze on her opponent. "You do not have the authority. Mr. Lowe is the name on the donation and—"

"Oh, but I do have the authority," Mrs. Lowe said. "I am afraid Mr. Lowe has been misleading you regarding who holds the purse in our family. The checks may have his name on them, but the Academy largely survives because of *my* patronage. And, as of this moment, my patronage is contingent upon your dismissal. You will collect your things at once."

For once, Madre was struck silent as she stumbled for a response. "Mrs. Lowe . . ."

Mrs. Lowe refused to acknowledge her and waved her maid forward, the box held in front of her. "Miss Vittoria will take that woman's place. After the performance, my maid will help you dress in this gown I have provided for a ball tonight that I am hosting at the Olympia Grande. Originally, the ball was to surprise Mr. Lowe for his birthday, but now I plan to hold it in celebration of your official debut as the prima donna of the Academy of Music."

"This is an outrage!" Madre stormed to the door and flung it open, and with a raised arm she summoned Maestro Rossi to her side, his son following closely behind.

"Maestro," she hissed, closing the door as if it could keep the company from hearing, "they are threatening my position."

"I was just informed," he said, tugging the wiry hairs of his muttonchops. "We cannot fight this tonight, Signora Vittoria."

She sent a glare at Delia. "Why are you not surprised? Please tell me that you knew nothing of this."

Delia shook her head, returning the magnificent gown to its box and readying herself to confess what exactly she *did* know.

"Of course she did not know," Mrs. Lowe retorted. "I held an emergency meeting of the patrons this morning, and if I pull my support, my friends will follow suit should the opera house refuse to release Mrs. Vittoria from her role and promote Miss Vittoria in her place. Permanently. As my parting gift to the Academy, I allowed your swan song with the first act."

"You will not dictate to me what the people want," Madre shot back. "And they want *me*."

"I *am* the people, and you should have thought of that before you lured my husband away from me." Mrs. Lowe snapped her fan in half. She cast the broken pieces of ivory and rich silk to the floor.

"He was no one's husband when I met him and was a great comfort after years of loneliness," Madre murmured, her fingers grazing Delia's box. "He was only ever mine."

"But he is lawfully *mine* now and has been my husband for five years." Mrs. Lowe lifted her chin and turned on her heel, calling over her shoulder, "Miss Vittoria, I suggest you dress for the second act. Your mother's career at the Academy is over."

Nine

Kit felt a little more than ridiculous in his costume that Millie Ford had designed and left at his door while he'd been at the athletic club. According to her note, the phantom was to make his great return in the second act during the ever-popular sleepwalking scene that proved Amina's innocence to her fiancé, Elvino.

The black silk cape with its scarlet lining was slightly longer than fashionable for a night at the opera, falling to his boot heels instead of his knees. For the black mask, Millie had included a bottle of glue to adhere it, which had taken some doing with getting the glue to dry while keeping the mask from sliding off his face. Twenty minutes later, it covered his forehead to his nose. But the *pièce de résistance* of the ensemble that had him groaning was the outlandish hat that appeared to have been inspired by a Regency pirate with a gargantuan black ostrich plume that curved from the back of the hat to his shoulder. As he *had* been present during the first opera haunting, he knew it was nearly a perfect replica of the first phantom's attire and he should've known it was part of the agreement.

He had been courting Elsie at the phantom's first appearance and had been a young fellow of one and twenty years when the first Academy of Music had been set ablaze in the basement. The fire was rumored to have been started in a fit of passion by the phantom because his chosen singer had not been named diva. It was a miracle that no one had been harmed in the fire. Afterward, the patrons showered the young Signora Vittoria with support, and an anonymous donor had provided the funds to have the building repaired. Until tonight, no one had dared question her place. But it seemed the memory of the phantom's adoration of Signora Vittoria had long since faded, and the haunting was only spoken of almost as if it had never happened, as if it hadn't been the catalyst for the star's rise to fame. After tonight, Kit would see to it that the rumors resurfaced.

He climbed to the walkway high above the stage, the walkway the crewmen had mysteriously vacated. He supposed Millie had seen to that detail, for she mentioned the director, Mr. Mapleson, was told of the plot and therefore made certain the crew would not hinder the phantom's mission. Kit glanced at his pocket watch . . . a half hour. He had been waiting for only half an hour? He adjusted his cape, thankful that the lights were dimming, announcing intermission was at an end. He would need to return to his box as soon as his part was concluded.

As a patron of the arts, he had to keep up appearances, lest people suspect he was the phantom. Like his mother before him, Kit had a love for the opera and had spent thousands on its upkeep and secured their family's box for the lifetime of the house, which hopefully would prove much longer, despite the Metropolitan's opening. Tonight, the Academy was nearing its impressive capacity of two thousand five hundred guests, as no one wished to go against Mrs. Astor in her attempts to save the Knickerbockers' house. Tomorrow, Ramsey would don the costume while Kit was seen at his box, applauding his starlet and keeping suspicion far away from him. *Ramsey is going to despise this costume.*

The thought made him grin as he attempted to readjust the mask, shifting under the weight of the deception he was about to engage in. *It's nothing dangerous or illegal. Only something to arouse interest in the theater once more. It's a play, and that is what the people are here to witness. A play providing the diversion they are so desperate to enjoy. No one will know it is you.* Yet his inner dialogue did little to still his racing heart.

As the strains of the second act began, he gripped the rail with one hand and eyed the golden rope that was attached to a net above the stage. He'd been instructed to pull the rope the moment Amina finished the bride's song.

His breath caught when he saw not Signora Vittoria in the burgundy wings but Delia, who was wearing a bridal costume for the next scene. Was she to sing tonight after all? It would make sense, what with the flowers he was soon to shower upon the stage.

Signora Vittoria, dressed in the same nightgown from the prior scene, shoved her way in front of Delia and entered the stage. She folded herself onto the bed of moss beneath a tree. The music changed, and Signora Vittoria became *La Sonnambula* as the village watched in fear that the sleep-walker might hurt herself. Arms spread wide, Signora Vittoria glided onto the board that slowly protruded from the stage as she walked, a feat that was impressive, but he supposed after all her years of practice, it was as easy for her as she made it appear. A *crack* sounded, and Signora Vittoria screamed, pitching over backward and into the orchestra pit. The crowd descended into chaos as the instruments minced themselves to an ungraceful halt, Signora Vittoria's moaning reaching him even up in the rafters.

Kit took in the scene, trying to deduce what had caused the accident. The plank was, of course, shattered in half, but it must have been tampered with to cause such an accident. He spotted Delia attempting to run out onto the stage to check on her mother, but Mr. Mapleson, the director, pulled her back before he himself strode onstage. Seconds later, the burgundy curtains closed behind him to hide the chaos of the company.

The crowd murmured over what was unfolding before them, those in boxes standing to see better as three stagehands, including Lorenzo, helped Signora Vittoria to her feet and whisked her through the pit door. Lorenzo, hopping up onto the stage and whispering something to the director, had the ladies in the audience in a twitter, likely due to the man's rolled-up sleeves displaying his well-defined muscles for all to see.

Mr. Mapleson lifted his arms to quiet the audience. "In what could have been a dreadful accident, Signora Vittoria is unharmed. She is being taken to her dressing chambers to rest. Her daughter, Miss Vittoria, will be assuming the lead. Please forgive us for the delay." The director bowed to the guests and then expertly cut through the curtain that billowed out in his wake.

Kit watched along with the crowd, wondering what on earth had caused such an accident, when the curtain opened once again. The crowd applauded politely as the stage lights focused on Delia, swathed in the wedding dress, stirring an ache within him at the sight. Her ebony hair fell freely to her waist and a crown of flowers encircled her head. With her arms outstretched, she became Amina once more.

The crowd's murmuring still hummed in the horseshoe of boxes, and Kit scowled, wishing he could silence them. Then, with Delia's first note, her rich tone silenced the room. And at the conclusion of the aria, Kit nearly forgot to pull the golden cord. As she bowed to her adoring audience, he tugged on the rope and thousands of scarlet rose petals rained down upon Delia. She raised her hands to catch them, her surprise and awe so genuine that the crowd roared with applause.

Sweat dripped into Kit's eyes beneath the mask, and he blinked furiously to clear his vision. *Now for the hard part.* He grasped a second rope, testing its strength to ensure its trustworthiness. It held. He perched on the top rail, his feet planted on the bottom rail, and drew a deep breath. Then he leapt off, the cape billowing out around him. His gloves whirred against the thick rope as he descended in a flash of black and scarlet, his boots landing on the deck with a thud.

Delia gasped at his appearance, the audience echoing her shock as the name "Phantom" filled the hall in hushed tones, people wondering aloud if it was truly *him*.

Kit the Phantom bowed to Delia and knelt before her, extending his hands with a single long-stem scarlet rose in his open palms, a gesture of the old ghost.

"Phantom," she whispered, her smile bright.

"My lady."

"It *is* him. It's the phantom!" a woman called.

"Are you certain it is him? I thought it was a myth," a

young gentleman in the front box returned. "Did he cause the plank to break?"

"Of course not. He's a romantic, not a murderer! Don't you remember the stories?" an elderly woman retorted.

Kit stood and placed a kiss atop her hand, the ladies near to swooning. He lifted her hand in his above their heads. "Patrons, behold the Academy's new prima donna—my lady, Delia Vittoria!"

Bowing once more, Kit escaped into the shadows of the wings and around the stage through a hidden passageway the company used between scenes. He scooted past a few Swiss maidens, earning curious glances from all, yet he did not contemplate if they would recognize him. Instead, he kept moving, following Millie Ford's instructions, which had him running for the stairs on the other side of the stage and up to the attic. Once there, he quickly shed his cloak and hat and put them in the box Millie had left him and that she would retrieve later.

He pulled at the mask, but unlike when it was drying, it did not budge. Just what sort of glue did Millie give him to use? *This is the last time I will trust her judgment.* He picked at the corners of the mask, feeling it move a bit. He tugged at it again and winced at the stinging it caused, but it did give a little more. Gritting his teeth, he yanked, sucking in a few choice words as it ripped away. He studied the inside of the mask and found a few long hairs from his pompadour that had been captured in the glue. "She better thank the good Lord I shaved this morning." He dropped the mask into the box. Next time he would have her affix ribbons to it. At the last moment, he remembered to pull his pant legs out of the tops of his high boots.

He took the stairs to the gilded lobby and slowed to a casual promenade, tugging at his black silk lapels to make certain his appearance led no one to think he was the phantom but merely a gentleman strolling about the lobby.

"Did you see what happened, Quincy?" Mr. Pruett lifted his glass to him from the refreshment wall. His sister was behind him, chatting with Kit's other chum from Willow Dupré's competition, Chandler Starling, a reporter for the *New York Starling*.

"You look quite red in the face. Are you well, old boy?" Chandler asked.

Kit tugged at his collar. "It's too hot in here with all these extra guests."

"I agree most heartily. The crush always overheats me as well," Miss Pruett said.

"Signora Vittoria's fall was quite the frightful business, wasn't it?" Kit shook his head. "I wonder what happened."

"Mr. Mapleson promised to provide me with an exclusive with some answers by tomorrow. I for one think it was the phantom's doing," Chandler said, downing his punch.

Miss Pruett flipped open her fan. "No man who showers a woman with roses could ever be capable of such duplicity."

Chandler lifted his brows. "Does everyone forget about the fire?"

"A fire that hurt no one and saw the Academy rebuilt into an even grander building. One might say he is a great patron as well as a romantic. Besides, who is to say it is the original? He haunted the Academy seventeen years ago, while this fellow seems mighty agile and far more romantic. The flowers he bestowed upon the woman mean the giver finds her a beauty, which guarantees his *protection* because of his love for her."

"The lady is a beauty to be sure," Mr. Pruett said with a grin. "All I know is our mother will be incensed that she missed tonight's events."

"Along with every other society family who did not attend tonight," Miss Pruett added.

"Tomorrow will prove to be quite the splash in the papers," Chandler interjected, his eyes bright. "I've finally got my front-page exclusive. I can see it now: *Phantom Returns! Romantic or Villain?*"

Kit was impossibly striking in his costume, so much so that Delia wasn't certain if it was just the thought of their outlandish plot that made her limbs weak or his dimpled grin. She fairly glided back to the dressing room, but at the yelling emanating from the other side of the door, she was brought to her senses in an instant. She could not be caught unawares by her mother's questions regarding the new phantom's patronage. Delia braced herself for battle and opened the door.

"They cannot do this." Madre's voice cracked as she sank back into the pile of pillows on her settee. "I have given them two decades of my life, Maestro Rossi. And they toss me out because of Mr. Lowe?" She dabbed her soiled handkerchief under each eye, coming away with a few streaks of cosmetics against the cotton. "It is not to be borne to be treated like a second-rate chorus girl they allow to fall into an orchestra pit in order to fire her." She narrowed her gaze at him. "You will discover the culprit behind the plank fiasco, won't you, Maestro? I could've been hurt if that French-horn fellow wasn't so large and obliging, allowing me to break my fall."

Maestro Rossi stuffed his hands into his pockets. "It *is* rather suspicious that the plank would give way like that, especially after your conversation with Mrs. Lowe. But if they rigged the plank, little Delia would have been the one to take the fall if you had complied with their wishes." He sighed. "And with such reasoning, I'm certain it will be ruled an accident."

"They must think me a fool to believe that." Madre threw herself back into her pillows.

"Do not allow yourself to get too worked up, Giovanna." Giuseppe tapped his throat with an index finger. "You may never be able to work again if you do."

Madre, who had never treated Giuseppe with anything but kindness, screamed and lunged at him, fingers curled into claws, which only made Giuseppe laugh as he easily evaded her attack.

"You ungrateful, disrespectful little clod." She snatched up a nearby book and hurled it at him, missing and sending it crashing toward Delia.

The thick copy of *Les Misérables* struck her above the eye, bringing tears to her eyes. "Madre!"

Madre's anger immediately dissipated. "*Perdonami.* I'm sorry, *cara mia.* I didn't mean to throw the book at you." Delia nodded as she ran her fingers over the spot, sighing with relief when she didn't find a lump or any blood. If it did leave a mark, she supposed she would be forced to resort to stage cosmetics. "Though no one would fault me if I did after what you did tonight, making away with *my* career. Who is Mrs. Lowe to just hand over the kingdom *I* have built? She's no one."

"Come now, Giovanna, jealousy is not an attractive shade

on a maturing woman, especially when it is directed to such a flower as your daughter." He winked at Delia, no doubt to further enrage Madre.

"Giuseppe, that is quite enough out of you. Mind how you speak to my star." Maestro Rossi rose to his full looming height, his shoulders broad even as they bent with age.

"Well, that's just the thing, isn't it? She is no longer your diva." Giuseppe leaned over the arm of the settee. "She is *no one's* diva."

Madre shook from where she stood beside the maestro. "Giuseppe, do I mean nothing to you? How can you speak such hurtful—?"

"It is not I who dare," Giuseppe said as he pulled a handkerchief from his pocket. He poured water from the washbasin upon it, soaking the linen and handing it to Delia.

Delia pressed the cloth to where the book had struck her, the coolness soothing the spot at once.

"Mrs. Lowe pulled her support the moment she discovered your dalliance with Mr. Lowe was still going on despite her first warning. You should know better by now how to behave." Maestro Rossi's eyes bored into Madre's.

Delia could have sworn she saw a flash of remorse in her mother's countenance, but as she only had the one good eye at the moment, the other covered with the handkerchief, she was more than likely wrong. Madre *never* showed remorse when it came to her one weakness.

"I warned you about your little trysts hurting your career one day." Maestro Rossi scowled at her, the glint in his eyes betraying his feelings. There were no *little* trysts when it came to his star. In his eyes, she belonged to him, as did her success—which meant her failures did as well.

Madre crossed her arms. "I have done nothing that hundreds of divas have not done before me."

"Yes, but you are not just any diva. You are *my* star, Giovanna. I could have trained anyone, but I chose you, the lowly little dancer with a gifted voice I turned from an ember into a blaze. And how do you repay me?" His voice shook, his eyes welling. "You marry Serenus Hearst and have a child together, putting the career I built for you on hold for *years* before calling for me to help you again. And once more I came to your rescue, only to be treated thus."

"I believe she repaid you with the ultimate insult, Father, by throwing it away on a gentleman who could never be anything to her and whose wife has seen to it that Signora Vittoria shall never see another night on the Academy's stage," Giuseppe finished, smirking.

Madre looked close to tears, but the maestro caught her arm and patted her shoulder even as his eyes narrowed at his son, who merely shrugged. With his father's constant pressing to improve his craft, and Madre's condescension at his attempts to improve her voice with a few new techniques, it was little wonder he wished to enjoy Madre's downfall, no matter how cruel.

"Why are you being so venomous?" Delia whispered, soaking his kerchief in fresh water once more, her back to Madre.

"She knows why," Giuseppe replied, crossing his arms.

She looked to Madre, then back to Giuseppe. "Because she refuses to take lessons from you? If so, I hardly think that is fair because you are nearly the same age as her career."

"No. She owes me," Giuseppe hissed.

A knock sounded on the door, and Hester hurried to

Madre's side with a letter, causing Delia to ignore Giuseppe's comment for now.

Madre took the message, pressing a handkerchief to her lips.

"At least try not to look so happy about this, Giuseppe. It is quite the blow," Maestro Rossi said as Madre unfolded the note.

"Though not the blow that you had hoped." Madre leaned into the maestro's arm for support, holding the letter open for him to read.

"Whatever do you mean, Madre?" Delia turned to face her mother. "Is it good news?" she asked, even as she ached with the thought of the patrons pulling their support from her and returning it to her mother.

"I mean, *cara mia*," she said and ran her fingers down the maestro's beard, "that the Metropolitan Opera House has offered me the lead role in their production of *Faust*."

"Such an honor," the maestro said. "A victory from the ashes, if you will."

"Just as it was before," Delia whispered, confusion flooding her senses.

The maestro gripped her mother's chin in his hand as he placed a slow kiss upon each cheek, the intimate gesture causing an infinitesimal shiver to run through Delia.

Maestro Rossi looked at Delia. "And with that, I must bid you farewell as my student."

"What?" Delia dropped the linen from her eye. "I will fail without direction. Maestro, I-I need you."

"It is not even a choice. Where my star goes, so must I." Maestro Rossi folded Madre's hand in his, placing them over his chest. "I will *always* go with her."

Madre shook her head. "My daughter needs instruction."

"Of course, but not from me. I am certain the rival house will not allow it."

Madre gave Delia a saddened smile as if to say she tried. "We will find a new instructor for you, Lia. Until then, I must announce our good fortune." Madre drew the maestro from the room, her head held high as she wove through the press of journalists and concerned admirers. She lifted her hand to the crowd, silencing them. "Since the Academy does not see to the safety of their opera company, I have decided I will not stay in such a building when the grandest opera house New York has ever seen has invited me to take my rightful place as prima donna."

The journalists erupted, but Delia closed the door to the chaos, pressing a hand to her corseted waist, sinking onto the settee. Without a teacher, her future on the stage would be short, even with the patronage of some of society's greatest matrons. "What am I to do, Giuseppe?"

"That is where I come in, little Delia." Giuseppe stepped forward and took her hand in his. "I have spent years at my father's side, gleaning his methods and studying new ones of my own in Italy and France. But you know what they say about prophets and their hometowns. In my father's eyes I will never be seen for more than that wayward boy I once was, but I know you do not see me thus."

"Of course not. Before you left for Europe, I saw your talent was beyond anyone your age."

He gave her a soft smile. "And it is time I thank you for that belief. If you would trust me to guide your voice, I know we can not only match your mother's talent but surpass it."

Hope burned in her belly. "When do we start?"

"Tonight." He rubbed his hands together, his expression sparking with ideas. "You will do something your mother never managed."

"And what's that?"

He opened the lid of the box Mrs. Lowe had left, reminding Delia of the maid who was likely still outside the door. He lifted out the gown, unfurling the masterpiece. "Get society to adore you by showing the world the lady you were born to be."

Ten

Please, enjoy a refreshment in the lobby as we wait for tonight's grand unveiling." Kit ushered Mr. and Mrs. Pruett from the porte cochere into the bright, gilded lobby of his hotel, turning to greet the next guests in the receiving line. As the owner of the Olympia Grande, Kit wished his sister's party to be the grandest he had yet to host, and as it was for Delia, it was even more important that it be spectacular. After his perusal of the rooftop garden, he knew it would be the grandest party of the season if all went well for the debut of the garden addition.

Beneath the lobby's six massive crystal chandeliers, the guests were already filling the space, wondering among themselves what could possibly be the surprise keeping them from entering the ballroom, which Kit prided himself on being one of the most ornate in the city. Their excitement charged the very hotel, for the Olympia's reputation was impeccable when it came to serving the elite, and the delay spoke of greater things to come than even Kit's famed ballroom.

He shifted from foot to foot on the marble tiles. With each

carriage slowing at the porte cochere to safely discharge its passengers, he searched for Delia, until at last he spotted her peeking through the open window of her hired carriage. He trotted down the steps toward her, eager to escort her to the paradise he was about to unveil to all, but *she* would be the first guest up the elevator. He opened the door, his grin fading at the sight of her. He did not stand a chance with this talented beauty. He shook that surprising thought from his head. *When did I start thinking of her in that light?*

"What?" She ran her fingertips over her silk half cloak. "Is it too much? Oh, I knew it looked like I was an impostor. I should just return home—"

"You are a vision." Kit grasped Delia's hand and gently tugged it, urging her to descend.

Her delicately embroidered silver slipper flashed beneath her silver gown that shimmered in the porte cochere's gaslights from the diamonds sewn into her bodice. Delia grasped his arm and released her train, which fell four feet behind her in two billowing bunches of ruffles cinched by silver ribbons and silk rosettes, all with pearl hearts.

Kit's chest filled with pride that *he* was escorting Delia tonight after her appointment to official lead soprano, even though he knew the part he was supposed to play. Still, he could not help but imagine what it would be like to truly be her escort.

"How can they not judge me for being an impostor?" Delia voiced her worry again, arranging her train after its being crushed in the carriage. "In a gown that is worth more than what I make in a single year, I can hardly feel otherwise. Such a costly gift has costly ties."

"Everyone here knows who you are and who are your

patron and patroness. No one will think you are pretending, because you have been selected to be prima donna by the Academy. You are, in all rights, a star. And you must come to expect their stares with the burden of your title now."

She pressed her lace-gloved hand to her chest. "I can hardly believe I am now the official prima donna."

The two footmen inside the Olympia bowed to him and held the double doors open, the man on the right sending Delia a brazen wink. Kit narrowed his gaze at the young man. "Do you have something in your eye, sir?"

The footman blanched, perhaps unaware of Kit's affection for the lady, though nearly the entire staff knew of it by now. Yet the men did not seem to care much about his romantic inclinations, not like the female staff did. Whether the footman knew or not, it was no excuse for such wanton behavior toward an honored guest of the hotel.

"Yes, sir, Mr. Quincy," he replied, giving such a theatrical twitch, it was obviously a lie.

Kit ignored the falsehood but made a mental note to have Ramsey observe the footman more closely. It would not do to have a man making the ladies at the Olympia feel anything but protected. The footman would not be warned a second time.

As they walked across the lobby's white-and-gray marble floors, Delia's grip tightened on his arm. Kit wished he could tell Delia that there was nothing to fear, but he had encountered these society women often enough to know that, save for a handful of ladies, their talons came out when threatened, especially by one so lovely as Delia, who could lure potential suitors away into a favorable marriage. He rolled his shoulders back. He did not like the idea of gentlemen paying court to her. He stole a glance at her. Her dark hair was pulled into a charming, albeit simple coiffure that was adorned only by three scarlet roses. *His* roses that he had sent to the dressing room? Was she silently signaling to all that she was taken by the giver?

It is a play, Kit. What right do you have to possess such thoughts? It was not as if he were *actually* courting her, and besides, they had only just met. After years without a single woman catching his eye following his heartbreak with Elsie, save for his brief time courting Willow Dupré, he had kept to his role as confirmed bachelor and enjoyed it. And yet this vibrant woman had changed everything overnight, and he didn't think he could ever go back to his rigid days of carefully laid-out schedules of calling, attending parties, and endless board meetings.

Kit guided Delia to his two elevators built by the esteemed Otis Brothers company, with their decorative gold-leaf gates of wrought iron. "Ladies and Gentlemen, I want to thank you for your patience. You will find soon it will all be well rewarded." He motioned to the elevators. "Tonight the party will not be a ball—"

The crowd began to murmur, the fans of the ladies fluttering in a medley of color. He lifted his arms to still their questions as his sister, Mrs. Lowe, joined his side.

"What do you mean 'not a ball'? Kit, I hired you for a ball," Mrs. Lowe whispered through her smile.

"That is to say," he continued, louder now, "it will not be a ball like any other you have attended, but the grand opening of the Olympia Grande's rooftop garden, inspired by ancient Greece. Tonight, you will be transported to a land worthy of fairy tales." At the flood of applause and gasps of delight,

Kit added, "Please, queue up and do not crush into the elevators. If two couples at a time ascend in each elevator, we will quickly have you all to the tenth floor safe and sound in just a few moments. There will be footmen upstairs to take your wraps if you find it too warm an evening."

His sister grasped his arm. "I cannot believe you finished the garden. I am honored, Kit, that you chose to unveil it for the party I am hosting."

He pressed a kiss to her forehead. "Anything for my little sister and her chosen star." He held his arm out to Delia. It felt so natural to have her at his side. Kit held his free hand out to his sister, but she waved him off.

"I will wait here for Lucian," she explained, "and greet the guests as they make their way upstairs, which is my duty as hostess." She spun on her heel and called to the nearest couple, "Petula, Damian! How wonderful to see you both tonight."

The elevator operator closed the gilded gates after Kit and Delia stepped inside, and soon they were rising and nearing the top floor. Kit stepped behind her and used his hands as a blindfold.

"Kit!" she protested, attempting to dart away, giggling.

"I don't want you to peek until we are off the elevator," he explained, laughing as the operator released the gates once more, knowing they only had a few minutes before the groups downstairs began to join them. "Keep your eyes closed as I guide you off."

"Don't let my train catch in the elevator!" she said, obediently keeping her eyes closed as she flung her hands back to catch her skirts. But Kit grabbed her train for her, inadvertently catching a glimpse of her dainty ankle in the process.

He dropped her skirts and took her hands, spinning her into place. "Now, open your eyes."

Delia's mouth dropped as she pressed her hands to her cheeks. "Oh, Kit."

He grinned as she observed the perfectly manicured boxwood topiaries and every flowering plant he could have set about the garden of evergreens. "I know this is most likely the rooftop's first and last party of the season before the weather turns, but come next spring I plan on introducing twice as many blooms."

She strolled through the garden, running her hand over the towering Corinthian columns supporting the roof that ran along the perimeter of the Olympia, offering a haven should it rain or simply a place to sit at a small table for two and enjoy the evening under the strings of Edison lights with their sapphire globes, strung from column to column across the open-air courtyard of marble, offering a romantic and yet festive air.

He smiled at the wonder in her enchanting green eyes as she stared up at the lights. On the stage at the far end of the rooftop, musicians began playing as the first guests arrived, and their numbers steadily grew with each elevator trip.

"At first, I didn't think there should be dancing," he said, "when I wished for the guests to enjoy the novelty of spending the evening atop the roof with the games I have arranged, but then I thought what better excuse to put my arms around you than to dance?" Kit bowed to her, watching her cheeks tint as he hoped they would.

Millie's bright green dress caught his eye before she reached them with her hands outstretched to Delia, taking both of hers. "I'd say tonight's performance was a smashing success, do you not agree?"

Kit grasped Millie's elbow, whispering, "I've been wanting to ask you. Surely, that stunt with the plank of wood—"

"Good heavens, no," Millie replied, then quickly schooled her features before anyone could see her distress at his question, as this was a party that would be written about for days to come in all the papers. "That certainly was not done intentionally."

"It seems far too strange to be a coincidence," Delia said. "If it was not arranged by the patrons, then we have another problem."

"Agreed. Thank heavens she was not hurt." Millie glanced about the rooftop and leaned toward them. "The police are looking into it, but of course people are speculating that the phantom is the one responsible, even though I tried to make your role of the romantic type."

"Miss Vittoria, I've been positively expiring to meet you. I'm Mrs. Hartford." An elderly lady joined their cluster, despite their obvious wish to converse in private. "I remember when your mother was out in society. We were well acquainted." She patted the base of her graying hair, arranged in the latest of fashions with diamond-studded pins.

Delia's eyes widened. "Oh? I have never met one of my mother's old friends from that period of her life."

Mrs. Hartford gave a little laugh and flipped open her fan. "I did not say we were friends, but I heard her sing the night the prince came to the Academy in the sixties." She lifted her monocle and studied the pergola with its grapevines extending from the Corinthian columns. The vines had been woven about as if they had spent years attached to the columns rather than just days.

"She often tells me the tale," Delia returned with a cautious smile. "One does not forget a meeting with the prince that led to her marriage with my father."

"Such a fairy tale for her, I'm certain," Mrs. Hartford said while vigorously waving her fan, despite the crisp air blowing over the hedge that bordered the roof and acted as a shield.

"A fairy tale, indeed, to sing for the prince," Kit interjected.

"Yes, but I was speaking of her capturing the attention of that English lord." The fluttering of her fan slowed as she realized Delia wasn't understanding her. "I'm, of course, speaking of Lord Rolfeson of Rolfeson Abbey. You *do* know the story of how your parents met? I am surprised Mrs. Astor has not brought up your father before now. Such a pedigree would open many a door."

Kit's stomach dropped. *Can her father be a lord?* If it wasn't bad enough that he held a woman nearly sixteen years his junior in the greatest of admiration, she was now so far above him in rank that the possibility of a match was that much further away. "The *Earl* of Rolfeson. I know of him."

Delia laughed. "*Lord Rolfeson?* I am sorry to disappoint you, but I do not know who he is. My father was a gentleman, which was why he was in attendance that night my mother sang, but he was *not* titled. His name was Serenus Hearst, and as he divorced my mother, such a story could hardly help me. I believe he is now married as well and they have a daughter."

Kit drew a deep breath and met the gaze of Mrs. Hartford before resting his hand over Lia's. "Serenus Hearst *is* the Earl of Rolfeson and resides in Rolfeson Abbey."

"Indeed," said Mrs. Hartford, "and the daughter you mentioned, Charlotte, has hair as regal as the sun. From what I was told in a letter from my English friend, the earl's infant son is his exact likeness." She eyed Delia pointedly. "You share his eyes, but not much else. And divorced or not, that makes you, his daughter, a lady in your own right."

Delia would have sunk to her knees if she had not been clutching so tightly to Kit's arm as Mrs. Hartford strolled away to greet a friend under the electric stringed lights, as if she had not just delivered life-altering news. "My father is an actual lord?" She pressed a hand to her cheek, her mother's stage name of *Lady* Vittoria making sense now, yet she'd thought it a jest to call herself *Signora*. She had referred to Father as Serenus, and only briefly, as though Madre could erase even that morsel of knowledge of Father from her memory.

But with the little pieces her mother let slip, and Hester's and Elena's memories, Delia had concocted a fanciful tale of the father she had always wanted, and in that story he had left for Europe on business, there to tend to his estate. He had become ill and was unable to return, and then after the death of her grandmother, whom she had never met, he stayed. She usually skimmed over the part of their divorcing, as it was too heartbreaking to imagine. For no matter how little Madre talked of him, Delia knew he had been the great love of her life, a fact that was difficult to accept as she was entertaining Mr. Lowe. Regardless, it was her dream and this was what she had imagined. In all her imaginings, however, she had never once thought her father could be descended from royalty—making her a lady, not only by character but by right.

"Lady Delia." Millie pressed a hand to her waist as if the news upset her stomach as much as it did Delia's. "How could the matrons of society have excluded that rather essential information? Do you think Mrs. Lowe knows?" she whispered to Kit.

"She said she had an announcement to make—" He halted and ran a hand over his mouth, then amended whatever he was going to say. "I would bet my horse she intends to announce it tonight to remind everyone of Delia's father. She knows how important the battle for the opera is to certain matrons and will use anything to gain an advantage."

Doors that Madre longed to have opened for her, inviting her inside, Delia added silently. *Why would she keep silent on such a score?* She ached to find a quiet corner to puzzle it all out with Kit, or better yet, take her leave and confront her mother. But now was not the appropriate time, not when Kit had planned such a grand evening for her.

"Did I overhear correctly that you are related to *Lord* Rolfeson of Rolfeson Abbey?" A Miss Grubb leaned forward into their little circle, excitement sparking in her eyes as she waved her brother over to join her.

The answer died in Delia's throat. How could she answer when she was struggling to breathe? She looked to Kit, silently begging him to save her. *Maybe Father's surname is common and he isn't* the *Serenus Hearst.* In truth, it did spark a memory of a giant man with strong shoulders and a soft smile directed down to her, an expression of complete devotion.

"She is his *daughter*," Kit answered for her with a smile that seemed forced. The admission brought a flock of matrons toward them, all speaking of the tale as if they suddenly recalled everything in perfect detail, despite the years of silence on the matter.

While everyone surely did not turn and stare at her as she imagined, she felt all eyes upon her. Her mother would be furious with her for allowing this tale to circulate. She had kept this information from Delia for a reason. It would not do to have it spread before she found out why it had been kept secret. Even now she could imagine the wildfire of society gossip flowing over the rooftop garden and spreading across the city. The gentlemen around her eyed Delia differently now, some with scowls directed at Kit, as if jealous of the attention he had been paying her all evening. If there was one thing she knew about high society, it was that matrons coveted the prospect of being related to someone with a title more than anything else for their children, even more than wealth itself.

"Kit?" she whispered.

He stiffened at her tone and bowed to the ladies. "I believe our star is feeling a bit parched. If you will excuse me, I must see to my lady."

Lady . . . The rooftop garden began to spin, then blur. She clenched her teeth. *You will not faint, Delia Vittoria*. But her clenching seemed to make the matter at hand worse. "Kit, I don't think I'm going to make it."

Concern flashed over his handsome features. "Shall I fetch you—?"

"Don't leave me," she moaned. Her ears rang, and spots edged her vision.

He grasped her elbow. "Lean on me." He expertly steered her through the crowd, glaring down any hopeful gentlemen, and procured a glass of punch as he led her to the corner where a trio of holly bushes formed a screen at the back of a wrought-iron bench. He helped her to sit and held the glass to her lips, the tang of the punch stinging her throat, yet her parched state required she drain the glass.

"Good. Deep breaths now." He set the glass on the ground, his hand at her waist oddly bringing her comfort.

She rested her palms on the cold iron of the bench and obeyed.

"Better?"

She nodded.

Kit chuckled. "Your silence does little to reassure me. Every time a woman has turned silent while alone with me, it usually meant she was ending things and moving on to greener pastures."

She lolled her head to look at him. "I'm just doing my best not to toss my accounts on your pretty new rooftop garden."

"Tell me, how can I help you?"

"My father is a lord," she whispered. "A fact which shouldn't make me ill, true?"

"That *was* rather surprising."

"And yet, even with a title, which would keep him under society's scrutiny, he still abandoned me and my mother." She laughed. "The irony of it all is that I used to dream that my father left me because he had so many responsibilities weighing on his shoulders. I never thought it could actually be true. Perhaps if I had a normal father with next to nothing, he would be at my side, protecting me from the world's harsh reality of so-called gentlemen."

He took her hand in his. "Delia, has someone hurt you? Or tried to hurt you?"

She squelched her rising tears. "Oh, many have tried, Kit,

but I am stronger than my mother. No one has dared touch me. No thanks to my father, but rather my God and my derringer pistol."

His brows shot up. "You carry a pistol?"

"Only to and from the Academy—and it is a fake."

"You carry a *fake* pistol?"

She shrugged. "It's from an old play, as I couldn't afford an actual gun. But the fake did just as well, and I only needed it once one night after a performance when I had misplaced my coin for a carriage ride home. I had to walk home past a group of rather nefarious-looking men."

He ran a hand over his mouth. "Oh, Delia."

"It's better than none," she said and clutched her arms over her stomach.

"We shall remedy that tomorrow." Kit placed his hand over hers. "And your father, titled or not, is a fool to have abandoned a daughter like you."

"You would never leave a wife and child, no matter how many properties you have." She looked up at him through her thick lashes. "You are too honorable."

"If I were so fortunate, no. I would never leave my family." He cast a glance over the back of the bench as if spying someone approaching. He held his finger to his lips.

She followed his line of vision and saw Mr. Pruett looking every which way, searching.

"That was close," Kit whispered. "I have it on good authority that Mr. Pruett has set his cap for you. You must be prepared for the gentlemen here to wage a battle for your hand. I fear you will have more than your share of proposals by the end of the season, what with a title now to go with your talent . . . and your beauty."

She shook her head. "Heaven help me. It has to be a mistake. I am no earl's daughter. Please, *Papá*, let it be a mistake."

"Isn't every young woman pleased at the idea of having a title and her pick of men?"

"Not me. I have never had the desire to court anyone . . . well, not since my girlhood when I learned my father was never returning." She rubbed her temples. "Marriage is . . . complicated."

"Not all marriages are." Kit pulled a leaf from the potted plant and rolled it in his fingers.

The wind rolled over the edge of the hotel's roof, stinging her bare arms. She rubbed them to keep the chill away. Kit sidled closer to her, causing the tremors to be not all from the cold. "Says the confirmed bachelor," she teased through chattering teeth.

He laughed. "I was speaking of my parents. My father loved my mother, and she was never the same after his death. When it came time for her to join him, she was eager to see him again, for she said every day apart was like another tear in her heart."

"A torn heart doesn't sound too enticing," she murmured, rising to peer over the edge. She watched the people below as they strode to-and-fro on the sidewalk. "No, I think I shall marry the stage, just as I have always planned, and travel the world."

Kit tossed the leaf off the building, watching it float down to the busy street below. "Never?"

"It would take an act of God to move my heart to matrimony."

"There you are, Christopher!"

Delia turned to find the lady from the bowling alley, dressed in a lavender brocade gown, dripping with jewels, complete with a tiara that most of the fashionable ladies donned.

Kit bowed, glancing sideways at Delia as if he were trying to gauge her reaction. "Lady Ellyson."

Delia's smile felt stiff. Perhaps having a title was not so unique after all.

Lady Ellyson waved her fan over her head toward a young man behind her. "Lady Delia, I want to introduce you to my cousin, who is dying to open the dancing with you."

Eleven

Before Kit even had the chance to protest that *he* wished to open the dancing with Delia, he was left standing on the rooftop without her, staring through the holly bushes at the brilliant star whirling in the arms of a most eligible gentleman on Kit's brand-new dance floor.

"Christopher?" Elsie rested her dainty hand on his arm. "Aren't you going to ask me to dance?"

He had forgotten that Alice Lexington never had been one to stand on ceremony, so he accepted the lady's hand and led her onto the dance floor, where Delia's gaze found his, confusion flashing through her expression.

"Seems we already have the matrons humming about the two of us coming together." Elsie smiled up at him before waving over his shoulder to a group of ladies.

He gritted his teeth. He knew Elsie had been flirting with him, but if there was a chance she thought he might be open to pursuing her again, he needed to correct her at once before the rumors forced him into a marriage he no longer desired.

"Elsie, I cannot allow you to hope that we can continue on

as we did before." Kit guided them past another couple, his voice low. "There is nothing left inside of me of the old days."

"What? But we had such a fine time this afternoon." Tears pooled in her eyes. "You would reject my friendship after I have been so vulnerable with you?" She dashed her fingertips under her eyes and whispered, "How could I not hope for a happy reunion when you have kept yourself single after all these years apart?"

"I do not mean to reject friendship, but I did not remain single because of you."

"Thank you for your honesty," she said, her voice rough, yet she made no move to leave the dance floor. "Surely our engagement meant *something* to you."

He clenched his jaw. "It meant everything to me, Elsie. You know that better than anyone."

Her eyes widened. "Then why are you casting me aside when we have only just reunited?"

"*Meant*. Past tense, Lady Ellyson. I know you were in India for the entirety of the time we were apart, but surely you have read the papers about Willow's competition and that I was a front-runner for her heart. I have not stayed shut away from society. I have lived and enjoyed my life."

She nodded. "As I'd hoped you would. But I want you to know, Christopher, we were meant for each other—give or take a few decades of life." She nodded toward Delia. "And if you are infatuated with that singer for now—"

"Don't call her that."

"Excuse me. I meant to say, if you are taken with the diva, I can understand and will allow this little fondness to decrease. And then I will be there, ready to give you the family you have always longed for, the family *your* mother wanted.

I have stolen your heart once. I know how to do it a second time." She pressed a kiss to his cheek, curtsied, and whisked away before the music ended.

Stunned, Kit glanced about to see if anyone had noticed, but as all were quite enthralled with the rooftop's entertainment, he decided to plant himself with the wallflowers lining the dance floor. He snatched up a glass of punch while keeping his eye on Delia as she stepped from the dance floor. She was swarmed by gentlemen, while he pretended to be observing the guests playing badminton on the court to the side of the dance floor.

Kit had convinced himself that she wouldn't mind his age, that he could offer her something that he could not with Willow, justifying their connection in his head as well as reminding himself that many of his set married young wives . . . though most who did so were widowers. *This isn't about you, Kit. The lady is confused.* And as much as he would like to be that supporting shoulder, he could not take advantage of her confusion.

"Lovely young lady you've brought tonight, Kit." Willow Dupré-Dempsey appeared at his elbow in a gold gown with a matching tiara sparkling in her dark curls.

He lifted his glass to her in greeting. After the first few times seeing Willow and her new husband upon his return from overseeing the building of his Charleston hotel, he was pleasantly surprised to find his decision to end his courtship with Willow had indeed preserved their friendship. Certainly, he had felt a twinge at the reminder he was still alone, but the feeling soon passed as he focused all his attention on the hotel project.

"I quite agree, Mrs. Dempsey." He smiled, admiring Delia

from afar. "I'm honored you and Cullen could be here for the grand opening of the garden."

"Cullen and I wouldn't have missed one of your parties, and I'm so glad I came if only to witness your happiness with the lovely Miss Vittoria."

"I met her three nights ago, so perhaps my happiness is more than likely due to the rooftop garden being completed at long last within budget." Kit chuckled, attempting to hide his affection for Delia, even as her laughter drew his gaze. He sighed. That should be *him* on the dance floor making her laugh, not Grubb.

Willow lifted a single brow. "In all your time courting me, you *never* looked at me with such adoration. I know you, Kit Quincy, and you are smitten. You have been waiting long enough for a bride, and I'm glad you seem to have gotten over that bit of nonsense of your being too old," she teased, reminding him of one of the reasons he had given Willow when he left the competition for her hand.

When it came to Delia, he felt her life experiences had matured her to the point that he almost never thought of their age difference—almost. He twisted the punch glass in his grip. "Is it absurd that after only three days at her side, I know I'd wait a decade if that meant she would love me?" he admitted, and for once he did not feel the guilt of the act, as if the performance were blending into a new reality.

"Why wouldn't she?" Willow accepted a chocolate confection from a passing footman's silver tray.

"Delia just informed me tonight that she doesn't wish to marry, and now that she is a rising star *and*, might I add, an earl's daughter, she may never have to."

"An earl's daughter?" Willow managed around her mouthful. Swallowing quickly, she brushed off her fingertips. "I really must make an attempt to get away from the office more often. You never know what news will come up next. Still, earl's daughter or not, whyever wouldn't she wish to marry you?"

He didn't feel right about spilling the reasons he had gathered from his time with her, but as it was Willow, an old and dear friend, perhaps she could give him some insight into the woman's mind. "She was hurt deeply by her father, and I believe that while she longs for family, she is afraid of being rejected. As for her aversion to marriage, there is no greater rejection than that of a husband turning his back to his wife in need, which her father did. And now that she has discovered she is titled, more questions will surely go unanswered unless the man shows his face—something he's not done since her childhood. But since he and her mother are divorced and he has remarried, there is no reason for him to return."

"Then you must convince her of your devotion," Willow said. "You must show her you are everything that her father is not. You are kind, compassionate, encouraging, and above all, faithful."

"And yet, despite possessing such qualities, I am *still* single and with little hope of that changing unless the lady in question changes her mind on marriage."

"Kit, we have spent time together and I know you, and ever since you pulled me out of that pond in Central Park, you have made me feel special and seen. You are a catch for any woman, but you may be exactly what Delia needs."

He grinned. "Goodness, I do sound like quite the catch."

"Now, go and *catch* her heart." Willow gave him a little

shove toward the dance floor. "And as we intend on going on being friends, I suggest you marry the sort of lady I would enjoy having for a friend." She laughed, lending a teasing tone to her command. "And from what I know of her thus far, she is the one."

He strode onto the dance floor to do just that, but as he reached out to her, the electric lights flickered twice before plunging the rooftop garden into darkness.

The music continued, undisturbed by the faulty modern bulbs as the footmen lit more candelabras, and in their flickering light, she saw a figure approach her. Delia's heart thundered at his scarlet phantom costume with an ivory skeleton's half mask concealing his face. Kit's second phantom costume was rather frightening, but she couldn't help but sway with the music, hoping he would at last ask her to dance. After all, as her escort, he should have opened the dancing with her. And during her time in the arms of another, she found herself searching for Kit, hoping he would cut in just to be with her. The revelation disturbed her, but even as she scolded herself, her heart raced again at the thought of his arm resting at her waist, of her hand in his, even if it would be with him in the phantom attire with all looking at them.

He bowed to her and extended his hand. She readily accepted it, but instead of pulling her into his arms and dancing, he guided her up onto the small stage at the back of the rooftop and murmured something to the pianist. The quartet at once followed his lead in playing from Act IV of Charles Gounod's *Roméo et Juliette*. She wrinkled her brow. *Doesn't Kit know it's a duet?* And how would she modify such an intimate song? She drew a deep breath and began to sing, a rich tenor joining her in perfect harmony. *Kit can sing?*

As if in a daze, she walked slowly across the stage toward him, her arms reaching as Juliette would have done, and she allowed him to embrace her from behind. Together they swayed with the melody and sang of the nightingale who called in the morning. At the final refrain, she opened her eyes and turned to Kit, awe washing over her.

"To the official prima donna of the Academy!" Mrs. Lowe raised her glass in salute, and all those on the rooftop followed suit. "To Lady Delia! Long may she reign."

She turned to share the moment with the phantom when out of the corner of her eye she found . . . *Kit?* Her cry was strangled as she whipped about to confront the man in the costume, who tore the top of a rose from its stem and tossed the petals at her feet. Grabbing a rope, he leapt off the side of the building. The women screamed while the men and Delia ran for the perimeter and were met with the fluttering cape disappearing into the shadows of the alley.

Kit took her by the arm and pulled her behind the stage and away from prying eyes. He grasped her hands in his. "Lia, are you well?"

She nodded. "I thought he was *you*. Where were you?"

"I went to check the electricity and the bulbs." He rested his head on hers and exhaled. "For future reference, let it be known that I sing about as well as a frog." He threaded her fingers through his. "Do not fear. I forgot to tell you that Millie mentioned needing a second phantom to allay people's suspicions about me, and well, I suppose she neglected to inform me of the particulars."

Relief flooded her being, as well as a good amount of

shame for allowing herself to be so caught up in thinking the tenor was Kit and that as such they were made for each other. At least the sentimental song would cover any genuine expression that had escaped from her treacherously hopeful heart and onto her face while onstage.

He drew her onto the stage where he lifted his own glass. "I hope you have all enjoyed the performance tonight, along with the unexpected appearance of the phantom." The crowd murmured but seemed to relax a bit. "Lady Delia will perform again before the end of the party. Until then, enjoy!" Kit cleared his throat as he assisted her down the stage steps. "Lia, I hope—"

"Good evening, Kit, old boy. Aren't you going to introduce me to the lovely Miss Vittoria, or should I say *Lady* Vittoria?" A gentleman with a dark pompadour stood before her, whom she recognized from the papers and the former Miss Dupré's competition as Mr. Chandler Starling.

"*Miss* is sufficient, Mr. Starling." Delia curtsied. "I have no desire to make a claim to something I am not certain even exists."

His grin widened, and she was at once aware of her mistake in not only speaking first but also admitting that she knew his name before they were properly introduced. She pressed the back of her hand to her cheek. The false phantom had rattled her more than she cared to admit. She needed to take care.

Likely noticing her flushed cheeks, Kit made the introductions quickly. "Chandler, may I present Delia Vittoria?" He smiled at the fellow. "Lia . . . I mean, Miss Vittoria, I would like you to meet Chandler Starling of the *New York Starling* newspaper tycoons, who, as we know, gave you that glittering review."

"I wrote it myself." Chandler rocked back on his heels. "I would have written it from my seat in the stands at the crest of the theater, but Kit's uncle, Elmer Bourton, took pity on me and let me into his box after bumping into me in the lobby." His grin spread. "And I have to say, you were a welcome treat. I want you to know you have the Starlings behind you, even if you sing at a theater that won't allow us to purchase any box seats because we are parvenus." He winked to soften his words.

Delia relaxed as Kit laughed at Chandler's jest, which could have been pointed if it wasn't delivered from such a friendly fellow.

"Well, I should speak with my uncle about letting you into our box," Kit returned. "Miss Vittoria, you may not be aware of this, but Willow placed Chandler, the pup of the group, with me as my roommate."

"Who was by far the *oldest* man in the competition," Chandler added. "I do miss our time together, but alas, business has kept me busy." He looked to Delia. "Before business calls once more, I'd love an exclusive interview with you, miss, and get your account on the phantom choosing you as his next songstress."

"I-I don't know. I wasn't prepared to make a statement of any sort, as the Academy hasn't officially made a statement confirming I am indeed prima donna."

"You have the patronesses behind you. It is as good as gold," Kit assured her.

"That's right. And my interview is nothing formal, just a quote or two, if you wouldn't mind. I couldn't tell my pa I met you and didn't try to get an exclusive, especially after a second phantom sighting."

Delia nodded. "As I well understand the pressures of a parent, I shall acquiesce to just a sentence upon the matter."

"Wonderful! Shall we begin now?" Chandler reached into his jacket and withdrew a small notebook and a pencil.

"The next dance is about to begin," Kit protested, lifting her hopes once more. "Can you wait until—"

"Perfect. Much better to have the interviewee relaxed than on edge. It leads to much better papers. I would be honored if you would dance with me, Miss Vittoria." He stuffed the notebook and pencil back into his jacket and bowed, extending his hand to her.

She could hardly say she was hoping to give Kit the next dance since he hadn't properly asked her, so she placed her hand in Chandler's. "It would be a pleasure." *And a welcome distraction from my fright.*

He led her onto the floor and bowed. The moment the dance began, he continued, "I hear your father is a lord. Would you mind telling me how it was you did not know that information? Or is this merely a ploy to earn your way into society's good graces?"

Delia stiffened at the disappearance of the jovial fellow she had just met moments earlier. In his place now was a reporter—one who might not have her best interests at heart. "I-I was simply never told of it."

Chandler's countenance melted into a smile again. "I'm sorry, was that too direct? My pa has been coaching me on leaving behind what he calls my 'blasted boyish bearing' and becoming more the hardened reporter like him."

"Clever alliteration of his, and I'd say it is working." She smiled through her apprehension. If only there were some way to signal Kit for help.

"Wonderful! I'll make a note to inform him of your reaction. As I was inquiring, how could you not know of your father's title?"

"That is a question that should be directed to my mother, but I truly had no idea. I never thought to ask if he had a title." She shrugged. "And why would I?"

"Because he is your father. Surely you were curious about him."

"Yes, well, I suppose every family has their secrets," she mumbled.

"Indeed, and those secrets make for the best articles." He grinned again as if that would work to put her at ease. "Let's move along to tonight's performance. The phantom has reappeared at long last. Do you know why he would choose you after he went through all the trouble of burning down the opera house so your mother might begin her reign after an absence—which would mark her marriage to Lord Rolfeson and your arrival?"

His eyes never wavered from hers in such a disconcerting fashion that she had to take a moment to think. She blinked. "What?"

Chandler shook his head. "How on earth did she keep that bit of information buried?"

"Perhaps when memories are unpleasant in nature, one does not wish to relive them," she murmured. She gasped that she had confessed such a thought aloud and missed a step. "Oh, do tell me you won't print that last part. Madre will have my head . . ." She slapped her hand at her second misstep.

"Good thing you were talking with me, Miss Vittoria. Others would not have been as generous or forgetful of a juicy morsel such as that, but I am a man who wishes to improve the reputation of newspapermen across the country and will of course honor your wishes. So, tell me, why did the phantom choose you?"

She couldn't lie, but she couldn't admit to it all being *the* patroness's idea that was being carried out by Millie. No one would believe her, and she surely would be cast aside in favor of another to save Mrs. Astor's own reputation. "Perhaps he believed it was time for a new voice."

"After a career that has spanned two decades, I'd agree, which is why I thought you were such a lovely change. I was not ready to see a woman well into her forties pretending—in heavy makeup, I might add—to be the young Amina, a woman not yet twenty." He chuckled. "Your mother, lovely as she is, tries her best to make that believable. You, on the other hand, a woman in her height of beauty and talent, make the opera seem as real as we are now."

She dipped her head, unsure how to respond.

"Now, can you tell me how you began singing?"

Delia was aware the instant Kit strode onto the ballroom floor, his focus trained on her and Mr. Starling whirling about. *Is he going to ask me to dance?* The butterflies began dancing in her stomach again. "I was still a young girl when—"

Kit tapped Mr. Starling's shoulder. "Excuse me, sir, may I cut in?"

Chandler sent him a scowl but relinquished his partner to Kit. "Very well, old boy. But we were just getting into the thick of it."

"Which is why I came to rescue my lady, as you said you wanted a quote, not a full-blown article," Kit chided.

Mr. Starling lifted his hands in defeat. "Very well. Steal her from me."

Kit bowed and drew her to himself, her pulse humming in her ears. His arm found her upper back, and the strong assurance it lent her was staggering. He waited for the beat and then in a fluid motion twirled her about the floor, expertly weaving through and around the others.

A dashing gentleman and *a dancer? How has this man not been snatched up by every eager mother wishing to make a favorable match for her daughter?* She spotted Mr. Grubb heading their way. "Can you turn us again?" she whispered.

Following her line of sight, he chuckled and spun her in the opposite direction of her would-be suitor. "Quite popular tonight, my lady."

"It is only due to the revelation of my birth," she replied. "Honestly, Kit, if you were not with me tonight, I could not bear it."

"To discover one is the daughter of an earl, I believe any young woman in your place would love to bear it," he teased, but she could see through to his concern, as if he were using humor as a shield.

Why does Kit feel the need to guard himself from me? "Well, for me, it makes things that much more confusing." She bit off the explanation for her feelings, hardly knowing exactly what that was after years of believing one thing only to discover it had all been a falsehood.

"Your mind is whirling."

It wasn't a question. Of course Kit knew. He always sensed her needs, anticipating them and listening for her moods before she even communicated them. How odd it felt to be so known by someone who had been all but a stranger days ago. Despite her efforts at distancing herself from all men, the few days she had spent with Kit had awoken something inside her that she thought would never exist. A spark that she was desperately trying to snuff out, especially at the reappearance of Lady Ellyson into Kit's life, lest everything she had worked for with her career and the protection of her heart be for nothing.

If it hadn't been for Hester, church and her faith, her life might have seemed forlorn to most, what with her isolated existence under the Academy's roof. But she had chosen it as a means to escape the cruelty of the matrons living in Gramercy Park, the ones who shuffled their sons to the other side of the street as she walked, pulled their daughters closer to keep her from influencing them with the louche stench of the opera house on her, and of the leering gentlemen who all assumed her character based on where she worked and who her mother was.

Yet Kit was *nothing* like them. He treated her with the respect she had been demanding from men her entire life. And with his treatment of her, she felt that carefully constructed brick wall around her heart slowly cracking with each day spent at his side.

She looked up at him, the silver at his temples drawing her fingers. She returned her hand to resting on his arm, forcing the desire to stroke his hair out of her. *What has come over me?* But deep in her heart, she already knew that it was Kit who had overtaken her heart and mind. With his kindness, his thoughtfulness, and the overwhelming security his presence offered, he drew her very soul to his.

Twelve

Delia shifted in her seat beside Hester in the front choir row on the mezzanine of First Presbyterian Church on Fifth Avenue. Usually, Reverend Hall's sermons transported her, but this Sunday, Delia had made the mistake of reading the newspapers before church, all of them fairly shouting that the phantom could return at any performance and Delia Vittoria was his choice—a titled lady in her own right.

The papers brought attention to her rank in English society, calling her the catch of the season. Some wrote that the phantom's return was impossible and that his absence since Wednesday's performance and the rooftop party had shown it all to be a farce. Others speculated that if the phantom had been in his twenties when he first supported her mother, he was still young enough to pull off the antics of old, and if it were indeed him, he should be put on trial for arson. Still others said the phantom was but a harmless theater lover, who had been made a scapegoat and so taken the blame for the real criminal. This opinion was shared by most socialites as tales of his romantic actions toward Delia swept through the city.

As a child, she had heard about a mysterious fire, until her mother had silenced the gossips. But perhaps now that things were being brought to light, Madre would tell her the tale. If what Mrs. Grubb said was true, Madre had been there and could offer her opinion of who the original phantom was, why he had chosen her mother all those years ago, and whether he was innocent.

Yet such questions would have to wait, for tonight Madre would begin her new role at the Metropolitan, and no doubt tomorrow the papers would boast of the new opera house stealing the Academy's star. It would be a blow to the Knickerbockers and their campaign for the Academy, but hopefully she could recover the attention the Metropolitan had usurped. Delia could not disappoint the patronesses, or her career would end faster than it had begun.

Hester pinched her. Delia jumped and turned to glare at Hester, who was frowning at her, her message clear. *Pay attention to the sermon.*

She discreetly observed the audience, hoping no one had witnessed the pinching, which she at once regretted as she spotted far too many matrons to keep her mind on the matter at hand. Delia's gaze rested on a father with his two young daughters seated on either side, his hand holding each child's hand. Watching how the father doted on them, she knew the little girls were safe, loved, and valued. They would never have to wonder what would happen to them. They had promising futures already provided for them.

She averted her eyes, that dull ache in the pit of her stomach reminding her of the many years since she had been in her father's arms and the tender memories that were carefully tucked away before last night shattered the illusion of him she had created. Before last night, she'd imagined how he missed her based solely on those fleeting happy memories she still possessed and the short notes on her birthday. How much must he be ashamed of her now that he had his own family—one that wasn't descended from Italian opera stars? *Apparently enough to remove himself completely from us.*

Madre had told her long ago that he had departed to manage his holdings in London and his country home and didn't have time for them. The answers to her questions of why he never returned varied, but all had the same ending: Father was not coming back, and Delia had given up asking herself why Father had left her . . . them. Now she knew better. A lord had many responsibilities, including producing a family worthy of bearing his crest.

Hester's pinch nearly made her shriek this time. She rubbed at the sore spot as the choir rose. Delia stood beside Hester and began the familiar hymn "Jesus, Lover of My Soul." Hester's crooning was enough to wake her from her thoughts and shift her attention to the present. As Delia began to sing, her cheeks burned. Her distraction would cease *now*. She rolled her shoulders back and allowed her voice to ring true.

"'Wilt Thou not regard my call? Wilt Thou not accept my prayer? Lo! I sink, I faint, I fall—Lo! On Thee I cast my care. Reach me out Thy gracious hand! While I of Thy strength receive, hoping against hope I stand, dying, and behold, I live. Thou, O Christ, art all I want, more than all in Thee I find. . . .'"

Her heart had certainly not been tuned this morning to any thought but that of the papers. Here she had been worrying over what men said about her career and the ramifications if she failed when it was not in her control. It never had been. Her father had abandoned her, but the Lord never had, not in life and not in her career. She would follow along with the patronesses' plans, but she would no longer bear the burden of the success of the Academy on her shoulders.

Papá, if society's favor turns away from me and the Academy, if my father rejects me as his titled daughter, and if Madre continues to accept a married man into her bed, remind me again and again, Lord, that you are all I need. You are all I have ever needed. And if all reject me, you hold my heart. I know you will cover and protect me in my father's absence and my mother's shame.

"'Just and holy is Thy Name, source of all true righteousness. Thou art evermore the same, Thou art full of truth and grace. Plenteous grace with Thee is found, grace to cover all my sin. Let the healing streams abound. Make and keep me pure within. . . .'"

Following the hymn, the reverend rose and the congregation bowed their heads as one for the final prayer, and then they were dismissed.

"What distracted you so, Delia?" Hester huffed as she buttoned her cloak, stepping onto the sidewalk of Fifth Avenue with the rest of the choir milling around them.

"Everything," she murmured, her stomach rumbling.

Hester reached into her reticule and removed something round covered with waxed paper. Unwrapping it, she gave Delia a glorious cranberry scone—too glorious to be Elena's creation. "I bought it as a treat for the walk home, but how can I enjoy it when your stomach is singing louder than I do in church?"

Delia broke the scone in half and handed the larger piece to Hester. "Thank you."

She waved her off and took a bite. "So, which was it, Mr. Quincy or the patronesses on your mind?"

"A little of both, I suppose." She kicked at a pebble on the sidewalk, watching it skitter and tumble into the street.

"His ears must be burning." Hester laughed around her mouthful.

"Why would you say a thing like that?"

"Because he is heading our way." Hester pointed up the sidewalk with her scone, where Kit broke away from the clusters outside the church, jogging toward them, slipping haphazardly on the patches of ice from last night's storm.

"Miss Vittoria!" he called, waving to her, but was caught by a gentleman on his way to her.

"He's here?" Even with nearly a thousand congregants, she was shocked she had not spied him in the crowd. She ran her hand over the front of her skirt, her favorite between the only two day gowns she possessed. It was emerald with ruffles down the bodice she had purchased herself with her earnings. A pity she had borrowed Elena's hideous brown cloak, as hers was still drying after washing it yesterday.

"You are as fresh as a spring day, Miss Delia, and twice as lovely," Hester assured her, patting her arm.

"Thank you, Hester." Her cheeks heated from the compliment.

"Under that cloak, that is." She clicked her tongue and shook her head. "Too bad you chose today of all days to wear Elena's spare cloak."

"Hester!"

"I'm certain he won't mind. That gentleman has been waiting long enough to find love. Did you know he was engaged nearly fifteen years ago but was fairly jilted, left at the altar? His fiancée, Alice Lexington, took off to India with her parents and within a year became Lady Ellyson." Hester dusted her hands free from bits of scone. "Elena told me all about it. Her sister worked for the Lexington family before they left. A tragic break it was, but rumor has it the lady has returned and has set her cap for him once more."

Delia jerked her head up from her appraisal of the cloak. "Kit Quincy was engaged to *her*?"

Hester's eyes widened. "Didn't you know?"

"I knew they shared a past, but that is all." Delia fiddled with the lace of her cuff, trying to swallow the lump in her throat. "I guess I should have supposed it was more than that with his being . . . well, perfect."

Hester cackled, clapping her hands together. "Look at you. After all this time, you have finally encountered a gentleman who makes you pause in your climb to the top of your career."

Unable to correct Hester that it was all a ruse for the sake of saving her beloved opera house and that Kit had been blackmailed into the role, Delia merely shook her head. And even if it wasn't all for play, how could she ever hope to truly be *noticed* by him? She might have a title now, yet she could not change the way she was raised. She would always be the little girl from the opera house with a shameful mother to any gentleman of good standing. "He's merely being kind."

"And why would Mr. Quincy do such a thing?" Hester smirked. "I think it is because you are now his favorite soprano. Your mother would be proud of you, landing a gentleman like that."

"I am doing no such thing," Delia insisted, glancing behind her. Her heart hammered with dread that others might overhear Hester and think Delia was just like her mother. Several men had requested to pay her call in the past, but seeing her mother's sordid pleasure with them, Delia couldn't help but be put off from the set. Because of Madre's loose ways, they always wanted something *she* would never give. *But Kit Quincy isn't anything like those men. He is a true gentleman.* Certainly, he was older than her, but with his age came a maturity that drew her, made her feel safe—something she hadn't experienced since the day her father left her. "If society thinks I am like her—"

"Hush now. Remember who you are," Hester chided, patting Delia's cheek.

She sighed and nodded. It seemed her revelation would take time to take root in her heart.

"Mr. Quincy is waiting, my dear." Hester gestured toward Kit, who was standing a few yards away, walking cane and hat in hand, waiting for her to turn to him.

Delia kissed Hester on the cheek and met Kit where he stood. His hair formed a perfect pompadour that was loose and falling to his shoulders, curling at the ends in a way that accentuated his fine jawline and Grecian nose. Did he know that was how she preferred he wear it? In the morning light, she could spy a dimple in his chin she had not noticed before. Surprising, for she had committed every detail of his face to memory. "Good morning, Kit. I didn't know you attended here."

"Good morning, Delia. I don't usually attend this church, but I wished to see you in the choir and then perhaps persuade you to take a walk about Gramercy Park with me?" he asked, swinging his cane, his look of uncertainty warming her heart.

"Don't you have more pressing matters to see to than taking your morning constitutional with me? I know being my escort is taking time away from your hotel duties."

"Which is why I hired a manager and assistant manager whom I can rely upon at all times. Nothing would please me more than to spend the day with you." He lifted his hands. "Though I do admit I have long since wished to take a walk inside Gramercy Park, but as I do not live there and therefore possess a key to that mysterious gate guarding your neighborhood's little garden of Eden, I was hoping you would allow me entrance?"

Delia laughed. "But are you up for the walk? It's over two miles away."

Kit rested both hands on his cane, grinning. "My lady, have you learned nothing about me?" He swept his arms out to the gig hitched to a charcoal mare not far behind him.

The leather-tufted bench seat would leave precious little space between a couple.

As if reading her thoughts, he nodded to the clusters of ladies gossiping behind their raised hands and fans and whispered, "They must have their show, eh?"

If only he were truly courting her. Would it be so terrible to pretend for just today that they were indeed a couple? *But I will have my memories, and years from now they will be all I have left of Kit.* That did it. She placed her hand in his, having thoroughly convinced herself it was the best course of action to enjoy the present moment and worry about the future later—preferably in the future. She rose on her tiptoes and pressed a kiss to his cheek, a thrill washing over her from the touch and her boldness. "My dashing Mr. Kit, let us be off."

His eyes widened, and she could spy a flush where her lips touched as he helped her into the gig. She wished she could shed the hideous cloak. She would much rather be pretty than warm at this moment. She settled her skirts as Kit rounded the gig, freed his horse, and climbed in beside her. He unwrapped his crimson scarf and wrapped it about her neck before draping a thick russet fur blanket over them both. "Must protect your voice."

He snapped the reins, and the mare sprang into motion, flinging her against Kit's shoulder as he guided the horse onto the busy street at breakneck speed, weaving about other carts, wagons, and carriages with such skill that it thrilled her. With the wind stinging her cheeks, she burrowed into the scarf, but all too soon they reached her residence and the park. Kit tied the horse and gig to the residence's hitching post and hurried around to assist her.

She drew in a sharp breath as his hands encircled her waist and easily lifted her from the carriage, slowly lowering her to the sidewalk. She pushed herself from his arms, despite her overwhelming longing to stay put. "You are not the first person to ask me to let them into the neighborhood's private park, sir, but you will be the first for whom I will make an exception to my rule." The wind swept between the residences, swirling her skirts and threatening to take her chapeau. She smashed her hand atop her head and dashed across the street to the park. Pulling the skeleton key from her reticule, she fit it into the gate that barred the entrance to the park.

"Well, this feels deliciously wicked to break the rules of an outsider being allowed into the sacred park." Kit rubbed his hands together, his enjoyment evident.

She laughed, pleased that the gentleman was so honorable

that he considered *this* wicked. She sighed as she attempted to quash her dream of a happy life with a husband at her side. She was meant to remain single. Her occupation left little time for a husband. She could not afford to allow sensibility to sweep her away beyond this brief window of time.

She pushed open the door to her sanctuary, being certain to lock the door behind her lest some curious passerby try to enter and she get in trouble with the rest of the community. Not that they ever spoke to her when they saw her, but a strongly worded note would appear on her letter tray as if by magic, citing her as the miscreant as though the very trees had been watching her.

"No wonder you wish to keep everyone else out." Kit released a low whistle as they followed the gravel path beneath the graceful branches, the giant maples losing their leaves even as they walked beneath them. "The place truly is a paradise." He offered her his arm.

A thrill passed through her at the feel of hardened muscle beneath the elegant walking coat. *Stop it. This is a farce, a play. Do not let your heart get involved just because he is so brilliant, kind, wonderful, and everything you could have ever hoped for in an honorable man. He has said nothing regarding a possible future. It is all in your head, Delia. Like always.*

"Tell me, Lia." He gestured toward the houses surrounding the park. "Do you have many friends in the area?"

"As you can imagine, sir, my mother's proclivities have kept many from my door." She ambled down the path, birds chirping in the branches overhead. "Most of my friends were made in my brief years at the day school I attended, during which time my mother began accepting her few choice callers before settling on the one. I've been wanting to ask, how is Mrs. Lowe bearing knowing Mr. Lowe's indiscretion?" *And his apparent disregard for her wishes?*

"As you might think." He gritted his teeth. "I've warned him, and she has cut off his funds until we are certain he has ceased his pursuit. She has Pinkerton agents following him at all hours in the event he seeks out your mother."

"And when they are caught together? What will Mrs. Lowe do? She's already taken the one thing my mother values."

"Mrs. Lowe is a woman of many resources. I would encourage you to speak with your mother about cutting ties with the man lest Mrs. Lowe take further action. Her influence does not stop at the doors of the Academy."

"I will try, but she doesn't like me to state my mind when it does not align with her wishes." Delia lifted her gaze to the rustling of the leaves. To her left, a pair of squirrels chased each other from branch to branch, their playfulness bringing a smile as she drew in a deep breath of the glorious morning air.

"What if you wrote to your father and asked him to return home?" Kit suggested.

"I've asked him a dozen times and will again, but I can guarantee you that once more will make no difference in his decision, and even if he did return home, I doubt Madre would listen. I do not blame him for staying away." *I only wish he had taken me when he left.* At the thought, another closely followed that if Father had taken her, she would not be here with Kit. And that thought did not sit well with her.

Kit frowned. "In doing so, he has kept himself away from you."

"Yes, but I have Hester and my work. I have a fulfilling life."

"Of course." He paused beneath the boughs and pressed a kiss atop her hand. "He is the one missing out. He is the one who should feel pain, not you."

"Oh, Kit, I . . ." Delia paused in her confession of how much his words touched her as she caught sight of two ladies approaching them. She quickly turned away from him to run her fingers under her eyelashes, then plastered on a bright smile. "As my mother says, I must save my tears for the stage. Must not let others see our pain unless they are paying for the privilege at the Academy."

He captured her hand again. "But never with me. I do not mind your tears. I want to share your burdens with you, Lia."

"That is a daring wish, Mr. Kit," she whispered.

"I'm a daring gentleman." At the crunch of gravel behind him, he spun around, lifting the brim of his hat to the two youngest Wingfield ladies of the house. "Why, if it isn't the Misses Wingfields. A pleasure to see you both. How are you faring?"

"Mr. Quincy." The older of the two, Ermengarde, curtsied, elbowing her youngest sister, Nora. Her gaze darted to Delia and back to Mr. Quincy, her eyes wide with curiosity. She knew as well as Delia that she had never been seen walking the park with anyone, not even with her mother, and especially not with a gentleman. "This is an unexpected surprise."

"I greatly enjoy spending time outdoors, and I know Miss Vittoria does as well. And as I have always wanted to see the park, Miss Vittoria was kind enough to oblige me," Kit replied, sending a smile to Delia.

Ermengarde nodded to Delia, a hint of a smile in place. "Oh? We do not see Miss Vittoria often here."

"I take most of my constitutionals at dawn," she explained. *Precisely to avoid running into anyone and being snubbed.* As a child, she had been tolerated as a playmate for Flora and Tacy, but the moment her mother began accepting callers, the parents of the park no longer wished their children to associate with her. It had been a horrible summer that year, and that was when she immersed herself in church and in the opera house, finding friends wherever she could, and when she had begun taking lessons, her tattered heart began to mend as her talent made itself known. She might not have a father's love, but she had her voice and a patchwork of family who cared for her. And as soon as she was allowed, she joined the choir with Hester. "How are your sisters, the ladies Flora, Olive, and Tacy, regarding their recent marriages?"

"Yes!" Kit interjected. "I read about it in the papers. It was unusual for three sisters to be married before summer's end. Did I read correctly that Tacy married Lord Peregrine?"

Nora looked surprised that Delia knew her entire family. Had she forgotten that Delia had grown up in Gramercy Park? "Yes, she did. Quite a whirlwind romance. Love never quite takes the expected route, does it, Mr. Quincy?" She batted her lashes at Kit.

Honestly. The girl is over twenty years his junior. Delia wished she could shake the starry-eyed gaze from the girl. *But can I fault her for her good taste?* Kit's character was nothing short of magnificent, with a physique to match.

"No, it does not." Kit raised Delia's hand to his lips once more.

Nora frowned as Ermengarde eyed Kit's hold on Delia. "We hope to see more of you, Mr. Quincy."

"You shall much sooner than you think if you will be attending Mrs. Dempsey's winter party?"

"As the two of us have been officially presented to society, we certainly would not miss the famed sugar queen's first ball in her new country manor," Nora replied, her smile a little too saucy.

Ermengarde curtsied once more and ushered her sister away, both sending backward glances at Delia.

Delia swallowed her comment to Kit that Mrs. Wingfield never allowed the lack of a daughter's age to keep them from attending balls before. *Mayhap it is because three of her daughters were married in a single summer and she is no longer able to hide the early coming out of each daughter. Or were their hasty marriages what are leading to a sudden clinging to the debutante's etiquette?* She shook her head free of that thought. The Wingfield daughters were the picture of propriety, no matter that Nora had come out a year sooner than most.

"Speaking of the party." Kit guided her to the bench. "Will you allow me to escort you to Willow's party in two weeks? I believe you received an invitation yesterday?" At her nod, he added, "Good. Good. It is a birthday surprise for Miss Flora—I mean, Mrs. Theodore Day—who will be in town visiting her family for the first time since she departed New York for her summer in New Orleans."

She bit her lip, regretting now only being able to purchase the one ball gown for Mrs. Astor's party, but perhaps she could wear the stunning silver gown again. Surely the rules of never wearing the same ball gown twice did not apply to her, for after this was over, what need had she of *two* insensible gowns?

"Unless there is another ball you wish me to escort you to instead?" he prompted. He reached for her cheek, paused a half second, then brushed a curl from her face. "Please, Miss Lia? I can think of no other I'd rather have on my arm than you."

Not even Lady Ellyson? The lines between the farce and reality were blurring at a rapid rate. She needed to retreat before it was too late. Yet she had promised the patronesses, and the idea of being on Kit's arm for an evening was entirely too tempting. "The honor is all mine, Kit."

For the next hour they strolled, speaking about whatever came to mind, until at last she forced herself to check her watch pin, recalling the hour and her lesson with Giuseppe. "We had best return. I have a prior engagement."

"Not with another suitor?" Kit teased, though a spark behind his eyes caught her attention.

"Would you have an objection if it was?" she teased back.

His brows rose. "Who is it?"

"My new maestro."

"Can a maestro be new? And you have a lesson on a Sunday?"

"New to me." She unlocked the gate, shut it behind them, and refastened the lock, dropping the key into her bag. "It is part of the occupation to practice whenever possible. Though you are correct in that I usually keep Sunday afternoons to myself, but again, he is new to me, and I will be performing a variation of arias for tonight's entertainment instead of the new opera *Norma*, which will begin on Friday."

"I do enjoy the variety performance," Kit replied, fiddling with his watch chain. "What is the name of your teacher?"

"It is Maestro Rossi's son, Giuseppe. He has been away

studying for years and has made quite the name for himself, though the maestro does not acknowledge him as a fellow master of the opera."

"Has he performed onstage?" Kit asked, assisting her across the street.

"He could be a leading tenor, but as he is a master of the piano, violin, and other instruments, he is determined to change the opera world through his teaching. And I am to be the pupil who launches his career."

He pointed to her front steps, where Giuseppe stood, scowling and holding a large box in one hand as he turned the bell with the other, the box tipping perilously. "Your maestro?"

"Giuseppe, you are early!" she called, gathering her skirts and taking the steps as quickly as she could. She reached for the box, but the moment she grasped it, Kit lifted it from her.

"Allow me, my lady."

"Finally." Giuseppe withdrew his pocket watch, tapping it with his forefinger. "Do you see what time it is?"

"I thought we were meeting at the Academy."

"We didn't set an exact time, so I came here. I figured we could practice in your parlor first and see how it goes." Giuseppe frowned. "I waited for ten minutes, and no one let me inside. Which is not a wonderful start for you, Miss Vittoria."

"We were all at church, and you know the walk is long for Hester from church and even farther from Elena's." She nodded to the box. "Whatever do you have in there?"

"No idea, but you really ought to inform your new friend that I am not a delivery boy." He motioned for her to open the door.

"Friend?" She paused with her hand on the doorknob.

"Miss Fort?" At her shake of the head, he added, "She's tall, talks a lot, brown curls."

"Millie Ford?" Kit and Delia asked in unison, glancing at each other. If Millie were involved, the phantom would be receiving his instructions next.

He snapped his fingers, pointing at Delia. "That's the one. Pretty lady. Can't seem to say no to pretty ladies. Now, shall we?"

Kit handed her the box and bowed to her. "Until tonight?"

"Tonight," she whispered back.

She reluctantly closed the door, smiling when a moment later she looked through the sidelight window and found him staring back at her from the street. She waved to him and, with the box propped on her hip, floated into the parlor, where she removed the lid. Her breath caught. A note sat atop the tissue and read, *For Willow Dupré-Dempsey's party.*

Delia lifted out a lovely gown of sapphire with a high collar of elegant black lace, its ebony buttons stark against the jewel tones of the satin. She held it out and sighed in delight at the three-quarter sleeves that ended in delicate black lace that would reach just past her wrists. She pressed the gown to her waist, unfurling it to find that the sapphire skirt melted into black lace with a matching hem. "Millie truly does think of everything."

Giuseppe removed a roll of sheet music from his coat pocket and plunked down at the piano seat, warming his fingers in a chromatic scale. "Except, apparently, to have a delivery boy do the delivering. Now, put down that confection and let us get to work."

Thirteen

Kit whistled to himself, swinging his cane as he trotted up the steps into the lobby of the Olympia the following afternoon. After a rather long board meeting at the club, he was looking forward to getting to work on his next pet project—planning a new hotel as soon as the Charleston hotel was open in the spring and profitable. While he had been set on the location being in California, he was beginning to reconsider, as it would mean leaving the East Coast. And a certain enchanting lady had him taking on the delightful task of selecting a new city. He was contemplating Savannah, yet he would have to make certain the numbers made sense before scouting out the new property.

"Kit! There you are! Thank the good Lord you keep such a tight schedule." Ramsey trotted up to him, sweat beading his forehead.

"What on earth is going on?" Kit whispered, veiling his concern from the guests milling about.

Ramsey gestured toward the elevators that were roped off. "I consider myself a fit man, but climbing six levels of stairs multiple times in a quarter of an hour would try even the Olympians."

Kit frowned, observing the workmen diligently attempting to set the elevators to rights. "And why would you have to climb the stairs so often? Why not just send the bellhop?"

Ramsey waved a note at him. "Read this."

Kit unfolded the hastily scrawled note. *"New tenant in one of the third-floor apartments complains of noisy neighbor."* Kit shoved the note in his pocket. It hardly seemed worth Ramsey's state, but as the fashionable apartments offered his steadiest stream of income for the hotel, it might speak to the reason behind Ramsey's ruddy complexion. "And have you addressed the situation?"

Ramsey whipped his handkerchief from his pocket with a snap and dabbed his forehead. "Of course, but the man making the noise is none other than *Mr. Beckby.*"

Kit sucked in through his teeth. "Oh no."

"Yes."

Kit rested his hand on Ramsey's shoulder and whispered, "I thought we had decided it was easier to keep room fifteen, the one sharing his wall, vacant."

"Trust me, I am well aware of that fact. But it was an emergency, and the lady was quite insistent, saying she would pay double the rate, which I tried to explain wasn't the reason why the room hadn't been let. Then she offered me triple, and how could I refuse when we are seeking to open a third hotel?"

"I'll see to it." Kit snatched up his cane at the middle and headed for the stairs.

"Thank you, but there is something else," Ramsey called after him.

Kit lifted a hand to him, letting Ramsey know he would handle the situation. It would be easier to relocate the woman to the suite he usually reserved for a bride and groom than to talk the eccentric millionaire in apartment sixteen out of whatever he had set his mind on accomplishing in his apartments. Last week, it had been learning to play the violin, which he had remarkably picked up in a short amount of time. Kit drew back his shoulders and knocked lightly on the door of apartment fifteen.

The door flung open, and he was met with the brilliance of Lady Ellyson, her golden hair swept into a coiffure with ringlets spilling over her shoulder, wearing his favorite color of royal blue that always set off her eyes.

"Why, Christopher!" She smiled. "How nice to see that you take such care of your guests that you personally see to our needs. Or is it simply that you wished to see to the complaint because it came from me?"

"I-I didn't know it was from you," he sputtered.

Her smile faltered for half a second as she leaned against the doorframe. "No matter. Now that you are here, though, perhaps you could ask Mr. Beckby to cease hitting the shared wall? It sounds as if knives are piercing the wood paneling."

"Knives?" Kit ran his hand over his face. *Wonderful*. He had to remind himself not to worry about the cost since Mr. Beckby had paid triple the going rate to cover his sins as a resident of the hotel. "So, besides the knives, are your rooms comfortable?"

"Quite. I was rather surprised to hear you do not let this apartment out. Isn't it rather a waste?" She motioned to the spacious salon behind her with its ornate crown molding, crystal chandelier, and luxurious furnishings.

"Yes, well, there are certain reasons"—he nodded to the next-door apartment—"that make it impossible for anyone to enjoy staying here, and it ends up costing me more to make the resident happy than it does to keep it vacant."

"Yes, Ramsey said as much to me," she said, "but I assured him I'm quite used to it, as my mansion was located almost in the middle of the marketplace in Calcutta. Though it was walled in, the noises comforted me. This last hullabaloo, however, concerned me because it is occurring directly adjacent to where I sleep."

Kit nodded. "To be clear, if I ask Mr. Beckby to throw his knives against the wall facing the avenue, you will be satisfied?"

"Entirely satisfied." Her lips quirked to the side. "And I must say, hearing your account of him, I plan on becoming friends with Mr. Beckby before too long."

Kit laughed. "I have to say you are one of the easiest guests I have dealt with in a long while."

"Well, it's the least I can do when you all have been so accommodating in letting me these rooms."

"Now, Ramsey mentioned an emergency? I hope everything is well."

She sighed. "Yes, but my parents returned home and wish to treat me as a child once more and take over the raising of my son. I, however, have been without parents to guide me for over a decade and must raise my son as I see fit. They think they can cure his melancholia with a strict regimen when I know what he needs is the freedom he had in Calcutta, surrounded with friends."

"Your son is here?" Kit peered over her shoulder.

"Thomas?" she called in a sweet tone toward the salon.

From behind the divan, a handsome chap of about four popped his head up, his baby-toothed grin stealing Kit's heart as the boy scampered to his mother's side. He clutched her hand at the sight of a strange gentleman in the doorway, his other arm protectively wrapping about a miniature three-masted Harlan & Hollingsworth yacht.

Kit knelt in front of the boy. "Hello, Lord Ellyson. I'm Mr. Kit." He pointed to the toy yacht. "You like boats?"

Thomas nodded, his blond hair falling into his eyes before Elsie gently swept it to the side.

"I have one in the harbor. I think you would like it."

His brown eyes widened under his thick lashes. "Could I see it?" Thomas asked with a slight lisp.

Kit looked to Elsie. "It might be good for him to be out of the apartments when Ramsey speaks with Mr. Beckby, in case things grow heated. Mr. Beckby is quite the passionate man."

"Oh, I hate to put out Mr. Beckby, but we would both enjoy the outing. Let me fetch his coat and my hat. Thomas, stay with Mr. *Kit*." She winked at Kit over the sobriquet she never could be persuaded to use in the old days. "He is Mother's oldest and dearest friend."

The boy showed his excitement, hopping from foot to foot, still clutching his toy yacht. "I love boats!"

"I'd have to agree with you, Thomas. I love boats, too." Kit waited as Elsie locked her door, then held out his arm to escort her and her son downstairs and outside to his carriage.

Reaching the harbor, they began walking along the boardwalk. Thomas's little mouth dropped open when he spotted all the boats, moored and gently swaying in the light wind, the waves lapping against their hulls.

Kit bent down to Thomas's level and pointed out to the water to his 232-foot triple-masted yacht with its black steam stack in the center, which he used only in his journeys to Charleston and Newport, for he enjoyed the challenge of the sail on short pleasure cruises. "And that one, Lord Ellyson, is mine."

The boy looked to his toy and then out to Kit's yacht, agape again.

"Would you like to go aboard her?" Kit asked.

"Can we?" He stared unbelieving at Kit and then twisted around to face his mother. "Oh, Mother, can we?"

She laughed and kissed his full rosy cheek. "Yes, darling."

Within moments, they were piled into the dinghy and being rowed out to the *Olympia*. Once aboard, the lad scampered over the deck with the first mate following close behind, answering every question he could manage.

"May I see belowdecks?" Elsie asked. "I remember when you were having her built, and I never got to see the finished product."

He nodded and waved her inside to the drawing room with its teak and mahogany panels that offered a manly air, while in the connecting dining room he had allowed for a brighter hue of sea-green wallpaper with platinum leafing that was illuminated by the skylight and portholes.

"Lovely," she said, taking in the dining room. "I love that you used my suggestion for the color."

Kit coughed as the memory he had so desperately attempted to squelch rose to greet him once more. "Was it?"

She laughed, resting her hand on his arm. "Don't be coy." Her mirth faded as she ran her hand over the mahogany dining table. "This was supposed to be *our* ship, sending us off to Europe for a dazzling month following the wedding."

He gritted his teeth. "Yes, well, I quite liked how everything turned out and would not wish to change it." *Despite the fact that you selected much of the interior design.* At first, he had hoped to follow Elsie to India to convince her of his love, but just as the ship had been finished, she had already become Lady Ellyson.

"Did you use the French walnut I picked out for the library?"

"Why, yes, I suppose I did." Honestly, he had forgotten how many things she had picked out, except for the nursery, which he had redesigned at once and converted into a storage room. "Shall we return now to the main deck? The nine staterooms are nothing extraordinary, just more of the same."

"More of the same." She smiled up at him. The merriment from her youth had not faded. "Christopher, you are too modest. This yacht is worth a fortune. Now, where is your kitchen? I want to see if you still have that ice cream maker I gave you."

Kit laughed, remembering her sweet tooth. "I believe it is in the kitchen, but alas, I do not have it stocked beyond the pantry items."

Her eyes sparkled. "Next time, then."

The hour passed quickly, and Thomas's spirits were quite high by the time they had returned to the hotel.

"What an enjoyable day." Lady Ellyson grasped his hand in the lobby. "I haven't seen Thomas so happy in a very long while."

He squeezed her hand and stepped back, then said farewell to Thomas, who was prancing from side to side in front of the elevators that appeared to be in working order once more. "I meant what I said. Thomas can play on the *Olympia* whenever he wishes while she is anchored in the harbor. I have already informed my crew of it. And should he wish to sail, I would be happy to show him."

Tears filled her eyes. "You don't know what this means to me. It gives me such hope that my sweet happy boy will one day return to me for good."

"Excuse me, Mr. Quincy. Lady Delia is here, waiting for you," his bellhop informed him with a short bow.

His appointment! "Ah, yes. Please tell Lady Delia I am on my way."

He motioned for the bellhop to cease speaking, but he supposed he wasn't clear enough, as the bellhop continued, "Very good, sir. She is waiting for you to be seated in the tea salon."

Elsie's eyes sparkled again. "Tea salon, eh? She must be quite the lady. I remember you talking with me about building that very salon, saying it would be the perfect meeting place for young courting couples. Are you courting her? Or playing with her heart?"

Kit bowed to Elsie. "Pardon me. Please, let my staff know if you have need of anything. The service at the Olympia Grande is unparalleled."

"I won't be giving up anytime soon, Christopher." She rested her hand on Thomas's head. "I always get what I want in the end. And what I want is you."

Fourteen

"You are thirty-eight, Quincy. The lady is even younger than Willow Dupré, and yet you continue," he muttered to himself, adjusting his cravat as he wove his way through the press of people in the opera house lobby on Friday night. A lady nearby lifted a brow at his talking to himself, and he sent her a reassuring smile that he was not in need of Blackwell's Island's asylum facilities.

The veiled pretense between assisting Delia because she was sweet and helping her because he couldn't keep himself from her side was all but gone now. For the first time since the competition for the sugar queen's hand, his routine had lost its luster. His business meetings felt longer, dinner conversations were mild, and even the thought of sailing off to Newport at the end of the season was no longer favorable if *she* was not to be present on the island. But he pressed on as he always had, because when this was over, all he would have left were his hotels to keep him busy.

And yet this afternoon he had stooped to a new low. He had skipped a meeting to discuss the paintings for his

Charleston hotel, avoided the ledgers for a third time, completely eluded Mr. Beckby and instead went for a stroll, escaping to another world, one filled with thoughts of Delia. Unbeknownst to Kit, those thoughts led him directly to the steps of the Academy and feeling more than a bit foolish. Until Delia, nothing could pry him away from his hotels during the workday.

Unable to keep himself from the chance of spying Delia onstage during rehearsal, he had slipped inside but kept to the shadows of his box and watched her run through her scenes for the next opera the company would be featuring tonight with the same tired sets they had used for years. But Delia had breathed new life into everything, and he was certain her *Norma* would be met with high praise. The lady truly was a marvel.

And that marvel is fifteen years younger than I, he reminded himself as the crowd halted. He shifted in his jacket as the house grew overly warm as the lobby narrowed, creating a bottleneck, but soon the theatergoers began moving again as each family made their way to their individual boxes. The overwhelming urge to shed his jacket subsided and he continued arguing with himself about his feelings for Delia.

However, the argument he had adopted for removing himself from Willow's competition no longer worked in the least. In fact, the more he got to know Delia, the more he thought that perhaps his age was just right for her mature outlook on life. Perhaps his age was even a draw for her, for she did not seem to appreciate the advances of the younger gentlemen clamoring for her.

He was bumped from behind, and when he turned to look

who it was, he found a note pressed in his hand and the back of Millie Ford in her turquoise gown striding away from him. *At last!* He was beginning to think he had the evening off from his phantom duties. Yet Millie knew as well as he that if the phantom did not show tonight, the thrill would lag.

Kit ducked behind some potted palms and broke the seal. He unfolded the note and studied her detailed map of how to reach his phantom costume and the place where his stunt was to take place. He crumpled the note in his fist with a groan. Contrary to the society matron's misguided belief, he did not possess the skills of a tightrope walker or that of the trapeze performer. And yet, even as he questioned his ability, he would still do all in his power to aid his lady with tonight's feat and fulfill his end of the bargain.

He cut across the lobby to the door marked STAFF ONLY and wove around the bustling footmen, who were attending upon the guests. They spared him only a passing glance. Being one of the highest-paying patrons, it was not uncommon for him to be seen behind the scenes, and they would assume he was there either for Delia or in search of Mr. Mapleson. He pushed through another door leading backstage, keeping to the shadows until he reached the winding wooden staircase. He began climbing, passing level upon level filled with old theatrical property and broken sets that had been set aside for repairs. Soon he came to where only the stagehands would venture to retrieve sets rarely used anymore.

Finally, Kit located the box with his costume in it. *This is ridiculous for her to expect me to do this,* he thought as he tightened the cape at his throat and then the strap securing the mask, grateful Millie saw the logic in not using glue again.

Footsteps sounded behind him. "Miss Ford told me you would be needing assistance tonight." Ramsey held up a harness. "I believe you are to attempt something rather dangerous, and she wished for me to act as your safety net, or rather, safety rope."

Kit exhaled in relief that he wasn't alone in this feat, even as he eyed the harness. "And this is supposed to hold me? Have you had any training in keeping someone from falling to his death?"

"She didn't exactly give me a lesson on how to work the pulley-and-harness system." Ramsey shrugged. "Still, it seems straightforward enough. Simply thread your limbs into the harness loops." He pointed at the four loops and lifted the straps with the buckles attached. "Then I buckle you in at the upper back to this iron loop thing and hook that to the rope I'm to use to pull you up and down, and voilà!"

"'Loop thing,' how comforting," Kit said. "Yes, you sound very familiar with this whole business." He flicked the brim of his phantom hat.

Ramsey motioned him forward. "Come now, you trusted me when we sailed to New Orleans and back, did you not, and there was that rather terrifying hurricane chasing us? Well, this is much less terrifying and very safe." He held up the harness and shook it, the buckles jingling. "At least from what Miss Ford tells me."

Kit sighed as he stepped into the harness, sticking his arms through the loops, then turning to allow Ramsey to buckle it together at the back. When finished, Ramsey adjusted the cape to hide most of the harness.

"There." Ramsey slapped him on the back. "We shall give the illusion of your flying from the rafters to the stage.

Remember, this is just a backup plan should you need to make a quick escape, or are unable to climb your way back up, or you slip—which would be highly embarrassing, as the phantom is supposed to exude a sense of manliness, and slipping has the opposite effect."

Kit eyed his friend. "Just how are you supposed to help me escape if I cannot climb my way out?"

Ramsey pointed to a pile of counterweights attached to the other end of the length of rope. "I use those to send you to the rafters."

"Please do not send me through the roof in your enthusiasm."

Ramsey grinned. "I can't promise anything." He held up a single crimson rose. "I was instructed that this was for you to deliver. Now, go and woo your lady like a man of legends."

Kit held the stem of the rose in his teeth and placed his foot on the double planks that hung suspended with ropes four stories above the stage and served as a walkway. They held. He gripped the rope rails and began moving, feeling himself sway with each stride. Stifling his fear of falling, he slid into the shadows of the rafters as Delia was about to take the stage for the opening act in Bellini's *Norma*. The set was far plainer than the Swiss village of *La Sonnambula*, what with its being situated in a forest of ancient Rome. He had never cared for this particular opera, even though it was touted as Bellini's best work. The plot was too dark in his opinion, no matter how rich the arias.

A movement below caught his eye, and on the platform of the second story, he spotted Lorenzo checking the pulley ropes. On the opposite side of the platform, a second stagehand minded the ropes and wheel to adjust the scenery onstage as needed. The men moved about their work, not noticing Kit two stories above them.

He shifted his weight on the platform, instantly regretting it as the boards tilted with him. He sucked in his breath and grasped the ropes tighter, his knuckles whitening. Besides the threat of plunging to his death, if Ramsey wasn't paying attention, this was going to be tricky with the theatergoers casting glances about every so often during the performance, hope and trepidation in their expressions as they anticipated the phantom's arrival.

Just as he expected, the whole of the opera house was filled. Even an elite family known to own a box at the Metropolitan was there with their debutante daughter sitting in the front of the box with a new beau at her side, her parents behind her along with her three brothers. The Wingfield and the Day family boxes were filled, and he spied Willow Dupré-Dempsey and her new husband in the Day box with Flora and Theodore. Seeing his friends, he felt a twinge of guilt for the deception. But if too many people knew his true identity, the illusion could backfire and destroy his Delia's dreams, and he could never allow that to happen.

The music swelled, and in just a few moments Delia would appear. Kit stretched his neck from side to side, readying himself. *I am about to plunge over sixty feet. Love has made a fool of you, Kit.* He tested the golden rope affixed to a hook in the ceiling and used for the heaviest of sets. Surely it would support him in his descent and his climb back to the top. Heaven help him if he slipped and Ramsey needed to use the harness to keep him from falling. If his friend looked away for half a second, it would be the end of Kit's grand romance.

He wrapped the golden rope about his hands and swung

a leg over it, the platform swaying wildly to the side beneath him. The moment she stepped onstage and the light found her, he would have a difficult time not losing himself in her song, as her voice seemed to grow in loveliness with her confidence. Nevertheless, he would wait until the final note to wrap both his legs about the rope, leaving the safety harness slack. The four-story drop would have any man unused to such heights feeling nauseated, but thankfully, due to his experience sailing the yacht, he stayed solidly planted on the rail and counted down the beats.

The time had come.

He shoved off, swinging down toward her, his cape billowing about him. The rush of wind nearly yanked the hat from his head, no thanks to the hatpin that had nicked his scalp earlier when trying on the costume for Millie, but the black ribbon tie held true. His boots landed with a thud on the deck, and miracle of miracles, he did not fall.

The crowd roared, cheering from the romance of it all. The ensemble looked to one another, as though questioning if this were part of the play and whether to continue with the opera as if nothing had happened. The orchestra kept playing, as did the chorus in their singing, even as the audience's murmuring swelled.

Kit strode forward, knelt before her, and pressed a kiss atop her hand. "With all my adoration, my lady." He presented the bloom to her.

Delia's mouth dropped briefly before a smile lit her face and she accepted the flower with appropriate curiosity, awe, and admiration. But as she had no idea of his plan, he knew she was genuine. As her fingertips brushed his, her eyes widened.

Kit whipped about to see Lorenzo charging at him, a couple of stagehands following suit. "Best of luck, my lady," Kit said in a gruff voice so as not to be recognized. He reached for his golden rope to climb back up, but it was gone. He looked to the rafters and saw it had somehow retracted. *Impossible!* He bolted for the wings, leaping for the set's makeshift tree branches. Using his momentum, he grabbed a branch and swung himself up to reach for a second branch. The fake leaves scraped his arms when the rope attached to his harness tugged to life, ramming his head into a trunk. He sucked in a choice word that was cut off as he was jerked again through the branches and sent soaring past the curtain drop, the crowd screaming and clapping as he hurtled toward the rafters. He came within a hairbreadth from the beam that would have rendered him senseless.

Ramsey grinned at him, his feet planted wide as he strained against the ropes, lowering Kit until his feet brushed the floor. Ramsey fixed the rope to the pinrail at the wall and dashed to his side.

"See? I knew I wouldn't accidentally kill you."

"Well, that is certainly good news," Kit panted. The harness loosened with Ramsey's unfastening it.

"It took three counterweights to get you through that copse, but the third nearly sent you through the roof." Ramsey clapped him on the back.

"We've got to move!" Kit ripped the cape from his shoulders, swept the costume into the box, then shoved it behind an old prop of a bush. He left the harness lying in a heap.

"What a rush!" Ramsey released a whoop as they trotted down the winding stairs.

"Quiet! It's not over yet." Kit ran through the stage door

and slowed his stride as he moved into the lobby, casually picking up a refreshment. They approached his box with the crowd still buzzing while the orchestra conductor attempted to garner some control to finish the opera. Kit shook hands with Ramsey as if they had merely met at the refreshment table.

The elder Mr. Pruett nodded to them in passing.

"Good to see you too, Ramsey. We must have that ride through Central Park sometime," Kit said for Mr. Pruett's benefit and then stepped through the burgundy velvet curtain to his box to join his uncle, Ramsey seeking his own box.

"Kit! You keep disappearing and missing all the action," Uncle Elmer huffed from his seat at the front of the box, his opera glasses gripped tightly in his fists. "If you were half the opera lover you claim to be, your pants would be sewn to that velvet chair. But no. You are always getting a refreshment and never think to fetch me one, I might add." He shook his head. "If your mother were here to witness your disruptive behavior, she would take you to task for entering and exiting at your will and not waiting until intermission."

"That's what I have you for, Uncle," Kit teased, keeping his breathing regulated as boots pounded past their box, most likely in chase of the phantom they would never find—at least he hoped they would never find. He had never quite worked out that part with the patronesses if he were caught. "Now, what did I miss?"

"What did you miss?" Miss Pruett called from the box beside theirs. "Only the most romantic act I have ever seen, Mr. Quincy." She flapped her fan, sighing.

Kit's chest swelled. If she thought it so, mayhap Delia did as well. Maybe she would see past the pretense.

"Miss Vittoria has quite the list of admirers, my brother being one of them." She gestured toward Digory Pruett, who already had an enormous bouquet of blooms of every variety imaginable ready to send to the stage or throw at Delia's feet. "He refuses to have them sent to her dressing room like every other fellow but wishes to present them himself."

The elation left him. "Digory was always a thoughtful chap."

"I forget that you two spent time together at Willow's." She shook her head.

How quickly society forgot their favorite bachelors and went on to the next eligible gentleman, and there was always a next with the nouveau riche set of parvenus.

"Odd as his fascination is, however, thank goodness he is now distracted by Miss Vittoria. My brother has been rather forlorn since the competition." She rolled her eyes. "I do not know how he became so attached to the idea of Miss Dupré—I mean, Mrs. Dupré-Dempsey. But honestly, this Italian star is a godsend."

If Digory physically brought her a bouquet, as her escort Kit should as well. He began to rise when his coattails yanked him back down again.

"Would you please sit down? You are going to miss the finale," Uncle Elmer said, tugging at his white tie.

"I need to fetch—"

"Sit." Uncle Elmer huffed on the glass of his monocle, wiped it with his handkerchief and set it in place, his scowl securing it as he raised the opera glasses with the curtain.

Quenching his retort at being treated like a lad, Kit returned to his seat and pondered how to woo a woman who did not wish to marry.

Delia's hands shook. Never before had she entered the lobby directly after a performance. But with a freshly scrubbed face and in her emerald ottoman silk and velvet gown from Mrs. Astor's party, she parted the curtains on her way to Kit's box. The group that met her sent her cheeks to heating at being caught where no opera singer had dared to appear before—in a Knickerbocker's box. The Pruetts from the box over were now in Kit's, along with Kit's uncle, but no Kit. *Where is he?*

"Miss Vittoria. What a surprise to see you here." Mrs. Pruett nodded to her, her daughter and son flanking her, the son bearing an enormous crimson bouquet.

"Kit—I mean, Mr. Quincy—invited me."

The group greeted her, all smiles and bows and congratulations flowing from them before the elderly men returned to their conversation and Mr. Digory Pruett presented her with a bouquet of every shade of red she could imagine.

"What good fortune. I was just about to depart for your dressing room to personally congratulate you, Miss Vittoria. I am enchanted by your voice." He grasped her hand in his, bowed, and kissed the back of it lightly.

She re-claimed her hand, then lifted the bouquet to her nose to disguise her discomfort. "Thank you, Mr. Pruett. The flowers are lovely."

His chest swelled as he nodded and stepped closer to her. "I was hoping," he whispered, "to ask you for a second dance at the Olympia Grande the other night."

"You must forgive my rudeness, for I received a bit of surprising news."

"If you need someone to confide in, please look no further. I do so detest seeing you distraught."

She released a nervous laugh as Kit appeared at the curtain with a gargantuan bouquet of his own, and she could not keep her smile at bay, relief flooding her entire being. Mr. Ramsey followed him inside, and Mr. and Miss Pruett caught them in a conversation at the entrance.

Mrs. Pruett joined her son and Delia, swaying with the gentle wafting of her painted silk fan. Its ivory handle, inset with diamonds, sparkled in the light. "Speaking of your surprising news, I read another piece of astonishing news in the paper recently."

"Oh?" Delia waited, not wanting to give Mrs. Pruett any information she was obviously mining for, and clutched the crimson bouquet in front of her as if it were a shield.

She turned to the younger Mr. Pruett. "Digory, I find I have taken a chill, and I left my shawl in our box. Would you be a dear and fetch it for me?"

He bowed to them. "Don't run away again," he whispered, hurrying through the box curtain.

Mrs. Pruett turned to Delia at once. "I read about your father."

"Yes?" She pressed her nose to the blooms and inhaled, delighting in their aroma as she casually glanced toward Kit, who met her gaze before he was forced to turn back to Miss Pruett.

"The Earl of Rolfeson . . ." She narrowed her eyes at Delia. "The only gentleman I know of with that name is Lord Serenus Hearst of Rolfeson, and he resides in Rolfeson Abbey."

"Yes, that is him." She was glad she could answer with

confidence, though she longed to have an honest talk with her mother about him.

Mrs. Pruett gave a half smile. "Well, I'm not entirely sure that is news I'd be spreading if I were you."

"I didn't." Delia blinked. "The papers did."

"Also, just because he is a lord, that does not make you a lady," she hissed, snapping her fan open to hide the anger behind her words from the rest in the box. "And if you have any designs on my son, I'd suggest you rethink such things."

"Pardon me?"

She gestured to the flowers. "I know your type."

Delia stiffened. *I knew I shouldn't have come here. Some things never change.* She drew back her shoulders. This time she would not bow to someone because they thought themselves superior simply because they had money. She was precious in God's eyes, and even if her father *had* abandoned her, she still had her character *and* title, and it was time to remind some patrons of that fact. "My type? I am an earl's daughter, which makes me a lady. Now, if I were a baron's daughter, I wouldn't have a title, but—"

"No, my dear girl." Mrs. Pruett paused, the endearment sounding quite the opposite of what was intended. "What I meant was that your mother must be married for you to inherit the title."

Again, heat flooded her cheeks. "Are you suggesting my mother and my father were not—?"

The lady flipped her fan closed. "Oh, do not get so flustered, Miss Vittoria. It is not so uncommon. I am merely speculating that given your mother's proclivities and that Serenus Hearst has a wife in England and has been married almost twenty years, it goes to prove that all is not as it seems."

Delia's stomach twisted. She could hardly breathe, but then it explained so much—her mother's secrecy and her father's absence. *I am illegitimate?* She shook her head. Madre had always spoken of divorce, but Madre didn't care to tell her when it had ended. Divorce was certainly scandalous, but not as scandalous as what Mrs. Pruett was suggesting. *But would a lord act in such a manner?* Even as the thought crossed her mind, she knew well and good that while there might be hundreds of honorable lords, some of them were capable of such behavior. She swallowed a moan.

"You may wish to ask your mother about Countess Emilie Hearst of Rolfeson. No doubt she would argue your claim to the title of lady. So, before you go counting your wealthy beaus, know that I for one will do everything in my power to refute your claim until proven otherwise if you do not cease your pursuit of my son." Without another word, Mrs. Pruett walked away.

Kit finally left the cluster behind and drew her to his side. "Are you well, Delia? You look flushed."

She pressed the back of her hand to her cheek. "Have you heard of a Countess Emilie Hearst of Rolfeson?"

He shook his head. "I am not in British society, but with Rolfeson in her title, I am assuming she means something to you? Did you mean dowager countess perhaps?"

"According to Mrs. Pruett, Lady Rolfeson is a title held not by my mother but by Emilie Hearst, my father's wife, as she believes I was born out of wedlock." She released a bitter laugh. "It seems Mrs. Pruett believes herself more acquainted with my family's state of affairs than I am." She pressed her handkerchief to her burning cheeks. "You'd best leave me or my family's crumbling status will crush you as well."

Kit handed her the armful of purple flowers. People on the opposite horseshoe of boxes gaped at them, some even going so far as to use their opera glasses to view the tableau. Kit lifted her hand to his lips, his eyes flitting toward the crowd, explaining his action during her intimate confession. "I am so sorry for her insinuations."

"Insinuations that very well may be true," she returned.

"Do not take her conjectures to heart. Speak with your mother if you feel you must. Until then, smile, my sweet Lia. Mrs. Pruett may be an old friend of the family, but she is a terrible gossip, and I would hate for her words to cause you distress—something she is only too happy to gossip about to the whole of society that whatever she told you *must* be true if you took it so hard."

Delia trained her expression and smiled at Kit, his kind eyes bringing her more comfort in a single glance than she had felt in years. *"Who are you?"* Hester's question washed over her, as well as the verses she had committed to heart. *"For thou hast been a shelter for me, and a strong tower from the enemy . . . I will trust in the covert of thy wings . . . For thou, O God, hast heard my vows, Thou hast given me the heritage of those that fear Thy name."* She would not allow the pointed arrows of Mrs. Pruett's conjectures to cause her to falter.

"Who are you?" Hester's voice again sounded through the chatter and the glamour surrounding her.

Title or not, her heritage did not belong to her mother and Serenus Hearst. She lifted her chin. *I am Delia Vittoria, child of God.*

Kit smiled. "There's my Lia. Now, are you busy tomorrow? I'd love to call upon you."

Fifteen

Delia hummed to herself as she unpinned her chapeau after taking her morning constitutional in the private park, happier than she had been in years. For as the days with Kit turned into weeks, her fame rose, and the doors of society were thrown open to her with her father's name being bandied about matrons' parlors as a titled lord. And whenever someone became rather nasty to her over Mrs. Pruett's claim, Kit was always there, shielding her, protecting her from any salaciousness. She sighed, thinking of her dashing Mr. Kit, which was how she referred to him in her heart. Because, almost against her will, she was falling for him. Her humming melted into a full aria as she twirled into the breakfast room.

"Miss Delia!" Hester panted from her climb up the stairs from the kitchen, flapping a letter in the air. "This arrived for you. Delivered downstairs by mistake just now."

Delia smiled at Hester's flushed cheeks, knowing the postman was sweet on Hester and was most likely still enjoying a pot of Italian coffee downstairs, taking a few moments' break from his route to be with his sweetheart. "You didn't need to rush upstairs. I could have waited."

"But this is no ordinary message, miss." Hester ran her fingers over the envelope. "I should have just brought it up to your mother, but it was addressed to you, and well, I didn't want you not to see the letter because she threw it in the fire."

"Why would you give it to her if—?" Delia gasped when Hester extended the letter, the handwriting clear. She snatched it up, studying the crimson wax seal that bore two swords crossing each other with *S. H.* on either side. Father hadn't written her since last Christmas, and as her birthday was a few weeks before Christmas, he usually sent one letter instead of two. And with it being only the middle of November, it was far too soon for him to send that letter. *Is he angry with me about the rumors?* She thrust her finger under the flap and broke the seal, uncertain why this man across the great sea had such an effect on her, and why, after all these years, she felt the need to please him when he didn't feel the same way about her.

Dearest Delia,

The papers have hailed you as the next Jenny Lind, calling for your tour in Europe. I am immensely proud of you for reaching such heights.

He's proud of me? Feeling a bit dazed, she read that line over and over until footsteps padded above her head. Madre was awake. She returned her attention to the letter.

I will be arriving in New York on the 15th of November to see you perform. Please inform your mother of my impending arrival and have the guest room ready.

S. H.

She looked up from the letter, squinting at the peeling paint of the once-opulent crown molding, desperately trying to recall the date. Surely he didn't mean to arrive so soon? The fifteenth was only two days away! How would she tell Madre?

Delia's hands shook as she rested the open letter on the dining room table, the scrawling script taunting her. Not only did her father finally say that he was proud of her, but that he was coming home. *Here!* She jerked to her feet, whirling about in examination of the room, uncertain of where to start. The entire house would need a thorough cleaning, yet she didn't have time for that, what with a new opera about to begin.

She thought of the coins in her reticule that were slowly accumulating with every performance. She had been saving them to purchase a new wardrobe. If she were to be a star, she would need a wardrobe to match her success and she could not rely on anyone's good graces any longer. But a good wardrobe would cost her a fortune. It was becoming scandalous to be seen wearing the same silver gown over and over, no matter how extravagant the piece or her attempt to alternate between wearing it and her emerald gown from Blanchard's. Even so, something had to be done, and she certainly couldn't clean the house alone. She sighed. The coins must be spent on hiring help. *But Father is coming home soon.*

Delia shoved the letter back into its envelope and slid it in her pocket, her panic rising between having to disclose the letter to her mother and the potential of losing her father's dear praise to the fire.

"What are you going to do?" Hester asked.

"I'm going to take a tray up to Madre's room." Delia reached for the coffeepot and poured her mother a cup, then gathered a plate of the choicest fruits as well as a bowl of the dreadful oats. She started up the stairs, the creaking floorboards announcing her presence before she could even knock.

Madre opened the door, surprise filling her expression at seeing the tray. She held the door open and motioned her inside, humming as she resumed her place on the divan.

"Good morning, Madre. What has you so cheerful?"

Madre lifted the newspaper in her hands, tapping her forefinger on a column with the glowing review for Madre's Metropolitan performance in *Carmen* that apparently outshone all before it. "I finally have been given a review to put all other reviews to shame." She lifted the coffee cup and took a sip, closing her eyes. "You must never take the glowing reviews for granted, Daughter, and never skip your lessons, even if it is for Mrs. Astor."

Delia smiled through gritted teeth and braced herself for the coming storm as she placed the letter on her mother's tray.

Madre took a bite of the juicy pear while lifting the letter and reached for her coffee as she read the handwriting. She dropped her cup, spilling coffee on the Persian rug.

Ignoring the rug, Delia waited for her mother to unfold the letter.

"He's coming here?" she shrieked. "After all these years, it took his *daughter* becoming a star to return to claim his family?"

Yes, and therefore most likely to claim only me, as you two have ended your marriage. Yet Delia didn't have the heart to correct her mother. She merely nodded instead.

Madre shrieked again and moved to shove her plate from the tray, but Delia snatched it up. "Madre, you know we do not have any china to spare," she gently chided.

"Let him see the squalor he left us in. The least he can do is replace our china." Madre hurled her oat dish at the wall, Delia flinching at the contents dripping down the faded papered wall.

"I'd hardly call a residence in Gramercy Park . . ." She left her thought unfinished when she saw her mother sinking to the floor before the fireplace, her morning gown billowing out.

"You don't remember what it was like," Madre murmured, reaching her hand out to Delia, silently begging her to join her.

Without hesitating, she went and knelt beside her mother, accepting her hand.

"I'm glad you don't remember what it was like before, along with the shame I felt after being abandoned by your father for his estate." She stroked Delia's hand in hers. "I could not have borne it if it hadn't been for my *stellina*. My one bright star in a sea of sadness."

Delia pressed a kiss to her mother's forehead. "I'm so sorry, Madre." She could not imagine how she would bear it if she had found love and her dreams had been granted, only later to be dashed. "But you carried on."

"Only because of you and my song." Madre rose, gliding toward her armoire, pulling out her boldest day gown of crimson. "I will be practicing all day with the maestro in my rooms."

"But we need to plan for Father's arrival," Delia protested, pausing to pick up a comb to smooth out Madre's hair.

Madre's shoulders sagged, exhaustion lining her features. "Delia, I cannot even begin to think about your father." She gestured toward the newly stained wall. "As you can see, I am completely unhinged where he is concerned."

She blinked at her mother's blatant honesty.

Madre began gathering the broken bits of china, sucking in her breath when she cut herself.

Delia crossed the room and wrapped her finger in her handkerchief. "Tell me."

Madre tugged at the tied end of the handkerchief. "Memories, the dark ones . . . pushed themselves to the surface, drowning out the good. And in that drowning, I became lost. I try never to think on those memories, for in loving him with all my soul, there is so much pain my soul cannot bear." She swiped her fingertips under her eyelashes. "But I suppose I do want your father to see that despite his leaving us, we are doing famously without him. Aren't we?" she whispered, a weak smile gracing her lips.

She nodded. "We are."

Madre pressed her lips into a firm line. "Very well. I have some funds I can spare. Make a list and give it to Hester and Elena. I know Elena has half a dozen nieces who could help set this place to rights." Her expression shifted to one of deep thought. "Yes. We must put on a good show for him and let him see what he has been missing."

"Why does that not comfort me?" Delia asked as she turned toward the door, her gaze falling on Father's picture on Madre's bedside table. After all these years, she had still not put the picture frame away in a drawer, not exactly the action of a divorced woman. Her stomach turned again at the thought of Mrs. Pruett's words.

Madre sank down at her vanity, jars of various cold creams spread across the top. She began dabbing the cream liberally over her face, after which she would no doubt nap as she usually did before a performance. Madre wiped her fingers on a cloth, her attention focusing on her daughter's reflection. "What is it?" she asked.

Delia set the comb on the vanity. "When did you divorce, Madre?"

She paused in lifting the comb to her hair. "Did we not already discuss this?" She drew it through once, the silky ebony locks flawless and shimmering in the gaslights.

Delia seized the back of the divan, steadying herself. "Yes, but several days ago I spoke with Mrs. Pruett, who said—"

"Whatever that woman said, be reassured that your father was mine before Emilie. I did indeed receive the title of Lady Rolfeson, along with the jewels owed me with that title." She rose, her heeled shoes beneath her dressing robe making her tower over Delia. "*Lady* Vittoria is more than a stage name, and when your father departed, I continued to use the title."

"If you were a lady by marriage, then why didn't you use the title to your advantage and open the doors to society? Isn't that what you always wanted?"

Madre snorted, flicking her comb onto the vanity, where it clattered against the crystal bottles of perfume. "Because I did try on my own and failed miserably. Without Serenus at my side to validate my claim, well, they didn't wish to associate with an Italian opera star, no matter my title. And when the divorce was announced, my so-called friends were nowhere to be seen, leaving you and me all on our own."

Delia moved to the vanity and righted the perfume bottles. She ran her fingers over the silver set of brushes and combs

Father had given Madre upon their marriage, another sign she could not ignore. "Then why would Mrs. Pruett say such a hurtful thing?" Her throat burned as she pushed the words out. "To insinuate that I was born out of wedlock?"

"Why do they all say such things, *cara mia*?" Madre reclined on the divan and motioned for Delia to fetch the blanket at the foot. "Jealousy, which led to their barring me from their precious parties. Be glad that you have been spared from them thus far."

Is that why you began to use their husbands? Out of revenge? Or was that before, and what was it that drove Father away?

Madre lifted the blanket to her chin and rolled to her side. "The money is in the drawer of my vanity. *Buona fortuna* with your performances, *stellina*. Please close the door on your way out."

Dismissed, Delia slipped away, but not before glancing over her shoulder to see tears rolling down Madre's cheeks. Questions still swirled within her, but now was not the time to discuss at length the sad tale of her parents' divorce.

No matter what a society matron had told her, and no matter her old maestro's barbs, she knew in her heart the truth—that she was worthy of love. Thanks to her mother's choice in callers, she knew what love was *not*. And despite her vow to never marry, the knowledge of her father's title gave her a bit of hope that regardless of her mother's tainted reputation and her career, society might still consider her to be worthy of Kit's attention as *Lady* Delia.

"What happened?" Hester's voice lifted her from the fog.

Delia smiled as she held up her mother's small purse, giving it a little shake. "A miracle."

For the rest of the morning, Hester and Delia created a plan, listing the greatest needs first and then the lesser points, such as providing a biscuit jar for Father's room. By midday, Delia felt more nervous than she had taking Madre's place onstage that first night so many performances ago. She snatched her shawl from the hall tree, determined to take a stroll in the park to clear her mind before she needed to nap and head to the Academy. She opened the door and was met with the carved handle of an umbrella on her head.

Millie gasped. "I am so sorry! I was about to knock." She pushed Delia's hair back, sucking in a breath. "Thank goodness. I could have maimed you for your performance tonight!" Her gaze landed on Delia's cheeks. "What on earth is going on? You look positively frazzled."

"That would be because I am." Delia grimaced, rubbing the sore spot. "I received some news."

"Good, I hope? But given your appearance, I think not." She settled on the top step in a cloud of copper tulle and satin.

Delia sighed and shared the tale to the last detail.

"Well, this will cause quite the stir," Millie said, "and I'm ever so glad you told me. What plans have you made for showing off Lord Rolfeson at parties?" She waved to the neighbors, who were departing in their carriage, sending curious glances their way.

"The only party I have on my list that I haven't yet sent the number who will be joining me is Miss Kemp's."

Millie pursed her lips. "That will not do. She is already dreadful, but if we allow her to host the first party with a *lord* in attendance, she will be unbearable for the remainder of the season."

"I'm certain more invitations will be coming forthwith."

Millie shook her head. "The only way to get ahead of Miss Kemp hosting the first party is for you to have a party here."

Delia's stomach roiled. If she had felt poorly before, she was near to fainting now. "We couldn't possibly. We don't even have a proper parlor, much less a ballroom."

"Hardly any of the elite possess large ballrooms, my dear girl, something you would know if you were brought out into society years ago as you should have been." She turned to peer through the dingy parlor window. "I'm sure this could do nicely for a dinner party of twenty couples."

Having never seen more than six people at a time in her parlor, the thought of inviting forty guests was unfathomable. "I wouldn't know where to start, and you haven't seen the interior."

"As our *patroness* has appointed me to guide you, I will have my people come over and arrange everything. You are too busy with the next opera to worry about anything else. You need only focus on a wonderful performance tonight."

Her stomach burned. If people attended, then the condition of their fading glory would no longer be a thing of speculation. "Millie, we do not even possess a full dinner set." She thought of the poor china cup that met its fate only hours ago.

Millie's eyes widened. "What? No! Certainly, in your attic—"

"There is nothing. And then there is the little matter of my mother's reputation and this being a house of ill repute."

"Yes, but your father is a lord, and a title covers a multitude of sins. These matrons are Anglomaniacs, and the only object missing in their illustrious feathered caps is a title. And *you*, my dear, hold the ticket to that title for their sons."

"I do not believe titles pass from females to their husbands," Delia muttered.

"You hold the title of *lady* and therefore connect the family to royalty." She waved her hand. "It will be quite the catch—a true American royal."

"I think it might simply be easier if I turn down Miss Kemp's invitation."

"Oh." Millie blinked. "I hadn't thought of that, but it would solve everything. I will speak with Willow about adding your father and mother to the list of guests."

"Ladies." Giuseppe appeared at the bottom of the steps, looking quite ashen, and swept away her momentary elation of being released from a horrid proposition. "I have some rather dreadful news. You are being replaced by your understudy tonight, my dear Lia."

"What?" Delia shot to her feet. "What happened?"

He ran his hand over his face and groaned. "Father attended your opera and had far too many things to say about your lacking execution to the Academy's manager, Mr. Mapleson. He made the decision to give your role to your understudy."

Millie rose, her fists clenched. "Not if *I* have anything to say about it."

Giuseppe's eyes widened at Millie, and Delia recognized a spark of interest there toward a lady he had admitted to thinking of as pretty. "I thank you for your support, Mrs.—"

"Not Mrs. It's *Miss* Ford." She grasped Delia's shoulders and propelled her toward the door. "Practice with your teacher as if nothing has changed. I have some planning to do. Good day." She gripped her closed parasol in her fist like a lance and took to the sidewalk, her heels clicking against the pavement at a brisk pace.

Before Delia could contemplate what Millie was up to, a boy in Kit's emerald livery trotted up the steps toward her, a letter in his hand.

"Miss Vittoria?" He grinned, displaying a gap between his front teeth. "I have a message for you."

"Elmer Bourton's table, please," Kit whispered to the maître d' of his fine dining restaurant in the corner of the Olympia. It had been a long morning of meetings, and he anticipated an even longer afternoon of being caught by guests of the Olympia. Despite the drop in temperature and impending snowfall, a number of them were complaining that he had closed the rooftop for the season.

He rolled back his stiff shoulders. He would have preferred to call on Delia during his noon break instead of answering Uncle Elmer's invitation to luncheon, but sometimes one did what one must instead of what one desired.

"Right away, Mr. Quincy." The maître d' wove about the white-cloth-covered tables with their gold plate settings.

Since it was only luncheon, the chandeliers did little to add light to the room, what with the wall of windows facing Forty-Ninth Street and Fifth Avenue, where his guests could observe the hustle and bustle of those passing without the clamor or smell from the animals pulling carriages, wagons, and carts, which, thanks to the wind, was quite putrid today.

The maître d' guided him to the far wall of his restaurant, around several elite couples to whom Kit supplied a nod and a smile, when a bright laugh caught his ear. He jerked his head up and saw not just Uncle Elmer at their table already dining. "Delia?" Kit laughed in delight in finding her there. "What are you doing here?"

"You asked me to come to luncheon with you." She looked to Uncle Elmer and sent him a saucy smirk. "Didn't he, Uncle Elmer?"

"Is that any way to greet a lady?" Elmer huffed and waved him to his seat, sending Delia a wink.

Kit leaned over in his chair, whispering, "Uncle, did you send a note? She no doubt gave up time rehearsing to attend luncheon."

"You caught me." He coughed to cover up his laughter. "Well, I did write it as you, Kit, so it might have been under false pretenses that I got her here."

Delia lifted her soup spoon. "And I am so glad you did, as it allowed me to taste your hotel's famed she-crab soup."

"A new delicacy I became quite accustomed to in Charleston." Kit bowed to her, snapping open his napkin. "And to be clear, Lady Delia, it is *always* a joy when you are near. Though I do apologize for the falsehood." He narrowed his eyes at Uncle Elmer.

"Well, when you refused to invite her to the house, what was I to do to get to know the girl?" Elmer grunted and amended, "The lady, I mean."

Kit rested a hand atop Delia's. "Uncle Elmer did not explain that correctly. He meant to say that I did not wish to bring you to his house, for he is at an exceedingly trying age." He gave a pointed look to the man as Delia smothered her giggle into her napkin. "Which I didn't wish to subject you to yet."

"I'm not entirely certain why you felt that way, as Uncle Elmer is quite the dear," Delia replied with a smile to the elderly gentleman.

What have these two been discussing? "How long have you been here?" Kit asked, but then the waiter arrived to take his order.

"Long enough to have already ordered and begun without you," Uncle Elmer interjected.

"I'll have the same as Miss Vittoria," Kit instructed the waiter, knowing that whatever his kitchens prepared would more than suffice.

"With all this courting going on, Kit, why haven't you brought her to meet me sooner?" Elmer asked Kit while patting Delia's hand. "She is positively enchanting."

"Well, I . . ." Kit began, then faltered.

She smiled and reached for her glass of water. "You are too kind."

Kit ground his teeth that Uncle Elmer had already formed a liking to Delia, and he couldn't bear the thought of disappointing him at the end of the opera season when Delia wished to part ways. But the mere idea of not seeing her again made his chest tighten. *Enjoy the time you have, Kit.*

"And I must admit," Elmer continued, "that I love her already, and if you don't marry her, Nephew, I may never speak to you again."

Kit, having just taken a sip of water, nearly choked as he set his glass back down on the table.

"Now, Miss Vittoria, how do you feel about Kit's hotel business? I for one thought it vulgar for him, a Knickerbocker, to get his hands dirty in business, but he seems to be doing well enough."

"I think Kit is brilliant in whatever he does," she replied, her gaze shyly meeting his. Her confession made his chest swell with pride that the lady thought him brilliant.

Uncle Elmer's brows rose. "Brilliant, eh? Well, he has another hotel in Charleston that will be opening in the spring. Would you feel comfortable traveling there for the opening and then each fall when you two are married?"

"Look!" Kit said, half rising from his chair. "The entrées." But as the waiter kept walking past them with a tray of entrées for another table, Kit resumed his seat.

"Well, it is something to consider when your career is blossoming," Elmer added, dipping his spoon into the crab soup, humming with each swallow.

"I wouldn't say *blossoming* when my understudy is taking the lead tonight."

"What?" Kit leaned toward her, grasping her hand. "When did this happen?"

Delia sighed, letting her own spoon rest against the lip of the bowl. "Right before I received the invitation to lunch. Seems I am not to be the rising star after all."

Panting caught his ear, and he twisted in his seat, rising at the sight of Millie approaching their table. His maître d' was attempting to flag her down, as she did not have an escort into the restaurant and was sweating profusely.

"I have news!" Millie blurted, gripping her side and nodding to Uncle Elmer, who was still sipping away on his soup. "Kit, we need to talk in private."

Sixteen

Kit was appalled at Millie Ford's plan for the phantom's performance tonight. Even though he would never terrify the new talent like the phantom of old to get the desired result, Millie determined that his phantom was not above showing his unwavering support for Delia by sending a message at the end of the first act, calling for his lady love to grace the stage by the end of the performance. Therefore, to once again bring Delia's name to the forefront of all the papers, and because Millie's plan took far longer to explain than it should have, Kit took his seat moments before the performance was to begin.

The curtains at the back of the box parted, and his uncle shuffled inside, his frown holding his monocle in place. "It's about time you got here," Uncle Elmer wheezed as he took his seat, pulling out a small brown bag from his opera jacket's interior pocket.

"I arrived before you." With his seat being in the front row, there was precious little chance Kit would be able to escape unnoticed. Why hadn't he thought of it sooner and sat in the back?

"I was at another box." Uncle Elmer rooted about in the brown bag before folding a black licorice into his mouth. "You know, your mother used to decorate this box with garlands of roses hung from the ceiling to the floor."

"I well remember." Kit smiled, glancing around the box as if he could see them now, along with the image of his mother. The opera was more than a passion for her. It had been her dream to be an opera singer, but alas, her parents only allowed her talent to be shown in front of guests in the parlor. He had grown up hearing her voice fill his home, and while he had not inherited her talent for singing, he had inherited her love of music.

"You should do the same," Elmer said around a mouthful of licorice.

"It would be rather silly for a grown man to have such decorations, don't you agree?"

"Then marry Delia and arrange the box for your bride as a show of affection." Elmer dug again into the paper bag filled with candy, the rustling sound bringing scowls from those seated nearby.

"Says the confirmed bachelor." Kit rolled his eyes, even though the notion of a wife to perform such gestures for was quite appealing to him.

"I wasn't meant to marry," Elmer said. "You, however, are." He pointed across the horseshoe ring of boxes to a group of ladies. "If you won't propose to Delia, what about one of them? You could have your pick, though you'd have to beat out a couple of those young pups for her hand. Still, I'd wager that you are far wealthier than you let on, what with that hotel business of yours—even if you took out a loan with William Waldorf Astor."

"I told you I did it as a favor to him. And I am happy as I am." Kit gave the same old reply and tugged on his evening jacket as he shifted in his seat, finding that it was no longer entirely truthful. Since Delia had set his past dreams alight in his heart once more, the prospect of remaining a bachelor had lost its luster. Delia was so often in his thoughts that it had caused his work on several boards to suffer, including those of his beloved hotels, to the point he had considered resigning from the boards he had been presiding over since his eighteenth year. But with his hotel growth, he supposed it was bound to happen unless he was willing to relinquish control to his managers—something he knew would prove impossible. He loved the work too much. *If you love the work so much, why are you taking away time from it to see a woman who will never marry you?* Kit cracked his knuckles. He well knew why.

"Well, I wonder if that happiness is due to that stodgy routine you tossed out, thanks to a certain young lady," Elmer said as if reading his nephew's thoughts. "Perhaps you do not wish for one of the society ladies because you have your heart set on someone else."

"Speculate if you wish." Kit flipped over the programme of tonight's performance just as the lights dimmed. He really shouldn't have invited Uncle Elmer to share his box this evening, what with his compulsive need to push Kit into the arms of any eligible woman within reach if Kit did not declare his heart was taken. *Yet how does a gentleman declare his heart is taken when the lady will not take his hand in marriage?* But to admit such a thing to his uncle? He'd rather leap onto the stage from the rafters again.

"Well, if you won't admit that it is the young Lady Delia

who is causing you such happiness, I won't feel remorse in telling you I invited Elsie, Miss Pruett, and her brother."

"Invited them to what?" Kit asked, studying tonight's programme featuring the French opera *Roméo et Juliette* by Gounod, even though he knew it by heart, thanks to Millie's perspicuous instructions. But perhaps if Elmer thought him reading, he would cease feeling the need to fill the silence.

"To join you both," a feminine voice answered from behind him.

Kit shot to his feet, snapping his jaw closed at the sight of Elsie and the siblings Pruett. Elsie had shed her mourning colors and was wearing a burgundy gown with a modest neckline. He swallowed and darted his gaze to Miss Pruett, who was dressed in a confection of pink, and to her brother, who was sporting a new pompadour that made him appear a great deal taller. He coughed, then bowed to them. "What a pleasant surprise."

"Surprise?" Elsie sent Elmer a wink. "Our dear Mr. Elmer Bourton made it clear that you were the one who asked him to issue it, as you were unable to do so in person. This is *your* box after all."

Kit would have words later with his matchmaking uncle.

"Lady Ellyson, you little traitor, to disclose such a thing to the very man I'm plotting against." Elmer shook his head. "And here I thought we were partners in our hope for Kit."

Kit held the back of the gilded opera chair in the front row for Miss Pruett on his left, then Elsie on his right, handing them each a programme that the staff had left for him. "Miss Pruett, I heard that you attended the Metropolitan. How does it compare?"

"Why don't you attend the Metropolitan with my brother

and me tomorrow? We have secured boxes there as well and are eagerly awaiting to see our dear Signora Vittoria as the female lead in *Carmen*. While the role was meant for a younger woman, the soprano's voice will not disappoint." She nodded toward the stage. "Unlike the young Miss Vittoria, who I heard is to be replaced tonight by her understudy. Is this true?"

Kit shrugged. "I do not know why she's being replaced. She has the voice of an angel."

"High praise indeed," Elsie said.

Miss Pruett shook her head. "Such a pity she isn't Juliette, as I wished to compare mother and daughter. We all know how often Signora Vittoria has played the role."

"It was most likely due to politics," Mr. Pruett interjected. "The patronesses must have had their reasons after all the support thrown Miss . . . that is, Lady Vittoria's way. But I too eagerly anticipate the younger Lady Vittoria's return."

"To those of us *actually* in possession of titles, I do wish you and everyone else in society would verify that fact before calling an Italian opera star *lady* anything." Elsie snapped open her fan.

Kit swallowed back his ready defense of Delia as Mr. Pruett and Elmer took their seats behind Kit and the ladies. The new Juliette's voice was pleasant sounding, but nothing compared to the rich dulcet tone of Delia's. No one compared to her, and he was certain the papers would reflect that even without the phantom's interference tonight.

"You must not be enjoying the new lead's voice?" Elsie whispered to him behind her painted fan.

He lifted his brows. Had he been scowling?

"You have not ceased fidgeting since the first note out of her throat." Elsie's eyes twinkled as if partaking in a secret with him.

"I'll not deny it." He chuckled softly and settled back into the velvet cushion, determined not to shift in his seat. Yet the anticipation of waiting for the ending of Act I, when he was supposed to leave to don his costume, was too great to bear for long. Perhaps he should excuse himself to the men's retiring room, but to be absent for nearly three-quarters of an hour with such an excuse would not be his first choice. Still, he didn't know what else to do.

He half rose when a flash of crimson in the wings caught his eye. He narrowed his gaze. "It can't be." *Millie wouldn't have hired the second phantom without speaking to me again, would she? After all her planning?*

"It is." Miss Pruett gasped, pointing with her fan. "It's the *phantom*!"

Kit shot up as the man in a crimson phantom costume and an ivory skeleton's half mask pulled Delia onto the stage by her hand. She didn't fight against him, but confusion marred her features at the change in plan.

He bowed on one knee before her, extending to her a single crimson rose, tied with a black ribbon on the stem. As her fingers enclosed the long stem, he stood, lifting her left hand in his right above her head. "*This* is Juliette!" he shouted, the acoustics of the house amplifying his deep voice.

The crowd erupted as the new talent fled into the wings, even as Delia appeared to be questioning the phantom, her eyes widening in horror when she realized he was not Kit. He could see her battling between acting as if nothing were amiss and fighting the phantom.

Miss Pruett grasped his arm. "Oh, Mr. Quincy! The phantom seems so angry. And not at all romantic."

Kit shifted her to her brother's arm and charged for the stairs, his heart pounding with what his mind could not contemplate—Delia was in danger. His darling Lia. He bolted for the lobby and through the staff area, ready to battle this fiend who dared lay a hand on *his* angel. He ran for the floor entrance, pausing in the wings as the company scrambled to complete the scene with the understudy's shaky voice.

Delia and the phantom were nowhere to be seen.

Alarm swept through Delia as the phantom drew her from the wings. No one stopped them. All were preoccupied with rushing to complete the first act. He led her to the narrow passageway between the wall of painted fabric that acted as the backdrop for each scene and the brick wall of the Academy. While he had the same build as Kit, this phantom gripped her hand with such possessiveness that it frightened her.

The moment his grip slackened, she shrank back, desperately searching for a weapon, but of course the crossover was the one place the company did not store theatrical property. She had only her voice, and she would not allow him to hear her fear. "What do you want?" She clenched her hands into fists. "I *know* you are not the real phantom. Were you hired?"

He inclined his head, the ivory skeleton's jawless mask making the action chilling. "That phantom impostor you speak of is not the *real* phantom. He is merely an admirer. A true devotee to the art would not hesitate to threaten the audience to ensure your place as diva."

His voice, while disguised, was powerful and full-bodied.

She thought to scream to alert the others, but if she could somehow recognize his voice, she could better serve the Academy. She simply had to keep him talking. "If you love the opera so, why set it ablaze so many years ago, sir?"

"They say it was me, but know this, to disrespect the Academy is not to be borne. Today was merely my warning to the director and the patrons. The lead soprano in *Roméo et Juliette* should sing like an angel or not at all," he growled, though his attention was focused on someone behind her. He drew his sword.

Delia gasped and scrambled back as he in one fluid motion grabbed one of the hundreds of ropes from the pinrail and sliced its end, sending him hurtling upward, his cape whipping about him. He vanished into the darkness as if he had never been there in the first place. She whirled about, searching for who had frightened off the phantom. *Kit.* She ran to him, slamming into his solid chest as tears streamed down her face. His arms wrapped about her, shielding her as the opera on the other side of the fabric concluded the first act.

"Lia," he breathed into her hair, which was flowing to her waist for the scene that had never occurred.

She knew she was ruining his shirtfront with her stage powder and tears. "Oh, Kit, I thought the man was you at first. But when I heard his cruel tone . . ."

"Did he hurt you?" He took her arms in his hands tenderly, turning them over and examining her wrists for injuries.

Losing herself in his care, she was unable to pull away even though she knew she should. People would talk. *I don't care.* She rested her cheek against his chest and breathed in the scent that was entirely unique to Kit. She froze. When had she come to recognize his scent?

"Whatever are you waiting for, Miss Vittoria?" Mrs. Lowe appeared at the stage left's entrance to the crossover, beckoning them both. "I spoke with Mr. Mapleson. Get onstage and sing the second act. Your understudy has been dismissed for hysterics and her outright refusal to continue singing under the circumstances."

"But the orchestra—"

"I support you and therefore I'd advise you to humor me. Sing now and prove to those nincompoops who pulled you from the stage once and for all that *you* are my star. Sing 'Ah! Je veux vivre' as if your career depended on it."

"You didn't pull her role?" Kit asked his sister.

Mrs. Lowe scowled. "Of course not. Someone paid the owner for the understudy to sing tonight and for tonight only. I wish for you to prove that such a move in the future will prove impossible because you cannot be replaced."

Kit took Delia's hand in his. "No one is forcing you to sing, Delia. If it is too much after what you have endured, just say the word."

She rested her other hand on his chest. "I can do this." Then Delia stepped onto the stage, closed her eyes to the audience's surprise, and began to hum the opening refrains of her aria "Ah! Je veux vivre." A lone violinist joined her and began to play, the rest of the orchestra following suit. She allowed the music to guide her as she hummed, swaying with the movement of the song until her voice spilled forth and all else was forgotten in the beauty of Gounod's aria. When she finished, she found the company in the wings with tears in their eyes, others with hands to their hearts, and still others simply staring, looking as lost in the music as she had been.

Mrs. Lowe stepped from the wings and lifted her arms. "Tonight, ladies and gentlemen, there was a message sent to us from the phantom. However, it was unnecessary. It is well known that I have long since chosen her. I will not punish her for being admired by the phantom, as she would have been chosen after all. Tonight you see that she is our true songstress and may have the lead as long as she desires. To the Academy of Music's official soprano diva, Lady Delia Vittoria, daughter of the Earl of Rolfeson." She clapped for Delia, the crowd joining in as cheers rang out for her, applause rolling in from every side.

The curtain was drawn for the set to be made ready for the next act. At Mrs. Lowe's departure, the company lifted Delia onto their shoulders and carried her from the stage, all of them cheering.

"She has saved the Academy!"

"The Metropolitan will not stand a chance now that we have her *and* the phantom's support."

"The man's a menace, but he makes for good papers!"

Delia looked about for the one face she wished to share this victory with and found him smiling up at her from the corner, standing alongside the rows of pulleys and ropes that kept everything in its place onstage. Kit's jacket was draped over his arm from the heat of many bodies crammed into the close quarters of backstage, and his queue was undone, sending his hair in thick waves to his shoulders. Truly he was glorious to behold. The company gently set her on the ground, Lorenzo stepping from the mass.

"I always knew that one day you would outshine even your mother." His eyes glimmered with such intensity that Delia fought the urge to step back, but as he draped an arm over

Bianca's shoulders, she relaxed. He had released his pursuit of her at long last.

"Thank you." She nodded to Bianca with a smile, hoping her friend would see her excitement for her that Lorenzo was at last paying Bianca special attention. But Bianca didn't smile back. She glared. "I'd best be on my way."

Lorenzo smirked. "Yes, we wouldn't wish to keep Mr. Quincy waiting for you too long, or else he might find another lady on whom to bestow his admiration."

Kit was at her side at once, scowling at the man Delia had once thought of as her friend. He turned to her and softened his look. "Are you well? Would it be too forward of me to ask your physician to call upon you to ensure your health after your scare?"

"Already done," Giuseppe interjected. "Delia Vittoria, I have never heard you sing so well."

"I've never before felt the threat of the phantom . . . not truly." She shivered and looked to Kit.

He reached for her hand, his fingers interlacing with hers. "And you never will again if I have anything to do with it."

"Do you think you could find him? I don't think he was ever hired by the patronesses."

"I will do everything in my power to discover the man responsible. I could not bear it if something happened to you." His gaze flicked to the herd of reporters stampeding toward them. "Lady Delia, you were sublime! Divine! Heavenly!" he exclaimed loudly enough for them to overhear.

The security from moments before ebbed from her bones. Of course, he was only acting as her suitor. She shifted away from him so he could not read her disappointment. She had forgotten that it was all a play . . . again.

"Miss Vittoria! A few questions?"

She nearly laughed in surprise at the sight of Chandler Starling, hair askew, notebook and pencil in hand. "Mr. Starling, what is your question?"

"Miss Vittoria, do you think the phantom is a threat to the Academy of Music?"

Lorenzo snorted, gathering the stool from the right wing where the understudy sat to watch the lead, keeping the path clear for moving the set from the stage. "I'd say *threat* is an easy assumption, sir."

Kit glanced down at her. What would this mean for his phantom appearances? *If Kit is no longer the phantom, the true phantom having returned, should he continue the charade despite the peril involved?* "I think passionate is a better term to describe the phantom."

Lorenzo ran his hand over his jaw. "We've seen this kind of passion at work before. I was just a boy working backstage, but I well remember it."

"You are referring to the fire of sixty-six?" another reporter interjected.

"Yes." Lorenzo shoved his hands into his pockets, grim-faced as he stared at Delia. "He's a dangerous one, Lia."

Chandler tapped his pencil to his notepad. "I'm not even certain he is the same man. People are thinking it was a romantic notion to have him return, treating him like some token from days gone by, for again the fire was never proven to be dealt by his hand."

Lorenzo scowled. "The man was a menace then, and he's a menace now. Unlike last time when he simply disappeared, he should be apprehended, put on trial, and prosecuted to the full extent of the law."

Chandler jotted that line down. "May I quote you, sir?"

He rocked back and forth on his heels, looking pleased with himself. "Name's Lorenzo Milanesi."

"Speaking of quotes, anything you would like to add, Lady Delia?" Mr. Starling turned, pencil at the ready.

"Please let it be known that I do not think the phantom of the Academy is a threat." She glanced sideways to Kit. This might ruin the farce, but she could not allow them to go on a hunt for the phantom when they might end up with Kit. The only way to preserve Kit's role was to make it so he appeared innocent. "I'll be the first to admit that the attention is flattering, but that is only because I do not believe him to be the phantom of old."

Chandler tucked his pencil and notepad into his jacket pocket. "Excellent. Kit, old boy, see to it that you keep the Academy's greatest star safe, won't you?"

Kit wrapped his arm around her waist. "No one will hurt her."

Lia looked up to him and nearly sagged into him. After always keeping a brave façade with her worries about the fate of her career and of what her mother might do and her father say, Kit was slowly chipping away at her safely hidden emotions that she only trotted out for the stage. When had pretense become reality?

"You're shaking," Kit said.

She gestured to her Juliette nightgown costume that Millie had instructed her to wear for their latest phantom scheme. Though thick enough for propriety with sleeves that fell to her elbows, the chill in the air made her wish she had remembered to slip on her shawl after her song had finished.

Kit draped his evening jacket over her shoulders before

grasping her hand in his, pulling her along through the wings and toward her dressing chamber. Thanks to Mrs. Lowe, it was her dressing room once again. Kit paused outside her room, reluctant to release her hand as he ran his thumb over the back of it. "I was terrified that you would be hurt or taken by the maniac."

She shook her head. "He didn't seem like he wanted to hurt me. But yes, he did frighten me when he grabbed me, and again when he spoke with me in the crossover."

"How do you wish me to proceed with our part, Lia?"

"I believe that will be up to Millie and the patronesses."

He nodded. "I shall send around a note. Acting the part of the phantom could mean arrest for me if they think me the phantom of old, when I have only showered you with my favor in blooms and a dramatic entrance or two."

"If it comes to that, I will testify on your behalf," Delia promised as she turned to look up at him, unwilling to release his hand as well.

"And ruin your career when the audience discovers you were in on the ruse?" He shook his head. "I could not do that to you."

"If it meant saving you, I'd take the risk."

He pressed kisses to the inside of her wrist and the top of her hand. "You are a dream, my lady."

Her heart pounded as she repeated his words in her head. "I would do it for any innocent man whose only crimes were those of helping me."

He gave her that delightful half smile that revealed his dimples, and she had to fight the urge to sink her fingers into his hair, which was so tempting in its unbound state. *What on earth is wrong with me?* She stepped back from him and his heady scent. "I'll be out in a moment." She looked to Kit from the threshold and sent him a smile as she slowly shut the door.

Delia nearly stumbled into her darkened dressing room that the assistant had forgotten to light and leaned her head against the doorframe. She closed her eyes against the intensity of the moment before, reliving his kisses. She pressed a hand to her chest in an effort to slow her heart. *Think of something else.* She *had* thought being confronted by the actual phantom would be the most terrifying thing she had ever endured, but no. Nothing was as frightening as the prospect of losing control of her heart to Kit Quincy. Never had she encountered a man who had treated her with such utmost respect and kindness, who did not care what her rather confusing past presented, nor her present line of work.

She moved silently though her dressing room to turn up the hurricane lamp on her vanity. She pulled the ribbon at the base of her neck, unbinding the tie holding her hair back.

"You were marvelous tonight, Delia."

She gasped and swung her wooden brush into the air, ready to beat the one who had spoken. She opened her mouth to scream, but something in his eyes stopped her. She knew this man. She had seen his face frozen in time, studied it for years in fact, searching for something of him in her own countenance. She lowered the brush to rest it in her open palm. "Father?"

Seventeen

Lord Rolfeson smirked and leaned heavily on his cane as he rose from a chair in the corner of Delia's dressing chamber. "Why are you looking so askance? I told you I would be arriving to see you. What did you think I meant? I certainly did not mean to wait until next week to witness your performance."

"I thought you were arriving the day after tomorrow." She wrapped Kit's coat tighter about herself, comforted by its weight. She clenched her teeth to keep them from chattering.

"I arrived early." He picked up a little bottle of perfume from her dresser and sniffed it, scrunching his nose. He gestured to the coat she wore. "You have a gentleman outside, I assume?"

"Yes, I, uh, in the confusion, I . . ." She gave up trying to explain it away, the stilted conversation unnerving her. "Well, I'd best change, so if you don't mind, I can meet you later at the house."

Lord Rolfeson ran his fingers over the stack of sheet music Madre and Maestro Rossi had neglected to take with them.

He paused on an old copy of Bellini's *Il Pirata*, his eyes misting over. He rolled it up and tucked it in his interior jacket pocket, half of it poking out haphazardly. "I hear you have been informing people of your title."

Her heart hammered to a stop. *This is why he has at last returned to us from across the sea. He objects to my using his title.*

He paused in his perusal of her dressing room and lifted his thick brows, his green eyes piercing her own. "Haven't you?"

She attempted to sift through her feelings enough to answer intelligently. "Not intentionally. I discovered it by accident when I was at a ball one night, and society took it from there. I have never introduced myself as such."

"Yes, well, that claim has brought about some rather uncomfortable complications for me." Lord Rolfeson strode across the room, his cane thumping with each step, emphasizing his slight limp. He resumed his seat, his cane gripped between his fists as he perched on the edge. "Complications I did not intend to ever occur."

"Complications in the form of Countess Emilie Hearst of Rolfeson Abbey and your other daughter?" She decided to test Mrs. Pruett's information.

"And son, who was born this past winter. Quite a sturdy chap." His grin faltered and he sighed. "So you can see why your using a title like that might cause a stir in my family and also the English papers, as it reminded everyone of my past."

"I am sorry to hear that, but as you *are* my father, it is not untrue." *Unless my title is null and void with the divorce?* Having little idea of the ways an aristocratic family tree worked, she wished she could voice her question, but it seemed vulgar to do so.

"No. It is not untrue. While your mother lost the title in divorce, you retained yours."

She felt light-headed from the sheer relief that both of her parents had confirmed the truth. It was not as Mrs. Pruett insinuated. She had not been born out of wedlock.

"But I have something else I need to discuss with you, something vastly more important."

More important than the circumstances of my birth?

"My wife has a desire to travel to the States and knows I purchased a place in Gramercy Park."

"Yes?"

"She is under the impression it is vacant and wishes to travel here for the Christmas season."

Surely he isn't asking me to make room for his wife under the same roof as my mother?

"I must have the deed to Gramercy Park," he stated simply.

"Oh. Is that all?" She released a short laugh. "Madre will never release her claim on the property." It was one of her final claims to the life that should have been hers as Father's wife.

He looked pointedly at her. "Your mother is only the trustee of the deed until you marry, and then the deed reverts to me and the problem is solved. I alone am the only one she may sign over the property to, which I will see occurs, one way or another. My wife may winter in New York, and then I may sell the property to cover my gambling debts, as Emilie has quite a firm grip on her purse strings."

The news sent her sinking onto her vanity stool. *So that is why Madre never sold, even though she hated being seen as less than all others in the neighborhood.* She ignored the second half of his explanation of his reappearance, basking in the warmth that he had in fact seen to her welfare before abandoning them.

"You didn't know," he supplied.

"Madre didn't tell me." She looked up to this man, and a spark from her childhood dreams burned to life, an image of his singing her to sleep, closely followed by a faint memory of his rich tenor worthy of the stage. *He does care for me.*

"Of course she didn't." He chuckled. "My darling Giovanna would not wish to paint me in a fatherly light after I left. But yes, before I returned to England, I made certain to keep your future secure and a roof over your head."

"Madre would never have let that happen." Delia rose to her mother's defense, for despite her tendencies to spend more than she ought, Madre had always seen to Delia's welfare, education, and training. No matter her being a diva and rather selfish, Madre loved her.

He smiled softly. "After nearly a decade of marriage to her, I knew well her spending habits. That is why I left the deed in your name, citing her as your trustee and myself as your guardian, to keep the property safe until you wed and it reverts to me. Therefore, I will need either her to sign it over or you to marry for me to present it to Emilie."

The warmth dispelled at his request. "Is Madre's shelter no longer a concern?"

"Yes, my dear, but you will no doubt be touring Europe next season, what with the reputation you are garnering, and I think a more modest dwelling will suffice for your mother. Perhaps another square? My source tells me there is a home in Stuyvesant Square available for a reasonable sum."

If Madre did as he requested, she and her mother would

likely be moved to reduced circumstances and then abandoned a second time, this time for good, with a home worth far less should they ever need to sell. "Is that why you were flattering me? So I can convince Madre to sign over our house?" she asked her father.

Lord Rolfeson rose to his towering full height. He possessed the physique of a man far younger than his fifty years. "I *never* flatter or say something I do not mean. Your voice is ethereal, I daresay a match for even your mother, whose voice I have not heard the equal of since I left—until this very evening." His eyes filled. "I still love Giovanna in my own way, you know, but life is cruel. There are things we cannot change even if we would give up a world of wealth. Nothing can alter the facts." He swiped at his cheeks with the back of his hand, and it took Delia aback to see such a powerful man grieve over a lost future. "But I will do right by you, my dearest little Lia, never fear. I have an English lord or two in mind for you who will pay a bride price to me because of your fame."

She jerked her head up. Did he know that was her preferred sobriquet? "How do you know that name?"

"I wished to name you Lia, but your mother insisted on the Italian *Delia*. I never could allow myself to call you anything but Lia."

If any of Madre's stories were true about Serenus Hearst, she would need to tread lightly, as the man was as charming as she had claimed, even when she well knew he was only after the money her marriage would allot him. "Yes, well, I do not think Madre would approve of just handing over the house, and I have quite made up my mind not to marry. Therefore, I do not see what can possibly keep you."

"Then we shall discuss it with her." He moved for the door. "Tell your gentleman you have your father to see you home. I'll wait in a hired cab for you outside. Do try to be in it in the next half hour, my dear." He threw open the door.

Kit turned, his countenance darkening at the sight of the strange gentleman, his hands fisted. "What are you doing in Lady Delia's dressing chamber?"

"I'm her father." He limped away without another word, his cane thumping a staccato beat in his haste.

Kit looked to her. "Are you certain it is him?"

She nodded. "And apparently, Lord Rolfeson says he is taking me home." She rested her hand on the doorframe, hesitant to ask, but she couldn't help it. "Will you join us?"

He grasped her hand in his. "I would not wish to be an intrusion."

"I haven't seen him in years, Kit. I do not know him," she whispered, tears rising, and she didn't know why.

For the second time tonight, he pulled her into his arms, and she rested her cheek against his sturdy chest, breathing in his security, wishing she could stay wrapped in this façade forever, where Kit adored her and she could admit to loving him with every beat of her heart.

"You can do this, Lia. You possess a strength that many can only dream of having."

I am so tired of being strong. Is it too much to ask for a love and *a career?* She shivered. With a past like her family's, not to mention her mother's present choices, it would take a man of extraordinary character to overlook her connections. "Thank you," she whispered, willing her tears to cease.

"I'll stand guard until you are ready to meet him, then see

you to the carriage and join you both until you arrive home." He held her at arm's length. "Will that help?"

"Immensely." She longed to beg him to see her beyond the upset of her father's return, but she couldn't allow him to see how much she had come to rely on him—care for him. How quickly this man had torn down the wall around her heart that she had built brick by painful brick. She released her hold on his arms and slipped inside her dressing room.

She sagged against the closed door. Her father was here, waiting for her. She had imagined this countless times, and now the man in Madre's photograph was alive to her as well. He was handsome as ever with strong shoulders still, and even though his step possessed a limp, power radiated from him—which she found unnerving. After a single meeting, she could understand Madre's loss of having such a protector in the face of society's rejection where she could sing for the elite, be lauded by them, but dine as one of them? Never.

At the delicate chime of the clock atop her vanity, she surged into motion. She would not keep her father waiting. She dressed in a simple gown and drew her cloak over her hair that she left in her stage arrangement, her locks falling to her waist, and in her haste she accidentally flung open the door, banging it against the wall.

Kit held his arm out to her. "I will miss escorting you home alone and our private conversations. Well, as private as they are with my driver within earshot."

She looked sideways at him. It almost sounded as if he meant it—as if she wasn't just a duty foisted upon him by the threat of the Astor loan, patronesses, and Millie. "I will miss it, too."

His eyes widened at her admission. "It does my old heart good to hear that."

"You are always making jests about your age, but I am beginning to feel as though you mean them."

"It is an *old* habit." He winked. "But no. Several months ago, I would have admitted to feeling old, but ever since the patronesses requested that I aid you in your career, there has been new life in my heart." He cleared his throat. "I have poured every spare moment into my hotels, building a legacy for a wife and family with whom I one day wish to share life."

Her heart hammered. *This is it. He is finally going to tell me about Lady Ellyson.* It would be lovely to hear it from his own lips whether Hester's tale surrounding his engagement were true.

He shrugged. "I had gotten too used to the way of things, and instead of growing bored with the momentum, I grew comfortable and allowed it to dictate that I was too old for Miss Dupré simply because I felt I couldn't offer her the adventure she sought. And it wasn't the first time I allowed that to happen."

"I am guessing the lady never requested that you save her career?" She smiled, wondering how on earth anyone would think or lead him to believe he was boring. Her breath still caught, recalling how he had swung down to the stage to offer her that first single rose.

He held the backstage door for her. "I'm afraid the ladies I was drawn to did not need me in that way. They liked my lineage . . . my money. To be fair, Miss Dupré was different. I only released her because I'd prefer to feel wanted, needed—to be first in her affections."

Is this man trying to make me fall in love with him? "Kit—"

"There you are," Lord Rolfeson called from where he was leaning against a lamppost, his arms crossed, the cane poking haphazardly into the walkway as if to keep people from passing by too near to him. A man in a valet's suit stood close by with a rolled-up newspaper in his hand, looking like he might swat anyone who dared to get near them both. Another man about Kit's age climbed down from inside the carriage. "You've been keeping my daughter too long, Mr. Quincy, and keeping my valet, myself, and Lord Kerr out far later than I had wished."

Lord Kerr? Had he actually *brought* one of the lords with him? "The fault lies with me. I had all my stage paints to remove and I—"

Lord Rolfeson ignored her. "Call in the morning, Mr. Quincy. There is a lot to discuss."

"He is joining us for the ride home." Her cheeks flamed. "And what could Mr. Quincy possibly have to discuss with you?"

"Perhaps the little matter that he has been seen with you about the city—many of those times *unchaperoned*." He scowled. "Something I do not appreciate, as she is intended for greater things than you, Mr. Quincy."

"I am not like the English ladies." Delia refrained from calling him Father. *Lord Rolfeson* was too formal, but *Father* far too intimate for one who for all intents and purposes had abandoned her as a child. "I have never had a chaperone."

Lord Rolfeson's frown deepened. "What?"

"A matter that will be resolved," Lord Kerr interjected as he bowed to her. "My lady, it is a pleasure to meet you at long last. Your beauty has been greatly understated."

She could sense more than see Kit stiffen behind her, but

to defuse the situation, she greeted the gentleman with a small curtsy.

Kit stepped up to her side. "Lord Rolfeson, I have no problem discussing anything with you in the morning. Any time spent in Lia's presence is to be treasured."

Delia felt her heart squeeze at his compliment.

Lord Rolfeson did not reply but instead climbed into the carriage. Lord Kerr held the door for her, motioning her inside.

She took Kit's hand in hers, silently asking him to follow her and sit beside her. To her heart's delight, he did.

It had taken nearly the whole of the drive to convince Delia's father to allow Lord Kerr to stay in the Olympia instead of the guest room of Delia's home, but with Delia's insistence that the house was not ready for a third guest, he had relented, to Kit and Delia's silent relief.

Kit hopped out of the carriage beside Delia's brownstone, holding his hand up to help her descend. He did not particularly enjoy the thought of leaving Delia with her father. The lady was clearly frightened of him, judging from her stilted conversation on the way there, but Kit supposed it was just nerves. Who wouldn't be nervous to meet one's parent practically for the first time?

He pulled her aside, thankful her father was too busy collecting his luggage with his valet to notice them, Lord Kerr overseeing the matter to be certain his bags remained behind. "Lia, if you need anything, send word and I'll be here as quickly as I can."

"Thank you, Kit. I-I don't like to admit how much I have come to rely on you."

"Well, I like hearing it." He pressed a kiss atop her hand. "And I mean it, Lia. I know he makes you uncomfortable, but you do not have cause to worry of his harming you, do you?" He looked sideways toward her father. After all, they didn't know much about the man.

"Oh no. Madre surely would have mentioned it. It's only that he is a stranger to me, and I do not know what to do with myself."

"I understand." He wished he could tell her just to be herself, but such advice seemed banal.

She squeezed his hand. "Please, return as early as you can in the morning."

"Come, Lia," Lord Rolfeson huffed, waving her toward himself, sending his opera cape flapping like the wings of a bat.

"Promise?" she said.

"Promise," Kit returned, his heart beating through his chest. Her act was gone, and now all he could see was something in her eyes he had never experienced. She truly did rely on him—trusted him implicitly.

After she disappeared inside the house, the lord, scowling at Kit, slammed the door behind him.

Kit was tempted to wait outside the home and watch them through the lace curtains, but if Lia had wanted him to stand watch, she would have requested he do so. He checked his pocket watch. Nearly midnight. With a sigh, he joined Lord Kerr in the carriage, directing the driver to the hotel.

"So, what brings you to the States?" Kit asked, forcing himself to treat the man as he would any guest staying at his establishment.

Lord Kerr swayed as the carriage turned down the avenue.

"Lady Delia. Her father wishes for me to take her off his hands, and, well, she has become quite famous in the London papers and therefore desirable. I plan to pay her court."

"And do you think the lady is agreeable to your little plan since I am already paying her court?" Kit clenched his fists at the arrogance of the man.

Lord Kerr snorted. "We all know that means little when it is I who hold her father's favor and a title to give to her children, righting the behavior of her own mother."

Thankfully, the carriage halted in front of the Olympia, saving him from saying something foolish. He clapped his footman on the back and motioned him toward the carriage. "Please see to it that Lord Kerr has everything his heart desires. Put him in the fifth-floor suite."

And with a wave to the lord, Kit slipped into his office, where he took in the piles of papers and letters from his various board positions across the city. It was time to resign his seats and focus on his two true loves—his hotels and, above all, his delightful Lady Delia. It was time to woo her . . . if she would only have him. Ignoring the late hour, he reached for a stack of notes and set to work, starting with one regarding the ever-popular Mr. Beckby and his latest hobby of playing the bagpipes.

Eighteen

The place looks quite different," her father commented, tripping over a book lying on the carpet.

Delia blushed as he picked it up and read the title. She glanced about the breakfast room she hadn't yet cleaned. Madre's cups and novels were still strewn about, along with wrappers of bonbons and one of Mother's dressing robes. She rushed to her father, snatched the book from him, and tucked it away on the tea cart. Then she grasped his arm, leading him into the parlor, desperate to get away from the shameful mess, praying he had not noticed the robe. She sank onto the divan, waiting for him to speak first, uncertain of what to discuss with him, though for years she had imagined sitting with him in this very spot.

Lord Rolfeson laid a hand to the side of the silver coffeepot on the cart that was undoubtedly stone-cold, being left over from lunch. He flicked the teaspoon in one of the dirty cups, the silver scraping against the chipped china rim as it swirled around. "Hester did not set this out for your return?"

"You know Hester?"

"Of course. She has been your mother's friend and maid since your mother's days in the Italian company's chorus." He chuckled. "Hester always wanted to be a chorus girl with your mother, but she was not Italian nor did her voice match her spirit."

"Speaking of Madre, there is no telling what time she will return, and you must be tired after your travels. Would you like me to show you upstairs to the spare room?" *Perhaps I can spirit him up into the guest room before she notices.*

"No. I think we should ring and have a pot of something hot made."

"Very well." Delia rose and headed for the door.

"Where are you going?" Lord Rolfeson scowled with his fist propped on his hip. "We need to speak with your mother. This cannot wait."

"I know, but if you wish for coffee, I must make it."

He ran a hand over the back of his neck. "I see. Well, lead the way to the kitchen."

The stairs creaked as she descended into the kitchen, which was far better equipped than anyone in the house knew how to use. But Delia always liked to imagine the previous owners and their hosting of grand parties that required a large kitchen and the feasts filling the long wooden table that bore scars from years of use. She reached for the half apron and wrapped it about her waist. She had learned from necessity how to accomplish a few basic dishes and the proper way to brew a strong pot of Italian coffee. Tea was not to be had in their house, which she had learned long ago was owing to her British father's taste for it.

Setting the coffeepot on the stove that thankfully Elena had kept stoked with wood before returning home for the evening, Delia began grinding the beans while the water heated to boiling. She gripped the pot's handle with her apron in one hand, and with the other she reached for the *cuccuma* copper pot, filling the bottom chamber with boiling water. She set the middle chamber, a metal basket of sorts, into the boiling water and scooped the grounds into it. Then she screwed the filter onto the basket and placed the pot upside down atop it. She wiped her hands and counted silently.

"I send you enough money to employ a cook." It was a statement, not a question.

"You send *Madre* enough for a cook, but that amount rarely makes its way down to the pockets of the staff."

"Then how do you employ them?"

"Loyalty, and half the time I am able to intercept the envelope from you." She bit her lip. "Madre still thinks you send the money every other month. At first, I tried to take them each month, but she caught on and I learned I needed to leave her some to have enough for Hester and Elena." *Has it been a minute or two yet?*

"Your secret is safe with me," Lord Rolfeson said, his smile flashing in the lamplight. Once again she could see the dashing demeanor that had dazzled her mother so much.

She counted in silence again as she searched the drawers, looking for the *cuppetiello* filter. Finding it, she flipped over the coffeepot contraption and set the paper cone over the spout to preserve the aroma, the dripping of the brew echoing in the stillness of the kitchen.

"You've done this often."

"After Elena showed me how, I make it at least once a day." She shrugged. "I find it calming."

"What are you doing here, Serenus?" Madre stood in the

kitchen doorway, her scarlet cloak's hood framing her ebony curls that still fell to her waist, fashioned no doubt for her performance in *Carmen*.

Lord Rolfeson's sharp intake of breath surprised Delia. He straightened from his place at the table. "My darling, you are exactly as I remember—a vision."

Madre drew back her hood, her expression softening a bit. "And you are as handsome as ever, Serenus."

"This leg hasn't been kind to me." He rose, limping toward her, leaning heavily on his cane. He ran his fingers over her cheek, brushing away a lone tear, then pressed his forehead to hers. "How I've missed you."

Madre shifted away from him, motioning Delia to pour her a cup of coffee, but as it had just been flipped, Delia chose to ignore her request rather than to explain that they must wait for the proper brew time.

"Something that could have been avoided if you hadn't deemed it unnecessary to return to Gramercy Park since you departed this place."

"You know why I stayed away, Giovanna." He stepped back and reached for her hand, weaving his fingers through hers. At the cough in the hallway, Lord Rolfeson turned and nodded to his valet, who clutched his lord's travel bag at his side. "Thank you, Parker." He looked to Madre. "Where shall I have the bags sent?"

"How about the East River?" She grunted and moved for the coffeepot, batting the cone to the floor.

Delia swallowed her protest that it hadn't been long enough.

"Now, my darling, such a thing is not to be borne, not when I brought such a lovely confection for each of you." He gestured toward the satchel, and Parker obliged. He lifted out two velvet boxes and held the longer one out to Madre and the other to Delia.

Madre slapped it away. "If I desire a confection, I can get it for myself."

Delia popped open the velvet box, gasping at the ring cushioned inside. It was a small gold insignia ring with two rubies that bore the initial R, which would fit on her little finger.

"For our Rolfeson seat. You are a lady, after all, and I want everyone to know you are my daughter." He lifted his little finger in the air. "The rings are twins, except I chose diamonds in the place of rubies. I thought rubies would suit your complexion."

"And how would you know what her complexion was?" Madre snapped.

"I left when she was six, not before she was born." He went over and slid the ring onto Delia's finger. "Do you remember our time together?"

"It is more a feeling than any one memory." She remembered happiness, a sense of safety, and being loved, until all at once she wasn't anymore. She wasn't anything when he left her. Just alone, as her mother had drawn inside herself. The ring felt cold against her skin.

"Do you like it?"

She held her hand up in the lamplight. It was tiny, not at all what her mother would have chosen, but exactly like what *she* would have picked for herself. Perhaps she did possess a fragment of Father in her. "Very much so. Thank you."

"Do not allow him to buy your good opinion, Delia." Madre narrowed her eyes at the valet. "If Serenus must stay, bring his lordship's things to the third floor, take a right, and his chamber will be the third door on the left."

"Thank you, my darling. And I was not telling a falsehood that you look as lovely today as the day I met you."

Delia watched her mother wavering between her fascination with her first love, his flattery, and the past seventeen years of loneliness and rejection.

"What would your wife say to such flattery?" She silenced him with a glare. "And why have you returned? Your wife has been holding your leash tightly for the past, what has it been, *two* decades?"

"Not quite that long, but you were always one to stretch things a bit, and Emilie trusts me."

"Despite the fact that you broke your engagement to her to marry me?"

He gritted his teeth. "She says that she has loved me the longest and I have always returned to her, and she knows I will do so again." He looked to Delia. "Back to the matter at hand, I have a few reasons for my return, one being that I heard our daughter was claiming her title as *Lady* Delia."

Madre whipped around to face Lia. "You've been doing what?" She turned back to Lord Rolfeson, a flash of alarm crossing her countenance. "I never told her to use her title. I promised you I would not, and I have held up my end of the bargain, Serenus."

"I know, Giovanna. I am not here to punish you. Lia says that she discovered it at a society event, which I thought was the reason why you stopped attending such things. If I had thought our daughter was going into society, I would have been better prepared to handle . . . things."

"I stopped attending because you abandoned me, and the shame of it all was too much for me to bear. I decided long ago I did not want the burden of answering the questions that would follow with your not being present at each event, especially once I noticed invitations ceasing and Delia's being excluded from playing with the children in the park. So I left society and never introduced Delia to spare her tender heart from being crushed. It was far simpler to allow people to believe her to be the daughter of an opera star who uses *Signora* as a stage name."

Lord Rolfeson shook his head and resumed his seat. "I wish it could have been different. You *know* that better than anyone."

Madre held her head high. "I cannot change the past no matter how much I wish I could, Serenus. I regret it all, but how could I have known that it would cause such pain when I didn't even know you existed—"

"What happened that caused you two to part?" Delia burst out, unable to keep the question inside any longer.

"A great deal." Lord Rolfeson leaned back in the wooden chair, which creaked in protest. "I do not need to stay here long, Giovanna."

"Of course you don't," Madre muttered, pouring herself a cup of the dark brew, stirring in a spoonful of sugar.

Delia brought Lord Rolfeson his own cup of hot coffee. "The reason I came here—besides dealing with the title nonsense—is because I would like to have the deed to this residence returned to my name and marry Lia off to a gentleman who is a suitable match for her."

He wished for both the deed *and* her marriage? Delia braced herself for the wrath to follow that request.

Madre slowly sipped her coffee and ran her finger along the sugar-dusted rim, sucking the crystals from her fingertip. "Do you think you can just limp in here and demand we return the deed to your name? And Delia to end the career I have spent years building for her? I think not."

"Well, there is a good reason why I need it—"

"Because you want to shame us further? Because you want to eject Delia from your house? And reject me? Again? Well, I have news for you—she *is* your daughter. And regardless of what that woman in England would have you do to tie up the loose ends of our marriage, you cannot treat your daughter as poorly as you have me." Madre stepped around the table and stood beside Delia. "You will not force her into anything against her will. You abandoned us once. Who is to say that you will not do so again if I sign over the deed and we are left homeless?"

"My darling, I would never purposefully hurt you. You know why I had to leave you, and you also know I married Lady Emilie to fulfill my duty as a lord. I had to have a son for my estate to continue to be held by the Hearst family."

"I might have given you a son if you had given our marriage half a chance."

"I gave it every chance." He rose from the chair and leaned against the windowsill, looking toward the streetlamps glowing along the street. "Lady Emilie is everything a man could wish for in a wife."

She snorted. "Lady indeed. What did you tell her, that I was your mistress? *Before* you met her?"

Delia's stomach flipped. "Father, is this true? You call us your second family?"

"I am not proud of it, but how else was I to convince a great lady such as herself to marry me when I was tainted with divorce from a louche opera singer?"

"I was faithful to you! You were the one who left me and

married another." Madre threw her hands into the air. "You drove me to do what I did with the others and Mr. Lowe. He shows me the love you should have freely given me—that you gave and took away." Her voice cracked, and she pressed her hand to her tiny waist. "Why couldn't you have left the past behind when I loved you with every breath of my body? I have *never* loved anyone as much as I loved you, and you took my heart, my hopes, and my dreams and crushed them underfoot the moment you stepped aboard that boat and left me."

Delia sank onto a chair, everything falling into place, her mother's actions making sense now. The way Madre sought approval and love. Delia felt her heart soften in understanding toward her mother and, heaven help her, Madre's choices. For all her faults, Delia knew that her mother still loved her father. Why else would she so desperately crave a man's devotion? Not that it justified her mother's scandalous behavior, yet the scorn for Madre's choice in men that Delia had long held on to turned to pity. "What happened?"

Lord Rolfeson looked to Delia. "There are things your mother kept from me prior to our marriage vows—things I did not know until my obsession for her had turned me into . . . Well, it cannot be said that I did not love your mother as fiercely as she claims to have loved me."

"And yet you wish us out of this house—our house."

Lord Rolfeson released a grunt that sounded more like a growl. "Giovanna, will you please be rational and sign over the document so we can end this part of the disagreement?"

Delia looked to her mother and Lord Rolfeson, and for the first time in her life, her father's image toppled from the pedestal it had too long occupied.

"I'm sorry, my lord, but I cannot." She grasped Delia's

hand. "I will not take away our daughter's home to please you. Long ago, I might have been persuaded, but time has taught me just how good your word is."

He shook his head. "Well, you can at least return to me the Rolfeson family jewels, Giovanna."

Madre rose to her full height. "I will not. By law they are Delia's. I was planning to give them to her on her twenty-fifth birthday."

"Yes, but you see, my dear, about a month ago, Emilie requested to wear them after years of pushing the matter aside. I told her they were packed away, and when I found them, they were in sore need of repair. I have only a few weeks before she asks for them again. She is determined to wear them for our anniversary ball."

"Such a story weaver you have become," Madre scoffed.

"When one comes from a colorful past, a well-woven tapestry is the best place to hide the facts. She believes I am on a business trip." He sat again and took a sip of coffee, his cup still nearly full. "See to it the jewels are on the table in the morning, as well as the deed, and I will leave you alone. If the deed is not signed, Giovanna, I expect Delia to be ready to entertain Lord Kerr."

Madre took another long draft of coffee, her back straight until his footfalls and cane sounded on the stairs, and then she slumped to the table, her hands covering her open mouth in a silent wail. Delia wrapped her arms around the woman who never cried and rocked her mother.

Delia wished she could admit to loving Kit, but seeing the effects of a love gone bitter, perhaps she was better off not knowing what it was like to have love and then lose it all.

Nineteen

Kit kicked his mount into a canter, his muscles basking in being strained as he cut through Central Park at dawn, the more leisurely riders moving out of his path and sending him a nod, or a wave if he knew them, which he returned with one of his own. Riding did not allow for conversation, which was exactly what he didn't need this morning. His thoughts were so full of a certain young lady that he needed to sort through them before calling on her and Lord Rolfeson this morning.

Part of him still couldn't fathom that he had allowed himself to fall in love again, not after Elsie and certainly not after Willow, and with a young lady even younger than Willow. Yet what he truly had wished for was a woman who adored him and him alone. And while some thought it a ridiculous thing to seek such adoration, he felt it was important for a husband to be as loved as a wife, with a mutual respect for each other. How else would a marriage last through the trials that were sure to come?

Certainly, Willow had treated him kindly, but he had been

just one of many gentlemen courting her. And Elsie had chosen adventure over keeping her promise to him, so it was difficult to trust Elsie's sincerity with her pursuit of him now. He didn't blame her for wishing to travel to India. She had been too bright a flame to stay tucked away in society, where she was destined to live a life of teatimes and calls as he built his hotel business. In the end, he was thankful to her for breaking it off with him, especially now that he had met Delia.

He had kept busy over the years, sinking his passions into his positions on various boards and accumulating enough wealth to use his own money instead of the trust's to open the first Olympia Grande. The second hotel was a strain financially, but that was just for the moment. What if Uncle Elmer was correct in his assessment—if Delia did not wish to marry him, should he marry another? What did all his success mean if he did not share his life with someone special?

He shook that thought from his head. The Lord had seen fit to keep him single all these years, but his lack of marital state did not make him or his accomplishments any less. He had hoped that one day he could share his life with a woman, yet he hadn't thought it would happen now, not after two serious relationships had failed. He had only recently made his peace with the Lord's apparent calling him to singleness, which had been clear until Delia waltzed into his life, closely followed by a lady whom he had long since surrendered to God. It seemed at long last the Lord was providing for his secret wish to marry—if only the lady he loved would have him. So, until she told him to leave her, he would continue to pursue her.

And while Delia was far younger than he was and he had

sworn not to behave like those old gentlemen who purposefully sought debutantes with their youthful exuberance and zest, Delia's innocence drew him. Her spirit spoke to him, and as long as she was free to marry, he would not be satisfied to offer his hand to anyone else. Lord help him. He was too far gone to hope to remove himself unscathed. Kit hummed Delia's melody from the night before, reveling in the thought of her.

"Humming to ourselves, are we?" Ramsey called, pulling his mount alongside Kit's horse, riding crop in his fist. "Seems like the old fellow has, dare I say it, found love at long last?"

"Aren't you supposed to be running my hotel?" Kit goaded, guiding his horse around a fallen branch.

Ramsey tapped his riding top hat. "I'm wearing my gentleman's hat this morning, so no. Are you humming an aria from last night's opera?"

Kit grinned. "And it may be because my heart is indeed taken."

"Truly?" Ramsey's jaw dropped as he flicked his hat brim upward, staring fully at Kit. "Not with Elsie?"

Kit shook his head. "She continues to press me into proposing, but—"

"But you are in love with the diva. Who would have thought? She's a fortunate woman."

"I would be so fortunate if she accepted my suit," Kit added as his horse pranced to the side, away from Ramsey's horse.

"Miss Vittoria hasn't yet?"

"I haven't asked."

"You nincompoop, whyever not?" Ramsey rolled his eyes.

"Did you not listen to any of my advice? Honestly, I do not know why I even try with you."

"I wish it were that simple, but the lady doesn't particularly wish to marry."

Ramsey's brows shot up. "Not for her mother's reasons, though, surely?"

Kit's grip on the reins tightened. "Of course not!"

Ramsey lifted his hands, sending his mount skittering a few steps to the side. "My apologies. It's only what everyone would think if you pursue her and she refuses to marry you."

"Then I shall sort through those rumors one fisticuff at a time," Kit growled.

"Do not start with me." Ramsey straightened in his saddle. "I will join you in the lady's defense."

Kit checked his pocket watch, snapping it shut when he saw he had but an hour before his call. "I must be going, but keep what I said to yourself about her not wishing to marry."

"Of course. After all, you *are* my source of income. The plight of the second son and all."

With a chuckle, Kit lifted his hand in farewell and galloped toward the club.

After visiting the retiring room to freshen himself, he shrugged on his coat and combed his hair into a tidy queue. He hurried through the club lounge, eager to call on Delia before heading to his hotel.

"I've noticed you have been spending a lot of time with that singer," a muffled voice called to him.

Kit glanced to his right to find Mr. Wingfield staring at him over the top of his morning paper, a pipe clenched between his teeth.

"Good morning, Mr. Wingfield. You mean Lady Delia?"

"That has yet to be confirmed, but yes, *Miss Vittoria*. I feel it is my duty, in memory of your parents, to warn you, Mr. Quincy. You need to think long and hard before marrying a girl who was practically raised in the Academy."

"Which I believe the entirety of the Knickerbockers frequent and hold in high esteem." Kit crossed his arms, unwilling to commit to sitting with the man.

"The opera, yes. The French dances held there when the opera is not occurring, not quite so much."

"She does not attend those, as the balls are not put on by the Italian company and are, as everyone knows, separate from the opera."

Mr. Wingfield lowered the paper in his hands. "I am only cautioning you to think about what you are doing before you are in too deep and put at risk your good reputation." He scowled. "Such as resigning from the boards you have presided over for twenty years just so you can flit about town with *her*. You might as well have pledged your troth to the girl."

Kit gritted his teeth and bade him good day, ignoring the calls from other gentlemen as he left the club on his way to his horse. He was about to mount when he spied a girl on the corner, selling blooms from her wicker basket. He led his horse toward the young girl and selected several flowers, gathering them into a petite bouquet. As he lifted another bloom, he thought of their diverse meanings and wondered how Fritz Blythe was doing, the budding botanist from Willow's competition who had shown an unhealthy obsession for Willow. While Kit had certainly judged the fellow, he couldn't help but compare his actions to Fritz's, what with the whole phantom business and deceiving society. He shook that thought from his head and finished off Delia's gift. It was decidedly *not* the same. He dropped a coin into the girl's open palm, her lips parting at the amount that he guessed was nearly what she earned in a week.

"God bless you, sir," she said, her gap-toothed grin melting his heart.

"And you, miss." Gripping the nosegay in one hand, he rode for Gramercy Park. Tying his horse to the post, he knocked on the front door, clutching the bouquet of blooms behind his back.

Delia flung open the door, her cheeks bright. "Kit! I mean—" She cast a glance behind her and corrected herself. "Mr. Quincy, thank goodness you arrived. Lord Rolfeson and my mother just arrived at the breakfast table, and according to my father, Lord Kerr will not be far behind."

"Oh? Am I interrupting your breakfast?" He shifted down a step. "I can return later."

"No! Let me just grab my wrap and hat."

"Why would you—?" But she had already disappeared back inside the house.

When she reappeared a moment later, she was threading a hatpin through the grosgrain ribbon as angry voices from inside spilled out. She quickly shut the door and sent him an apologetic smile. "I do not think now is the best time for Madre or Lord Rolfeson to be receiving anyone. If we take a turn, I'm sure before long they will have calmed enough to receive you."

"I don't suppose you will make me carry these blooms in the park?" He grinned, holding them out to her.

"How lovely." She held them to her nose, closed her eyes,

and inhaled. "'The forward violet thus did I chide: sweet thief, whence didst thou steal thy sweet that smells, if not from my love's breath?'"

"What is that?"

"I was just quoting Shakespeare." Her cheeks blossomed. "I read his works far too often for research into his characters I portray by the various librettists."

"So, you think I smell like a violet?"

"Oh no! I was, uh . . ." She held up the bunch. "The violets made me think of sonnet ninety-nine. You smell far manlier, like the outdoors and wintergreen . . ."

She averted her eyes and looked away, but he could tell she was hiding her blush and that pleased him. *Perhaps there is hope for a Mrs. Quincy in my future after all, with little ones to fill my empty home.*

He took her hand and threaded it through his arm, waiting as she unlocked the gate and then took a seat beside her on what she had come to consider as their bench in their many promenades.

"Lia, I know you do not wish to marry, but after several conversations this morning, I think it is important that *you* know once and for all where I stand so there is no confusion."

She stiffened, her heart following suit. "What do you mean?" she whispered. *Is he going to end my dearest daydream?* It was only right, for she had allowed the farce to become all too real, both in her heart and in her head.

"From the moment you corrected me—yelled at me—that I was mistaken regarding your actions that first night, you stole a piece of my heart. And every moment I have spent with you since, I have given you another piece, and another, until I find that my entire heart now is in your possession."

She forced herself to meet his gaze, to read anything there that might reveal a flicker of doubt behind his words. Instead, she found only promise and hope and truth.

"And if you would allow me to *truly* court you, I could not be happier." Kit grasped her hand in his. "I hold you in the greatest of affection and—"

"And if you were a *gentleman* at all, you would have sought Lord Rolfeson's permission before pressing his daughter into giving you an answer," Lord Kerr barked, his expression stormy.

Delia jumped to her feet, scattering the fallen leaves underfoot. "Lord Kerr. How did you get inside the gate?"

"You left it open, my dear." His features softened for a brief second, until he focused on Kit grasping Delia's hand in his own, silently offering her the strength she needed, and then the thunderous expression returned. "My lady, will you please allow me to escort you home, where we may get to know each other in the proper way? After all, your father has all but promised a happy union between us."

Even though she had yet to give Kit her answer, she was irked that her father would think he could command her to allow this man to pay court to her, as if she were a debutante and not a woman grown. "If I wished to marry Kit—I mean, Mr. Quincy—no one could stop me from doing so."

"Lia, do you mean that? That you would reconsider your stance on marriage, for me?" Kit took both of her hands in his now, turning her toward him.

She wished she could have been alone with him for this moment, to explain her answer. She loved him more than she ever thought possible, but there were things she had to do first before becoming his bride. "Not during my first season, no."

"There *is* hope, then, afterward?" Kit asked with a longing in his voice that was echoed within her.

She gazed up at him. "Yes, Kit. There is hope."

He pressed his lips atop each hand. "My darling, you have no idea how happy you have made me that one day you may agree to be my bride."

"While this is all very moving, it has no bearing on whether your father shall bestow his blessing." Lord Kerr extended his arm to her once more, wiggling his fingers and bidding her to take his arm. "This is most untoward. Allow me to return you home. It does not do well for your reputation to spend any more time alone with this gentleman."

Delia wove her fingers through Kit's and rose on her tiptoes to whisper, "Forever seems an appropriate amount of time to promise to be your bride."

"Forever with you is not long enough," Kit murmured in her ear, sending chills down her arm. "Lord Kerr, I assure you, it is I and not you who will be seeing . . ." Kit was cut off as a group of ladies taking their morning constitutional rounded the corner.

"Did I hear someone say 'Lord Kerr'?" Mrs. Wingfield interjected, her fingers whitening on her carved parasol handle as she motioned her two daughters to flank her.

Kit had never been so glad to see the woman. Capitalizing on Kerr's momentary distraction, Kit reached for Delia's elbow, keeping her beside him as they stepped through the gate. “Did you mean what you said? You were so against even the idea of marriage not even a month ago.”

“I did mean it, Mr. Kit,” she replied. “But it is up to you to convince me to change my mind as to when a wedding might occur.”

Twenty

Delia was jostled in her seat when the carriage hit a tree root as they turned down the lane toward Willow Dupré's country estate just outside New York City. The arrival of Lord Rolfeson and the eligible Lord Kerr had caused such a stir that overnight it seemed all in society had sent invitations to their door. And for once Madre was invited. While Madre pretended to be above such happenings, Delia could tell that her mother was thrilled to have the doors open for her again, along with her father's adoring gaze that he had been showering Madre with for the past few days since his arrival. Delia was more confused than ever as to what had happened to separate them, if Madre was faithful as she had claimed, and Lord Rolfeson still loved her . . .

If there was such affection between them, why had they separated? She couldn't keep her smile from spreading as she watched Lord Rolfeson clearly enjoying Madre's company, who sat beside him. Both were laughing, a scene Delia had imagined as a child, that the gentlemen spending time with her mother were really her father. In her imaginings, her father was never this adoring and Madre never so jovial . . . and there was never a lord beside her, crushing her skirts.

Delia ran her hand down the sapphire silk gown from Millie, admiring the black lace at her waist that matched the lace of her high-collared neckline. Together with the gold cornet of diamonds and gold South Sea pearls, bracelet, and earrings to match that Father had presented her, it was an ensemble befitting a lady with a title.

"I brought you something else." Lord Rolfeson leaned toward her and handed her a thin square box, his smile not quite reaching his eyes. "You cannot rightly wear that simple cameo with such a gown. Wear this instead."

Delia's fingers trembled as she opened the velvet-lined box, gasping at the diamond brooch within. She had never worn one stone, let alone so many. "Lord Rolfeson, it is too much."

Madre arched a brow at the extravagant gift, but shockingly she remained silent as Lord Rolfeson lifted the brooch from its box, gesturing for her to turn her back to him. He loosened the bow at the base of her neck to remove the cameo so she might pin the diamond brooch in its place.

"Not for the daughter of an earl. I want all to know you are mine." He admired the jewels at her throat.

Lord Kerr's eyes sparkled in the moonlight spilling in through the carriage window. "And remember, there is more where that comes from if you decide to accept my suit."

She touched the gems, wishing the jewels were not a bribe to release their home on Gramercy Park through her marriage but rather a symbol of her father's affection. She didn't know why he didn't just purchase another New York residence, especially when he obviously did *not* have financial troubles with gifts like these. Or perhaps lords did not divest themselves of the family jewels and possessed coffers of jewels from generations of nobility? *But surely he wishes to keep the family jewels for his other children and therefore must have the deed to our house to relieve his finances and continue their lifestyle.* He must love them far more than he pretended to care for her, for why else would he come all this way to protect their futures when every letter she had ever written requesting his return was met with a resounding no?

She didn't know his motives, but she didn't dare refuse Lord Rolfeson's gifts after last night's argument with the threats flowing between her parents. While they still seemed to love each other, the fighting was unbearable at times. Yet she supposed a broken vow of such depth caused the sort of hurt others could not understand. From what she gathered from her third-floor bedroom, Madre had threatened Lord Rolfeson with something that could have him arrested, while her father had begged Madre to see reason—which left her wondering what on earth her mother could have over her father that was worse than Madre's philandering ways with Mr. Lowe.

Even in the dim light of the carriage, she could feel Madre's eyes lingering on Delia's jewels, coming at last to rest on the cameo clutched in her daughter's hand, the same cameo she had gifted Delia on her thirteenth birthday. She hated to remove the necklace that Madre said was her family's one heirloom, but she couldn't refuse her father even though she disliked the pretentious air the jewels lent her. After her father left, she would return to being a woman of middling means.

She looked out the window, spying torches lining the drive

all the way up to the massive castle-like manor the Dempseys had just finished renovating—at least that is what she had been told. As soon as the carriage halted under the porte cochere, a footman in silver livery stood at the right of the double doors, accepting each guest's invitation. A second held out his hand to assist her from the carriage, while a third who was just inside removed her cape.

Delia joined the reception line, searching for anyone she knew—well, searching for Kit mostly. After their sweet conversation in the park, she ached to spend time with him alone, which had been nearly impossible given her father's hovering and Lord Kerr's attention. Speaking of Lord Kerr, she glanced over her shoulder and sighed in relief at the single ladies chattering to him. She returned to looking for Kit and was met with the gazes of a cluster of women she had met previously. She smiled and nodded to the ladies, who all but turned up their noses at the sight of Madre behind her in a crimson gown. Their confusion was evident when Madre clutched the arm of Lord Rolfeson and he pressed a kiss to her forehead. Whispers began to swirl about, making Delia's head dizzy as they proceeded down the reception line.

"Lord Rolfeson." Willow greeted him with Cullen, who was quite the giant beside his petite wife. "Signora Vittoria, Lady Delia, and Lord Kerr. How wonderful for you to join us at our first ball at North Manor."

"Your home is lovely." Delia curtsied, wondering how it was Willow and Cullen Dempsey could make a castle feel cozy despite its vastness, crystal chandeliers, and the gold leaf that covered every inch of molding.

"Thank you," Willow replied. "We haven't yet finished

everything, but we are hoping the old underwater ballroom will be fit to host a party before the end of the season."

"Underwater ballroom?" Delia quirked a brow.

Mr. Dempsey laughed. "Nonsensical, isn't it? I must admit the eccentricity of a tunnel leading to a ballroom under the lake behind the house intrigued me when we were viewing the place before we purchased it."

"You must tell us all about it once you greet your other guests," Lord Rolfeson interjected.

Greetings completed, Delia slipped away from her parents and Lord Kerr, moving around the ballroom floor, unable to keep herself from searching. It was as if her heart knew Kit was near, and if so, she too must be near him to keep her heart beating. But the moment she was spotted in the crowd, she was swarmed by gentlemen. She greeted each but soon grew uncomfortable with their attention. Making her excuses, she hurried into the crowd, hoping for a bit of anonymity there. Well, as much as one could obtain with a crown atop one's coiffure. Punch glass in hand, she found a place along the far wall and scanned the room once more, her heart dipping at the sight of Kit, who appeared at long last in a well-tailored black evening coat.

After weeks at his side at such gatherings and their very recent confessions of affection, followed by three full days of rehearsals with Giuseppe when she had not been able to speak with Kit alone, she ached to run to him. But decorum kept her planted along the wall. Sipping her drink, she allowed herself to delight in the sight of him in his coattails and brocade neckcloth, his hair tied neatly back into a queue. The silver streaks at his temples gave him a decidedly masculine edge over the other men who had approached her tonight. Surely there was no one in the ballroom half as dashing as Kit Quincy.

Willow and Cullen climbed the massive stone staircase along the side wall of the ballroom, where Willow lifted a glass in the air. "Ladies and gentlemen. As you know, tonight is our first ball at North Manor in honor of Flora Day. When she arrives, we must all shout our congratulations on her birthday. Until then, Mr. Dempsey and I would love to invite our prima donna to sing for us tonight."

At the enthusiastic applause, Delia was about to step forward to claim her place when Madre swept across the floor, joined the orchestra, and whispered her instructions regarding the song. As the room hushed, a few murmurings through the introduction's notes brought Delia's attention to the back of the room, where Mr. and Mrs. Lowe stood listening. Mr. Lowe appeared excited at the sight of Madre, while his wife pressed her lips into a thin line.

Delia's cheeks burned, not because her mother's voice wasn't perfection, but because she always had to be center stage no matter the place and who might be in attendance, even though she would never intentionally take her own daughter's limelight. Delia moved to the edge of the crowd, intent on escaping to the powder room for the duration of the song. *Heaven help us if Father spots Mr. Lowe and the man's adoring smile directed to Madre.* Finding Father in the crowd, she saw he was so enchanted with Madre's singing that he had not taken notice of the Lowes' arrival.

"Pardon me, Lady Delia?" A footman approached her, holding a card between his two fingers, a tray of appetizers in the other hand. "This note is for you." He handed her the card.

She thanked him, flipped open the card, and read it.

Come to the underwater ballroom. I need to speak with you in private.

Your Phantom

She fought back a smile in case anyone was looking and tucked the note inside her dance card. Her heart beating wildly, she wove through the crowd to where it was said a tunnel from the house led to the underwater ballroom. She paused at the double doors, eyeing the golden ropes blocking the way that separated the closed tunnel from the rest of the home. It was obviously not ready to receive guests, but Kit would never suggest she do anything improper. More than likely he had a message from the patronesses about their mishap with the other phantom, and she had to receive the message in private now that her father and Lord Kerr were keeping such a close eye on her.

She checked behind her. It could be catastrophic if her reputation was damaged, but seeing as all were enthralled with Madre's aria, she ducked under the ropes, her enormous bustle catching on the gold cord. She pulled her sapphire skirt loose, making the rope sway between the two wooden poles holding it in place as she shoved open the door, which released such a groan she fairly jumped. She darted inside and closed it behind her, not risking even a glance to check if anyone had seen her. She blinked at the change in light, pleased to find that Kit had thought to leave a few torches lit down the pathway to keep her from stumbling in the darkness.

Her heeled slippers echoed on the marble floors of the tunnel, and the closer she came to the ballroom, the brighter the unearthly glow emanating from the chamber grew. She was so preoccupied with trying to determine the source of the glow that she slipped on a streak of jade slime that was leaking through the tunnel's ceiling and onto the floor, leaving a long trail behind. She clasped her skirts in her hands, terrified she might mar the beautiful gown. She shuddered against the chill in the room that once had been stunning. Crossing the threshold into what must have been the ballroom, she gasped. The glow emanated from the moon, which was shining through the lake and mottled glass dome. Once finished and cleaned, all would be more than impressive.

In the moonlight and flickering firelight, she found the floor in the ballroom changed to a pink marble that would gleam when polished and further reflect the moon. Its walls were adorned with slabs of the same pink marble. The molding was decorated in gold foil, although the slime oozing from the edges of the glass dome above had taken away from the grandeur as it made its way down the marble, clinging in clumps to the gold-leaf sconces lining the room.

"Kit?" she called, his name echoing in the chamber.

"I knew you would come if you thought the note was from him." The man in the crimson phantom costume appeared from the pink marble wall, his towering body effectively blocking her exit, his ivory skeleton mask grinning as he tilted his head this way and that, much like a snake testing his prey.

Delia gasped, accidentally dropping her train and stumbling over it in her haste to leave. "Kit!" she screamed into the tunnel, desperately hoping he would appear. "Kit?"

"Do you think I mean you harm?" The phantom laughed and extended his arms to her as if to embrace her. "Quite the contrary, my lady. I have a proposition for you."

She gathered her skirts over her arm and stepped back from him, even though it gave the phantom an eyeful of her silk-stockinged calves. "What do you want from me?"

"Merely to say that Signora Vittoria's voice will fade from memory by the time we are through."

"I thought Madre was your chosen one?"

He paced beneath the burning candles of the sconces, the light shadowing his features further. Drawing his rapier, he extinguished each wick with a slice of the blade as he rounded the room. "Signora Vittoria abandoned her place as my angel when she chose the Metropolitan instead of waiting for me to save her again."

His angel? Delia suppressed a shudder. "And if I do not wish to be a pawn in your game?"

"We both know you have ambitions, so why pretend you do not, other than to preserve your honor?"

"You are right." Her words brought a maniacal grin to life beneath his mask as he reached the last sconce. "I do wish to be diva, but not in an underhanded way."

"And having an impostor pose as me is not underhanded?" He laughed again, pausing as his accusation found its mark. "Do not disappoint me, my lady, or there will be consequences. We could do great things together, if only you would release your infatuation with Kit Quincy. The man is no different than the rest. He will use you and leave you. And if you need proof of it, look to your mother. She left my protection and joined with Lord Rolfeson, and unlike what I would have done, he abandoned her. I would never leave you, Lia."

She clenched her fists to keep them from trembling at the mention of Kit's name, reminding herself that he might only be speaking of Kit as her suitor and not as the impostor phantom. "Who are you?"

But he had already vanished in the shadows, taking the light with him, save for a lone candle that sputtered dangerously in his wake.

"Lia?" Kit's voice rumbled down the tunnel from the entrance.

"Kit?" she cried, even as she glanced over her shoulder to find the phantom had reappeared once more, sword drawn. "Kit!" she screamed.

"Remember our agreement," the phantom warned, "or else Kit will be the one to pay the price." Then he snuffed out the last candle, plunging her into darkness.

"Lia!" Kit's footsteps pounded on the marble.

She flew in his direction and rammed into him, his arms engulfing her and his solid chest comforting her.

"Who was that man? Did he hurt you?"

"Kit, I thought you had summoned me," she murmured into his chest, her eyes slowly adjusting to the moonlight. "I was foolish. Stupidly foolish."

"Did he hurt you?" he repeated, holding her at arm's length, looking her over for injuries in the moonlight.

She shook her head. "He didn't touch me, Kit. He said that he is the real phantom. His build and distorted voice matched the man from the Academy and the hotel, but I still do not know him."

"If he bothered to distort his voice with you, that means you most likely *do* know him." Kit held her close as the strains of violins flowed into the tunnel from the double doors.

"Your heart is pounding," she whispered, her hands gripping his lapels as if he were anchoring her.

"Because I have never been so frightened for another in all my life."

She looked up to him. "You worried for me?"

He took her face between his hands. "You know you are far more than the next star of the Academy to me, Delia."

She lifted her chin, hoping, wishing he would kiss her at last, but he pulled away and wrapped his arm more firmly about her waist. "How did you know where to find me, Kit?"

"I didn't. I spied the footman giving you a note, and it took me a few moments to get through the crowd, only to discover you had gone into the tunnel. Then I heard him speaking . . . I am beginning to think he did indeed set fire to the Academy." He rested his forehead against hers. "Please, don't go running off by yourself, Lia, at least until we can discover this madman's true identity. I have no doubt that, whoever it is, he was invited to this party, because Willow's staff would have sent anyone who was not invited away at once."

Her cheeks burned at his gentle admonishment. Even if the note *had* been from Kit, meeting a gentleman in a dark, secluded place would brand her, leaving her reputation just as tarnished as her mother's. "I won't," she promised.

"Good." He lifted her hand in his and kissed it. "Now, let us escape this place before he returns."

Hand in hand, they half ran to the double doors. But when Kit attempted to turn the handle, the door did not budge. "It's locked."

"Oh no!" She tested the handle for herself. "Can't you just break down the door?"

He chuckled. "I thank you for the vote of confidence in my strength, but I'm afraid I cannot simply bust open the door, because then—"

"Then my reputation would be in tatters." She nodded. "Well, if we do not get out of here before people realize we are both missing, and we cannot find another way out, my reputation will still be destroyed."

"But we *will* find another way. I doubt the staff used the family's entrance, which means there is a servants' entrance somewhere. However, we must find it in a timely manner."

Having no other light than that of the glass dome, they carefully made their way along the tunnel, searching for signs of the phantom's entry and possible exit points. With her hand secure in Kit's, she found she wasn't frightened of the phantom's return.

"Look." Kit pointed to a ladder in a short secondary tunnel that branched to the left and appeared to be a service entrance. It did not have the lake above it. "This must be how he entered and exited."

Climbing to the top of the ladder, Kit pushed against an iron hatch. It did not budge. "Or perhaps not. Don't fret, my lady," Kit called from the top rungs, shedding his evening coat and handing it down to her.

Her arm brushed the wall beside the ladder, and she heard the faintest jingle. *A key?* She lifted the ring from the wall, overwhelming relief filling her that her father would not be tearing this mansion apart looking for her, which he likely would have done were she to disappear for longer than a quarter of an hour. "Kit?"

"I will see us out of here, and if I cannot—" he pressed his shoulder against the metal, grunting with the effort—"I will break down those double doors myself and come back around to fetch you from wherever this hatch leads."

"Yes, but . . ."

His strained exhale divulged the amount of effort he was putting into shoving against the hatch, which probably kept him from hearing her. The hinges groaned. He dropped his shoulder and wiped his brow with his forearm. "I think a few more shoves will weaken the rusted hinges enough to break through."

"I appreciate your efforts, Kit, but mayhap this would help?" Delia lifted the keys and gave them a little jingle, drawing his gaze as she reached up to place the key ring in his hand.

Kit laughed. "And here I was hoping to impress you with my strength."

"Oh, I assure you, I was quite impressed," she replied.

Keys in hand, he climbed up another rung and located the keyhole. The hinges groaned again in protest as he pushed upward. "Watch out!"

Dirt, grass, and heaven knew what else rained down, and she leapt backward to protect her gown.

"It worked!" She clapped her hands. "Where are we exactly on the grounds?"

He stood on the third rung from the top, half of him out of the tunnel. "In the gardens," he answered. "So, the man could have been a party crasher, but surely the squeaking of the metal would have echoed down the chamber and alerted us of his exit as we waited by the door, and the debris would not have been so heavy. That means the man used the double doors before locking us in the tunnel. He is somewhere inside North Manor as we speak."

Twenty-One

Kit slowly rose from the tunnel hatch at the left of the lake near the back of the manor. The sounds of merriment drifted through the windows and across the grounds. Three couples were milling about. Kit squatted down as Delia's head popped up, and he grabbed her arms and lifted her out of the tunnel. Quickly they slipped behind a cluster of pointed topiaries, his lips brushing the tip of her nose. He found himself fighting to draw a breath at the nearness of her.

"Kit?" She placed a hand on his arm.

"You are lovely, do you know that?"

She drew her hand over the front of the sapphire silk he had never seen her don before tonight. "I hope it is not marred from the tunnel."

"You look lovely," he repeated, his fingers weaving through hers as he so often found himself doing lately, and lately she had not been pulling away. *Too lovely. I will have to be diligent indeed to keep the other gentlemen at bay.* "We will have to wait a moment more here. There are too many guests about the grounds."

"Were you nervous about coming tonight?"

The question was so odd, it did the trick in shaking him out of his stupor brought on by being so close to her. "Nervous? No, why would I be?"

"Well, you were late in arriving. I thought that perhaps with the party being here in Willow Dempsey's new home, and as one of the final gentlemen who courted her, you might feel—"

He shook his head. "I have cared for Willow as a friend for years, ever since she was a young girl." *Should not have said that, Kit, old boy.* "And that affection, though it did alter from friendship to romance for a bit, did not cease with my being in the competition and did not discontinue with my stepping away. Rather, I think stepping away helped to preserve our friendship, returning Willow and me to that former bond. Granted, I may not have wished to visit her in the weeks following my departure"—*due to my broken dreams after having developed feelings for Willow during the competition for her heart, despite what the papers said about the contrived situation*—"but I assure you, our purely platonic relationship has completely returned."

He looked Delia in the eyes, the wondrousness of having her beside him in the moonlight doing things to his heart. He ached to draw her into his arms and kiss her, but having such thoughts was exactly why he needed to check again. *Blast.* All the guests had returned to the ballroom. Satisfied no one was about, he led her through the garden.

"Wait! Your jacket!" She pulled him back just shy of the veranda steps and made quick work of dusting the dirt from his coat, her fingers lingering at his hair.

She bit her lip and looked up at him in such a way that Kit lost all thoughts of propriety and leaned forward to accept her kiss when the gong sounded and Willow called out, "Teddy and Flora's carriage! Quick, everyone, hide!"

Kit and Delia scurried toward the farthest doors to their right, where he remembered the parlor to be when the mansion belonged to the Grant family. But the moment he flung open the door, he found not the parlor filled with guests attempting to hide, but a study with papers stacked on what could only be Willow's desk. The back of it was up against a second matching desk that held papers as well but in a more disorganized fashion, which he supposed belonged to Cullen. He couldn't help but be touched by the love Willow felt for her husband by not only welcoming him into her business but also working beside him quite literally in the business she so loved.

"Are you certain we should be in here?" Delia whispered.

"No." He peeked through the crack in the door. "But as Miss Flora—I mean, Mrs. Day—is approaching the foyer, we cannot rightly dash out across to the parlor." He sent her an apologetic smile. "I'm sorry you will miss the surprise for Flora. From what I've pieced together, Mrs. Day was a friend of yours."

"We were friends, but not as close as we would have liked. Her parents would no longer allow us to play together once Madre began her exploits. We have only spoken in stolen moments in the park in passing throughout the years, but even in those brief moments, I know she considers me her friend as much as I do her."

He could feel the tremble in her hand that he still clasped and had little desire to release. "Have I told you how lovely you look tonight?" Footsteps sounded in the hall. "Pretend to laugh at something I said. Someone is coming in."

"Lady Delia." Lord Kerr's voice held a tone of annoyance as he held a glass of punch in each hand and looked to Kit and then back to her. He held out a glass to her. "Will you join me?"

Delia cast Kit a smile and, with a gentle squeeze of his arm, slipped into the brilliant ballroom with Lord Kerr, who did not cease his scowling glances back toward Kit.

He followed a few yards behind them, his brows rising at the sight of the gentlemen already about Lady Delia. He thrust his hand into his waistcoat pocket, where he kept his mother's engagement ring secured to his watch chain. He felt the hard sapphire encircled by woven silver and imagined the ring on her finger at the end of the season. It had been easier to envision before Lord Rolfeson gave credence to society's claim of her title. Overhearing the wishes of Lord Rolfeson from others in attendance, Kit was now certain the lord did not desire to leave his daughter behind again, which meant if she did not love him as he hoped, Delia would be leaving for England and the story of his youth would repeat itself. As Elsie had left him for the courts of splendor India had to offer, so might Delia for the courts of the queen, despite her promise that he could hope.

"Mr. Quincy." Willow greeted him with a wobbly smile as she stood next to him, surveying her guests. "I did not have a chance to tell you when you were in the reception line for fear I would be overheard, but there is a guest tonight I thought you would like to be made aware of before you were taken by surprise."

Kit scanned the room, wondering who could have caused Willow to feel nervous, seeing as she was the hostess. "Is Cullen aware of this person's presence? Or do you need me to bring it to his attention so he can dispose of the unwanted guest?"

"It's not like that, but, uh, one of the guests brought a friend . . . who is actually an old friend of yours of a sort." She picked at her nails, a habit he had learned meant she was truly uncomfortable. "And I am sincerely sorry for it."

"A friend? Did more than one guest bring an unannounced friend?" He stiffened. Perhaps that was how the villain managed to steal into a private party.

"The Walden family brought her, and I couldn't say no, as she was already standing in my doorway. Mother could have managed it, but I could not." Her lips pulled into a thin frown.

"Willow, surely a woman's presence isn't cause for such alarm—"

"Christopher, so good to see you!" Elsie waved to him with her silk fan.

Willow lifted her hands, palms out toward him, and backed away. "Again, I repeat my earlier statement. Please excuse me."

He couldn't be angry with Willow, but why tonight of all nights would Elsie decide to attend a party she had not been invited to? His gaze found Delia in the crush of gentlemen, concern flaring that her father was not nearby. What if the phantom was in their midst? He had to get to her before she found herself in danger again.

"Elsie, I apologize, but I really must be on my way."

"Thank you for being so candid," she murmured, but made no move to leave. "But why are you in such a hurry? You are at a party! We must dance." She giggled and handed him her dance card. "I will not object to your claiming a second dance as well."

"Lady Ellyson."

Hurt flashed through her eyes. "Mr. Quincy."

He gritted his teeth. He had hoped he could avoid this, but if he were to have any chance with Delia, he needed to make things clear. "Lady Ellyson, I need you to cease this idea of us."

"You make me sound like quite the pursuer." Her cheeks blossomed. She whipped out her fan to disguise her complexion. "When in fact you were the one who did all the pursuing, promising to love me forever. Surely our engagement meant *something* to you—your vow meant something to you."

"It meant everything to me, Elsie."

Her eyes widened. "Then why—?"

"Because that vow became void when you married Lord Ellyson and I moved on." He secured two drinks from a passing waiter and handed one to her. "Besides, you know I have been spending ample time with Lady Delia, which has also been printed about in great length in the papers."

"True," Lady Ellyson said. "But surely you, a man of such rigid scheduling, would prefer a simpler life than that of being the husband of an opera star, who no doubt plans to tour Europe. Imagine the life we could share together with my son here in New York now that I've decided to settle down here—that is, if you were to propose."

He ran his hand over his jaw. A few years ago, the idea of having a second chance with Elsie would have seemed like an answer to prayer . . . until Delia.

Reading his answer on his face, she ran her hand from his shoulder to his upper arm just as she had in the old days. "You are certain? Because it is not in my nature to linger in the past longer than a few days."

At his nod, she extended her arms. "Then let us have one last dance together."

He didn't care that his life was not full of adventure before Delia, and neither did Delia. Yet Delia had unwittingly changed him. Before Delia, he never would have thought to don a phantom costume and fly from the eaves in daring maneuvers simply to aid a diva's blossoming career. But he never felt for anyone like he did for Delia, not even Elsie.

She laid her hand against his cheek. "You were always my rock, Christopher. Miss Vittoria is a fortunate woman."

The intimate gesture caused his gaze to shift to Delia, who gaped at them from across the room. Not caring about etiquette and abandoning a lady on the dance floor, he whirled them toward the corner, bowed to Elsie, and presented her to Uncle Elmer, who laughed in delight.

"Why, Alice Lexington, always a pleasure. Tell me, how is living next to Mr. Beckby?"

Kit didn't wait to excuse himself, but hurried to claim Delia from Noah Walden and Clyde Billings.

"Lady Delia, will you do me the honor of taking a stroll with me on the veranda?"

She slipped her hand around his arm, the action warming him after his shock, and nodded to Walden and Billings.

"How is Lady Ellyson?"

If Kit hadn't been so concerned about what she might think, he would have grinned. She had lasted all of twenty seconds before her curiosity had gotten the better of her. Yet his mirth faded as he held the door for her, the crisp evening stinging his cheeks. "She is well enough."

She straightened her shoulders as if preparing for him to declare that she was correct in thinking all men were double-crossing cads. "I was told she is staying at your hotel."

Kit winced inwardly. He hadn't mentioned it before to keep her from assuming the worst about him, but here she had already known and was waiting on him to explain. "She wished to revive the past, but I made it clear that I have moved forward and have no desire to return to what we once were." He ached to reassure Delia of his affections for her alone, but instead he waited.

"Oh." Her lashes flitted up for just a moment, but it was enough for him to see her relief.

The ring hidden in his vest pocket pressed against his abdomen, but he could not wait until spring to let her know without a doubt how he felt about the matter, even if he had to wait to ask her to be his alone. "I have made it no secret where, or with whom, my heart lies."

Her gaze met his, her eyes wide in the moonlight. "Where?"

He took her hand and laid it over his heart. "In your hands, and you must do with it what you will. I am at your mercy, my lady."

Delia didn't even feel the cold as she walked the length of the verenda with Kit, arm in arm. When she had first seen the woman graze her hand down Kit's arm, her heart stumbled in her chest, drawing the very breath from her. And while doubts swirled about her mind, questioning Kit's character, she knew he had done nothing but display his respect to her and reassure her of where his affections lay.

While her fears and news of where Lady Ellyson was staying fought to shatter the beautiful moments with Kit, she pressed the verses to the forefront of her heart to silence the beast within with the truth. "*When my heart is overwhelmed: lead me to the rock that is higher than I . . . I will trust in the covert of thy wings.*" She quieted her fears, resting in the Lord's calling to trust in Him. *Lord, you have shown me again and again that Kit is nothing like the men who call on Madre, or those who made advances on me. Kit is a man of honor, a godly man who protects the vulnerable—a man after your heart. But if Kit and I are not meant to be, lead me to the Rock that is higher than I, for you are my shelter . . . just as you have always been.*

"Delia?" Kit's eyes held nothing but concern. "You do believe me about Lady Ellyson, yes?"

She nodded, returning her gaze to the shimmering lake.

"I know you wish to continue your first season without complications, but I do not want to leave you with any doubt. I have come to admire you greatly, my delightful Lady Delia. I wish to be with you for the rest of forever—to cherish you, honor you, and support you in your dreams. I would never ask you to give up the stage, for your voice is too beautiful to keep to myself, and even if I selfishly did, I couldn't keep you from being a star—you shine too brightly to ever be set on society's shelf. I realize a proposal is not what you wish for at the moment, but know this. I love you with everything I am, and the moment this season ends, I intend on asking you to become my bride."

She pressed her hand to her mouth, the dream—the beautiful dream—of a happy marriage filled with a mutual love and a husband who would support her career was actually being promised to her. *Lord, thank you for your faithfulness, for blessing me beyond measure.*

At her silence, he added in a rush, "I know that in the end you may not even wish to marry me, but I want you to know my intentions on the subject are the same as they were two weeks ago. I am in love with you, Lady Delia, and I will be faithful to you alone forever if you'll have me."

Her throat was too constricted to speak, so she allowed her arms to trail up and around his neck. "Kit." She drew out his name as if it were the sweetest word to ever pass her lips. She lifted herself onto the tips of her toes and pressed her lips to his, a thrill flowing through her. She did not wish for the kiss—her first kiss—to end. And as Kit pulled back, she could see it affected him as much as her. He rested his forehead against hers, and they laughed softly at their shared secret.

Five months seemed like forever away now that she knew what the end of the season promised. She shook her head loose of the romance clouding her eyes, laughing in delight. But the phantom was here, and she could not afford to be caught unawares once more. There would be plenty of time to dream at the end of the season, a lifetime to dream . . . if Kit did indeed ask her to be his bride.

Twenty-Two

Kit applauded as wildly as the younger gentlemen who threw roses at Delia's feet, calling for more. The performance of *Roméo et Juliette* ended in three encores and could have continued to a fourth, but Delia was at last released by Mr. Mapleson, who stepped onto the stage to bow with Delia's curtsy and signaled the drawing of the curtain.

"Goodness, you would think it was the Queen of England onstage with all the applause and fanfare," Elsie commented from her seat beside Uncle Elmer.

Kit leaned forward to inform Uncle Elmer of his taking his leave, but the man was so busy laughing with Elsie about the good old days, he had scarcely spoken to his nephew for the entirety of the performance.

"Your company is a balm, Lady Ellyson." Uncle Elmer patted her gloved hand. "I would be honored should you join us in our box again next week. Do say you'll attend?"

Kit barely kept himself from rolling his eyes at his uncle's words.

Elsie didn't seem to mind as she dipped her head and

bestowed a smile on his uncle that, if memory served him right, was her flirtatious smile. Was the woman so determined to have a second husband that she would wish to marry a man over *twenty* years her senior? The lady certainly did not waste time. It had not been twenty-four hours since he turned her away. At least now she might get what she desired.

The curtain behind him parted, and Millie sank down beside him with the barest of greetings to the others in the box and mumbled, "Do you know how much trouble I am in with a certain society matron for you *not* appearing tonight, especially after *le Fantôme de l'Opéra* appeared the other night?"

"Is that French for the phantom of the opera . . . ?" Kit lifted his brows at the whispered name.

She waved him off. "It added an air of mystique and I don't have time to come up with a better code name. The point is, we should have done something. Mrs. Vittoria is pulling ahead in the polls."

"We agreed that if I made an appearance every performance, it would lose its romantic element, and you do realize you are the one who schedules the appearances along with the mastermind plan?"

She frowned. "I am aware, Kit. The point is that we must *act*, and I do have a plan, thank you very much."

"Honestly, even if we had something slotted for tonight, I am hesitant to act. I do not wish to rile *le Fantôme* into doing something that could harm Lia." He turned in his seat to make certain Elsie was still engrossed in conversation with Uncle Elmer. "And you are taking polls now too?"

She looked pointedly at him. "Unlike you, I take any missive from a certain society matron as seriously as a missive from the president."

"And I don't? Did you forget that my livelihood was threatened?" Kit retorted.

"What's this about a missive from the president?" Elsie interjected. She sent him a smile as if that would melt the awkwardness of this evening when it was becoming abundantly clear that she had set her sights on his uncle.

Millie gave Kit a look of warning before turning a smile on Elsie and extending her hand. "I do not believe we have met."

Alice lifted a single brow at the offered hand and slowly extended her own. "Of course we have, Miss Ford. I'm Mrs. Alice Lexington Dawson, Lady of Ellyson Hall."

Millie's eyes widened in feigned innocence. "Alice Lexington? Why, I hardly recognized you! That shade of silver does wonders for you. But, Lady Ellyson, you know better than to eavesdrop, so I am afraid I cannot answer your question. Please excuse us." Millie grabbed Kit's arm and hauled him into the swarming hall leading to the lobby, tucking him behind a potted palm.

"I know you were only rude on my account, but I have long since made my peace with her," Kit said.

Millie crossed her arms. "Well, I have not. You forget that I was the one who dragged you from your house and back into church and out of your depression. Those were not easy months."

He pressed his lips into a firm line against those dark memories after being left. "Yes, but thanks to the Lord and you, I have forgiven her and moved on with my life."

"Which means you owe me. Now, here is the plan I have concocted. And before you protest, know that this took me nearly all night after Willow Dupré-Dempsey's ball to compose, so listen well. And no, I am not open to suggestions." She peered through the branches of the palm. "Do you wish to discuss it here or at your hotel over coffee? I think coffee would be splendid, as this is a rather lengthy strategy."

"Then I suppose it is a good thing I do not have plans for this evening after the opera, for Lady Delia is spending it with her family."

Delia finished the final touches on her gown and hair in her dressing room, readying for her private birthday dinner with Father at Delmonico's, for which she had to stop home first to collect Father. The difference after Lord Rolfeson's publicly claiming her was astounding. Delia had never felt so conspicuous. She was now an officially titled lady and not just a talented singer with a whispered-about heritage. She could feel the audience's respect during her arias, something she had longed for and fought to possess, and now that she was finally getting it, she couldn't help but wish she would have received it without the title. Yet she was not above accepting their praise, not when so much was at stake for her and for Kit.

Throughout her performance, Delia glanced up to Kit's box even though she greatly disliked seeing Lady Ellyson there. However, it appeared she was with Kit's uncle. *Could that be the desired illusion they are casting?* Stop *it. Kit wishes to marry* you. *Are you so uncertain of his affections as to suspect everyone? Kit is* not *your father nor your mother's conquests.*

She stepped out of her dressing chamber and was met with the familiar crush of reporters that was a little less tonight since neither of the phantoms had appeared. She instantly did not sense Kit's presence among them. She frowned. He was always there waiting for her. She excused herself from the group and dared to peek into the lobby, the bevy of society's elite keeping her safely behind the door, when she spotted Kit behind a potted palm with another lady. She stiffened. The only reason for a gentleman to linger behind a potted plant with another lady was not one she wished to consider. Shaken, she slammed the door shut and pushed past the company members calling out to her, rushing for the rear exit to where Lord Rolfeson had a carriage waiting for her. Thankfully, he was not inside.

"Delia!" Lorenzo's call stopped her from closing the carriage door. He trotted up to her, handing her a nosegay of violets. "You were wondrous tonight."

"Thank you." She smiled down at him, grateful her years of training could help her dry most any tears upon a moment's notice. She accepted the gift, burying her nose into the blossoms to compose herself. "This is so kind of you, but are you certain Bianca won't mind?"

He shrugged. "She knows we have been friends much longer, and if she has a problem with our friendship, then she may leave."

Torn between her loyalty to Lorenzo and her loyalty to Bianca, she didn't reply but fiddled with a sprig of baby's breath.

"I hope you will get past this awkwardness between us, Lia." Lorenzo swiped off his cap. "I miss the ease between us."

She exhaled, relief flooding her. "I would love that. I've missed you." She grasped his hand. "I shall take these as a sign of our renewed friendship."

"To friendship." He grinned and slapped his hat back into place. "Better get back inside for cleanup duty. *Buona notte*, Lia."

"*Buona notte*, Lorenzo."

As the driver directed the closed carriage to Gramercy Park, Delia gave in to her torn heart. Tears spilled onto her cheeks as she clutched her handkerchief to her mouth to quell the sobs. Why did she allow herself to think Kit was unlike the others? Lady Ellyson would forever hold his heart as his first love, much like how it seemed Madre still possessed Father's heart. Was it true what Madre claimed, that first loves always had a hold on the other's heart? She moaned. *Papá, let it not be so. I cannot bear it.* The carriage rolled to a halt, and she fought to compose herself lest her father join her in the carriage and find her nose swollen from crying. But the minutes ticked by without her father appearing, so she let herself down and into the house, where she heard murmuring coming from the parlor.

"You ruined our beautiful marriage, Serenus," Madre sobbed.

"That's just fine to put that utter failure on me," Father said with a snort. "Considering it was *you* who had a child outside of our vows. Is Delia even *mine*?"

Delia gasped, dropping her reticule to the floor in such a resounding clatter, the parlor door flew open and Father's eyes widened for half a second before a flash of pity passed over his expression.

"My darling, I did not know you were home." He ran a hand through his hair. "I should have been watching for you. I never willingly would have allowed you to hear that."

Madre waved her into the room, her expression oddly

compassionate toward Delia. She glared at Father. "You should know just by looking at her, Serenus, that she is undoubtedly yours beneath the coloring I gave her with the way she holds herself and the shape and color of her green eyes."

"And the boy? How do you explain his presence?" Father grunted.

Delia looked at her father in disbelief, then turned back to her mother. "I have a brother?"

Madre gave a slow nod. "A half brother."

"When?" The single word sounded strangled to her ears. But perhaps the timing would explain everything and why her father would not, could not, forgive Madre.

Madre sighed. "I had a son when I was seventeen, a year before I met your father."

"With her beloved maestro." Father gritted his teeth. "She chose the one man she knew would hurt me the worst. He had been obsessed with her for years. Giovanna knew how I hated him and yet she chose to keep it from me that he had fathered a son with my beloved bride."

"Serenus, I was but a child myself when he seduced me." Madre clutched Father's sleeve, desperation lacing her every word as her nails dug into his arm to keep him at her side. "And when I met you, everything fell away. There was only you and me. I gave up my career to be your wife. Is that not proof enough that I loved you? I gave up everything to be with you, and it still wasn't enough!"

"Including the baby?" Delia whispered, shocked that her new teacher was in truth her brother. "Giuseppe is my brother . . ."

Madre nodded again, tears filling her eyes. "That was the hardest part. We decided after Giuseppe was born that my career was too important to jeopardize with my having a family so early, so the maestro took him and we separated."

No wonder Madre always insisted on calling him Giuseppe instead of Signore Rossi . . . as if she were holding on to the last thing that could connect them in her world of secrets and lies.

Madre sank onto the divan and continued, "But when I met Lord Rolfeson, I decided to retire from the stage. So Maestro Rossi departed for Italy to train the boy to become a great master himself while training a new rising star. As you can imagine, after his departure, our platonic relationship returned in its fullest form."

"And this did not drive him into a rage that you chose to marry another when you had Giuseppe with him?" Delia pressed her fingers to her temples, desperate to understand what on earth was happening.

Madre shrugged. "It did not matter. When I married your father, I gave up my career, until sixty-six when I decided I missed the stage too much, despite how much I loved being your mother." She grasped Delia's hands. "Raising you helped ease the loss of Giuseppe."

"Her desire to return to the stage was when she sent that blasted telegram to Maestro Rossi that ruined our lives. The maestro returned to coach her for the position, and my jealousy rose as a result." Father clenched his jaw. "I did everything to please you, Giovanna. You know that better than anyone else. I was nearly driven mad by my adoration for you."

Madre twisted the handkerchief in her hands. "Your father never truly believed my relationship with Maestro Rossi was innocent. Even so, the maestro accepted that if he wished to be a part of my life, he needed to remain my teacher. For we would be nothing more if I was to rise to fame as a titled singer."

"I'm assuming that's when Father discovered Madre's secret of having a child with Maestro Rossi?"

"I discovered it in the spring of the following year when she was awarded the position as diva, during one of their many lessons, and little Giuseppe began to resemble your mother far too much to be coincidental." Lord Rolfeson sagged against the fireplace mantel, the crackling of the burning logs in the hearth filling the room.

"And yet Giuseppe's obvious age, marking our time together, never convinced your father that the affair was long since over."

Delia sank onto the wing-back chair, unable to bear the weight of the scandal that would crush them all if word of it circulated. *Even if he truly does have feelings for me, Kit would never have me now . . . not with this shame woven into the very fibers of my family's tapestry. A child out of wedlock, abandonment, divorce?* She swiped at her cheeks, tears greeting her fingertips. "Was I never to know of my brother? We have been friends for so long . . . we could have been so much more. I thought I was alone in the world, and now I find I have a half brother living in the same city."

"I never wished for you to feel that way." Madre rested her hand on Delia's shoulder. "Keeping Giuseppe apart from our family pained me more than you could ever know, but in revealing my secret, it would have destroyed any chance of your making a good match."

"And that is the great secret." Delia felt as if she were not in her body, but a member of the audience watching a tragic opera from the boxes. "And after all these years, it will still destroy us all."

Lord Rolfeson flicked his cigar into the flames and turned from the mantel. "And so you can see how our once passionate marriage crumbled under the weight of your mother's lies, and *why* I felt it my duty to marry you to a highborn lord to cover your mother's shame."

Madre narrowed her gaze. "If you loved me as much as you said you did, I think we could have gotten past it and no one ever needed to know. After all, I gave up my son for you."

He shrugged. "It is done. I have Lady Emilie and my children. Things are more complicated than our bruised pride and shattered dreams."

"Then how do you suggest our way forward? Because I refuse to sign over Gramercy Park or allow you to marry off Delia."

Delia was quite warmed by her mother's passionate defense. "Thank you, Madre, but he must only hire a lawyer to see us out of the house. You may as well sign it over to him, and we can move quietly to Stuyvesant Square."

Madre released a short laugh, tinted by rage. "One would think that, but he *knows* why he can never request it. If he goes to the lawyers, I will play the card I've been holding for years—one that will destroy him."

A chill swept over Delia. There was something else they were not telling her. She looked to Father. "You mentioned a great burden, but Giuseppe is Madre's, not yours . . . what does she have over you?"

Father crossed his arms, his eyes stormy. "I cannot and will not say."

At the rap on the front door, the trio paused.

"Hester!" Madre shrieked through the open parlor door. "Hester?"

Delia pushed herself up. "She's probably asleep in her room, Madre, which means she could never hear your shrieking, much less a knock at the front door." She looked pointedly to her parents. "But I am not finished with my questions yet."

"You say that as if you have power over us, my dear." Father sniffed. "I will only reveal what I wish to reveal and nothing more."

Madre rested her hand on Delia's cheek. "One day I will tell you, but trust me, in knowing you will find no comfort."

Delia swallowed her ready rebuttal and instead ran her hand along the foyer's chair rail in a daze to answer the call. She twisted the bolt and opened the door, the sharp wind cutting into the foyer, lifting the dust atop the grandfather clock along the wall as it chimed the hour.

"There you are," Kit whispered, sagging against the doorframe, a light dusting of snow on his opera cloak. "I didn't know what to think when you weren't in your dressing chamber or waiting for me."

"Why would you worry?" The image of him with Elsie still cut her deeply.

He ran a hand through his hair. "I honestly thought the second phantom may have made an appearance and taken you with him."

"Oh." She felt a twinge of guilt. "I didn't think of that when I left."

He did not wait for an invitation to enter but closed the door behind him as he leaned down to her, his forehead nearly touching hers in an attempt to force her to meet his gaze. "I'm no fool, Lia. I know you saw Lady Ellyson in my box, but you must believe me that it was my uncle who invited her. Apparently, my uncle is pursuing the lady."

She lifted her gaze. "He really would do that to you?"

Kit removed his top hat, the action causing the flakes of snow to fall from the brim and land on the marble tiles, melting at once. "He figured I'd had my turn with Lady Ellyson and that if it hasn't worked out by now, it never will, so perhaps she should try a courtship with him."

"And you do not mind?"

"I prefer it."

"And the woman behind the potted palm with you?"

He groaned. "So that is why you left? That was Millie—discussing another one of her harebrained ideas."

"Oh." Her cheeks burned with the shame of her doubting him, even as the secret between them wrenched her soul.

He gave her a slow smile, his hand cupping her cheek, his icy touch cooling her skin. "Does that help?"

She returned his smile with only half of herself, the shattering of before making every movement labored. "Kit, there is so much you do not know." She averted her eyes for fear he would read the scandal in her expression. "And if you did know, it would ruin your good opinion of me. My father's title cannot cover this many sins—it's too much for any mortal man to bear."

"Do you not know me at all, Lia?" He lifted her chin. "I love you, Delia Vittoria, and I will never leave you or forsake you. You are a woman pure of heart, full of life and joy. I would be fortunate indeed to have you by my side in life."

The secrets pressing against her heart eased a little. "But the things you do not know surrounding my birth . . . won't they crush us like they did my parents' marriage?"

He stroked a curl behind her ear. "We are stronger than their secrets."

She ached to seek sanctuary in his arms, but propriety prevented her. Her fingers inched forward, and she gave in to the impulse, weaving them through his. "Convince me, my Kit. Convince me of your love for me, for life's scars will take time to fade."

"It will be my pleasure, my lady." He swept her hand into both of his and kissed it. "Until tomorrow?"

"Until tomorrow, my Kit."

Twenty-Three

All morning long, Delia had been rehearsing how to tell Giuseppe the news, and her hands would not cease their trembling. She drew in a deep breath and straightened her shoulders, determined to face this new truth with courage. Pushing open the door into the small rehearsal room, she squinted in the dim light. "Giuseppe?"

"Over here." He rose from the piano. "Sorry. I forget sometimes to light all the gas lamps, an effect of working alongside my melodramatic father for too long." He went over and lit the sconces along the wall, turning them up until the brightness banished every trace of darkness. "Well, after last night's performance, I think we have some more work to do."

She blinked in the light. "Are you remembering the same performance as I? I had *three* encores with standing ovations."

"Yes, but the theater was not as full as the Metropolitan. And because of that, I think I can prove to Father that you still need work before I make a star of you, and you fill up the

Academy because of *my* training." He cracked his knuckles and resumed his seat at the piano, running his fingers up and down the ivory keys in a chromatic scale, flying over each half step.

She had debated long into the night whether to tell him. She considered the risks of bringing someone new into the secret who might spread the word. But the idea that a long-awaited sibling had always been near brought tears to her eyes. *If only he knew.*

"Whoa now. I didn't mean to tease you too harshly. I thought you would take it like always." Giuseppe stood and gently rested his hands on her shoulders. "You are usually so stoic when it comes to criticism that I sometimes forget you are your mother's daughter and might be as susceptible to that horrid female habit of hysterics."

"Hysterics?" She gave him a light shove, laughing at his clear attempt to cheer her up through riling her. Her smile faded as she shook her head. "It isn't that. I discovered something from Lord Rolfeson and my mother that has shaken me." She lifted her gaze to the man who had always been so kind to her through the years—her brother.

His grin spread once more, his dark eyes sparking. "They told you at last, then. You know the secret of our shocking prima donna?"

Her jaw slackened. "You *knew* I am your sister? For how long?"

He shrugged. "Father did not wish for my affection for you to grow beyond that of friendship, so he told me when I was fifteen, after you just turned thirteen." He snorted. "As if I'd ever think of you like that, but it still gave me a start. I wanted to tell you at once, but he made me swear not to do so or my lessons would be taken away and also any chance of surpassing my father's fame as a maestro." He rubbed his hands together. "Well, I'm glad we got that out of the way. Now, my little prima donna, shall we get to work?"

Delia shook her head. "You may have had years to think things over, but my world has tumbled on end."

"I'm hardly someone to tumble your world, my dear *sister*." He winked and, grasping her hand, twirled her into place beside the piano. "Just consider me the brother you always wished you had, or actually the brother you wished you *hadn't*, given the way my presence destroyed your parents' marriage." He grimaced as his joke turned sour.

"I would never wish your presence away, Giuseppe. You are my oldest and dearest friend." She took his hand in her own. "Not only that, you are my older brother. And no matter the poor choices my mother has made in her life, you are the greatest gift anyone has ever given me."

Giuseppe's mirth disappeared as he rubbed his sleeve over his eyes. "You always were a sentimental girl. Now, if I am ever to reach that legendary fame of my father, we'd best get to work!"

After a couple of hours of her lesson with the steady vocal warming and familiar albeit challenging opera, she was ready to enjoy the afternoon with Kit, even though her heart wrenched at what was to come. For though he had promised her his undying love, surely in the light of day where her shame was in full view, he would see reason at last and divest himself of her. The thought of losing him made her heart shudder, for she had found her afternoons with Kit even more appealing than singing on the stage . . . and that was something she didn't think she could ever relinquish now that she had a taste of it. *What does that say about my heart and Kit?*

"What is the phantom planning today?" Delia asked, twirling her parasol, plastering on a bright smile as if to keep him from guessing the maudlin thoughts he knew were plaguing her as they walked about Central Park.

"No phantom discussions today or farce of any kind. Today I am simply your Kit." He bowed, presenting her with a small box, and led her to a nearby bench. "A day late, but happiest of birthdays to you, my lady."

She smiled. "How did you know? I never told anyone, and my dinner with Father was canceled, so I know you didn't discover it through your set."

"Giuseppe." He grinned.

She paused in unwrapping the gift, her face paling. "You spoke with him today?"

"Yes, most days after you rehearse in fact. When you are freshening up or fetching your cloak, I ask about you and he is happy to oblige. Today I was fortunate you took longer to ready yourself. It gave me the chance to prepare something I was saving for your Christmas present, which was in turn, why I was late for our walk."

She nodded politely. "I need to have a talk with Giuseppe about his blathering about me."

"The man has good taste in students, and he cannot cease his boasting of you." His grin froze. "Should I be jealous of your maestro?"

She snorted, her eyes widening. "No. Absolutely, decidedly without a doubt, no."

"That was rather unequivocal."

She drew a deep breath, glancing at Kit in such a way as though this were the last time they would share such a moment. The glance prickled his skin and made him want to clench his hands to brace himself. *Lord, please let her not be ending our time together.*

"About Giuseppe, there is something I need to confess."

His heart tripped over itself. "Yes?" He barely released the single word.

She stared at him. "Giuseppe Rossi is my brother."

"Your brother?" He rubbed his forehead at the news.

"Well, half brother. My mother had him with Maestro Rossi before she met my father, when she was but a girl herself," she quickly amended.

His jaw dropped before he snapped it up. "Well, one could never say that our lives are not full of surprises, even when one thinks there couldn't possibly be more."

She handed the unopened box to him. "I suppose you will want this back? As it is not flowers. I know what such a gift means, and I do not wish for you to feel tied to me any more than you might already feel."

He scowled. "Do you think my affections for you are so fragile?" Seeing her trembling lip, Kit was reminded of the examples of marriage and love she had while growing up—a love that abandoned, a love that vacillated—not exactly a firm foundation on which to put one's trust. "To love, truly love, is more than a brief infatuation that withers at the first sign of adversity. Love withstands even the harshest storm. I know how to hold fast when all seems lost."

"How?" she whispered, dashing her fingers beneath her lashes. "Life's storm has battered me to the point of breaking these past few days."

"I have been studying in the mornings to find an example of perfect love that one might understand when one has never had it, and I was reading in First John, chapter four. Are you familiar with the passage?"

"Hester used to read that particular chapter to me." She scrunched her brows as if trying to draw the words from her memory. "Is it the one about Christ's love for us?"

"Yes! As believers in Christ, we have a perfect example in our Lord. John states, 'God is love and he that dwelleth in love dwelleth in God, and God in him. Herein is our love made perfect, that we may have boldness in the day of judgment: because as He is, so are we in this world. There is no fear in love, but perfect love casteth out fear: because fear hath torment. He that feareth is not made perfect in love. We love Him, because He first loved us.'" Kit pressed her hand between both of his, praying his words came across as he intended. "I am by no means perfect, but we both serve the Lord who is, and because of His example, I know how to love you. Attempt to set your fear aside, Lia, and trust in the Lord that if He has placed our hands together and given us each a pure love for the other, no one can pull us apart."

He returned the box to her lap. "I know such trust does not come overnight, but know that I intend to love you until the day I die—if you allow me."

Delia dipped her head, her cheeks stained with tears. "For years I have been seeking shelter under my Father God's wing, seeing Him as my heavenly Father, but I hadn't really considered that His example of perfect love was an example of a bridegroom's love." She laughed. "I should have, but I suppose one can be so focused on what one does not have that they do not see that they in actuality *did* possess an example of perfect love all along." She lifted her gaze to him. "I trust you, Kit Quincy," she whispered.

"I will not forget what that trust costs you." He lifted her hand and pressed a kiss atop it. "Thank you."

She slowly opened the box and gasped. She lifted out a circular gold locket with a raised rococo edge and a single diamond in the heart of the etched rose. "It's stunning. I've never seen such a lovely locket." She turned it over in her hand, rubbing the gold, her fingertips finding the latch and flipping it open. "Where is your photograph?"

He took the locket from her and placed it about her neck. "That, Lia, is the second part of my gift."

"Kit?" She lifted a brow. "You may not know this about me yet, but I do not particularly enjoy surprises. What is the second part of your gift?"

Laughing, Kit took her hand in his and led her to a more secluded part of the park, where a gentleman stood with a box camera with four lenses atop a stand. Kit swept his arms out wide. "I've arranged for us to pose together for some *cartes de visite*, and I thought it might be unique to have the locket in the picture with us and put that picture inside the locket."

She pulled him to a stop. "You cannot be serious. Not to mention how untoward it is to have our pictures together before any official agreement . . ." She broke it off when she saw him grinning. "And what if someone walks by and sees us in such a fashion?" Her cheeks turned pink again.

He couldn't help but chuckle at her flustered state. Once more he captured her hand and pressed a kiss upon it. He couldn't seem to keep himself from kissing her these days, and as her lips, luscious and beguiling, were out of the question, he settled for her hand. "My lady, whenever you say the word, an agreement will be struck and announced to the world. Until then, if anyone sees us posing together, they shall know that we are courting. And our posing for a photograph shows yet again my intentions toward you." He met her gaze. "Marriage and marriage only."

The photographer, a short, thin man with a gap in his front teeth, smiled at Kit. "Quincy, you didn't tell me the young lady was so beautiful that she will put my setting to shame."

The color in her cheeks deepened. Kit ran his thumb over the bloom. *May I always bring such color to her cheeks. She is too lovely.* Kit nodded at the great care the photographer had taken in decorating the arbor with purple blooms, which Kit had requested as a token of the very first bouquet he gave to Delia. "Thank you for getting this together so quickly, Gallier."

"No need to thank me. My bill will reflect any trouble I have taken, along with the change in date and time." He winked and then turned his attention to Delia. "Now, I understand this photograph is for a locket, and as such, you two will have to forgo the usual pose for courting couples."

"What?"

"Nothing you wouldn't do in a ballroom, miss, in front of all of society," Mr. Gallier assured her.

"Very well," she murmured, her gaze fixed on the ground of the arbor that was scattered with violet petals.

"Good. Now, Mr. Quincy, step behind her. Miss, rest your arm about your waist so your fingers may grasp his, as if you are performing a turn in a waltz, while keeping your other arm arched over your head. The picture will seem as if I am capturing you in the middle of a turn. Quincy, you will hold her hand in an arch of your own."

Kit guided her into the pose. "For a woman of the stage, you are quite reluctant to act."

"And now you must look at each other," Mr. Gallier added, "*really* look at each other with all the love in your hearts."

Delia's lips parted. "Really, Mr. Gallier, I hardly think—"

"Easily done for me," Kit whispered, stilling her protest.

"Simply a pose as if you were dancing, miss." He raised his hands in defense. "And I chose a place and time when most will not be walking in this area while still allowing for optimal light." Gallier stepped toward them, his hands ready to adjust her. "May I, miss?"

She nodded, and he helped guide her into position next to Kit. Her delicate hand felt so right in his, and with her tucked into his side, her body warmed him in the crisp afternoon. He smiled down at her, and she shyly peeked up at him through her lashes, a small smile meeting his.

"That's it! Hold that expression, Miss Vittoria and Mr. Quincy," he urged, quickly moving behind the camera.

Kit leaned toward her. With all their talk of love, he couldn't help but wish to kiss her. She shifted back.

Mr. Gallier grunted, peeking back around from his camera. "Miss Vittoria, you must hold still or I will have to take it all again."

"That was my fault, Gallier," Kit returned.

The photographer scowled. "Lean closer to her, Kit. You *must* convey the love you feel for her through your expression or else it will seem hackneyed. This moment will fade over the years, but my picture will last for a lifetime."

"I don't ever see this moment fading," she whispered up to Kit. "I daresay I have a picture forever burned into my mind."

"And hopefully your heart?" he asked. If she would only accept his proposal instead of a promise to hope for more.

A family walking their three little yapping dogs passed them, curious gazes on the couple in a dancing arch frozen in motion.

He could tell she was fighting shifting away from him. "Keep your eyes on me, Lia. Don't mind them. Keep your focus on me."

Delia had never considered herself to be a weak woman, but her knees were threatening to give out if the photographer did not make haste and take the picture. The scent of Kit pulled her to him, and she felt as if she had taken leave of her senses with the sheer longing springing inside to just rise onto the tips of her toes and kiss him until they were both breathless.

"I could hold you like this forever," Kit whispered.

She could feel her cheeks heating again. "I don't think we are supposed to talk, Kit."

"When we danced before, we were moving too swiftly for me to fully concentrate on how well you fit in my arms. It is as if we were designed for each other, my lady."

"Kit! Such things you say . . ."

"Do *not* move, Miss Vittoria, the light is almost just right," Mr. Gallier scolded. "The sun is just about to splay among the leaves and give the illusion of a heavenly blessing upon your love."

"Sorry," she whispered.

"I have never met anyone like you, Lia. I have never felt for anyone the way I feel for you. Your spirit and drive and innocence pull me—"

"My parents harbor secrets, Kit, secrets I have yet to learn."

"I know enough about your family that if I haven't been frightened away by now, nothing will . . . unless you send me away."

"I will never send you away," she admitted before she could stop herself. "I don't think I could ever be as happy as I am with you in this moment. If I hadn't met you, life would be so much less complicated . . . and so much less exciting." She smiled up at him. "My heart and home have been broken for so long, it was beginning to seem normal to me, until you stepped into my life and showed me how full my heart could be—how love can transform everything."

"And as I shall never leave you, I suppose we are left with only one option," Kit whispered, kneeling before her. "Marry me the moment the season is over, my delightful Lady Delia. Marry me and allow me to applaud you through life and the stage and forever throw roses at your feet as your most ardent admirer."

She cupped his cheek in one hand and bent toward him, giving in to a sweet, chaste kiss. "Well, then you'd best purchase a flower shop in preparation to throw flowers at my feet—a lifetime's worth."

He reached into his waistcoat pocket and removed the ring. The gem caught the last rays of the sun. She gasped at the sapphire encircled by intricately woven silver as he slid the band onto her finger. He rose and swept her into his arms, whirling her about the little alcove, laughing.

Gallier stepped out from behind his camera lens. "Well, Mr. Quincy, I can honestly say I have never captured a proposal before, but you two will have a nice start to your wedding album."

"Album?"

"You didn't think I was only taking one picture, did you?" Gallier chuckled. "I managed to capture eight poses, the last being the kiss."

She blushed that their kiss was forever captured, but what it symbolized was ever sweet—a life together with the love of her dreams.

"I will have them delivered within the week, Mr. Quincy, along with the bill. Now, you two enjoy this moment without me here to interrupt it."

Kit guided her to a bench that held an overflowing picnic basket, showering her with all her favorite treats. The two spent the sunset in blissful planning and hope for the future, until the last light waned and propriety pulled them to their feet.

As they prepared to exit the park, Kit said, "I was hoping to take you to dinner after we change, and Millie will be joining us not only to celebrate but also to act as chaperone."

"Lovely! She is the only one I wish to tell tonight of our understanding." Delia smiled as she admired the ring on her finger, basking in its brilliance.

Kit held her hand out and frowned. "Then you'd best keep that finger covered, because I believe the size of it alone will give our secret away."

She pulled her glove over the ring. "There. Besides the obvious bulge, it will do nicely."

"I think I may need to purchase some gloves for you with

a slit in the left glove to show off your ring, lest the gentlemen get any ideas."

"They will always get ideas as long as I am on the stage, my Kit, but never forget that I am the one who will be turning them away, for I have found my one true love and I desire no other."

Twenty-Four

Delia smiled back at him from the top step. "I will be ready in half an hour or so."

"I'll change and return posthaste." Kit lifted his hand in farewell to his future bride and then turned to his driver. "I'll meet you at the end of the block." The air was too delightful to spend shut up for very long inside a carriage, but as time was of the essence, he could only spare a few moments.

"Mr. Quincy!"

Kit's humming halted at the man's strident tone. "Sir." Kit nodded to Lord Rolfeson, who limped toward him, his cane thudding his disapproval.

"It's 'my lord' actually." Lord Rolfeson stared at him in a manner that could only be described as a glare.

"Pardon?"

"You called me *sir*, which is quite a few notches below my position, though I suppose you Americans cannot be expected to know such things." Lord Rolfeson crossed his arms and leaned against a lamppost, the electric light casting shadows under the lord's eyes.

"I do know that, but I was surprised to see you, sir." At the pointed stare, he amended, "My lord."

Lord Rolfeson pursed his lips, his chiseled jaw making the action appear dangerous. "I have not said anything because I did not wish to upset my daughter, but I can no longer stay silent, as you have once again returned my daughter home without a chaperone in the carriage."

Kit ran his fingers along the brim of his hat. "Yes, but there was a chaperone directly prior to the brief ride here, and there will be one for the evening portion I have planned for Delia."

Delia reappeared atop her front steps, her gaze finding her father confronting him. She gathered her skirts in both hands and hurried toward them.

Lord Rolfeson scowled. "Her title if you please, *Mr.* Quincy."

Kit gritted his teeth against the gentleman's obvious attempts to belittle him. "Yes, Lady Delia. But as we have grown in our relationship, we have taken to calling each other by our Christian names, leaving off terms of pomp and circumstance."

"Her title is not to be *left off.*" Lord Rolfeson rested his hand on Delia's shoulder as she joined them.

"Father, Mr. Quincy really must be on his way. Our reservations—"

"Lady Delia is my daughter and will be treated with respect, no matter her position onstage or who her mother is."

Kit nodded. "She absolutely deserves respect, and any man who dares to show her anything but respect shall be met with my fist."

Lord Rolfeson's brows rose, a hint of a smile at the corner of his mouth. "Good. We agree upon something at last."

"I'm certain we agree on a lot more, beginning with our affection for *Lady* Delia."

"Affection?" He looked to his daughter. "Do you feel affection for this man, Daughter?"

Delia looked to Kit as if to gain courage and slowly pulled off her glove, revealing the ring that shone like starlight.

At his sharp intake of breath, Delia looked up at him, eyes wide. "Father?"

"Yes, you have certainly shown her your affection." He ran his hand over his face. "I wish I had known about this prior to the ring being placed on her finger, but I suppose I should be happy that she is at least with a gentleman of your caliber, Mr. Quincy."

"You are not angry, Father?" She twisted her hands.

"I could never be angry with you, my sweet." He stroked her cheek with the back of his hand. "As you know, I had only hoped that as soon as this opera season was complete, I could marry you to Lord Kerr and take you home to England with me and so leave this sordid life behind once and for all." He sighed. "But my hopes shall be dashed once more it seems."

Kit squared his shoulders, determined to prove to Delia's father that he was not some young man fresh from university. "Never fear, my lord. I will treat your daughter like American royalty."

"Psh. She *is* royalty—English royalty," Lord Rolfeson scoffed.

"Father . . ." Delia chided.

He chuckled. "My apologies. I am simply getting used to the fact that my hopes will not be realized. Please forgive me as I adjust my thinking." He smiled at his daughter. "Will this young man make you happy?"

Kit stood taller and smoothed the front of his jacket. He had not been called a young man in some time.

She smiled at Kit and answered, "Marriage to Mr. Quincy would bring me joy beyond measure."

"Then I give you both my heartfelt blessing."

With a little cry, Delia flew into her father's arms, tears rimming her eyes. "Thank you."

"I know I gave you reason to doubt my love for you, my sweet Lia. It broke my heart to leave you so many years ago." He pressed a kiss atop her curls. "Now, go dress while I keep Mr. Quincy company."

Delia sent Kit a grin over her shoulder as she hurried inside to change.

The jovial father disappeared as Lord Rolfeson turned a scowl on Kit. "Look. I did not travel all the way to America with Lord Kerr to have my plans wrecked."

Kit stiffened.

"Still, as my daughter's marriage to you will prove useful in my acquiring the deed to Gramercy Park as I intended, I *will* give my blessing, but on one condition."

"Yes?"

"For my trouble, you must agree to pay double the amount Lord Kerr agreed to pay for marriage to my daughter, the toast of New York." He paused and looked Kit in the eyes. "I require two million dollars, and as you think my daughter priceless and you claim you are American royalty, the sum should not pose a problem. And if you do not agree or if you think my blessing superfluous, I still have influence in the opera community and could see her dreams for a tour dashed with a few lines of my pen. As for her finding work in the States, I recently discovered a bit about her that would see her expelled from decent society."

Kit swallowed back his anger at the man's threats against his own daughter.

"Or is your love not as strong as you declared? Will you refuse to pay the price for your bride-to-be?"

"She is everything to me," Kit snapped. "What kind of father would use his daughter to blackmail his future son-in-law?"

"One who has nothing to lose."

"Except your daughter's love," Kit shot back.

"I do not need her affection. Money is what I require." Lord Rolfeson gripped his cane, tossing it from hand to hand. "Or I will tell the world she is illegitimate and undeserving of the title of lady."

"What? I thought you were married to Signora Vittoria."

"I did as well, until recently." He shook his head. "But it turns out there is documentation stating otherwise."

"Why would you tell me this? Surely you have not told as much to Lord Kerr."

Lord Rolfeson grinned. "To insert a secret between you and my daughter as well as to test if you truly love my daughter enough to marry her, sullied as she is."

The man is a lunatic. While Kit would surrender all to be by Delia's side, two million was far more than he had in reserve for any overage during the construction of the Charleston hotel in case the worst happened. He rubbed the back of his neck. "I propose something that might be far more palatable to you and your wife. If you leave the Gramercy Park home to Signora Vittoria and keep your threats to yourself, how would you like to own my home on Madison Avenue? The house is worth a fortune."

The lord grinned. "I'm listening."

Entering the Olympia Grande's restaurant was nearly too intimidating for Delia only weeks before. Now, as a titled lady and engaged to the powerful Kit Quincy, she held her head high as Kit held the back of her seat at the round table set for four in the honored center of the restaurant. She slipped into her seat.

"Millie has a guest?" she whispered to Kit to keep from being overheard by the other guests, who were eyeing them with marked interest as she removed her gloves, her ring shimmering in the candlelight as she smoothed the sapphire skirt of the gown she had worn to Willow's party, which matched the ring to perfection.

"Yes, she does!" Giuseppe called from her elbow, sending her nearly toppling over in her seat. The lovely Millie, wearing a magenta evening gown, hung on his arm, the couple beaming.

Delia snapped her mouth shut to keep herself from asking how her brother and society mentor had grown in their acquaintance, waiting as he seated Millie and then took his own seat. "I know you have met, but what brought on this unexpected turn?"

"I'm always about backstage these days," Millie replied, unfurling her napkin and placing it over her lap. "And one evening, after your performance, your new maestro kindly rescued me from a most dire situation—"

"Dire situation?" *How on earth did I miss that?*

"Yes. An old beau with his new wife happened upon me, and, well, Giuseppe saved me from certain death by extreme humiliation and even went so far as to escort me home."

"And I returned with flowers the following day before our lessons, and I have been returning with flowers every day since." Giuseppe grinned. "Millie made me promise not to tell you. She wanted to see that expression painted on your face this very moment."

My dearest friend and half brother in a relationship? Delia smiled into her crystal glass as the gentlemen placed their orders, her joy complete.

The meal was the finest she had ever had, yet she strongly suspected it was because of the company she was keeping and the ring weighing down her hand in the most delightful reminder of her promise to Kit.

"Why, Kit, what a pleasant surprise." Mrs. Lowe rested her hand briefly on Kit's shoulder before clenching her fan in both hands in front of her swollen abdomen.

"Jocelyn!" Kit rose to his feet, bowing over her hand. "I am thrilled you happened upon us, for tonight I wish to share the most wondrous news."

"News?" Mrs. Lowe's smile spread.

"I am getting married."

Her jaw dropped slightly, and she shifted toward Millie, who shook her head and held both hands up to display the lack of a ring. Mrs. Lowe's gaze came to rest on Delia's hand. "To none other than my star, Lady Delia Vittoria?"

"The same." Kit grasped Delia's hand, lending her comfort.

"May I offer my most sincere congratulations, my dear Miss Vittoria." Mrs. Lowe's voice was muted so as not to be overheard, but she was unable to disguise her concern.

Delia smiled up at the lady, who had unwittingly allowed Delia's dearest dreams to come true. "Thank you, Mrs. Lowe. Without your patronage—"

"No need to thank me." Her generous smile faltered as her husband left a conversation and joined them.

Mr. Lowe met her gaze, her stomach churning at the sight of his glancing about the table looking for Madre. She had seen him too many times in her parlor to make polite conversation with him. She twisted the ring around her finger.

"Congratulations, my little Delia." He grinned down at her, his left eyelid drooping and betraying his inebriation.

Mrs. Lowe pursed her lips. Kit tensed, his free hand balling into a fist while Delia merely nodded, wishing the moment to pass.

"Christopher?"

Delia looked up to find Lady Ellyson with an elderly couple, whom she assumed to be her parents. She groaned and at once stifled the sound. While she knew she had nothing to fear with Lady Ellyson, it was still her special night, and the less drama, the better.

"Seems we should have chosen a different restaurant," Millie whispered, giving voice to Delia's thoughts.

Kit bowed to Lady Ellyson and the older couple. "Lady Ellyson. Mr. and Mrs. Lexington. It's been some time."

"We heard the restaurant murmuring about an announcement." Mrs. Lexington and her family's gazes shifted to Delia's hand. "You are *marrying* the girl, Christopher?" Mrs. Lexington's cheeks turned pale.

"Take care, Mrs. Lexington," Kit warned softly.

"But marriage? I thought you said he was happy to see you, Elsie?" Mr. Lexington hissed to his daughter.

"And I thought you said you had reached an understanding?" Mrs. Lexington added, glaring at Delia as if she were the *other* woman.

Delia brought her left hand to her glass. "Yes, there has been an understanding reached. I am marrying Mr. Quincy." She displayed her ring. The ladies at the tables surrounding them gasped and fluttered their fans at the news as whispers of their undying love flowed through the restaurant over the ramifications of the phantom's reaction when he discovered her duplicity.

"I'm certain you are indeed happy with the match, but we are not when it is our daughter who will suffer from your entrapping a gentleman into marriage. Mrs. Lowe knows the pain of that suffering more than anyone," Mr. Lexington harrumphed.

"Father!" Lady Ellyson interjected. "I told you that we had an understanding but that it ended, and I am happy because it is his uncle who has his eye on me."

Mr. Lexington's arrow would have found its mark only hours ago, but now she ran her finger over the sapphire. He knew everything about her and still he loved her.

With Mrs. Lowe looking as though she might faint, Kit stepped between the groups.

"Come now, Mr. and Mrs. Lexington, do not put on a show for society's sake. Everyone dining tonight knows I have been escorting Delia for the season."

"For a season, yes, but you have been Elsie's escort for nearly her entire life, Christopher," Mrs. Lexington whispered into her handkerchief.

"And you want to throw it all away on *her*?" Mr. Lexington scoffed as Giuseppe shot to his feet, fists clenched and eyes flashing. But Mr. Lexington was not finished. "A girl with only a bit of talent to set her apart from her kind when my daughter is a *Knickerbocker* like you? Your mother—"

"Would have adored his Lia," Lady Ellyson interrupted, resting a hand on Mr. Lexington's arm, her knuckles whitening from the pressure of her silent warning.

"Thank you, Lady Ellyson." Kit lowered his voice while keeping his expression neutral for the guests. "Mr. and Mrs. Lexington, you will kindly treat my future wife with *utmost* respect or else step away from our table at once."

Mrs. Lexington lifted her nose in the air. "Be glad you did not marry that one, Elsie. His manners leave much to be desired."

"Yes, heaven forbid a man actually defends the woman he loves," Mrs. Lowe said as the dessert arrived and she pulled her husband toward the door. "What father would want that for his darling daughter?"

Delia's swelling emotions were mollified at last, the tension easing with the Lexingtons' swift departure and the men returning to their seats.

"I cannot believe their treatment of you." Millie shook her head and tapped her spoon against the crème brûlée top, cracking the crust of sugar to get at the vanilla custard beneath. "But I must admit that Lady Ellyson has matured. I think she and Uncle Elmer will make a good match after all."

Delia shrugged. "I appreciate her defense, but I have been treated thus my entire life . . . until Father laid claim to me."

"It doesn't make it right," Giuseppe interjected.

"No, it does not," Kit agreed. "And I have quite made up my mind to ban Mr. and Mrs. Lexington from the Olympia for their treatment of you."

"Please don't. I'd hate to cause more friction between you and your set." Delia grasped his hand. "But take comfort that since I've met you, Kit, I have found I do not need the approval of others. As long as I have my God and you at my side, I need no one else."

Giuseppe coughed twice into his fist and lifted a single brow. "Pretty speech, but I am feeling rather slighted, as I was not included in that group."

Delia patted his hand. "Of course I need you and my friends as well. You all enrich my life significantly. I only meant that I have finally found peace in knowing I am complete in Christ, even without the praise of man or the love of my father."

Twenty-Five

Kit didn't particularly enjoy the height of the rafters above the stage nearly fifty feet from the deck, but it did allow him an excellent view of the opera. He sat on the walkway boards, his feet dangling off the edge of the scaffolding. But since he had a firm grip on the rail and this was not his first time up here, he was feeling more comfortable with it. In fact, it reminded him of being aboard a ship, high up in the rigging.

If only his stomach would cease twisting over the secret he held. *But at least she will be safe.* This afternoon he had completed the trade with Delia's father—his mansion for Lord Rolfeson's signature on the contract, the transaction witnessed by lawyers. The contract was to take effect in two days, leaving Kit precious little time to pack his personal belongings. Nevertheless, Delia would be spared from the threats of her father, and Signora Vittoria would keep her home for the rest of her life.

At Delia's first notes of her duet, he couldn't help but smile as he watched his fiancée, stunning as always in her performance in *Roméo et Juliette*, although he had to admit he was glad it was the season's final performance of this opera. He only hoped that when the company began a different opera, it did not require such tender love duets between Delia and her tenor counterpart. As they embraced below him, Kit grimaced at the innocent-enough staged affection with a feigned kiss, which was all the more difficult to watch now that he knew what it was like to be wrapped in her lovely arms, to kiss those lips like he had under the arbor yesterday afternoon . . . His hand slipped and he flailed, grabbing for the rail. He grunted at his own stupidity.

For tonight's performance, as instructed by Millie, he would attempt a feat so daring, it had even him feeling nervous. Even so, he had to keep up the ruse of the phantom's obsession with her during Act V, while Kit Quincy had been seen for the first four acts. As soon as he completed this feat, Ramsey was to don the costume and appear once more as Kit returned to his box, or else people might suspect that he and the phantom were one and the same. If, however, they did leave for Delia's tour at the end of the season, it would bring about a natural end to the phantom ruse.

The lights dimmed for the famed death scene, and Kit got to his feet. "Here we go."

"You *dare* return, scum." A voice hissed in the darkness. "After you stole the hand of *my chosen one*?"

Kit pulled himself up and slid into a ready position, even as the planks swayed on the ropes beneath his feet. "Show yourself."

"Why?" the maniacal voice laughed.

The voice sounded as if it was coming from above him. Kit twisted around but saw nothing. "Fight me like a man and not like the coward you are for hiding behind that mask for the past twenty years."

The phantom dropped from above, landing with a soft thud on the boards with practiced precision. His grin spread under his ivory mask. "You wish to fight me with your hands? How quaint." He drew a rapier from within his cape, pointing the blade at Kit, the gleam catching in the light from the stage below. At the crescendo in the music, the phantom lunged at Kit.

Kit ducked, the blade slicing the feather from his hat. Kit wrenched about, searching for something with which to defend himself. He spied a wooden pin in the rail that did not have rope anchored to it. He bolted down the planks, keeping his hands along the roped rail. He grasped it in both hands and jerked downward, splintering the pin from the rail. He whirled around in time to catch the rapier on the stake, the metal planting itself in the wood, the force of the phantom's blow causing Kit's footing to slip on the boards. He sank to one knee, his leg dangling over the edge of the planks. The phantom bore his weight down on the blade. Kit shook with the effort to keep the blade from his throat.

"You dare pretend to be me and have footing like that? Pitiful," the phantom spat. "She deserves more than you."

With a mighty shove, Kit sent the phantom scrambling backward, freeing the stake from the blade. Kit swung at the man again with the splintered pin, making contact with the phantom's arm, but the man did not stop. Instead of falling back, the phantom slammed his shoulder into Kit's chest, sending him over the ropes.

Kit seized the rigging, snagging a rope and dangling above the set, where no one was aware of what was going on above the curtain drop line. He stretched his hand out to grab a second rope to swing himself back to the safety of the planks when the phantom reappeared with the lantern Kit had kept near the exit.

With a grin, the phantom held it over the edge. "Let's see how they love you after you endanger the audience and their loved ones."

Kit's eyes widened as he looked to where the lantern would fall. There behind the set was a thin line of black. He was going to set the stage on fire. "No! Delia!" he yelled, but the ensemble drowned out his words.

"Can you fly like me, Pretender?" The phantom then released his hold on the lantern, letting it fall and then shatter on the black line. He sliced his rapier through the rope, and Kit plummeted to the stage as it erupted into flames.

In between a breath and the next note, Delia heard them overhead. She looked up to see Kit dangling from a rope in his phantom costume, with the second phantom slicing through the rope as fire exploded from behind the set. She screamed and ran for Kit as he dropped toward the deck, landing on a roof of the set's village. He rolled off the roof, hit Juliette's balcony, and fell to the stage in a heap of black.

The crowd was silent for a moment, as if trying to comprehend if this were part of the play, and then all detonated into chaos as the fire roared to life.

The company ran for the fire buckets as Delia rushed to Kit's side. "Phantom?" She dared not use his real name. "Phantom?" *Papá, Lord God, please! Please . . .*

He groaned, turning to her, blood dripping from a cut in his head, his hand clutching his ribs. "My love."

"Thank the Lord." Tremors threatened to overtake her, but at the shrill whistles of the police and the growing danger, she wrapped his arm around her shoulders as if he were taking her away. "Can you walk? Everyone will think you set the fire. We must get you away before you are taken."

He grunted and nodded. "Not far, though."

She wrapped his fingers around her upper arm. "Act as though you are taking me by force."

He pulled her to himself, leaning heavily over her as she cried out, giving the impression of being in great pain. But the Academy was in pandemonium, and if anyone noticed her, no one was coming to her aid. She guided him through the set to the one wing she knew was not occupied.

"Lia!" Lorenzo cried from the stage, grabbing a policeman's rifle and pointing it at Kit. "Let her go, Phantom."

She gasped and Kit glanced up, obviously in a haze as he tilted his head at Lorenzo's command. The pinrail to Kit's left splintered as Lorenzo's shot split the air, the gunfire drawing the attention of the police. Suppressing a scream, Delia staggered with Kit into the shadows of backstage, disappearing through the door that led to the basement of the building. She shut the bolt of the door behind her, the iron cracking in the dense air.

"We have to keep going," she said. "If Lorenzo finds you or leads the police to us, in his state, I doubt he will believe our story but will shoot first. They have been wanting to punish someone for years over the burning of the Academy, and your age fits their story." She grunted under his weight as they shuffled down stone steps that spiraled into darkness, feeling her way along the cold wall with her free hand.

"How do you know where you are going?" Kit asked, his voice strained.

"I grew up here, Kit," she whispered. "I used to come down here during Madre's performances. It's below the stage and trap room, where you can hear everything and still be alone." She paused, feeling along the wall. "It's still here," she murmured, her fingers finding the tinderbox. She struck the match and lit the torch she had long since abandoned, light spilling into the chamber. She helped him to the floor, leaning him against the stone wall, and untied his mask.

Kit looked awful. The bruises under his eye were deepening, and the blood from the cut in his forehead trickled down his chin into his collar, soaking it crimson. As to his clutching his side, she hated to think of the possible ramifications of his fall. "What happened?"

He filled her in quickly and shifted his weight, groaning. "I am lucky I had the presence of mind to launch myself toward the set's roof. It broke my fall fairly well, but I think I may have bruised my ribs and I certainly hurt my leg."

She bit her lip. She hadn't even noticed his limp. "Where?"

He pointed to his shin, and she tentatively lifted his pant leg, gasping at the blood oozing from a gash. "It looks like a nail pierced you and was dragged down during your fall."

He nodded, accompanied by another grunt. "Sums it up well. Feels like it too."

She twisted her hands. "I cannot bring you back up there now. If they see that Kit Quincy is injured, they will put it all together and arrest you."

"They won't hurt me."

"Fear makes people act in ways they never normally would. If they think you threatened their families with the fire, they might attack you, or may never believe you *didn't* do those things. Besides, no one else outside our circle knows there's a second phantom. They only know of the one who adores me, who once again proved his jealous nature by setting a second fire."

He nodded. "What do you suggest we do, then?"

"If I can sneak away and find you a fresh set of clothes, perhaps we can get you home. Then I'll get a doctor to tend to your wounds. If someone asks, I can simply say I escaped." She traced his jaw with her finger. "I don't know what I would have done if . . . if . . ."

He placed his fingertips on her lips to silence her fears. "I didn't. I'm fine."

"You need help."

He wrapped his arm over his rib cage. "Yes, but you may want to wait for an hour. They are swarming the opera, and if they spot you and you say you escaped, well, they will know the phantom is not far away. But if they don't find you, they may take the search elsewhere, which gives you a chance to get help without being caught."

As much as she wished to argue, she couldn't debate his logic. Delia crossed her arms to keep herself from shivering.

"You're cold."

He notices me, even when he is in such pain? How she loved this selfless man. "Juliette's costume isn't exactly the warmest gown to wear in the depths of the Academy in winter."

He held his other arm open to her, and she moved into his embrace, the events of the last hour catching up with her. She rested her head on his shoulder, mindful to avoid his injuries. "I was so afraid I lost you, Kit. I love you more than anything."

His arm tightened about her. "If a fall is what it took for you to profess your love, I'd fall again."

"Kit! You shouldn't say such things," she admonished, tilting her head up to meet his gaze. "I was foolish not to tell you how I felt before. I believed that by accepting your ring, it was declaration enough, but when I thought you had perished in that brief moment, I regretted not telling you most heartily." She lifted her lips to his. "I love you, my Kit."

Kit's throbbing ribs woke him, yet he stilled at once at the feel of Delia resting her head on his shoulder. Her delicate breathing made him loath to wake her, but as the swelling in his ankle had doubled while he had slept, he knew it was time to seek help. "My lady? I think I need a doctor."

She immediately stiffened and pushed herself up, the sleepiness in her eyes making him grin, even though the action caused his lip to split once more and he tasted copper bitterness on his tongue.

"I can't believe I fell asleep. I am so sorry, Kit." She scrubbed her hand over her cheeks, giving them a little slap as if to chase away her exhaustion. "I only meant to rest my eyes."

Kit couldn't admit to being sorry to have spent time at her side, yet the swelling of his ankle was dulling the pleasure. "You needed to rest, and we needed to wait long enough for the panic above to abate."

Pushing herself to standing, she went over and rummaged

through the little shelf at the corner of the basement and withdrew a jar. She handed it to him. "I used to bring a loaf of bread with jam down here. I clearly don't have bread, but the sweetness of the jam might help to dull your hunger."

Kit lifted a brow at the dust-covered jar. He popped the lid and sniffed the contents. *Blueberries*. "How old is this jam?"

She grimaced. "About two years. I haven't been down here in a long while, being the understudy and all. But there was a time when Madre was excessively harsh in her critique of me, when I was first promoted to understudy, and I would retreat down here. She was only trying to make me better, but at the time the method stung, until I realized that if I listened to the heart of what she was saying, I would in fact better my craft, and eventually I stopped coming down here." She pressed a kiss to his lips, her sudden warmth blunting the ache of his body. "I'll be back, my Mr. Kit."

"And when you do, please continue kissing me. It is the best medicine I have ever tasted."

"That is unlikely, as I will be bringing aid." She laughed and sat back on her heels.

He pulled the cape from his lap and wrapped it about her shoulders. "This will keep you warm and cover your costume."

She kissed him once more before disappearing up the winding stairs, leaving him in the cold with only the memory of her sweet kiss and the flickering torch for light and warmth.

Twenty-Six

The fire had long since been extinguished by the time Delia reached backstage. It seemed only the set had been damaged, but reporters still milled about, taking down anyone's account of the evening. When they spotted Delia emerging from the shadows, she was soon surrounded, all of them clamoring for her story. With flowing tears worthy of the stage, she pleaded a need to change and begged them to wait until she had gathered herself before telling the tale. She then darted into her dressing room, sagging against the closed door in her relief that she had a few more moments to compose her tale.

"You are safe." Madre cast aside the blanket and rushed from the divan, throwing her arms about Delia in such a rare show of maternity that Delia failed to embrace her before Madre pulled away, dashing her knuckle under her eyelashes. "Did the second phantom hurt the gentleman pretending to be the phantom?"

"How do you know the man is only pretending?" Delia asked.

"Because I know who the real phantom is *not*, and I know it is not Kit," Madre replied. "How is he? Your Mr. Quincy."

Delia's jaw dropped. "How could you possibly know it was him? No one but a handful of people know his identity."

Madre moved to the closet and removed Delia's plain day gown, setting the navy cloth in Delia's arms and motioning for her to turn before assisting her out of the costume. "It doesn't matter. How can I help you?"

Delia shook her head against her mother's unusual actions. "Kit needs a doctor and someone to help him move from the basement to his home. I was going to ask Giuseppe, whose career is just as much at stake as mine, and, well, there is the whole big brother aspect that makes me believe he will do just about anything to help me."

"*Molto bene.*" Madre nodded. "Very good. I will fetch Kit with Giuseppe while you send Mr. Lowe to Kit's home."

"Mr. Lowe? Madre—"

Madre lifted a single brow. "You know I do not know many doctors, and besides, the only one we *can* trust is his cousin. Mr. Lowe is the obvious choice with the most to lose if he spreads the tale."

"And the most to gain." Delia pressed her lips into a thin line. "Are you certain Mr. Lowe will not use this as leverage to get what he wants?" *What he wants being you.*

"He most certainly will attempt to use this as blackmail, but I will make Mr. Lowe understand once you fetch him to me at Mr. Quincy's residence." Madre gathered their cloaks and reticules.

"And how can we do all this without the police seeing Kit in his condition?" Delia asked, shrugging on her own outerwear.

"Simple. You are to give the performance of a lifetime to distract them with your heroic tale, describing a man so vague that no one and everyone fits his description," Madre responded, threading a pin through her winter hat.

"Lie? To the press?" Delia twisted her beaded reticule.

"To everyone." Madre sighed at Delia's hesitation. "My dear, think of it as a play, a performance, which is what we do for a living. Give the people what they want, a show to never forget, and make certain that you mention it was Kit who saved you."

A play. Just as Millie had said all those months ago. "But won't they be expecting him to be at my side?"

"That is where the doctor comes in. Say he was injured in the rescuing of you, by which time Giuseppe will be able to have Kit in his opera clothes and ready to prove that he was not the phantom."

Delia rubbed her forehead. "All of which I should have thought of directly after the fire as a solution. And to those who question my running from the stage with the phantom? What do I say?"

Madre waved her hand. "Tell them you were overwrought with hysterics. Men will always believe a woman to lose her wits. Just be careful to mention your clear mind now, lest they throw you in Blackwell's Lunatic Asylum on Blackwell's Island."

Madre flung open the door, and they were greeted by a mob of reporters, all clamoring for the full story. After spinning a tale that left her stomach in knots but as close to the truth as she could manage, with Kit being a hero, Delia escaped from the company and reporters to take a hired carriage to Madison Avenue to the Lowes' residence. She dismissed the carriage and rapped on the door, wringing her hands as the butler fetched Mr. Lowe. The gentleman appeared quickly, his eyes widening at the sight of Delia on his front stoop.

Mr. Lowe closed the door behind him and stepped out onto the snow-covered steps, crossing his arms over his chest against the cold. "Miss Vittoria. Is your mother well?"

"I am not here to discuss my mother. Kit is in trouble," she said through clenched teeth.

His eyes darkened. "What sort of trouble?"

"He's hurt and needs you to attend him in his home."

"Hurt?" To his credit, concern etched the lines of his face. "Why on earth did you come to me then? I haven't practiced in at least five years."

"Because, despite everything, Kit trusts you."

"Come. Wait inside." He held the door open for her.

"No thank you." She pulled her wool cloak tighter over her gown. She'd rather freeze.

He nodded and disappeared back inside. When he returned moments later, he was gripping a slightly squashed doctor's bag in one hand and an umbrella in the other, his opera cape across his shoulders. He tugged his top hat into place. "Let's go."

They hurried down the avenue with Mr. Lowe holding the umbrella aloft, the snow and wind fighting against it as icy gusts pierced her clothing and made her limbs numb. *Thank goodness it is only two blocks away.*

She trotted up the steps of Kit's mansion and tested the doorknob. She had never seen the inside of his home. The door swung open, and she and Mr. Lowe slipped inside.

"Kit?" she called, the dawn's light already beginning to glow through the window.

"He's in here." It was Madre's voice coming from the next room. She rose from her place beside Kit.

Delia sank down beside him, kneeling on the hardwood floor of his front parlor that was decorated in pale peach and cream hues, most likely done by his mother. If she wasn't so concerned for him, she would have smiled at the sight of Kit stretched out on the settee, his feet hanging over its dainty arm.

She stroked his hair from his face. "Kit, are you awake?"

His thick lashes fluttered and he glanced up at her through one eye, the other swollen. "My Lia."

"I've brought Mr. Lowe."

Mr. Lowe surged into motion, checking Kit for injuries. Without ado, he removed Kit's soiled shirt, and Lia gasped at the sight. Purple splotches marred his surprisingly tanned chest. Madre caught her staring, and a smug smile slid into place that had Delia whipping her back to him. Engaged or not, staring at the man's bare chest was forbidden.

"Modesty is all well and good, little Delia, but I did not dismiss you from the room because I need your assistance to keep him upright while I affix the bandages about his torso. He has broken ribs."

"Broken . . ." Her knees weakened. "Where's Giuseppe? Can't he help?"

"He had to leave," Madre said, turning her own back to the sight as she pressed her hand to her mouth, looking a bit green.

"Delia! Kit needs you," Mr. Lowe snapped.

For Kit. She could do this for Kit. She knelt beside him, and the doctor placed Kit's arms on Delia's shoulders. "Don't move."

The feel of Kit's hot skin against hers chased the chill away while the heaviness of his arms surprised her. Kit smiled, their foreheads nearly touching.

He grunted against Mr. Lowe's tight wrapping. "Well, this almost makes getting broken ribs worth it to have you so near."

She shook her head. "Such nonsense. If you would've waited a mere handful of months, we would be wed and you wouldn't have to be broken to hold me."

Kit's brows rose. "Such scandalous talk, Miss Vittoria."

Her cheeks burned that Mr. Lowe and Madre overheard her. She shifted away from him, eliciting a groan from Kit and a glare from Mr. Lowe. Her arms at once found their way under Kit again, supporting him.

"There. That should take care of the worst of it. A few broken ribs from a fall from that height is not so bad, Cousin." Mr. Lowe gave a shrug. "And, well, that black eye is an improvement. Makes you appear more dashing and debonair to the ladies." He looked up to Madre. "May we speak?"

Delia lowered Kit to a pillow even as his body tensed and he attempted to rise from the settee. "Lowe, if you so much as leave this room with—"

"I only wish to speak with her . . . to say goodbye." He motioned for Madre to join him in the foyer.

"Very well, but leave the door open," Kit grunted, twisting his head to keep his eyes on them.

Pounding at the front door jarred Delia. Kit was still without his shirt. Though the wrapping covered him considerably, whoever was at the door would surely want to see him. She lifted the shirt to help Kit into it when the rapid beat of the cane on the marble foyer made her panic.

Father limped into the parlor and glared at Delia, who was still assisting Kit with tugging his shirt over the bandages. Her lips parted to assuage his anger, but then she snapped her jaw closed. Nothing could save her from his wrath after seeing her in such a compromising position.

Madre and Mr. Lowe followed Father into the room. She shot to her feet but could not defend herself.

"Hester told me the truth," Father began. "You were out all night, and now I know why. You were with this man, who, judging from his wounds, was no doubt masquerading as the phantom." He pointed his cane at Kit, but instead of shouting . . . he grinned? "Didn't take you too long to claim her after signing on the dotted line."

Broken ribs or not, Kit rolled off the settee to rise to his full towering height. "I have treated her as my fiancée with only the deepest respect. Besides, you know very well of my intention to marry her just as soon as she agrees."

Delia whispered to Kit, "What is he talking about, signing on the dotted line?"

"It does not matter."

"It's not what you think, Father. Kit is not the original phantom and has done nothing wrong," she quickly informed him.

"Misleading the public comes to mind. Isn't that some sort of crime in the States?" Father chortled. "What a trip this turned out to be—scandal, secrets, conspiracy."

"Oh, Serenus, the man did nothing wrong, and *you* of all people know that." Madre returned to Delia's side, wrapping her arm about her daughter's waist.

Father scowled at her. "You have no right to defend anything or anyone after what I discovered."

Lifting her head, Madre said, "Do you think I still care about what you think? Even when Delia marries Kit and leaves me homeless, at least she will be far away from you."

Delia reached her hand out to Kit. His large hand engulfed hers at once.

"You will never be homeless, Signora Vittoria. I have seen to it that you do not have to move."

"What?" Madre and Delia exclaimed in unison.

"We have struck a deal, your Mr. Quincy and I." Father ran his fingers over the carved head of his cane. "I have given my blessing as well as my vow of silence regarding your birth in exchange for this mansion." He turned about the room, nodding. "I believe it will suit my wife quite well."

Kit growled, "*Silence* being the key word, Serenus."

Delia gasped, spinning toward Kit. "You didn't . . ."

He brought her hand to his lips. "I would give all for you, my darling, if it meant that you would be safe."

"Safe? What is Father holding over you?" she whispered.

Madre sighed. "Over you, *cara mia*. Your birth. Our marriage was invalid, as I was still in the process of divorcing Maestro Rossi."

Delia's knees weakened, and she felt Kit's arm wrap about her shoulders as the last thread of any social acceptance snapped. She cringed at the ugly word so many gentlemen used to deny their children respectability and society, branding them as pariahs—the *unwanted*. Not only was she an iniquitous opera star's daughter, but she was also the illegitimate daughter of the lord she had been claiming as her true father. "You knew?" she whispered to Kit as he lowered her to the settee, taking the seat beside her and holding her hand.

"Yes," he answered, drawing her gaze to his, and she found

nothing but love shining in his eyes. "I know all, Lia, and I would marry you tonight if you would have me."

"I do not think you should wed, at least not tonight," Madre interjected. "People will think something did indeed happen when we all know Delia's character. Instead, let Kit announce it at a ball with your father's approval and then have the society wedding that you deserve, which will squelch any rumors."

Father narrowed his gaze at her. "You would risk her reputation?"

"I believe I am saving it." Madre looked to Kit. "What do you think?"

"You both have valid points, but I will leave the choice to my bride-to-be."

Her mind spun at the news of Kit's complete love for her, recalling the verses from First John that Kit had shared with her. *"God is love; and he that dwelleth in love dwelleth in God, and God in him. Herein is our love made perfect, that we may have boldness in the day of judgment: because as he is, so are we in this world."* She straightened her shoulders, trusting God and trusting Kit's love. "I will marry you after the opera season, my darling, if you don't mind the wait."

Kit squeezed her hand. "I've waited my entire life for you, Lia. I will not mind waiting a few more weeks."

Kit paid no mind to their audience and was leaning to kiss her when Mr. Lowe coughed into his hand, reminding him of who all was there.

"I'd better return home." Mr. Lowe picked up his bag. "Mrs. Lowe will be wondering where I am as I was only downstairs fetching a book when you called."

Father clenched his fists at the man's presence but remained silent for once.

"And not a word of what has happened this night," Kit instructed.

"On my honor." Mr. Lowe bowed his head in agreement.

"How about on your wife's trust fund?" Kit replied.

"Done." Lowe shoved on his hat and bid them farewell, the front door banging shut behind him when the house gaslights flickered.

Kit slowly rose from the settee, his senses racing, and held Delia to him.

"The phantom," Delia said, her arms tightening around Kit. "He's here. He's here to take me from you."

Kit kept her hand fast in his and gripped the poker from the fireplace. "I will not let him harm you."

The house plunged into darkness, the ladies gasping in surprise.

"Who says I would harm her," a man's voice hissed.

"Who are you?" Lord Rolfeson shouted.

Kit whirled toward the phantom's voice as Delia cried out and her hand slipped from his. He heard a thud against the floor. "Delia!" Then a rod smashed into his ribs, and he sucked in a breath, dropping the poker. Delia moaned.

"I have her!" Signora Vittoria replied from the floor.

"Too bad you did not bring your rapier this time," the phantom said. "You will not steal the Academy's songbird. I will not lose Delia, not after all these years of waiting for her."

Kit heard the scrape of a blade being removed from its scabbard. He dropped to his knees, but he could not find the poker. Squinting in the darkness, he could make out the shape of the phantom. Kit lunged for the man's legs, cutting him down and sending his weapon spinning across the floorboards. The two men grappled with each other in the dark. The phantom managed to wrap his hands around Kit's throat while pressing all his weight into Kit's broken ribs.

Kit rammed his fist into the phantom's nose, the audible *crunch* sending a shudder through the man as light flickered and filled the room, thanks to Lord Rolfeson. But the phantom still did not release him, his maniacal grin eerie beneath the ivory mask. Spots dotted his vision, but he caught sight of Delia seizing the rapier and holding it to the phantom's neck.

"It's over! Release Kit at once."

The phantom panted, his shoulders rising and falling. He lifted his hands in the air, slid off Kit onto his knees, and sat back on his heels. "You would choose him over me, Lia? Truly?" he asked, his voice no longer disguised.

Kit took the rapier from Delia and bent toward the phantom, reaching for his mask.

"Wait!" Delia's strangled cry halted them. "Let me," she said, both tenderness and pain flashing in her eyes.

Kit cradled his ribs with one arm and gave a nod, motioning her forward.

Delia knelt and rested her left palm on the phantom's chest, and with her right hand she slowly pulled at the black ribbons securing the man's mask. She gently tugged the ivory mask free. "I hoped it wasn't you."

Twenty-Seven

"Why, Lorenzo? Why would you do this?" Delia whispered, staring at the mask in her hands and back at her childhood friend.

"You know why," he murmured, his hand catching hers.

At Kit's grunt, she pulled away from Lorenzo.

Madre shook her head. "Such theatrics? Why didn't you simply try to woo her away from Mr. Quincy?"

"When the phantom first returned, I wanted to protect you, so I searched out his lair in the theater that I remembered catching him in during my first week at the Academy, learning the ropes with my father. Searching the room, I found his original costume and decided that the only way to catch the phantom was to pretend to be him and to anger him, forcing the phantom to confront me at last, for now I was no frightened little boy." He chortled. "It did not take me long to figure out that the bumbling phantom was Kit. So I decided to continue on with the charade for you, Delia—to truly become the phantom of old who would stop at nothing to see your career a success. I figured if I helped you, you would—"

"Feel indebted to you," she finished, her heart hammering. "The plank, that first night Madre almost died . . . that was you?"

"No!" Lorenzo's refusal was so passionate that she actually believed him. "It was an accident, or some malicious act by another's hand, but it was not my doing. I love you too much." His voice cracked. "I want you to remember that I love you—to never forget, no matter the wretched ending of my plan."

Kit gritted his teeth. "What I want to know is, if you knew where to look for the phantom costume, did you know the true identity of the first phantom?"

"As a child, I did not know his name. But his face is seared into my mind." Lorenzo's eyes flashed. "I was sworn to silence, fearing for my father and mother's safety. I saw what the phantom was capable of. No one else really believed he could be violent, but I knew better. I saw the way he watched Signora Vittoria, his possessiveness. And now that I know your name, you no longer have any power over me or my family, *Serenus Hearst*."

Delia felt her vision blur. Yet Kit was there, wrapping his arm about her, bolstering her, just as he had from the moment he became her ally. She did not give in to the darkness. She would not. She stared at her father. "It was *you* all those years ago? Your limp . . . it was from the fire, yes?"

Madre nodded, stroking the hair from Lord Rolfeson's eyes. "He was always so strong, so devoted to me, but he was not like you think, Lorenzo. He did not set the fire on purpose, nor did he wish to harm anyone—he was only ever a romantic."

Lord Rolfeson's hard eyes met Madre's and then took in

the rest of the group, his shoulders relaxing as he sat up, his hand resting on Madre's. "Well, I suppose my secret is out now, Giovanna, so I have nothing left tying me to you besides memories."

Delia turned to Madre. "Why didn't you tell me?"

"I couldn't," Madre replied.

"But why?" Delia clenched her fists. "And do not think of leaving anything out. I want the *whole* truth. No more half-truths."

"Because I was using his secret of being the phantom and the fire to hold him captive to my will—to make him add that clause in the deed to keep us from being homeless for years, to keep him sending us money so that you did not grow up in Five Points, where little girls disappear too often." She swallowed. "I did it to protect you, *cara mia*. Gramercy Park would be your home until you were safely married, and that woman your father left me for would not get her hands on it."

"What a lovely introduction." A regal woman stood in the doorway of the parlor in a traveling suit of the latest fashion, a fluffy petite dog with a pink bow atop its head in her left arm, and a traveling case in her right hand.

"Who in the blazes are you?" Kit snapped, keeping the blade trained on Lorenzo.

"That is no way to greet my wife." Lord Rolfeson scowled. "No matter what I have done, she is a lady through and through, and as of tomorrow, this will be her house."

"For your information, I did knock, and Serenus's valet let me inside." She frowned at Kit as she sailed into the room, pressing a kiss to Father's cheek. She let down her little dog, who at once leapt onto the antique wing-back chair beside the fireplace. "I've missed you, my darling."

Is she as mad as Father? Father is obviously a psychopath, and here Lady Rolfeson is kissing him as if he has merely been away on business.

"Now, what is this about your being held captive by this woman?" She lifted a single brow at Madre.

"This is the woman you chose over me?" Madre looked down her nose at Lady Rolfeson, which, given the lady's height, was a difficult feat to achieve.

"And this is the woman you *left*?" Lady Rolfeson smirked in return, obviously enjoying seeing Madre disconcerted. "No wonder you did not wish to return to New York."

Madre shrieked and lunged for Lady Rolfeson.

Father held Lady Rolfeson behind him, protecting her from Madre's sharp nails, taking a claw to the face before he released his wife and grabbed hold of Madre. "Giovanna! Stop, my love. There is nothing left hidden, and nothing left to fight about." Father looked to Delia. "Thanks to your Kit's signing over the deed to this beautiful mansion, as far as the world knows, your mother and I were married and parted, and I married again. A rumored divorce is scandalous, but as an earl I have certain privileges, and I will see to it that you will not be the source of scandal when you tour in Europe."

"So, as you dropped Lord Kerr from your plan, I take it that you didn't know about Madre's duplicity until recently?"

"Very recently. Yet this is what I have been waiting for." His half grin grew wider, his voice shaking with glee. "It is the leverage I needed to finally exact my revenge."

"Oh, my darling . . ." Lady Rolfeson patted his cheek, raking her fingers through his hair, combing the golden locks from his face. "How tortured you must have felt in the waiting. I wish you could've shared your burdens with me. You know the doctor says it helps you not to have an episode."

"Episode?" The woman made little sense. Delia looked to Madre, who merely pressed her lips into a thin line. "Are you ill, Father?"

Lord Rolfeson's scowl deepened, and Lady Rolfeson sent her a discreet nod and patted his arm. "Look on the happy side, my love. You are free now that your *mistress's* blackmail is not so secret anymore. She can no longer hold on to you with her threats, as this fellow has informed this entire room of your past." At their quizzical looks, she shrugged. "I arrived a while ago, and the conversation was so enthralling, I decided to listen in and assess the situation before announcing my presence."

"Certainly, her blackmail is invalid now, but what about his charges of arson?" Kit interjected.

"Yes, I burned the first opera house, but by accident," Lord Rolfeson admitted. "I loved Giovanna, and when I saw my wife was miserable without her career, I tried to get them to appoint her as diva, using my influence and money. They said no, so I came up with the phantom idea and began haunting the theater, asking for them to appoint Giovanna, until at last I followed through on my threat. But I never meant to cause such damage."

Lord Rolfeson ran his hands through his hair, his eyes darting about the room. "I started the fire in the basement as a warning, but it grew out of control and consumed the building. I severely regretted the spread of the flames, but I paid to have the Academy rebuilt, hoping to nullify my sins. It was an accident—one I regret every day." He looked to Madre. "Yet it was the leverage your mother needed to keep me a part of her life once I discovered her love child with the maestro—which we now know is indeed her legitimate son. And *you*, Delia, are in fact *my* love child, which saddens me. And yet my children in England are spared from a shameful connection in that they are truly mine and you are not."

"Still, the shame of your arrest will follow them through life," Kit said.

He waved him off. "Quincy, have you yet to learn the power of a title and money? You cannot touch me."

Kit took a step closer, fists clenched at his sides. "I will be sending for the law, sir, to take you down to the station, where they will decide your fate."

"I think not." Lady Rolfeson strode to the doorway, her little dog leaping from the chair and following at her skirts. "Agent Durand, will you please come into the parlor now?"

Delia and the group exchanged glances as a man clutching the brim of a bowler hat stepped into the room, his reddened forehead coated in perspiration. He flashed his badge to the group and nodded.

Lady Hearst rubbed her fingers together and extended her hand as if to admire her jeweled rings. "I have brought one of your famous Pinkertons with me, so I shall rely on his advice before we take any measures to include the law. What is your take on all this, Agent Durand?"

"Well, Lord Rolfeson, lucky for you, the United States follows a little something called the statute of limitations. And the time limit for your crime has long since passed, as I'm sure any judge will agree, since you rectified the situation monetarily."

Lord Rolfeson dropped his hands from tugging at his hair. "So, I am free?"

"Well, as you made reparations for the burning down of the opera house and no deaths occurred, the limitations of charging you have passed, and I see no reason why I should have to bring you in to the station," the agent said. "But I will be bringing this up to my captain, so I think it would be best if you both stayed in the States for now, Lady Rolfeson. At least until we get this matter behind us."

She nodded emphatically. "I agree completely. I wanted to spend the Christmas holiday in New York City in any event, so this works out perfectly." She softened her gaze at Delia. "I have heard so much about you over the years, and I wish I could request that you join us for the holidays, but you'll have to forgive me if I do not."

Agent Durand looked to Kit and Lorenzo. "Now, why don't you tell me what is going on here?"

Delia pulled Lady Rolfeson aside as Kit filled in the agent. "After all Father has done, you are accepting his actions with an outrageous level of grace."

"I have loved your father since my girlhood, and there is no other man for me. When he returned from England, I knew he was not quite well—that he had been broken by your mother. But I suppose your father evokes a passion in his partners that makes us as mad as he." Lady Rolfeson nodded to Kit. "He seems like a good man. See to it that you treat him better than your mother did your father."

Delia returned to Kit's side, keeping her back to the sight of Lorenzo being taken away by Agent Durand. Kit grasped her hand and led her to the breakfast room for a modicum of privacy.

"Are you well, Kit?"

"Well enough to tell you that I will not allow you to back

out of our engagement on the grounds that you think me so weak as to bend to society's will." He grasped her hands in his. "I do not care if you were born an earl's daughter or born without a father's name. I love you, Delia Vittoria. *You.* Please, do not leave me. Now that I know what it is like to have your love, I think it would destroy me if you—"

She placed her hand over his lips. "'There is no fear in love; but perfect love casteth out fear: because fear hath torment. He that feareth is not made perfect in love. We love Him, because He first loved us.'" She lifted her hand. "I trust you with my heart, Kit Quincy, and I respect the man you are more than anyone I have ever met. I have no desire to part from you, my love, now or ever."

Twenty-Eight

Lord and Lady Rolfeson were nowhere to be found the following morning, and it wasn't until two weeks later that Delia received a letter from her father and his wife. The one from his wife proved to be the most interesting of the two, as Lady Rolfeson sincerely apologized for the underhanded manner of her husband, and she had Kit's mansion returned to him. This greatly softened the blow of her next paragraph in which she explained that she did not trust another country's criminal justice system. She was using her title and lands to protect Lord Rolfeson, who for all intents and purposes was now confined to their estate in England to live out the rest of his days under her care instead of being admitted to an institution, which was the doctor's recommendation. After everything that had occurred with her tortured father's time as phantom, Delia was thankful he would at last have peace—as long as it was far away from Madre, herself, and her husband-to-be.

Violins playing "God Rest Ye Merry, Gentlemen" caught Delia's ear and pulled her out of her reverie as she ascended in the elevator of the Olympia Grande to the rooftop garden for her Christmas Eve engagement party with Kit. She ran her hands over her ivory silk gown with its matching fur-trimmed mantle, a thrill still running through her at the sight of the sapphire ring shining through the slit in her left glove. The wrought-iron gate opened, and she strode out onto the marble floor of the rooftop garden, gasping at the electric lights strung from one end of the roof to the other and back, creating a ceiling of twinkling lights. Evergreen garlands with clusters of red berries were wrapped around the Corinthian columns with massive crimson bows tied about each column's middle.

Kit had made certain the four fireplaces along the perimeter were blazing and their mantels decked with garland along with a row of candles, offering warmth to any chilled guests, while footmen offered hot chocolate, steaming coffee, or tea. In the center of the garden stood a Christmas tree, twenty-five feet high, decorated with strings of electric lights that had the guests marveling at the novel way to light the tree. Beneath the branches were the wrapped favors she and Kit had selected for each guest from Tiffany's. Kit had insisted that they were going to have their engagement party done in style, and so she had relinquished her concern and enjoyed every bit of the process of planning their party, which was to include quite the surprise for Kit.

"You are a vision." His deep timbre and arms embraced her from behind.

"Kit!" She twirled to find him in his dress coat, his hair looking dashing, hanging in loose waves to his shoulders. She ached to run her fingers through his locks.

"I believe I have greeted enough guests, and we should

open the evening with the first dance of the night," Kit whispered in her ear.

Her heart tripped at the thought of her surprise for him tonight. "I thought you would never ask." She accepted his offered hand and allowed him to guide her onto the dance floor, acutely aware of all those encircling them, including Flora and Theodore Day, and Willow and Cullen Dempsey, the women beaming over their happiness for their friends and the gentlemen grinning, her mother standing to the side and looking very pleased.

"It almost makes me wish we could stay in New York after the opera season, seeing all the support we have here," she whispered.

"Will you miss it too much?" Kit turned her under his arm.

"I think it is time for me to move onward. The Academy has been my home for as long as I can remember, but for me to grow as a singer, I think a new challenge will keep me reaching." She laughed. "Though I may not have been as brave as I let on if Giuseppe hadn't agreed to travel with us to Paris as my maestro for the prima donna position."

"Your brother is a wise man and knows you will be famous beyond your mother, and he wishes to align himself with you."

"He is not selfish, though. A move of such magnitude is not to be taken lightly," she replied, thinking of the time he would be losing courting Millie in person.

"No, but he is wise and ambitious—much like me." He grinned.

"Are you hesitant about leaving your hotels in the States, even though you found that property in Paris? I'd never wish you to feel that I would ever choose my career over yours."

"I'd trust Ramsey Gunn with my life, so I know without a doubt he can run the Olympia Grande hotels without my interference, especially now that the pressure added by William Waldorf Astor's loan has abated since I sold the Madison Avenue mansion to Uncle Elmer and his future bride and used part of the funds to repay Astor. Like you, I am looking forward to the new challenges ahead with jumping into the European hotel industry." He laughed. "It feels like quite the adventure, and I know I have been accused in the past of not having an adventurous spirit. But with you at my side, everything is an adventure. I am all in with you, my lady, and I am never looking back to my carefully constructed days."

"You are a wonderful man. And I cannot wait to see your sailing skills in motion on our journey to our new home." Delia rested her head on his chest and breathed him in, her soon-to-be husband. Unbeknownst to Kit, she had given her last performance at the Academy tonight. Saying farewell to her friends had been harder than she had thought it would be, but it was time. Though it would be strange to journey to a new place and begin again, she was ever so grateful to have men like Kit and her brother supporting her. She straightened at the clamor of church bells from below, smiling, knowing that they were for her.

Kit paused in their dance to lean over the edge of the building, curious as the rest of the guests as to why the bells were ringing at this late hour as snow began to fall in a delicate dusting. Millie, the architect of the surprise, darted onto the dance floor with the bouquet of purple blooms in her hands and set the bridal wreath and veil atop Delia's head along with a kiss to her cheek.

When Kit turned back to her, his jaw dropped and the

world faded from view as he ran toward her, slipping on the dusting of snow as he reached her. She wrapped her arms about him to keep him from falling, but they tumbled to the ground with her atop him, both laughing.

"It's time to begin a new life with a love I never thought possible. Marry me, Kit?"

He drew her to standing and cupped her face in his two strong hands. "My delightful Lady Delia, I thought you would never ask." Kit pressed a kiss to her lips that stole her breath and her heart forever.

AUTHOR'S NOTE

Dear reader, thank you so much for joining me for the conclusion of the AMERICAN ROYALTY series!

Being from a New Orleans Italian family, it was fun to dive into the history of Italians in America, especially the Italian opera companies. As an avid opera and Broadway fan, there is nothing like listening to operas for research purposes! Best excuse ever to rewatch and listen to *The Phantom of the Opera* for the millionth time.

Bellini's operas *La Sonnambula* and *Norma* and Gounod's *Roméo et Juliette* did occur during the Academy's opera season, as well as Bizet's *Carmen* in the Metropolitan's season, but I took some liberty with the timing of the operas and, for the purposes of this story, had them featured a little earlier or later than they actually were performed—judging from the 1883 *New-York Tribune*'s schedule. Also, the opera season took about a four-week break for the Christmas and holiday season starting December 7, but as I wished for a Christmas wedding for Delia, I fictionalized the date of Delia's final Academy appearance.

Madre's meeting the prince, though fiction, was inspired by the prince's ball hosted at the Academy of Music in October 1860, which was the perfect place for her to meet an English lord.

The fire that the original phantom started really did occur in 1866, and while the origin of the fire is unknown, it is rumored to have been lit in the basement, spreading to the upper levels in a matter of thirty minutes. The fire tragically claimed the lives of a few innocent bystanders. While this event did indeed result in the Academy's being rebuilt, I added a bit of fiction as to who started the fire, how bad it was, and why. I also allowed Lord Rolfeson to be the one who rebuilt it instead of the owner of the Academy.

Mrs. Astor, in actuality, did not attend either opera house's opening night, as she left town as a means of conveying her utter lack of interest in the new opera house and therefore showing it was no true threat. However, the battle for the opera house to remain for the elite was quite real. For the purposes of my story, I had her attend opening night. While Delia, as our fictional prima donna, did her best to keep the Academy of Music afloat, the Academy did not fare well, and Mrs. Astor deemed it necessary to rent a box from the Metropolitan. In its second season in its war against the Metropolitan Opera House, the Academy floundered and eventually was forced to close its doors. But then Delia went on to sing in the Paris Opera House, so I'd say she did just fine without her old home.

Mrs. Astor's nephew, William Waldorf Astor, did not get along with Mrs. Astor. When leaving America, as a parting gift, William tore down his family's home across from Mrs. Astor's on Fifth Avenue in 1893 and built the Waldorf. In retaliation, Mrs. Astor's son moved his mother and built in the place of her home the Astoria. The feud eventually ended, and the two cousins merged the hotels via a marble corridor called Peacock Alley into what we now know as the Waldorf-Astoria brand. So I thought it would be fun for Kit to have a hand in William's interest in the hotel game.

North Manor's underwater ballroom is inspired by Whitaker Wright's underwater conservatory in Lea Park. The photos of the Victorian gentleman's abandoned dream are quite eerie with a hint of romance.

Want to know more about Willow Dupré, Cullen Dempsey, Teddy Day, Flora Wingfield, and what exactly happened during that outlandish competition they are always going on about? Check out the first two books in the AMERICAN ROYALTY series, *My Dear Miss Dupré* and *Her Darling Mr. Day*. Happy reading, friends!

ACKNOWLEDGMENTS

I cannot believe that the AMERICAN ROYALTY series has concluded! It has been a dream, a joy, and an honor to write these novels for Bethany House.

My Dearest, Darling, Delightful Mr. Dakota (see what I did there?), I love you more than words can express. Thank you for being my greatest supporter and inspiration. Every hero I write possesses a dreaminess that I find in you.

To my babies, I love you with all my heart and am so proud of you.

To my family, Dad, Mama, Charlie, Molly, Sam, Natalie and Eli and nephews, thank you for always being so supportive of my writing.

To my beta, Theresa, thank you for always providing me with great feedback in those very, very rough first drafts that help my characters and plot grow!

You may not know this, dear reader, but I have been a fan of the wrestling sport since I was a young teen and have gone to countless tournaments, including the Olympic trials, where I cheered for my favorite wrestler of all time, whom

I consequently tracked down to assist me in making Kit's wrestling scene authentic—a huge thank you to "Wild Man" Sammy Jones on the U.S. World Team, my younger brother and partner in many a crime.

To the team at Bethany House, my acquisitions editor Dave Long and senior editor Luke Hinrichs, thank you for all your hard work! To Anne, Raela, Noelle, Brooke, Serena, Amy (who is now a full-time writer but who was a huge part of this series) and the Bethany House team, you are amazing! I am thrilled to be a Bethany House author!

To my agent, Tamela Hancock Murray, thank you for all your hard work and constant encouragement.

To the reader, thank you for reading Delia Vittoria's story. I hope you enjoyed the series! If you did like the novels, please take a moment to leave a review on your favorite bookish website. If you want more updates on where I am in the writing process and behind-the-scenes news, join my newsletter on GraceHitchcock.com.

And to the Lord, thank You for being with me through every storm, for being my place of refuge, for loving me, and for being the perfect example of true love. I will sing of Your goodness and mercy forever.

Grace Hitchcock is the award-winning author of the AMERICAN ROYALTY series, as well as a number of other historical novels and novella collections. Grace is a member of ACFW and holds a master's degree in creative writing and a BA in English with a minor in history. She lives in the New Orleans area with her husband, Dakota, sons, and daughter. To learn more, visit her at GraceHitchcock.com.

Sign Up for Grace's Newsletter

Keep up to date with Grace's news on book releases and events by signing up for her email list at gracehitchcock.com.

More from Grace Hitchcock

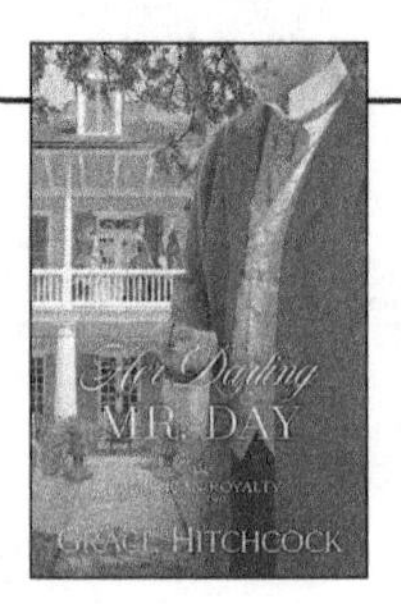

A very public jilting has Theodore Day fleeing the ballrooms of New York to focus on building his family's luxury steamboat business in New Orleans and beating out his brother to be next in charge. But he can't escape the Southern belles' notice, nor Flora Wingfield, who is determined to win his attention.

Her Darling Mr. Day
American Royalty #2

BETHANYHOUSE

Stay up to date on your favorite books and authors with our free e-newsletters. Sign up today at bethanyhouse.com.

facebook.com/bethanyhousepublishers

@bethanyhousefiction

Free exclusive resources for your book group at bethanyhouseopenbook.com

You May Also Like . . .

Upon her father's unexpected retirement, his shareholders refuse to allow Willow Dupré to take over the company without a man at her side. Presented with thirty potential suitors from New York society's elite, she has six months to choose which she will marry. But when one captures her heart, she must discover for herself if his motives are truly pure.

My Dear Miss Dupré by Grace Hitchcock
American Royalty #1
gracehitchcock.com

After uncovering a diary that leads to a secret artifact, Lady Emily Scofield and Bram Sinclair must piece together the mystifying legends while dodging a team of archeologists. In a race against time, they must decide what makes a hero. Is it fighting valiantly to claim the treasure or sacrificing everything in the name of selfless love?

Worthy of Legend by Roseanna M. White
The Secrets of the Isles #3
roseannamwhite.com

When their father's death leaves them impoverished, the Summers sisters open their home to guests to provide for their ailing mother. But instead of the elderly invalids they expect, they find themselves hosting eligible gentlemen. Sarah must confront her growing attraction to a mysterious widower, and Viola learns to heal her deep-hidden scars.

The Sisters of Sea View by Julie Klassen
On Devonshire Shores #1
julieklassen.com

BethanyHouse

More from Bethany House

Discovered floating in a basket along the canals of Venice, Sebastien Trovato wrestles with questions of his origins. Decades later, on an assignment to translate a rare book, Daniel Goodman finds himself embroiled in a web of secrets carefully kept within the ancient city and in the mystery of the man whose story the book does not finish: Sebastien.

All the Lost Places by Amanda Dykes
amandadykes.com

Captain Marcus Weatherford arrives in Russia on a secret mission with a ballerina posing as his fiancée, but his sense of duty battles his desire to return home to Clare. Clare Danner fears losing her daughter to the father's heartless family, but only Marcus can provide the proof to save her. Can she trust Marcus, or will he shatter her world yet again?

In Love's Time by Kate Breslin
katebreslin.com

In 1942, a promise to her brother before he goes off to war puts Avis Montgomery in the unlikely position of head librarian and book club organizer in small-town Maine. The women of her club band together as the war comes dangerously close, but their friendships are tested by secrets, and they must decide whether depending on each other is worth the cost.

The Blackout Book Club by Amy Lynn Green
amygreenbooks.com

BETHANYHOUSE

Printed in the USA
CPSIA information can be obtained
at www.ICGtesting.com
JSHW081057150424
61183JS00003B/142